IN THE
PLACE OF
FALLEN
LEAVES

IN THE
PLACE OF
FALLEN
LEAVES

A Novel

TIM PEARS

DONALD I. FINE, INC.

New York

For Annie and Emma

Acknowledgements

For advice, faith and encouragement at various times during the writing of this book, I'd like to thank especially: Sean Hand, Joan O'Donovan, Alison Charles-Edwards, Mark Hayhurst, Alison Halsey, Clifford Pugh, Emmanuela Tandello-Pugh, Michael Borst, Maida Suarez-Rogers, Juliet Burton, and my mother, Jill Scurfield; and Alexandra Pringle, to whose editing the book owes more than the author would like to admit.

And to my teachers: Mervyn Charles-Edwards, Bill Pears and David Charles-Edwards – love and gratitude.

CHAPTER ONE

Morning

It was the summer the world stopped turning on the spiral of history, the summer we spent waiting for the world to begin again, when the sun hung above the village and poured a hot glue that slowed everything down.

'This idn't nothin',' said grandmother in June, recalling the drought of 1976, when the earth swallowed lambs, and the electric summer after the war when people got shocks off each other whenever they touched. By August, though, both those things had already happened, and even she had to admit it was worse.

Shadows were pushed back into awkward corners, and it was there I first noticed things being moved around, as the spirits of the house made space for themselves in their diminishing refuge. Gradually, though, objects themselves took on a life of their own and moved without the spirits' help, rising from the surfaces of furniture through empty air that the heat had squeezed even gravity out of.

Mother was unable, eventually, to ignore the autonomous flight of pillows on the landing, and salt and pepper pots that raced each other across the kitchen table. But she couldn't tell anyone because the same thing was said to have happened around Rosemary, an aunt who'd thrown herself into the quarry pool long before I was born, so the village was deprived of another exorcism, last seen when one of the newcomer families claimed that their brand-new house was possessed by an incubus who was tampering with the children's dreams. A large crowd had gathered with candles. At first they felt let down as the Rector simply traipsed through the house with his mind on other things, and whispered some diffident prayers. But then the spirit, bored with so feeble an adversary, swept out of the house in a miniature cyclone of sugar and dust and soared off towards Dartmoor, leaving a faint nutmeggy odour in the porch.

Worried should a surprise visitor discover that our home was turning into an aviary of household utensils, mother went through the house methodically sticking the ashtrays to table-tops, Ian's chess medals to the mantelpiece and even fruit to the fruitbowl with double-sided tape, a makeshift arrangement which proved successful, the house becoming calm again right up until the period of confusion that came much later on.

Throughout that summer there were hours and hours between first light and the actual appearance of the sun, and they were the only habitable ones in the day until the fleeting relief of dusk eighteen hours later, when the droopy rich purple of love-lies-bleeding would come back to life by the kitchen door and the air be filled with the aroma of sweet-smelling tobacco plants that grew beside the stream.

Our farm was the last dwelling along the lane going out of the village towards Haldon Forest. Opposite us was the Old Rectory with its thatched roof, in which grandmother could remember putting fragrant grasses to soothe the troubled dreams of a previous occupant's child. Next door to us was another old house owned by outsiders, who themselves lived on the other side of the world and rented it out to summer visitors. It had a small pond inhabited by goldfish, which used to jump out of the water whenever someone slammed the front door, but which when the pond dried up in July had disappeared off the face of the earth, leaving no trace except for a mysterious quiver in the whiskers of our cats.

It was Thursday morning, 6 September 1984. I lay in bed, ignoring mother's shouts from below. I'd turned thirteen just the week before and Pamela, my older sister, had given me a rather useless multicoloured glass mobile which I hung in the window: I stared at the colours which hovered on the wall in front of me, and wondered if I could risk closing my eyes without slipping backwards into sleep.

The sun had woken up in a valley beyond the ridge with the church on it, across the village from us, and yawned a slow, luxurious breath of blue into the sky. That was when the work was done: Ian and Tom had been sleepwalkers in the darkness, but the light found them and grandfather repairing fences or docking lambs' tails, imbued with a senseless optimism that this day might be different. But it never was and, drawn out of bed by the steam from mother's bread that wafted through the house, I'd find my brothers as always sitting glumly by the stove, drinking their mugs of tea, for the sun had again come rising behind the steeple and let go its dragon's breath into the steep combe of the village, burning off the tenuous morning mist that clung to the stream still trickling along the groove it'd scored, in more abundant times, through the heart of the village, while the sun's rays shafted into the kitchen upon the customary pandemonium of women at that hour of the day. While Ian and Tom sat by the stove, immobile as bulls, we darted around them.

'I called you twice, girl,' said mother as I came in the door. 'You'll be late for school.'

'Had 'er nose in some bloody book again, shouldn't doubt,' said Tom.

I searched for my stuff in the confusion of the kitchen, but piskies had come in the night and hidden them.

'Where's my swimmers, Mum?' I moaned.

Pamela swept into the kitchen in a flurry of bags and clothes and make-up; her perfume floated in behind her, without ever quite catching up. Lipstick bouncing on the tiled floor and keys and coins and bracelets jangling, she gulped half a glass of apple juice without pausing for breath and grabbed a slice of buttered toast as she passed the table.

'I might be late back, Mum. Rehearsal tonight,' she muttered breathlessly on her way to the door.

'And how'll you get 'ome, might I ask?'

'I'll get a lift,' she replied, stepping outside; and then, over her shoulder, 'Don't you worry.'

3

Her scent lingered in the kitchen as she scattered the chickens, all except the cockerel, who'd galvanized them hours before with his crowing and then strutted foolishly around the farmyard, courting the resentment of his beady-eyed brood as they waited for the sun to rise behind the church, and pecked at the grit and dust.

'Where's our breakfast, mother?' Tom demanded.

Mother was at the stove, elbows a blur at her sides, into which tomatoes and mushrooms were sucked, and from which eggshells came spinning into the bin. The boys lifted their heavy limbs from the easy chairs on either side of the range and lumbered over to the table as mother turned with the enormous frying-pan and slid sizzling food on to their plates. She cut thick slices of bread; steam escaped from the loaf and vanished.

'Hurry up, girl, the van'll be gone,' she exclaimed.

'My swimmers is disappeared.'

'They's underneath the newspapers in the corner there.'

She was the only one who could outwit the piskies. I went back upstairs to get dressed. Already the sun was squeezing the air out of the house; now and again a slate would crack above my head, and timbers creaked as the last traces of sap were sucked out of them, moaning as they warped. The Honeywills' donkey brayed in a distant field. I looked out of the window. Ian and Tom tramped across to the barn, heads down, to join grandfather, who always carried his mug of tea out of the house and into the yard when he heard the rest of us getting up.

Back in the kitchen the smell of fried food thickened the air and settled on the walls. Mother was feeding the cats; she lifted a fishy hand, licked her handkerchief, and wiped a smudge of jam off my cheek.

'Let's 'ope there's school today,' she said, and I left the house.

CHAPTER TWO

School

By that time in the morning the tar in the road had already gone soft and chips of gravel floated on it like hundreds and thousands on top of trifle; some of them came loose and stuck to the soles of my shoes as I walked up the lane between the high hedges people kept up around their gardens.

The others were all up at the Green, which we called the Brown: the year before, the Rector had purchased it from Joseph Howard with Parish funds and organized a work party to clear the brambles, lay turf and erect climbing frames, so that children would have a recreation park like in other villages, but the boys dismantled the climbing frames to make goalposts and they played football all day till after dark, crying: 'Use the free man, Platini!' or 'Hoddle's on his own!', frightening their wilting parents with the madness of their exertions. What few hardy tufts of grass on the Brown had survived their battering were killed off by the sun. Even now, waiting for Fred's van, they were dashing red-faced after a plastic football, like a herd of bullocks chasing a sheepdog. Nan Dyer leaned against the doorway of her almshouse, a cigarette in her mouth, gazing out at the younger girls turning cartwheels in the dust, showing their white knickers. The older girls stood around the telephone box, whose thick red paint was blistering. I wanted to turn cartwheels too.

The last to arrive was always Jane Ashplant, who would come scurrying up Rattle Street, so steep she had to lean right into it and almost use her hands to clamber up. Those people blessed with a long life cursed the founders of the village,

5

since not a single path ran level for more than five yards, further punishing their arthritic joints. The houses had been built on the irregular sides of a deep gash in the hillside sloping down from Haldon Forest to the Teign Valley and they looked, on the occasion the Rector took Jane and me up the church tower, as if they had been frozen in the midst of tumbling, one on top of the other, into the stream. The village was all lopsided and everyone looked down upon, or was looked upon by, their neighbours.

The old people cursed the village founders, but they'd been clever men and women who chose a site where every dwelling was in as bad a position as any other: those living up on the ridge by the church could amble down to the shop but had to struggle home, while those of us around the stream complained all the way up to the post-box opposite the telephone, and for people in the middle every journey had its trials, so that no one had anything more to complain about than anyone else.

Jane came over to where I was standing by the telegraph pole, and tried to squeeze into its shadow.

'Think there'll be school today?' she asked.

'In't no reason to be. 'Tis still the same, innit?' I replied.

We could hear Fred's Escort van coughing and rattling up the hill. Girls who'd forgotten not to lean against the phone box came away with red stripes on their white shirts, while the boys emerged from a cloud of dust. Fred leapt out and unpacked his milk crates, stacking them as always in the telephone box; the eight of us at Comprehensive squeezed into the van and we bumped down the hill, sickened by the smell of spilt milk.

Fred shuttled us down to the Teign Valley road in between milk rounds. He kept a cigarette end on his lower lip, and his teeth were stained brown. He had also taken snuff three times daily throughout his adult life, and his nose was ruined: it dribbled, and he was constantly having to wipe it, but if one of us pretended to be congested he'd let us take a sniff, and as you felt those peppery grains tickle your nostrils you understood how someone could become addicted to sneezing.

6

At the main road we'd spill out and Fred would turn the van with a furious crunching of gears and race back up the hill to collect the Primary School kids, while we waited for what seemed the ever less likely appearance of the school bus.

Slag heaps advancing from the granite works had brought the other side of the Valley right up to the road, and a cloud of grey dust was already rising behind them. The kids from Teign Village, a few hundred yards up the opposite slope of the Valley, joined us at the crossroads. Living that bit closer to the main road connecting the villages of the Valley both to each other and to the world outside, they had a superior stock of new rumours with which they proceeded to indulge us: the teachers' strike had been dramatically resolved in arbitration on the stroke of midnight; the army were being brought in to supervise the playground; Japanese midgets had succeeded in repairing the air-cooling system. Johnathan Teignmouth too came walking along the Valley road, and stood apart.

Presently Fred came tearing down the lane with ten minnows packed into the van, and we parted to let him through, tyres squealing around the corner, as he drove them off to Chudleigh Primary. We hung around getting bored with each other and annoyed with the wasps that had proliferated in that sultry cocoon of a summer: Sally Green was allergic and she moaned if we didn't keep guard, batting them off with our pencil cases. We were all willing the coach to turn up half-filled with the Christow and Bridford lot, and take us to the school I hadn't yet seen, but by the time Fred reappeared it obviously wasn't going to, so we'd pile back into the van and be taken home. Fred leaned forward to urge the van faster, chewing the cigarette end with his lips, while his milk curdled in the telephone box.

As I walked back with Jane we'd hear the rattle of the crates behind us. She'd been my best friend; we went through Primary and Middle schools together, just as Daddy had gone to school with her father. He was a mechanic down at the granite works now. He spent so much time on his back, under the diggers and dumper-trucks, that at night he slept in a chair.

I used to stay at their house some Saturdays; Jane and I would keep awake talking with a candle. Jane was always the first to drop off, and then she farted in her sleep, silently, as dogs do.

Now we wondered whether we'd ever get to Comprehensive, and I told her of the time, back when grandmother was growing up on Dartmoor and people rode their ponies off the moor to school, when schooling was suddenly made free and people stopped going, suspicious of something that had no value.

'Susanna would ride 'er pony if 'er could, all the way to Newton,' said Jane.

'So would I if I had one,' I agreed.

'See you later, any road,' we told each other at her gate.

The silence throbbed. Behind it could be discerned a distant hum that droned throughout that strange summer. Back inside our house the silence was deepened by the breathing of the cats, who sat curled up on the tops of things, and by grandmother's snoring as she took her morning nap in the sitting-room. I tiptoed along the dim passage and paused by the kitchen. There was no one there. The grandfather clock in the hallway ticked behind me, and the washing-up steamed on the draining-board. Then I saw that mother stood unbreathing by the window in chequered sunlight, cupping a mug of tea. All at once she leaned forward and carefully placed the mug on the floor before dropping to her knees, her hands spread out on the tiles.

'Why,' she sobbed to herself, 'dear God, do it not get no easier?'

CHAPTER THREE

The Quarry Pool

Back home from another useless trip to the Valley road to wait for the phantom school bus, I'd find Daddy upstairs in the bath, gazing along the islands made by his stomach, penis and toes, or studying irregularities in the plaster on the ceiling. I felt the water: 'It's cold! Come on, let's get dry.'

He proudly showed me his fingers, their skin corrugated by wet wrinkles. Mother would come in time to dry his hair, vigorously rubbing it with a towel as he sat on the side of the bath, though it would have dried within minutes anyway during that summer, when on Mondays the washing had dried by the time mother hung the next lot on the line. As the reservoirs emptied and the water authority banned the use of hose-pipes and watering-cans and urged entire families to bath together, so mother did a wash only every fortnight at first and then once a month, out of a sense of civic responsibility, but it didn't matter since we wore fewer and fewer clothes anyway and all began to look as foreign as auntie Maria up in the poet's shack.

We sweated so much we'd go whole days without needing to pee, and when we did we had to go outside to save flushing the toilet. With no school I'd head off to the quarry pool, not to wash off my sweat but to seek relief from the heat in the black water.

I'd walk through the village, past Rotten Row, where Granny Sims and her sisters and all their families lived, with the Post Office and General Store in the middle – a bare room with a few provisions stocked on wooden shelves – and Elsie's sweetshop in the end cottage. Our family was rare for the way the men went out of the village to find a wife, but even so the natural inbreeding of the village was exaggerated in Rotten Row: mother said that Granny Sims forbade them to come out of the Row to marry, and it's true that it was inhabited by a chaos of generations, of babies begotten by a bewildering variety of parents, all mixed up, so that even Granny Sims, who prided herself on her intricate knowledge of everyone's affairs, was perplexed by the confusion of her own family, with an unaccounted child here or a mismatched aunt there. They seemed to sleep wherever they found themselves when they were tired and mothers fed whoever happened to be around their table at mealtimes: when I whistled to see if anyone wanted to come swimming I never knew what child would emerge from which door.

On the way to the quarry pool I paused at the lip in the hill where the stream, after struggling through the village, could drop down the steep incline to the Teign below.

I took the telescope from the sawn-off branch of the beech tree there and made sure that the widowman heron was still down by the pool, maintaining his vigil on the overhanging rock, staring through his lonely reflection on the water's surface. Beyond him, beside the river, a skein of mist lay strung along the Valley, as if the steam train of grandmother's memory had returned along the disused railway line during the night and left its vapour trail tangled among the treetops.

As the sun burned into the Valley, the big house over on the estate rose through the mist, its enormous windows all boarded up and holes gaping in its tiled roof. Tracking across the deserted lawns to the waterfall I could make out kids from Teign Village or Hennock cooling themselves beneath the long cascade, seeking a kind of refuge just as rich people had when Napoleon declared war, and wealthy Exeter families fled from the impending invasion along the narrow lanes and up the steep hills to this remote asylum. The 8th Viscount Teignmouth had welcomed them all, each new arrival with ever greater warmth, not because of the rent he could charge them but because his family had acquired the politeness of aristocrats, and when the last of them departed after receiving news of the Battle of Trafalgar without giving him a farthing for his hospitality, they left the orchards bare, the granaries ransacked, the kitchens upside down, the terraced lawns rubbed out and everything in an even worse state than the Diggers had left it in a hundred and fifty years before, or the hippies would a hundred and fifty years later.

After seeing reminders of grandmother's history I'd put the telescope back in its place and follow the stream down. The water in the quarry pool was so deep that beneath the surface it stayed cold all summer and gave you cramp when you least expected it. No one was supposed to swim out into the middle, and when now and then one of the older boys forced himself to, his fear was there for anyone to see in the disturbed muscles of his face as he struggled back.

The little kids went skinny-dipping, but we didn't. Between swims we poked around in the scrubby copse that'd grown over the mineworkings around the pool, and into which the widowman heron retreated when we disturbed his vigil on the projecting rock that we dived off. We'd see how long we could lie in the sun without moving, until our backs sizzled, and then we'd leap into the water with a hiss.

The older girls didn't want to dive, they just hung around whispering to each other and waiting for the boys to come over. But the boys were busy showing off their ever more complicated somersault twists and ducking each other. At the beginning of the summer, after I'd left Middle School for ever, I copied the older girls. Jane was happy to join them, but it was a tedious way to spend time, and soon I became the only girl that summer who learned to do a double backward dive. The boys resented that, and the girls looked the other way.

No one bothered with towels: the beads of moisture that came out of the pool with us vanished from our skin, but by the time we'd climbed to the beech tree our clothes would already be damp again.

Grandmother's very first Christmas in the village was the

wettest in living memory: it even rained on Christmas Day itself, an unheard-of phenomenon.

The church was full for the communion service, and afterwards, while the women were preparing dinner, the men in squeaking boots and uncomfortable hats strolled around the village, despite the drizzle, smoking and conversing over each other's gates. Two of them, Joseph Howard and grandfather, ambled along the lane beside the village stream, discussing the barter of a new set of window-frames for a rocky slope of land behind the church, and before they knew where they were they found themselves at the end of the lane, beside the beech tree above the granite quarry where grandfather had briefly worked, looking down upon a sight so baffling they could only stare at it in silence. Yet even so others were drawn inexplicably in their direction and joined them, equally awestruck by the spectacle. When their daughters and sisters were sent out to call the men in to dinner they found the village deserted, and even though they searched separately for various fathers and brothers they all found themselves propelled in the same direction.

The women of the village sweating around the stoves, after calling from their kitchens, finally stepped outside and proceeded to follow each other without consultation, pulled not by their will but rather by impulses so far out on the edges of their senses that they were unaware of them at the time. It was only afterwards that they were able to infer from traces in the sediment of their memories that they must have been drawn by the inaudible screeching and the blurred tilting of wings of seagulls, and by the intangible taste of salt in the air, because that was the only explanation for them joining the rest of their families around the beech tree beside the lip in the hill where the village stream dropped to the Valley below. And then they too were dumbfounded by the sight of the great quarry transformed into a black, bottomless pool of water.

No one moved.

They barely breathed.

There was no conflict raging in their hearts, wondering

whether to develop murderous intentions towards their employer, the 14th Viscount, for having them work in so dangerous a place, or on the other hand to thank Christ for delivering this natural catastrophe on the one day of the year when not a single person was working there. They were simply overcome by the spectacle. But then someone dropped forward, no one knows whether they stumbled or even fainted, whereupon everyone else too fell to their knees in relief and praise for the Saviour who'd been born on Christmas Day, the one day of the year everyone, even the night-watchman, had a holiday, and who had saved forty-seven villagers from what grandmother assured me was the worst form of death, that of drowning, because it's the most lonely.

When I got back mother was cutting Daddy's hair in the kitchen. He picked up a cluster that had fallen in his lap, and considered the mixture of black and white hairs with a frown on his face.

'I can't 'ave 'ad a bath since us all painted the pig-sty,' he decided with a rare note of conviction, although he was wrong. In reality the Howards had been the first and only ones to make the mistake of whitewashing a farm building that summer: the whole family got snow-blindness and had to stay inside wearing dark glasses for a week, nursing their eyes with hot flannels boiled in rosemary-scented water. Mike said it even hurt to watch television. I helped Tom take care of their animals, scattering hay from the trailer like we did in winter.

Before she'd let Daddy out to play, mother made him lie down on the settee in the front room and listen to one of the records that Pamela brought home from the library in Exeter. Mother said it stopped him getting wrinkles. He lay still as a boulder in a stream and let the torrent of notes of a harpsichord sonata pour over him. He couldn't hold them and didn't try, but simply let them slide over the smooth surface of his mind.

I got itchy waiting: in common with my elder brothers and

13

sister I had no talent for music. Mother had installed a piano when she first became pregnant, with Ian, and after that she knew when she'd conceived because she'd awake one morning with an illogical tune nagging at her mind which she'd have to root out on the piano. It was the only time she ever played, she said it was good for the baby in her womb and that we'd be born with a lifelong love of music, but the tactic failed with each of us in turn. After I was born she never played again, but she kept the piano tuned none the less in the hope that some inspiration might yet awaken in one of us a sleeping talent.

The piano tuner wore a black suit and tie, and he had the solemn bearing of an undertaker. Grandmother and mother and Pamela would argue over his age in the kitchen while he adjusted wires and tightened screws until he was satisfied with our cheap piano's tone and pitch, and then he'd reduce them to enchanted silence with his rendering of one of Liszt's *Consolations*. At one time he'd almost had to give up his practice because half the husbands barred him from coming into their houses while they were out at work, with his sad bearing like a droopy flower and his suspicious hair lotion whose aroma hung around the piano for the rest of the day, because they could sense that women felt a need to comfort him.

'Of all times to be in this line of work,' he said in his high-pitched voice when he joined us for coffee in the kitchen, 'I find myself in the twentieth century. The Dismal Age of the Decline of Music. It's up to you women to keep it going, you know, you'll have to carry the responsibility now: men have lost their sensitivity. I don't know what I'd have done without the newcomers.'

The piano tuner had made his biannual visit from Chagford one Tuesday morning in July, plagued, as he was all through that mournful summer, by a small swarm of midges that gathered around the tuning fork, attracted by its hum, under the illusion that it was made by the wings of a female mosquito.

14

CHAPTER FOUR

Laying Hedges

Ian, my eldest brother, was the one who ran the farm now, but he never chose to. He didn't seem to mind, he always brushed everything off.

'I never 'spected to do what I want with my life,' he assured me, 'there's few people gets that lucky.' But you could see that underneath his calm manner he was in a constant state of fretting and fidgeting: the uncertainties of a farmer's life tied his insides up in knots. He could never work out, despite hours spent at his desk making calculations, how we would ever make any money given the incalculables of the weather, health and disease, cattle-market prices and foreign competition, vehicle maintenance and capital investment, but, most of all, time. It was always working against him. He started his day, after a few hours of fitful sleep, swinging out of bed and punching the alarm clock in a single movement. In the bathroom he wiped himself with one hand and brushed his teeth with the other, he combed his hair as he shaved, he pulled his shirt on at the same time as he tied his shoelaces, at breakfast he gulped his tea while his mouth was full of food, and he carried on through the day in the same way, except that he somehow managed to do it with an air of calm efficiency, as if he were acting in this way purely as a controlled experiment, which saved him from looking like a madman.

Despite Ian's efforts, though, time always seemed to catch up and overtake him and when, exhausted, he collapsed on his bed in the early hours of the morning, all the things he still had to do seemed to pile up on an imaginary conveyor-belt and glide contemptuously past, a succession of tasks undone, floating by him as sleep dragged him under, into tomorrow. I thought it was a unique and absurd affliction that possessed my brother, until I got to know the Rector and discovered that he suffered exactly the same.

Ian hid his impatience from most people, but if they watched him they'd have noticed the way he tightened the curls of his hair with one finger when he appeared to be at ease. And they might have wondered why he was so thin: he consumed prodigious quantities of food, as much as Tom did, but without adding any flesh to his wiry frame. Mother told him he kept a worm inside his body which ate up all the surplus calories, so that he could have the pleasures of gluttony without its consequences; he sometimes failed to make sure that the toilet had managed to flush away the evidence of his appetite, leaving a large turd floating in the bowl.

The only time Ian made no effort to hide his impatience was when he thought he'd be late for football, which was every Saturday afternoon. He'd rush across the yard, socks or shin-pads spilling from his sportsbag, rev up his yellow ex-British Telecom van, lurch forward then brake suddenly, remembering something he'd forgotten, lift off the door whose hinges he never got round to fixing, lean it against the side of the van, come scrambling back into the house, demand to know who the hell had hidden his tie-ups, eventually find them where he'd left them the week before, dash out again, leap into the van pulling the door behind him, and screech out of the yard in a turmoil of dust, burning rubber, and panic-stricken chickens.

The only escape that Ian found from time's unblinking scrutiny was in his insomniac's refuge of the early hours, listening to the sounds of the sea on his short-wave radio as he played another game of chess against his computer. He couldn't understand how, in the middle of the chaos and confusion of life that teemed around him, something of such beauty – and nothing more than a game, at that – could exist, an infinitely renewable, unfolding secret waiting for him to make the first move and develop into another unique pattern of intrigue and delight. It was truly incredible. When I started going to church on my own, after mother stopped, he used to tease me: 'Don't be silly, maid, there b'ain't no God. Unless he was the one what invented chess. I could make some sense out of that.'

'Come on, mother,' I said, while the record was still droning on. 'Can't I take Daddy out yet?'

'Stop your bloody moaning, maid. Why don't you play with someone your own age for a change?' she demanded. 'What's Jane doing?'

'I don't know,' I replied. 'Go on, mother, you can see he wants to.'

Mother made Daddy put on his dark jacket, 'because it keeps the heat off', so she said, but I knew that really it was just because she liked him to look smart. We ambled across the farmyard through the fetid air that drifted from the barn, past the gaggle of cackling geese loath to leave the stagnant pond, between the hens pecking some illusory sustenance from the dust, and into the lane. Sweat broke out across Daddy's smooth forehead, and his soft cheeks reddened.

We carried on out of the village. Since the sun hurt our eyes we opened our ears instead. All I could hear was the strange hum that hovered behind every other sound throughout that summer. Earlier on, when it first became audible, there was widespread unease at the idea that Mrs Corporal Alcock's tinnitus had become contagious, and people bent over and shook their heads or used knitting needles to try and dislodge the singing insect in their eardrums. Soon, though, people had to make a special effort to distinguish it from everyday silence and it no longer irritated anyone, except for grandmother, who had recognized the first symptoms of cholera. Her own great-grandmother had died in the epidemic that decimated Exeter, and she would choose inappropriate moments to ask relatives and strangers alike who passed through the house whether they'd felt a sensation of giddiness recently or a feeling of uneasiness in their stomach, and she warned us to look out for what she described as rice-water motions.

Soon the hum was consigned to the background and there was a faint squelching as Daddy's heavy boots were absorbed by gravel swimming in the liquefying tarmac. Gradually I extended the range of my hearing: a whine emerged from the blurry clouds of gnats and midges that hung over the meadow to our right, and we passed a thrush in the hedgerow whose liquid runs of melody were constantly abandoned and begun again. Then from what seemed a long way away came a tinkling of silver bells, and I shielded my eyes to see if I could catch my first glimpse of the procession of Buddhists who were rumoured to have turned Whiteway House over Haldon into a monastery and filed through surrounding villages begging for alms.

I couldn't see anything, but then I looked down at my feet and found we were walking through an entire army of toads.

'Watch where you're treading, Daddy!' I yelled.

'Runnin' Belinda!' he exclaimed. 'There's hundreds of the little things.'

We stood still to let them pass. They were hopping laboriously along the lane, as disorientated by the sun stealing their ponds as they had been ten years before when the useless plots of land on the steep slope below the church were sold, and enormous yellow bulldozers invaded the village to gouge out platforms on which to build houses for commuting newcomers. With one scoop a bulldozer's bucket removed the tiny bog where grandfather could remember collecting frogspawn. The Simmons family, first of the outsiders to move in the following winter, woke up one spring morning to find their house besieged by hundreds of croaking toads, the smallest of which had squeezed under the doors and hopped up the stairs to the bathroom. They returned every year, following the stars, to tamper with the dreams of the Simmons family with their mournful croaking, more melancholy even than the braying of the Honeywills' donkey. Even when the toads grew silent it took only one of them to croak and set off all the others again. The children had vague but

18

guilt-ridden dreams, until they finally persuaded their father to dig a goldfish pond in the garden.

The tinkling tribe of toads seemed endless, and by the time we'd passed through them all we'd reached where the lane forked left up to Haldon Forest. From over in Barton Wood came the tap-tap-tapping of a woodpecker, while the plaint of sheep at the heat of the sun expressed the whole world's discomfort. The feeble trickle of water in the stream labouring towards the village was virtually inaudible, and was replaced in the spectrum of sound by the chiming of church bells for an hour well past: the air was so dry and thin that they came in dissonant waves, like a spring being unwound, all the way from Exeter Cathedral.

We stood at the junction. Close by, a meadowlark elaborated phrases of notes in a new song. The air that was so dry in my throat was liquid to look at. Towards Shilhay, moving amongst his herd of sorrowful cows, was the shimmering but unmistakable silhouette of Douglas Westcott, as he carefully picked ticks off his cattle and squeezed them, in tiny eruptions of blood.

Douglas was the bull-like recluse who'd left home, grandmother told me, the day his father chided him for his bestial table manners. He rose from the table without a word. His mother found him packing everything he needed into a holdall no larger than a lady's handbag. 'I'm going to find out whether the world looks like the maps say it do,' he told her, and strode through the front door. His father ordered that no one should step over that threshold before Douglas did, and from then on they entered and left the house only through the kitchen. Once when Stuart from the shop was delivering a box of groceries and, receiving no answer to his knocking, opened the door to leave them in the porch, old Westcott saw him from the barn and stilled his heartbeat with a bellow. He marched over, picked Stuart up by the scruff of his neck, carried him to the drinking trough, and dropped him in.

Summers robbed the beechwood door of all its juice, and

thirst bent it; the rains made it swell; the winters froze and cracked it. The house settled further upon itself.

Douglas appeared in the farmyard after twelve years, seven months, two weeks and six days away. When the family, who had heard his heavy flat feet approaching, had greeted him, then his father bade them gather as he ceremoniously opened the front door. But it was stuck fast, warped into the frame. He pushed and then he kicked it but he made no impression, except when he put his shoulder against it and felt, in his fury, fine shards of bone splintering off his scapula. As celebration turned into embarrassment Douglas fetched the big axe from its usual place in the barn, pushed his father out of the way, and with one swing clove the door in half so that it swung open, one side on the hinges, the other on the catch. He re-entered the house, and they knew then that he had changed for the worse.

The afternoon was at its height: the sun had just begun its slow descending curve towards Cornwall and was slumbering on the wing. A drowsy hornet drifted by. The harsh air rasped my throat as I inhaled, and my eyelids felt heavy as velvet.

'I'm thirsty,' said Daddy. In the hedge to our right I spotted a ripe blackberry, and as Daddy reached over to pluck it another appeared, then another. Soon his lips and tongue were stained purple. He lay down in the shadowed verge and fell asleep, and I joined him.

I dreamt of a man forcing his horse through waist-high snowdrifts up on to the moor, and of the woman, grand-mother with hazelnut hair, breathing on a window pane as she waited. I dreamt that as I lay sleeping an insect flew from my mouth. People gathered round but wouldn't wake me. Suddenly they were gone and I woke gagging on something in my throat. I hawked but it wouldn't budge. I knew I should try and eat it, to save from choking, but the idea of swallowing a tick was worse than dying. Then I was saved by my own body, which sprang my neck forward in convulsive retching until I felt the insect tumble on to my tongue. I opened my mouth and gently lifted it between thumb and forefinger, but it had gone and turned into a freshly cut twig. At that moment my ears opened: a fury of thwacking and crackling bore down upon us, and as I looked up old Martin the hedge-layer saw me too and stopped working.

'Alison!' he exclaimed, and then as Daddy stirred, 'Georgie! Oi didn't see 'ee down in the ditch there.'

Old Martin sunk his bill into a stout sapling and proffered a hand to help Daddy to his feet.

'Fell asleep, did 'ee? Goods a place as any I s'pose, though 'tidn't wise to sleep out in the 'ot. You's all flicketty, maid; you must both be parch-mouthed. Come and 'ave some tea.'

He poured us a cup from his thermos. The liquid soothed my burning mouth and throat, and as it trickled down my gullet and into my stomach it brought me alive.

'Thank you, that's better,' Daddy said, returning the cup to old Martin, who poured himself a little and sipped it slowly. His face and bald skull were glazed in a film of sweat. He cleared his throat and gobbed into the hedge.

'You been out walkin' then?' he asked Daddy.

'Yes,' I replied for him.

'See anything about?'

'Nothin' much,' I said.

'See Douglas out with his cows, mazed bugger?' he asked, because he always wanted to know everything. When he'd asked all his questions, we leaned into the heat, saying nothing.

'In't you gettin' 'ot and tired workin' out in this sun?' Daddy asked after a while.

'I loves it, bay. 'Tis winter makes me slow at my age. Sweat's my lubrication, I works better with it. Why, us 'aven't 'ad a summer like this since 1976, though I don't s'pose you'd callhome that, Georgie. No, the 'otter the better for me. Only trouble is it gets lonely; the rest of you lazy buggers is sleepin' all day!'

Old Martin could talk the hindlegs off a donkey, as grand-mother put it; he was the friendliest man in the village.

'I never ought to be layin' 'edges this time o' year, I don't mind tellin' 'ee. You should cut young wood in winter, and the older ones early spring, or late autumn if you prefers. Not summer. Trouble is I don't want to get behind, like, or they'll start usin' a tractor-saw and make a bloody mess of everything. You seen over Bridford?'

I shook my head.

'They's pullin' up 'edges and puttin' fences in their place. Old boy up there's out of a job. They says to 'im, they says, "Look at it practical, like. With 'edges you can lay eight yard a day on yours own, or fifty yard with another bloke. But a man on his own can fence a whole field in a day." "Where's the birds gonna nest then?" he says to 'em. Farmers 'as always been greedy, like, no offence mind, but now 'tis worse than ever 'twas.'

Old Martin was the friendliest man in the village, and the most lonely. Even dogs slunk away from him, snarling, and he made televisions flicker on the rare occasions he was invited into someone's front room. He'd been laying hedges for years, like his uncle before him. According to grandmother, at the end of the last war, when half a dozen young men returned to the village, old Cecil recalled the ingratitude that had greeted him when he came back from the Somme in 1918, and so he passed over his contracts to his nephew.

Now Martin drained his cup and screwed it back on the flask. Picking up his heavy maul he said:

'I better be back to work afore I cools down,' and I wondered how he'd be able to do that even if he wanted to. Daddy hung around to watch him thumping stakes into the middle of the saplings he'd already plashed. He put all his energy into it, but I felt like I saw him as Daddy saw him, and there was something illusory about his movements, as if someone else were really performing them. At last Daddy couldn't contain his curiosity any longer.

'Where's Martin the hedge-layer?' he asked. 'Is you his uncle or what?'

Old Martin stopped and turned, his nut-brown forehead wrinkled with irritation at Daddy's familiar question.

'I'm Martin,' he said, pointing to himself with his bill. 'I'm the 'edge-layer, Martin.' He returned to his work, and I pulled Daddy on along the lane back towards the village.

He was quiet for a moment, but was soon looking around to see what was happening in the world. Through the thick sluggish air a barely perceptible breeze surprised us, brushing past our faces. Then, to our left, across a field a scattered cloud of thistledown came floating. We climbed over the gate, and all across the field soft white burrs attached themselves to us, until we entered the huge, overgrown vegetable garden of the rectory.

CHAPTER FIVE

Cool Sanctuary of Stone

From his room my brother Tom had a clear view of the field between the rectory and the new houses. It was where Susanna Simmons grazed her palomino pony. Sometimes she would just visit him, as he stood by the fence, licking the block of salt she renewed every week.

She always took an apple or a carrot with her, and offered it on her open palm. The pony mouthed it carefully, with his thick and clumsy lips, to avoid biting her.

After he'd swallowed it she stood beside him, stroking his neck, and they nuzzled each other, Susanna inhaling the sharp, sweet horse's smell with her eyes closed, as she ran her nose across his skin. It seemed to Tom as if she were about to sink her teeth into the animal's flesh. He watched her as she blew her breath into the pony's nostrils: its body became quite still, and Tom felt, himself, the pony's pleasure.

The Old Rectory had been the first building in the village in which glass was installed in windows, and people queueing to pay their tithes were perplexed to see themselves inside the house as well as outside where they stood, even though according to grandfather a full millennium had passed since the Romans had glazed the basilica in Isca just ten miles away.

When they built a new rectory up on the ridge along from the church they made an even bigger house, with rolling lawns at the front and a steep vegetable garden the size of a football pitch round the back. Now that the Rector's family had long since grown up and left home and he had neither time nor appetite to cultivate it, he made only occasional

24

forays into what had become a jungle to seek out the few hardy plants whose chemistry withstood the onslaught of weeds: cucumbers and rhubarb and sweet potatoes.

Daddy and I picked our way along paths dictated by the whim of the Rector's footsteps, avoiding brambles and nettles, until we arrived at his front door.

I pushed the rectory doorbell and lifted the letterbox flap in order to hear the copper bell ring in the back hallway, and echo through the twenty-six empty rooms surrounding the Rector's study, into which he retreated during his brief moments of respite, to continue the metaphysical contemplation he'd refused to abandon despite a lifetime's ministry among people who ignored his ideas, though it would most likely have been the same anywhere else, since he had been so handsome that people weren't able to look at him and absorb what he was saying at the same time. Instead, the men made jokes about his schoolboy looks and their wives fought remorseless silent struggles for the best pews. When at last time found him out at the age of fifty-five and overnight his face crumpled and his jet-black hair turned white it was already too late, for they'd long grown deaf to the obscure theology he proposed, simplified though it was from the lucid perceptions that came to him in his study, surrounded by twenty-six empty rooms, where he speculated upon new aspects of unconsidered truths.

When I got to know him and asked why he had so many rooms between him and the world he said he needed the space, though their number was irrelevant and might just as well have been three, for the space he needed was immeasurable.

The echo of the doorbell finally died in an abandoned dining-room, and no sound of footsteps came.

The church door was wide open but we hesitated in the porch: an old man was sitting in the front pew, his gaze directed at the altar. I was going to knock and ask if he minded us coming in, but Daddy looked at me and put a finger to his lips. We stepped stealthily in and sat down in a pew at the back, escaping from the torpid heat into a cool sanctuary of stone. I could feel the perspiration drying on my skin, cool and tingly.

My nostrils filled with a smell of must and moisture, an ecclesiological smell, as tangible as the enticing ordurous aroma that rain lifts from cow-pats. It was ever-present inside the church, exacerbating worshippers' incipient rheumatism and almost encouraging enough signatures on Granny Sims's biannual petition for the incense and holy water of High Church ritual to sway the three nonconformist priests whose ministries she oversaw, as well as allowing atheistic families to taunt their neighbouring believers with the claim that praying gives you piles.

Yet it was all an illusion. In reality the air was bone dry: it nibbled at the edges of the brittle leaves of the huge Bible spread across the lectern eagle's wings, and following the old man's gaze to the altar I could discern the candle there disappearing, consumed by its descending flame.

Dead flowers in dirty glass vases had shed their petals on the window-sills. On a boss in the centre of the nave roof three rabbits shared three ears of corn, keenly scrutinized by the eagle on the lectern, its savage beak prepared at any moment to break through its wooden shell, throwing off the huge Bible, which would disintegrate on impact with the stone floor, and sink its claws into those three rabbits that clung stupidly on to the ceiling. Corporal Alcock had told me during the Falklands war that an eagle's talons are even sharper than the kukris of the gurkhas, alongside whom he'd once fought, and who broke the morale of the enemy at Goose Green, scalping Argentine conscripts as they slept.

The old man in the front pew was still motionless and facing the altar, the candle almost all eaten up. In the window behind, flanked by two female saints, the folds of their softly contoured skin and pleated robes flowing through the glass, sat a resolute Christ with a sickle in his hand. Running across the bottom of the window were the words: 'Thrust in thy sickle and reap, for the time is come to reap, for the harvest of the earth is ripe.'

Beside me Daddy shuffled. He entered the aisle and slowly

approached the old man. As he did so he could hear a dry whisper, but there were neither angels nor bats fluttering in the high roof, the wings of the saints remained rigid in glass, and there was no wind anywhere in the world to play around the steeple. It was only as he came right up behind the man that Daddy realized that the sound was that of the man intoning a barely audible, sibilant whisper.

'Hello,' Daddy exclaimed.

The man rose, tall and stooped, looking down on him. He was wearing a dog-collar, so Daddy recognized the Rector all right, but I knew how startlingly old he must have looked to him. A smile further creased his delicate skin into a cobweb of wrinkles.

'Hello, Georgie. How are you?'

'All right, Rector,' Daddy replied, his voice all disturbed. The Rector stepped out of the pew and Daddy took a few hesitant paces backwards, then stopped and stared at him.

'Rector,' he asked, 'does praying make you old?'

The Rector looked sad, and reached a long, bony arm towards Daddy's shoulder, but Daddy stepped backwards again and it fluttered there like a chicken's useless wing. Daddy turned and rushed out of the church.

The Rector watched him go. Behind him, the big candle guttered and died, releasing a plume of smoke.

'Hello, Alison,' the Rector said softly; and then he cheered up as he walked towards me. 'What are you doing? I'd have thought with no school you'd all be out playing. I wish teachers had gone on strike in our day.'

'There's no one to play with, really,' I told him.

'Had an argument?' he smiled.

'Not really. They're just stupid I suppose. Last time Jane and Susan came round they ended up with Pamela in her room, doing the dancing from Bananarama's video. She hasn't even got a big mirror.'

'Sounds like fun.'

'You should try it,' I said without thinking. 'I suppose I better see where Daddy's got to.'

*

I stepped into the still sweltering afternoon. Daddy had carried on out of the graveyard and past the old Gospel Oak whose roots still baffled gravediggers. I sat down against a headstone in the middle of the churchyard and closed my eyes. I could hear bees buzzing around the few wilting flowers placed on two or three graves. A centipede crawled onto my leg. It was the same colour as my skin. I tugged a stem of grass and tried to annoy the insect into biting the grass with its pincers, but it just crawled dumbly over my knee.

Into the silence came a tuneless whistle, attempting a martial tune. I looked round the side of the headstone and saw Corporal Alcock the organist limping stiffly into the churchyard, accompanied by Chico, his serpentine dog, and I felt happy again. Invalided out of the army in 1944 after being hit by shrapnel, which according to his wife would work its way out of his body, fragments appearing unexpectedly under the surface of his skin which she would pierce with a needle in order to remove them, Corporal Alcock had insisted ever since on being addressed by his rank. Any new arrival in the village he would plug with subtle but insistent questions to ascertain whether or not they'd been in the services, and if so what rank they'd achieved, because he was mortified by the possibility of failing to call his superiors 'sir' at the end of every sentence. He carried his bad leg as rigidly as his ramrod back, and treated everyone with the same impenetrable formality: there was no hint of deference in the manner of his salute to superiors nor condescension in his attitude even to us children. When I came out from behind the headstone he stopped and leaned away from me, gaining in width what he lacked in height by clasping his hands behind his back and thrusting out his shoulders.

'Been in the church, Alison?' he barked.

'Yes, Corporal Alcock.'

'Good girl. Us can't let this 'eat get us down, can us? In the desert you know, with one mug of water for all our washin' purposes, us shaved every day without fail. 'Tis a matter of morale.'

'Yes, Corporal Alcock.'

'Keep yer chin up.'

He limped on towards the church, spine as proud as ever despite the fact that he was approaching his nemesis, for it was only because the organ unmanned him that he was not just tolerated but even cherished as organist for the monthly family service, when the congregation would struggle to overcome the cacophony he produced in return for the sublime pleasure of witnessing his inevitable humiliation. Tone deaf, Corporal Alcock began each hymn unerringly on the wrong note, losing the battle as soon as he started. The rest of the hymn would take off like a runaway horse that only became more frenzied as he attempted to whip it into submission, with the congregation trying to catch up. Occasionally, drenched in sweat and back arched over the keyboard like a wrestler pinning down his opponent, he'd finally force the tune to an abrupt standstill, only for the voices to gleefully carry on past, challenging him to catch up with them. Then he'd explode into action once more, inflexible legs pumping the pedals and stubby fingers crashing down upon the keys. With unfailing courage Corporal Alcock persisted, even through that merciless summer when the newcomers' domestic animals, driven mad by the heat, would gather in the porch to miaow and howl their accompaniment. After each hymn, in the residue of insuppressible giggles, he'd bend limply forward, heaving breathlessly. Yet by the end of every service he'd fully recovered his composure and would march stiffly home behind his wife, oblivious to the ridicule and admiration of everyone.

I could hear him begin practising, the organ an untameable beast, as I passed through the lych-gate, and I hurried on, catching up with Daddy in the square by the Brown. Over in the almshouse, Nan Dyer, blurred by cigarette smoke, shrank in her doorway: she was even smaller than Corporal Alcock. 'Get out of the sun, maid,' she called at me in her broken voice. She'd smoked so many cigarettes that she spoke with a growl. She was also, grandmother told me, the last of the choirsingers in the village: she'd sung all the right notes in the wrong way for forty years, until her vocal chords were shot to pieces.

'You'll go soft in the head if you stays out in this sun,' she growled.

I looked around for Daddy: he was on the Brown, hanging by his knees from the crossbar of one of the goals, grasping it with his hands. His jacket had fallen down and hung behind him, and he was gently rocking.

When we stood down on the Valley road, waiting for the school bus that didn't appear, Johnathan Teignmouth stood always apart. He never spoke to anyone, because as soon as he opened his mouth people made fun of his aristocrat's accent, braying at each other like donkeys. If anyone spoke to him he answered not with words but by raising his left eyebrow, turning down the sides of his mouth, and gazing off in another direction. Out of the corner of his other eye, though, he watched everything that went on – the banter, the fighting, the laughter; all that he was excluded from. Standing aloof from the crowd, he managed to look both contemptuous and as if he was about to cry. But it was much easier and safer to laugh at him than to approach him, so I kept my distance.

The next morning the bus again failed to show up, because the strike was being maintained, teachers still refusing to take classes so big that remembering everybody's name, never mind teaching them, they claimed, was a proven impossibility. I went home, changed, and got straight back out to go swimming. Tinker followed me, padding along the lane, panting for breath. I reached the quarry pool and dived in on my own, feeling safe to do so because if anything happened I knew Tinker would throw herself in and doggy-paddle to my rescue.

I floated on my back, propelling myself slowly to stop from sinking, looking up at the sky. If I bent my head right back the world was turned upside down.

I climbed out on to the overhanging rock, and was sat there enjoying the brief sensation of water still on my skin, before it evaporated, when Tinker started barking. She went over to some bushes and stopped in front of them, bared her teeth, and growled. Standing beside her, I could make out some shapeless form amongst the branches and leaves, and colour in the shadows.

'You better come out, whoever you are,' I said, 'or I might have to let this mad dog loose.'

'No need to, actually,' a voice called back, 'quite all right; I'm c-c-coming out right away. Keep hold of your hound.' Johnathan Teignmouth crawled from the bushes. Tinker growled all the more. Johnathan looked nervously at her, his eyebrows twitching. He was pale and skinny in his shorts and tee-shirt. The only reason one or two of the boys never went further than making fun of him was because a relationship of masters and servants that had lasted for hundreds of years couldn't be set aside overnight, and saved him from the bullying that he was otherwise ready-made for.

'Might it be an idea to stop him growling?' he asked nervously.

'He's a she!' I told him. 'Anyway, what was you doing in there?'

'Nothing,' he replied. 'Just looking for b-b-birds' nests, actually.'

'Don't be stupid. Birds don't build nests in little bushes.'

'Don't they? No, I didn't find any. Can't you stop her growling?'

'Maybe I can. Wouldn't do no good.'

'Why not?' he asked worriedly, not taking his eyes off Tinker for a moment.

'She'll only stop if she thinks we's friends. We'll have to shake hands or something.'

He extended his arm towards me, but Tinker bared her teeth, and he quickly withdrew it.

'It's all right, girl,' I said, and stepped forward and shook his hand. Tinker looked at us for a moment, then went and lay in some shade under a bush.

'Did you come to swim?' I asked him. 'I never seen you swimming.'

'I don't know that I do,' he replied.

31

'Come on!' I said on impulse. 'I don't mind going in again.'

He'd stopped twitching and blushing by now. He furrowed his brow in concentration, glanced up at the path, and then smiled: 'That's a jolly good idea.'

He followed me onto the overhanging rock, and removed his trainers.

'You can't swim in your tee-shirt,' I told him. 'You'll have to take that off.'

'I'd rather not, actually.'

'All right, if you don't want to. Go on then, you can dive in first.'

His left eyebrow rose. 'I don't dive, if you don't mind.'

I looked him up and down, beginning to regret my soft-heartedness. I should have let Tinker keep him trapped in the bushes until I felt like going home. He wouldn't take his tee-shirt off, and he couldn't even dive. He was no use to anyone.

'I suppose you *can* swim?' I asked sarcastically.

'I think so,' he said.

'What do you mean you *think* so? Don't you know? Either you can or you can't.'

'Well, I suppose I can, then,' he replied, the side of his mouth lifting in an ironic and superior smile. It made me suddenly furious.

'We better find out, then,' I said, and I stepped forward and pushed him backwards off the rock into the water. He was so light and skinny it was like pushing over a bundle of bean-poles: his body offered no resistance, falling into air. He somersaulted backwards, landed with a splash in the water, and disappeared.

I leaned over the rock, and peered into the dark water. Gradually it recomposed its placid surface. And he was gone. My heart rose into my throat, and I could feel it thumping there. 'Please, please,' I pleaded, 'come back, come back.' But the water was still.

I took a breath and dived in.

When you went deeper than a body's length in the pool, you couldn't see anything: it was all dark, like being under-ground, and I had to feel around for him, but my hands found nothing but water. I came back to the surface for air, and went back down again, twice, a third time, frantic, and a fourth. But I could only go down so far: he'd slipped down the steep side and into the depths of the pool. I kept on going, diving and coming up for air, hoping against hope that he would somehow still be no more than a few feet below the surface.

I kept trying till all my strength was spent, and I could hardly drag myself out of the pool.

I lay on the rock, shaking with fear, breathing hard to get my breath back, wondering already how I'd tell what I'd done, and whether I'd tell the truth. I started to cry, and looked up, and my heart stopped because there was Johnathan, standing twenty feet away, beside the water, looking at me with the side of his mouth raised in an ironic smile.

I chased him all the way around the pool. When I caught him up he was still laughing, and I was still mad with anger. I threw myself at him, and got on top of him.

'You bastard idiot!' I screamed. 'I thought you was dead. Don't laugh! That's the stupidest trick anyone can play. You must be mad.'

I raised my hand and was about to hit him but the next thing I knew Tinker was beside me, barking. Only she wasn't growling at him this time, she was pushing and nudging at me.

'Get off, you stupid dog!' I cried, but that just made her more excited, and I had to get up and move away. Johnathan laughed even more. I sat on the rock, my head swirling.

Eventually Tinker calmed down, and Johnathan stopped laughing.

'I'm sorry,' he said. 'But you shouldn't have pushed me in.'

'You can fuck off!' I yelled with my back to him. 'I don't want nothing to do with you. No wonder no one talks to you, if that's what you're like.'

When I turned round he was staring at the ground. His contemptuous look had vanished completely, leaving only the impression that he was about to burst into tears.

'Oh, I didn't mean it, you idiot. Don't be a baby.'

He looked at me, and then back down at the ground.

'Teach me to dive?' he asked.

'Don't try and make fun of me again, bay, or I really will get you.'

'I c-c-can't dive. I *can* swim, I admit, but I can't dive. No one's had time to show me how.'

'You don't have to be shown, you just does it.'

He wiped the sweat off his face. 'I'm scared to,' he whispered.

I got up. 'All right, then. Watch this.'

It was the beginning of our friendship, that Friday when we should have been in school. Whenever I went down to the pool on my own he'd emerge from out of the scrubby wasteland and we'd swim together. But if anyone else was around he never appeared, and I realized that he must have gone there every day, and stayed in hiding. We lay on the rock, drying off and blowing through grass and throwing pebbles. His pale skin burned in the sun, but he wouldn't leave until he heard someone else scrambling down the bed of the dried-up stream. Then his ears pricked up like a dog's, he'd sit bolt upright and say: 'Is that the time already? I ought to be going, actually,' and whatever I said made no difference. He gathered up his things in an instant and disappeared.

He was a good pupil: he did whatever I told him to, diving in with one hand or with his eyes closed, and even backwards, even when the very idea made his teeth chatter with fear. He stood rigid on the rock and stared hard at the water, his thin body trembling. Then he closed his eyes and screwed up his face like he was trying to swallow a mouthful of disgusting food, and launched himself forward.

It was strange to see someone who was so frightened by life: it took him a huge effort to overcome himself. At first I wanted to make fun of him, like everyone else; but it didn't take long for me to realize that in reality I'd never known anyone with so much courage.

CHAPTER SIX

Grandparents

My grandparents slept in a room at the other end of the corridor from mother and Daddy. Unlike most children in the village, my elder brothers and sister and I each had a room of our own, sandwiched between them. There was even a guest room next to the bathroom, where no one ever seemed to stay but over whose twin beds mother spread out patterns of material, strange shapes that bore no resemblance to the human body, from which she sewed clothes on an antique Singer, as if she were making dresses and shirts for mysterious, misshapen relatives who never arrived.

Grandfather and grandmother were as different from each other as it was possible for two such old people to be. 'We's two opposites come together to make a whole,' she confided in me one evening, taking grandfather's hand and cackling with pleasure at his embarrassment, as he struggled to concentrate on the wildlife programme on television.

Grandmother had an answer to every question, which she gave without pause for thought but with total conviction, and she held opinions on any subject that arose.

'Never trust a doctor,' she'd told me when I came home from Primary School one day with my arm aching from an innoculation. 'They makes money from fooling healthy folks into thinking they's sick.'

'But I told you grandma, 'twas a nurse.'

She shook her head. 'Same thing nowadays.'

'You'd sooner find a good-natured Cornishman than an honest policeman,' she assured me, spitting into the dust, on one of the rare occasions a Panda car cruised surreptitiously through the village. 'Why don't they leave people alone, prying into country folk's affairs. Git on back to the city, where you belong!' she shouted after them.

Grandfather, on the other hand, had few words. "Er's got enough for the both of them,' mother told me. Grandfather kept his own counsel. When someone addressed him, even one of his own family whom he'd known from the day of their birth, he shuffled from one foot to the other, unwilling to look you in the eye, blushing behind his ears and preferring to reply to grandmother, as if she was the one who'd asked him the question; or if she wasn't there, then he'd look at the ceiling when he spoke to you, fingers fiddling with his pipe, his whole body afflicted by the discomfort of speech.

I'm not sure anyone knew grandfather well, but everyone was aware of his reputation, not just as one of the wealthiest farmers in the district but also as a man of legendary guts, all because of two acts of bravery he'd committed in his youth. It wasn't grandfather who told me, of course, it was grandmother. She told me her stories with such conviction that I had to remind myself that she hadn't actually witnessed them herself.

'He were no more than a boy of ten or eleven year old, younger than you is, maid,' she said, taking my hand in her own roughened fingers as we sat on the sofa. 'He pushed past his own father and run into a blazing barn, and come out through the flames leadin' their pair of 'orses.'

I tried to imagine grandfather as a young boy but it was difficult, and the image got confused with that of Johnathan, so that I saw a pale, skinny boy with grandfather's stubbly face pulling two huge carthorses out of the fire.

In fact, it was the second display of bravery that really earned grandfather his reputation: when he left school at fifteen, his father was unable to justify his joining him on their farm that was little more than a smallholding, and so he fixed his son up with a job at the Viscount's quarry down in the Valley.

The Viscount had recently committed the grave error of appointing a Cornish foreman, and grandfather had only been working there a matter of weeks when the Cornishman, a squat, red-faced man, caught sight of him relieving himself in one of the small side-tunnels underground. Back at the surface grandfather's gang were stopped by the foreman. He didn't single grandfather out but put his hands on his hips and addressed them all together.

'You Devon bloody shirkers!' he roared. 'You works here same rules as the tin-miners: you eats in your own time, you shits in your own time. And you, lad,' he added, pointing a finger at grandfather, 'you're docked a penny from your wages.'

Grandfather felt his blood bubble and rise, it coursed through his fifteen-year-old body and made him seethe, but he could still think clearly. He knew instantly that he was resigning himself to a life of comparative poverty, on a casual farm-labourer's wages – unaware that the rest of the village miners would soon join him – when he stepped forward and with one punch sent the Cornish foreman back across the Tamar, with his jaw broken in so many places it was said that for the rest of his life he lived on a diet of soup sucked through a straw.

It was the first and last time grandfather ever struck anyone in anger. Nowadays he only got cross when city ramblers, having lost their way in the forest and wandered into our valley by mistake, left gates open; and when people were cruel to their animals. That was the real reason, rather than his shyness, as people assumed, that he'd never belonged to the Young Farmers, and also turned down annual invitations to join the organizing committee of the Christow and District Agricultural Show: he'd seen how other men treated their livestock, without dignity, and it was beyond his comprehension.

Grandfather never even raised his voice, except when he was on the telephone: when the first red phone box was erected across from the almshouse, grandfather had used it to order supplies from the grain merchants in Newton Abbot, and he shouted so loudly, since he couldn't believe that otherwise it was possible to communicate with someone miles away, that everyone in the village knew his business. It was a habit he never got round to breaking: even years later, during that summer when the air became so thin that the sound of trains entering St David's station in Exeter, nine miles away, could sometimes be heard in the Valley, fooling grandmother into thinking that the railway line beside the river had been reopened overnight, even then I'd be suddenly startled by the sound of grandfather shouting down the telephone, as if beside himself with rage, as he ordered 'FIFTY HUNDRED-WEIGHT OF FERTILIZER; YES, YOU HEARD RIGHT; SIXTEEN SACKS OF GRAIN; THE USUAL, BAY; SIX-TEEN, YES, AND TWO DOZEN TEN-GALLON DRUMS OF NITREX; DELIVER MONDAY, FREE-MANTLE ... YOU SHOULD KNOW BY NOW, ON ACCOUNT!'

Grandfather had come home from the quarry on that day of his dismissal and looked around for work, but the only jobs to be had for miles around were at the slaughterhouse at Longdown. He paid a visit, only to please his parents, and he was so put out by a pile of wishbones stacked up to the ceiling, by the fact that everyone who worked there appeared to be short of fingers, and by the way they had to yell to each other because they were going deaf from the squealing of the pigs, that he resolved never to take any of his animals, when he took over the farm, to die in such a place.

He came home and told his parents that it was no use, he'd just have to help his father with the twelve-head herd of cows in their paltry field, and make a bit of cash at other people's harvests, just as the family had always done it.

'In that case,' his father asked him, 'what else is you goin' to do?' because the only way they survived then was by supplementing their income with a specific craft, each small farmer in the village acquiring a different skill.

Grandfather, though, had neglected to consider this; yet he didn't like to appear stupid in front of his own father. He leaned back in his chair, took a puff on his clay pipe, blushed

38

behind his ears, and glanced around the room for inspiration. He took the pipe out of his mouth and exhaled its smoke through his nose. 'I thought I'd be, like, the window-maker, father.'

His father considered this option, and nodded. 'In't no window-maker hereabouts, bay. Don't see why 'e shouldn't earn a couple or three shillings from that, now and 'gain.'

During the summer that starlings stunned themselves against polished glass and wooden window-frames buckled in the sapless heat, grandfather had long since become one of the richest farmers for miles around, his ownership of property having spread like ink across the tapestry of fields, ignoring parish boundaries, on the map that Ian kept pinned above his desk. But even now grandfather was glad to abandon his agricultural chores at a moment's notice to go and repair someone's sash-cord windows somewhere in the Valley, because that instantaneous, unconsidered choice of a flustered fifteen-year-old had proved to be grandfather's vocation in life.

'Windows let in the light. We'd still be in darkness without them,' he told me. 'And we looks through them out at the world. Think about it, maid, you won't get it straightaway.'

He pressed a plug of tobacco into his pipe with his thumb. 'They tried to tax windows once; we bloodied their noses then, all right. They won't try again in a hurry, even this lot.'

Grandfather had begun by making a pair of wooden panniers that sat astride his horse, to which he strapped sheets of glass, coils of cord and strips of beading. He put some of his father's tools in a canvas bag, and went around the larger houses in the villages of the Valley replacing broken glass and perished sash-cord, refilling cracked putty, gluing split parting bead, planing wood swollen by the rain, adjusting joints warped in the sun, and renovating rotten sills, until he was a proficient enough carpenter to set up a workshop in one of the outbuildings, where he could construct complete window-frames in the quiet winter months. He'd gradually collected all the tools he needed, and summer evenings after tea, in his workshop that always smelled sweet and enticing, he used to show me what each of them was for: a gauge with two pins for making mortise and tenon joints; wooden planes of the type first brought to Devon by Joseph of Arimathea; a set of chisels grandfather inherited from his own grandfather; a line of small nuts strung together to lead sash-cord down the box, which was called a mouse; and a cabinet scraper 'for a finish smooth as yer skin, Alison'.

His carpenter's tools were grandfather's most precious possessions, and he treated them with the carelessness of a toddler its toys. One wall of his workshop was covered with nails to hang the tools on, their shapes outlined in felt-tip pen so that he could put each one straight back in its proper place without having to think about it; yet that wall was almost always empty. Instead the work-bench was invariably cluttered with hammers and handsaws and boxes of nails, screwdrivers and files were scattered higgledy-piggledy on shelves or on the floor, and if grandfather couldn't find a wooden mallet it was because it was more likely to be lost in the pile of shavings by his electric saw than hung in front of its black outline on the whitewashed wall.

The only exception to this strangely careless behaviour was the fastidiousness with which grandfather looked after his set of chisels and gouges, which sat in a rack within arm's reach of the work-bench. He sharpened them for an hour on Saturday afternoons, even if he hadn't used them all week and had no plans to. Ian and Tom knew they could borrow any of grandfather's other tools without asking, but he wouldn't let anyone use his chisels, and to prove this was not out of meanness he bought each of them their own set on their sixteenth birthdays.

'When you uses a chisel proper,' he told them, 'it should look like an extension of your own arm.'

You could make out all the lines and creases in grandfather's hands because minute particles of the earth he'd tended for a lifetime had collected in them. He liked to pick up a handful and inspect it, rubbing it between his fingers. That summer he watched it turn into dust and blow off his palm.

However long his day he was always the first to bed, and would wait there for grandmother to join him before falling asleep with his rough, flat hand enveloping hers, and it was then that he made up for his reticence during his waking hours, because as soon as he dropped off, lying on his back as always, he was transformed into a monster beside her.

She couldn't believe it was only breath entering and leaving his mouth that rumbled and resonated from him. She would dream of being at the railway station with the steam train bearing down upon her and wake up as it was about to hurtle into their bedroom, only to realize it was just her husband snoring his monstrous snore beside her.

When their children were young she was sure it would wake them, because in the silence of three a.m. her shy husband's thunderous snores rattled the bed and shook the rafters and reverberated along the corridor. She pinched his nose, clamped his mouth shut and told him to 'Stop snoring!', which he obediently did without waking up. But then instead of going back to sleep herself she was unable to do anything other than lie there, perfectly still, mesmerized, waiting for the inevitable trombone of his windpipe to start up again; and she would curse herself as much as she did him.

It never once occurred to grandmother to seek refuge in another part of the house. She just buried her head under the pillow and tried to count cows until she finally fell asleep, exhausted. In the morning, however, grandmother always awoke from her sporadic rest with a smile on her face, while grandfather, despite his eight hours of deep, uninterrupted sleep, would greet the day in a foul mood.

To the end of his days grandfather carried a stick of chalk in his pocket. Pottering around the house, he'd stop and run windows up and down as if to fan the room, and if they snagged or squeaked he'd rub chalk into the runnels.

Grandfather possessed a number of habits of an earlier generation: at breakfast, while we all sat around the same table on which as a boy he'd had his tonsils removed by the local doctor, grandfather chose to eat his porridge standing up, the better to encourage its digestion. He consumed a large bowl of porridge every morning of the year, even at the height of summer when no one else could stomach even the thought of it, and he washed it down with mugfuls of sweet tea.

He also chewed the inside of his cheeks. I used to think he was grinding bits of oatmeal left over from breakfast, stuck between his teeth, but grandmother would say: 'Look at 'im, he's chewing the cud again,' and she was right. It was a habit he'd acquired from cows. In the same way that grown-ups unsure of themselves grow to resemble their more powerful wives or husbands, so grandfather had assumed something of the character of cattle, and would quietly ruminate when his mind was preoccupied. Later, though, as he saw his herd dwindle in the heat, he would become increasingly agitated, and chewed the inside of his mouth to pieces.

CHAPTER SEVEN

Winter

When I was a little girl in the valley of fallen leaves, every winter snow hypnotized us. We dragged our toboggans up the road through Haldon Forest and then careered across a vast field sloping down from the Folly, until the year that the owner of the field, an Ashton farmer, appeared with a bus conductor's ticket-machine and started charging, because word had spread and whole carloads were coming out from Exeter.

And we skated on the frozen surface of the quarry pool. I found grandmother's old pair of skates in the bottom of a cupboard: Ian oiled their rusty buckles and perished leather and brought them back to life.

Grandmother had used them when she was a girl, racing with her brothers along frozen leats, built by the engineer Sir Francis Drake to bring water down off the high moor. By the time my feet were big enough to fit them grandmother was too crippled to walk through the village to the beech tree, and anyway too blinded by her cataracts to have made sense of the blurry movement below. But when I was small she used to come. She'd bring a blanket and flask and sit herself up by the tree while we slithered down the bed of the stream into the Valley. Completing a daring slide or jump I'd glance up for the gratification of her audience and glimpse her there like a statue, patiently engrossed in the recurring choreography of children scoring patterns across the ice, while her nose turned blue and she warmed her hands around a plastic cup of tea.

That previous winter, though, was the coldest of all.

A terrible frost had seized with numbing severity on the village. People were unable, through stiffened lips, to enunciate words properly, uttering sentences that sounded as if they were back to front. Tom's cider in the pantry solidified, the bottles that held it cracking into shards which fell away. Even thoughts iced up in the mind. Trees split asunder at night. The quarry pool was covered with impenetrable ice, far too thick for poachers' holes, and rooks fell to the ground frozen in their flight.

People stopped going to church, impatient with benumbed fingers fumbling with the pages of their hymn books, disenchanted by the sight of their prayers turning into steam before their very eyes. The Rector plundered parish funds to buy a portable gas heater but it was inadequate to sustain the congregation, which dwindled to half a dozen of the toughest old men and women, who sat dotted around the church in their customary pews, shivering, rather than come together for warmth. Grandmother gave up the struggle to kneel before the altar at which she'd worshipped every week since her wedding. She declined grandfather's offer to drive her up the hill and pick her up again afterwards, and instead accepted the Rector's, that of bringing communion to her in her own home.

Mother, too, stayed at home, claiming that it was no good for anyone freezing for their faith, that what God wanted was upright honest believers, not hypothermic martyrs. She said she'd start going again as soon as God saw fit to bring us spring, though in fact she never did. She was glad of the excuse to give up a weekly ritual she'd continued only out of duty: she took it as a mother's obligation to shepherd her children to church in the same way as she packed us off to school. One institution instilled values, the other knowledge, and she assured us often of their importance. Yet she showed little interest in the content of those values, or that knowledge. Her own domain was not the mind but the body: she clothed and fed us, kept us warm and healthy.

Neither did mother consider it necessary to continue going to church herself in order to validate its relevance. Ian, Pamela and Tom had each dropped away after their confirmations, just as they'd all left school as soon as they could; in Ian's case mother almost wept with frustration as she argued with him to stay on at Newton Abbot Grammar and gain the grades that would enable him to escape. But she knew that he would bow instead to the persuasion of his grandfather and uncles, and take Daddy's place on the farm.

I had a test in school that winter, and I knew I'd do badly. Half of it consisted of written sums, the other half mathematical problems we had to answer in class. I confided in grandmother, and she said: 'Go find me some ladybirds, Alison, to go with your breakfast. In't nothing better for the memory.'

'Yuk,' I said, 'I wouldn't eat them poor little things. Anyway, there aren't any, Gran, 'tis the middle of winter.'

'So 'tis,' she replied, disconcerted.

I was still fearful, and when it was time to leave I said to mother: 'Why should I have to go to school? I don't want to.'

I wasn't being serious even as I said it, it was just a last-minute moan before the inevitable, but mother spun round from the sink, soap suds flying from her hands and floating around her as she cried: 'Cos if you don't, maid, you'll get the belt.'

So I was surprised when mother said to me, one frozen Sunday morning: '*You* don't have to go to church neither, Alison,' and I was even more surprised when I heard myself reply: 'But I wants to, mother.'

Granny Sims brought blankets to church and handed them round for people to spread across their knees. There was a tab on the corner of each one that said 'Virgin Wool', and I thought they'd been darned specially for church services. I shared one with Maria, and she let me snuggle up against her to keep warm. She smelled of starch and cats and the mints which she sucked through the Rector's sermons, whose words she couldn't understand.

When Maria had first moved into the village, before I was born, a couple from some place further along the Valley used to give her a lift to the Catholic church in Chudleigh. Then they moved away, and for a time she walked there every

Sunday along the back lanes, until the Rector managed to convince her that she was welcome in our church, where we worshipped the same God, after all, and so she started taking communion from an Anglican priest. It was in church that she uttered the only English anyone heard from her lips, because she learned to repeat the meaningless syllables of the sung responses.

Hers was the loveliest voice in the village, even if age had thinned it, and the newcomer families would stop what they were doing and listen to her singing Portuguese lullabies to herself when she came to collect their ironing, just as the other servants in the big house across the Valley used to pause outside the library as she dusted books to the rhythm of folk-songs her mother had once sung.

Here in our church Maria imitated as best she could words whose meanings she preferred to ignore, singing with her eyes closed.

> O Lamb of God, that takest away the sins of the world, have mercy upon us.
> O Lamb of God, that takest away the sins of the world, have mercy upon us.
> O Lamb of God, that takest away the sins of the world, receive our prayer.

I sometimes took Daddy to church with me, but something kept him apart, and he chose to sit at the back, trembling with cold. I rejoined him after the service, and together we watched Corporal Alcock blow out the candles, and his breath turn to flame.

The real reason I kept going to church was because I could see that the Rector needed me. Even Joseph Howard, who was Granny Sims' fellow churchwarden, opted to spend Sunday mornings by his open log fire, so there was no one to take the collection or distribute the hymn and prayer books: such menial tasks were beneath Granny Sims' dignity, for she saw herself not as a humble functionary of the church but as its conscience, scrutineer of the suspect ideas of yet another nonconformist parson.

So I arrived early and placed hymn books not just in the regular attendants' places but, on the Rector's insistence, in all the pews, 'because, Alison, we can never predict when people might turn towards God'. I collected the offerings in a little cloth satchel, a muffled jangle of coins, and brought it up to the altar. The Rector took it from me as if I wasn't there, and I returned to my place accompanied by the offertory hymn, an uneven contest in which the few frail voices were no match for Corporal Alcock's furious organ, having to concede defeat and forlornly follow him as best they could, wherever he chose to go.

It was one brittle Sunday morning while I was helping Corporal Alcock light the candles with a long taper, that the Rector popped his head round the vestry door and, pulling his surplice down over his shoulders, said: 'Alison! How would you like to be my server?'

After church I ran all the way home, forgetting Daddy dropping further behind me, to tell grandmother.

'Like I always told 'ee, cherry maid, you's my cleverest girl of all,' she said, 'us've never 'ad one of they in our church before.' Then she furrowed her brow and asked: 'By the way, girl, what do it mean?'

I soon learned: it was my job to put the chalice and paten in their little niche, ready for the Rector to consecrate the bread and wine at the altar, and to pass them to him when the communicants knelt at the altar rail; I handed him his hymn book, opened at the appropriate page, when it was time for him to sing, and his leather-bound Bible when he had to read the Epistle; and I exchanged his glasses for the bifocal spectacles he wore to deliver the sermon. Within two or three weeks I'd learned the simple procedure of the service, and the Rector for his part soon relied on my hand being there to take his Prayer Book and fold his stole, as if I'd been assisting him for years.

He told me that when he was an industrial chaplain in Crewe he had a whole phalanx of acolytes, sons of railway workers with ruff-collared surplices, who got in his and each other's way. They flanked the Rector and his curates in a procession up the aisle during the opening hymn, led by the eldest boy carrying an iron cross that had been forged in the Works foundry, and they had a number of esoteric tasks to perform during the services, waving incense-carriers to please God's nostrils and tinkling a tiny bell at certain intervals to wake people up. When he came down to Devon the Rector dispensed with those superstitious trappings of idolatry, as he called them, and in all the years of his ministry in our village I was his one and only server.

Mother gladly atoned for her absence from church by sewing me a plain white surplice. While I was trying it on Ian told me: 'I looked up what you is in the dictionary. They calls it the celebrant's assistant. You must be mazed, girl.'

When the Underhills had another baby I broke the ice in the font so she could be baptized, and I started helping the Rector home after services, carrying his heavy black cassock and his frayed silk stole.

A short way up Church Lane from the phone box, Maria sat in a chair on the patio in front of the old poet's shack in which she lived, feeding the birds. If it hadn't been for the thick hedge of shrubs and small trees, she could have looked down upon the village. Jane and I used to wriggle through a gap in the wall around the village hall yard and into her garden.

'She in't never been with a man,' Jane whispered to me.

'Where?' I asked.

'You know!' she replied.

But we soon shut up and lay there, patiently watching and waiting, because the reason we crawled into the edge of her garden was so we could witness the spectacle of blue tits and chaffinches alighting upon her shoulders.

I hung the Rector's vestments on a coathanger on the back of his study door, while he reheated himself some coffee and lit a cigarette, and after that I might have been invisible. He never invited me to stay or told me to go home: it was clear that I was welcome to do as I wished.

I explored the empty rooms of the rectory like an archaeologist, gathering evidence of past lives: a small red button, from a child's dress long since discarded; two miniature items of furniture, a chair and a dresser, in the corner of an otherwise empty room upstairs, as if they'd been shrunk by a magic spell; and on the inside of a cupboard I found a black and white cutting of a team of footballers in long shorts and thick shin-pads, looking much older than they do today. Their names were printed underneath, and I memorized the first one or two so as to impress Ian when I got home. But he interrupted me after the first name and reeled off the rest: 'Carey, Aston, Anderson, Chilton, Cockburn, Delaney, Morris, Rowley, Pearson, Mitten. There's some reckon they was the best team of all.' He paused, as if recalling a particular game he could never actually have seen. 'Of course,' he continued, ''tis a load of old rubbish. Their memories is lyin'.'

There were no women's smells in the rectory: no aromas of flowers or herbs or the scent of perfume. The Rector's study smelled of books and cigarette smoke, and in the kitchen the fierce odour of fried bacon was dispelled only by fresh pots of coffee that he made sporadically through the day. The rest of the house, except for his bedroom and bathroom at the far end of the upstairs corridor, was as if deserted, abandoned when the Rector gave away all his excess furniture, or rather sold it at rock-bottom prices, so that instead of insulting the poorest families in the village he gave them the satisfaction of striking exceptional bargains.

That emptiness made the rectory seem even more enormous than it already was: our home wasn't a quarter of the size and there were eight of us living in it without being squashed. While I wandered through the huge rooms I could occasionally hear the Rector emit a strangled, long-drawn-out sneeze that reverberated around the house. I wondered whether Fred provided him with snuff, but one day I was coming down the stairs just as the Rector emerged from his study and was suddenly seized by a spasm that bent him double, and it wasn't a sneeze but a cough.

There was barely a trace of the Rector's family in the house. His wife had run away with someone someone knew, in a scandalous incident whose details no one could recall because the Rector, instead of creeping back where he came from with his tail between his legs, had stayed put and brought up his three children alone, and grandmother told me that people were so impressed by that stubbornness that they were too busy taking it in turns to clean the house, cook meals, weed the vegetable garden and invite his children round for tea, to make fun of him. By now, few could even remember his having children: they'd all left home so long ago that most people treated him with the circumspection of a bachelor priest, and on the rare occasions his grown-up children came to visit him they slipped into the village and out again with the stealth of deer.

It was during the last frosts of winter that the widowman heron came into our Valley. He came soaring silently above the trees of Haldon Forest and glided low over the village. I tugged Daddy's arm by the beech tree and we watched, spellbound, as he floated grey against grey and with a lazily regal, captivating flapping of his wings made a wide circle in the sky. Then, seeing his reflection in the water below, he descended towards the quarry pool, where he landed without a shudder on his spindly legs, settled himself on the outhanging rock, and folded his nightwatchman's wings.

One item of furniture remained in the old drawing-room of the rectory: a vast, gilt-framed mirror above the mantelpiece. It was pocked with bubbles and distorting flaws. I was drawn to it, and stood in the empty room, scrutinizing my uncertain reflection in its antiquated glass.

If he thought he'd be undisturbed for any length of time, the Rector removed his dog-collar as soon as he'd put a saucepan of coffee on the stove. He walked with a firm stride and his limp only made him look more purposeful. He told me that he'd known the exact moment that would lead to his hip replacement operation: he'd gone for a walk with his young children on Dartmoor. It was drizzling, and they came to a five-bar gate. The Rector stepped ahead of his youngest daughter, placed a hand on the top bar and sprang forward, reaching over with his other hand for the middle bar, and keeping his legs out straight behind him he sailed over the gate in a perfect vaulting motion. He told me that in the second or so between his grip slipping loose, so that his limbs spreadeagled in every direction, and feeling his back thump against the granite ground, he had time to reflect, or rather some part of his mind scolded him, that for this moment of proud carelessness he might well pay for the rest of his life. So it would prove.

'And it was also the moment I knew, and I don't mean as an intellectual abstraction but I actually realized inside, that one day I'd die,' he said.

When he was young he'd known the physical exhilaration of running so fast you left yourself behind. Maybe that was why he drove his Triumph Vitesse like a madman around the blind-cornered lanes of our Valley. He'd had an athlete's self-confidence in his body that came from the certainty that he could outrun a rampaging bull or catch a departing train, if ever such emergencies might arise, right up until at the age of fifty-five his angel's face had suddenly crumpled into a web of wrinkles, his dark preacher's hair went white, his hip started aching at night, and he admitted to himself that for some years he'd been approaching the bathroom mirror instinctively breathing in.

His body had turned against him. It was like a mutiny, or the betrayal of an unspoken pact, at first in the grumbling of dissent from some inner recess, which gradually became more audible and constant, until there came a time when always some part of him ached, or burned.

Even so, the Rector was a man in control of himself. His otherworldliness was not that of a vague or absent-minded dreamer but rather of a fierce idealist whose aims were unrealistic. His authority was so measured and articulate that he always appeared calm; Maria was the only one who could discern that within his resolute body his insides churned with the need to get things done before time ran out, because time was always slipping away. The Rector marvelled at patient people, and had to stop himself from despising them.

He was always impatient. He never had any time, because there was so much to accomplish and so little time. His driving was notorious throughout the Valley, and the only advantage of his discovery of the Triumph Vitesse, another model of which he got hold of after each accident, with its awesome powers of acceleration, was that you could hear its throaty engine coming from a long way off. Many a driver had raised a fist as he roared past them within an inch of their own vehicle, only to lower it when they glimpsed the blur of his dog-collar. Mother was aware that he sometimes took me along for the ride when he went to visit a parishioner on one of the outlying farms, and she disapproved because she knew, as did everyone, what a terrifying driver he was.

His most hair-raising accident had occurred one Christmas night: he'd taken Midnight Mass at Bridford, a nearby village which didn't have its own priest, and was coming back along the Valley road. A blizzard had blown up while he was in church, and the road was already covered in a thin icing of snow, while a cascade of thick snowflakes continued to fall. A number of cars groped their way along the road, bumper to bumper, and he came up behind them. Even though he had nothing to get home for except sleep, he must have been driving with the usual impatience that gripped him behind the wheel: he tried to overtake the entire line of cars with a burst of acceleration on the slippery snow. His was the first car to start skidding and the rest followed suit, as if in imitation of his, and six cars started skating along the Valley road, in a blizzard one Christmas night.

The miraculous powers of the saviour born that day must have intervened, as He had when the quarry was flooded on another of His birthdays earlier in the century, because even though all six cars were write-offs not a single person was hurt.

*

The Rector wore a freshly ironed white handkerchief in the breast pocket of his jacket, although when he had to wipe a gob of phlegm off his lips he used a crumpled one from his trouser pocket.

'Well, Alison,' he said, 'it's a gentleman's habit to carry a spare handkerchief.'

'But why?'

'For emergencies,' he replied with a grin, suggesting notions of gallantry that came from an earlier time, and another place.

I watched how the Rector made his coffee, putting three spoonfuls into a pot, filling it up with hot water, and stirring sixty times. I learned to guess when he wanted another mug and would take it into his study just as he was rising from his chair to go and make it himself. The time this saved him the Rector spent talking with me. He told me about a woman blind from birth, who dreamed in rich and startling images that she recounted to him in detail; and of another woman, who also lived in one of the many identical back-streets of Crewe, similar to the single street in Teign Village across the Valley, who was cleaning the windows of her house and fell off the chair she was standing on. They put her to bed, and when she woke up she looked at them with surprise and spoke in a gibberish no one had ever heard before, but which sounded as if she was taking the mickey out of them. One by one they brought all the foreigners they knew of to her bedside to see if they could help, until the owner of the Chinese takeaway thought he recognized a word here and there. The string of visitors ended with a Professor of Philology from Manchester University, who identified her utterances as being those of a dialect of Mandarin that had become obsolete in the seventeenth century. She came to her senses after a week in this condition, with no memory of it. Instead she shooed them away from around her bed, telling them she couldn't lie around all day when she was in the middle of cleaning windows.

The Rector lit a cigarette and flicked the lit match towards his overflowing wastepaper basket. The flame died and was replaced by a tail of smoke in its spinning orbit.

'How did she know that language?' I asked him. 'Had she lived another life in China?'

'What do you think?' he replied.

Sometimes when he left the house the Rector switched on his tape-recorder, and later we would listen, ears to the speakers, to distant voices, trying to make out what they were saying.

Midway through the mornings of that summer my brothers were beaten back inside by the heat of the day, and returned with the dogs, swearing at the sun. Tom sweated more than other people. He'd kick shut the door of his van, because the metal was so hot it burned his fingers, and come across the yard red-faced and wiping his brow. The first thing he did, even before pouring himself a mug of tea, was to fill a plastic basin with cold water and take it outside, which he wouldn't have bothered to do if mother hadn't insisted, since even she couldn't bear the pestilential smell that erupted into the room when he took off his heavy workman's boots. Then he peeled off his dripping socks and put his feet in the basin, and as the water hissed Tom closed his eyes, and sighed with pleasure.

Freed from her duties of a sheepdog, Tinker sometimes followed my scent and I'd find her lying with her paws crossed in the shadows of the rectory verandah, calmly waiting to accompany me home, taking upon herself responsibility for my whereabouts, since no one else at home noticed whether I was here, there or nowhere.

Tinker would shepherd me back to the house, see me through the door and then pad over to the barn, since she wasn't allowed to follow me inside. She accepted her banishment with dignity, loping across the yard without a backward glance, but it seemed to me we were doing her wrong, because it hadn't always been like that.

Tinker was born two years after I was, and when she was a puppy the house was as much her playground as it was mine. She bounced around after me, nipping at my ankles and flopping down when I did, with a permanent air of mischief and expectation. She chewed everything she could get her teeth into, dragging grandfather's boots and mother's slippers into corners and silently destroying them even as we searched for her underneath beds and behind chairs. She took match-boxes from off table-tops and scattered their contents across the sitting-room floor; she carried mother's kitchen aprons up the stairs and deposited them in the bathroom. But no one had the heart to scold her with more than a brief, unconvincing reprimand, because her puppy dog's eyes could soften the hearts of even the hardened farmers of our family.

I was just learning to talk then, so mother later told me, and Tinker was the only one with the patience to listen to the rambling monologues of a toddler: she sat up and stared back, cocking her head this way and that, as if trying to follow a convoluted line of argument.

The fact is she thought she was a human being. She refused to drink from her dish of water by the back door, waiting instead for people to leave a half-drunk cup of tea on the sideboard, whereupon she would stick her snout inside and drain it. It was the same with food: mother used to buy uncooked dog meat in bulk from the grain merchants, which filled the house with a foul smell when she boiled a huge pan of it each Monday. When she set a bowl down for Tinker she turned her nose up at it, fixed mother with a look of reproach, and walked out of the kitchen with her tail in the air. She preferred a bowl of cornflakes for breakfast and a mug of sweet tea. Later on, when she thought no one was looking, she'd creep back into the kitchen and gollop the dog-food down in two or three mouthfuls, but it didn't affect her appetite for people's left-overs, which she would delicately remove from their plates with her long tongue and sneak off with, to consume in a quiet corner.

At night Tinker slept full-length on the floor beside my bed. At the slightest sound, of an owl hooting in a distant wood or a mouse scrabbling along the rafters, her little tail would start thumping on the carpet in her sleep. On the other hand she woke up of her own accord every few hours and would bark to be let out, whine to be given some attention, or miaow for a saucer of milk in imitation of the cats. I always slept through her howling: mother was the one who had to attend to her whims. She complained that it was like having another baby in the house.

Tinker slept with her paws crossed from the very beginning, and also inherited from her grandmother the habit of climbing on to a chair, placing her front paws on the sill and, ears pricked back, watching the world through the window. When a chicken crossed the yard, though, or a car passed by along the lane, she didn't seem to see them. Instead her eyes would suddenly stare, her snout point forwards and her head track intently across the yard when there was nothing there: she seemed to be scrutinizing the traffic of another dimension.

Strange things upset her. She never got used to the vacuum cleaner, and whenever mother hoovered the carpets Tinker would bark and growl and try to nip the nozzle until she knew she was beaten, and then she fled from the room with her tail between her legs and hid under my bed. And although she had the genes of generations of sheepdogs in her, a sheep had only to fix her with its gaze, the way sheep do with puppies, to make her run to us for safety.

She preferred human beings. In fact, she wouldn't leave people alone. She nibbled grandfather's toes as he watched television, licked Pamela's face with her long tongue, and she climbed up the arms of grandmother's chair and on to the back, so that she could drop unannounced into grandmother's lap. She drove everyone to distraction and they would flick her snout or pinch her ears and tell her to go away, stupid dog, leave me alone, go and annoy the chickens. But then she'd look up at them with her dog's eyes, cock her head to one side and make them feel guilty despite themselves, until they felt so bad they apologized to her and grandma invited her on to her lap, or grandfather fed her gobbets of bread by the side of his chair when he thought no one was looking.

The paradise we shared in the house was ended by her sudden expulsion: one night the house was surrounded by all the dogs in the village, who appeared without warning, one after another, to sit in the yard and howl in the direction of my window, until Tom turned the hose on them.

When I woke up in the morning Tinker wasn't snoring by my bed, as usual, and she wasn't in the kitchen or the sitting-room or chewing a towel in the bathroom or anywhere else in the house. Finally I had to break the news to mother: someone had stolen my puppy in the middle of the night. Mother stopped what she was doing and looked down at me.

'For one thing, girl, 'er's not your dog, 'er's grandfather's. And for another, 'er lives outside now,' she told me. 'And I don't want no tears,' she added, on that day grandfather decided Tinker was old enough to earn her keep, and from then on she had to sleep with her grandmother, Nipper, out in the barn. During the day she learned from her the craft of a sheepdog, and she was forbidden from ever entering the house, until in the October of that sad summer, when in the life of a dog she was almost a hundred years old, grandfather would ask her to share his vigil beside grandmother's bed.

I was beginning to realize that the questions that preoccupied me were those to which no one knew the answers. 'What happens to animals' souls when they die?' I demanded of mother, but she only told me to stop mooching around the kitchen, getting under her feet. 'Don't worry about their damn souls, maid, get yourself busy, go collect the eggs like you should have done s'morning.'

'Why did rich people go to the moon, anyway, when poor people was starving on the earth?' I asked Pamela as she made up ready to go out, and she said: 'I'll take you to the moon when you're a bit older, little sister. Here, try this lipstick, it's more your colour than mine. Don't go away now, you wants to start learning these things in good time.'

Ian might have told me things, but he was too busy. When I found him leaning forward with his head resting on his desk, dozing after lunch and catching up on the sleep insomnia had deprived him of, I prodded him awake. 'What time is it?' he asked, looking round anxiously.

'Two-thirty,' I informed him. 'Ian, you tell me: why are the pine trees bleeding? Something's happening to the forest.' But he'd already picked up his pen and was back doing the accounts where he'd left off, and all Ian said was: 'I'll talk to 'ee later, Alison, ask me tonight, I've got to correct these 'ere for the broker now, the berk. Pass me my calculator.'

No one would give me any answers, no one that is except grandmother, whose answers only conspired to complicate the issues I was trying to clarify. 'Of course there's people 'ere from other planets,' she affirmed, 'there's no end of stars in the galaxies, so it stands to reason. But there's no end of dimensions 'ere, see. Where do you s'pose souls and spirits live? Think about it. People from other planets hides in them dimensions and watches us. Anyway, they'd rather mix with the dead than the living, and who can blame 'em? I think I would.'

Often her answers had nothing to do with the question. 'How often is you s'posed to pray, grandma?' I asked her, hoping to learn something with which I could impress the Rector.

'Regularity,' she said, 'that's the answer. And not after breakfast neither, always before. Keep regular, girl, stay healthy.' More than anything else, it was grandmother's recitation of these useless maxims that gradually made people oblivious to the sound of her voice. She only wanted to share the experience of her long lifetime, but without realizing it she was somehow being forced to pass on, along with her own wisdom, the advice she'd been given as a child. Strictures concerning personal cleanliness, a person's duties both in the household and in the outside world, trite religious imperatives, these and many more would fall from her tongue on deaf ears, apart from mine. The trouble was that often I couldn't tell the difference.

'I like the sound of your grandmother,' said Johnathan.

Blimey, I thought, next thing he'll want to meet her, so I changed the subject quickly.

'Have you heard about all these unemployed?' I asked him. 'Ian says they're going to start riding out of the cities on their bikes and ask for their old jobs back.'

Johnathan stared at the surface of the quarry pool. 'I wish

Tolstoy was still alive,' he said gloomily. 'He would have had an answer.' And then he jumped up and said: 'Come on, race you to the middle!'

The Rector, though, was not only prepared to listen to my enquiries, he responded as if pleased to discover someone who shared his concerns.

I asked him why people fought against those they had most in common with, and he told me all about intolerance, about the war he'd fought in even though Jesus said to turn the other cheek, and he told a joke about a man stopped in a quiet lane in Northern Ireland in the middle of the night by masked gunmen. '"Are you Protestant or Catholic?" they demanded.

'The man trembled, but inspiration came to him: "I'm an atheist," he told them.

'"Yes, but are you a Protestant atheist or a Catholic atheist?" they asked,' said the Rector, roaring with laughter which turned into a fit of coughing that bent him double. But he came back up smiling and carried on talking, about Jews who believe that the Torah was with God before He created the world, it existed in heaven; about Sunni Muslims who not only maintain that the Koran existed before Creation, they emphasize that it was in Arabic. He couldn't stop himself from laughing again, and I began to realize that he joked when he was most serious. 'They had trouble getting Muslims to sign the Universal Declaration of Human Rights,' he told me, 'because they didn't agree with freedom of worship, since there's only one God: Allah. It's as bad as the Christian Churches, who decided most of the world, not yet introduced to Christ's teachings, lived and died in a state of sin.' He shook his head at things beyond his comprehension.

'Where is God, anyway?' I asked. 'In the church? Do you have to go there to be with him?'

He lit a cigarette and looked at me. 'You know very well that's simplistic nonsense,' he replied. 'The church is merely symbolic, a place to help us concentrate our thought and energy. Are you teasing me, Alison?'

'No,' I said, 'I just don't understand how God can be

everywhere. I know if he exists he must be everywhere, but he can't be inside things and inside people and in the air and . . . everywhere.'

'I know. It's hard to grasp,' he agreed, unhelpfully. 'It's funny, Alison, you know,' he reflected, 'you're just a little boy asking questions – "What's this mean? Why do people do that?" You grow up but inside you're still just a little boy asking questions. Except that the next thing you know there's a boy or girl beside you asking you the very same questions.'

The Rector told me that when he was young he was convinced that other people saw the point of life. He could not imagine that anyone else suffered from the same inability to find purpose as he did. He could find no fixed point inside himself, no sense of self beyond a vapid personality that sensations, experienced in the flow of time, blew into ever changing shapes. He knew he had no substance. Whereas others' actions, speech, movement, their very physical being, spoke of purpose.

It was only gradually that he realized he was no more purposeless than others, that the inherent busyness of their being, as observed, was an illusion created by the fact of observation. As he lost his awe of other people, his expectations of them, he realized not only that truth would not be given him by others, but that he had to find it within himself.

I told him about an experiment we'd done at Primary School, dipping a piece of string into a beaker of blue liquid, and how a crystal formed on the end of the string, as if out of nothing.

'That's why we're here, Alison,' he said, seizing upon the metaphor with his eagerness of a preacher; 'we're simply souls dipped into time, in order to substantiate ourselves.'

And yet although he thought he'd lost his awe of other people, he still felt himself insubstantial, and thought he saw glimpses in others of their greater solidity. He never saw himself as others saw him, a tough, obstinate man of impractical ideals and unshakeable integrity.

Sometimes I saw him through his study window, bent over

his desk, surrounded by twenty-six empty rooms. A lifetime of writing baptismal and funeral addresses, letters, articles, diaries, notebooks and parish magazines had given him arthritis, so that after completing a sermon his hand was like a claw: he had to extract the pen from between his fingers with his other hand and massage it back to normality. He thought it pleasingly ironic that as his sermons became a little more liable to be worth listening to, they gave him an increasing amount of pain to write.

At such times I thought he must be the loneliest man in the world. But he wasn't really lonely, just alone. His mind was too intent upon the elusive truths he was pursuing to reflect on the futility of ever communicating them to other people.

He had no friends, but occasionally he went out to supper with one or other of the newcomer families who spoke the same as he did, without an accent. None of them came to church, and he felt at ease in their company, where he could argue freely.

The Rector knew that most of the villagers felt uncomfortable when he visited, even those he'd known for forty years. He remembered when he first arrived from Crewe with his wife and children, 'to get the nits out of their hair and fresh air in their lungs', he said.

In fact he'd nearly turned round and left before they'd even unpacked: at the first service he took the church was full, and he realized that he'd made the right choice, that country people hadn't lost their spirituality as had happened to those forced to live in city slums and slave in factories. Half-way through his sermon, a complex dissertation based on the Gospel reading of Christ's dictum that it was easier for a camel to pass through the eye of a needle than for a rich man to enter the kingdom of heaven, a red-faced farmer in one of the back pews stood up and heckled him:

'You don't know what you're bloody talking about, man! I had to work for my money!'

A woman near the front turned round and shouted back: 'Leave him be, Gordon! Hear him out!' And the man sat down.

A couple of minutes later, though, another man stood up:

'You clergy's hand in glove with the rich! You give every-thing away like Jesus and walk about in sandals and I might come back and listen to you,' he declared, and marched out.

He'd never been heckled in the pulpit before, and a cold sweat turned to ice on his back. He got to the end of his sermon in a blur.

Afterwards he was surprised to find a number of men outside, who had sat smoking in the graveyard while their wives were inside. He introduced himself, as he had to the congregation. 'Don't bother,' said one old man. 'You'll never get me into that there church. I 'ad enough of bowing and scraping when I was a bay.'

'We idn't afeared of God no more,' another told him, as they walked away across the churchyard.

The following week's congregation was half the size of his first, because, as Granny Sims told him, they'd only come to size him up. He discovered to his dismay that he'd taken over from the latest in a long line of priests overfriendly with the Viscounts, patrons of the living – with their family's special pew, their crypt beneath the church, their founder's portrait on the wall – conniving in their exploitation of the people of the village. They'd performed the difficult task of reading the scriptures and then interpreting their opposite meaning. No wonder he wasn't trusted here. His predecessors had made themselves comfortable, taken pains not to disturb anyone, and enjoyed the old-fashioned life of a country parson: they took their tithes from tenant farmers far worse off than themselves; they employed two men to take care of their vegetable and flower gardens; and they sang lusty hymns, which helped keep people's minds off the words in the Bible they ignored.

And more than any of these there was the fact that he came from a different social class. 'I'm afraid there's not much mention of this in the Gospels, Alison. Christ doesn't seem to have allowed for the English class system. It's not as simple a problem as the one faced by the inhabitants of Babel, because we appear on the surface to be speaking the same language.'

So he invited the 14th Viscount over for a drink. He was a

short man with broken spectacles held together with elastoplast; he wore thick corduroy trousers and a thin cardigan, with a spotted bow-tie. The Rector had expected an arrogant and empty-headed aristocrat, but instead found a charming and open-minded drinking companion. Even so, he declared that he was sorry, it was nothing personal, but things had to change, this priest was not going to be the Teignmouths' lackey as others had, he was on the side of the oppressed, the downtrodden, as he was obliged to be by his collar and his conscience, and that was the plain and simple truth.

The Viscount accepted another gin and tonic and said yes, how true that is, and what a good idea it was to make a fresh start, a number of his ancestors had done that from time to time, it shook things up. He said he'd support the Rector in his efforts with all the means at his disposal, and how pleased he was he'd agreed to his induction.

The Rector tried to tell him that he was missing the point, there was a problem here that the Viscount couldn't solve because he was it, but he got his words tangled up, since it wasn't in his nature to declare war on a man he'd only just met and who, besides, he found agreeable.

'Don't be so serious, old chap,' the Viscount told him. 'You're as outmoded as I am. People resent being subordinate to God as much as they resent being subordinate to another human being. One day this rectory will be converted to a different use, just as our estate will, sooner rather than later according to my accountant. A priest will drive in from far away to take services in a crumbling church for senile parishioners, living out the servile pattern of their childhood. And when they die, we'll all be able to live in a world uncomplicated by notions of God and the afterlife, and other such nonsense.'

The Rector felt on firmer ground discussing religion, especially with an atheist: 'It might be easier to live in a world uncomplicated by food; unfortunately we need it. That's the way we are. And tell me this: why are you atheists as unhappy as we are?'

'Quite frankly I don't care enough to call myself an atheist.

The essential attraction of religion is to safeguard against extinction. But since the church has recanted the fearsome threat of Hell, and with it fear, why should I even bother with such an absurd preoccupation? I'm better off concerned with whether my wife still loves me.'

'Ideas change, of course. What used to be imagined as Hell we now perceive as non-advancement; we're here to evolve spiritually; not to do so means you'll start again in the same place, or drop back. You see, you're just lazy; representative of this generation.'

'I don't deny it,' he replied. 'I try to enjoy life.'

'That's the problem. We've adopted this notion that the goal of life is happiness. What a lovely idea! And how far from the truth!' And he launched into a lengthy exposition of the fallacies of this human foible, in the middle of which the Viscount, not used to the Rector's drinking habits, promptly fell asleep.

The Rector also discovered, to his dismay, that his first sermon was to be the only one that anyone seemed to listen to: they had an ability to switch off and think of other things while he was presenting them with the challenge of the Gospel message, or else to take from his radical but complex arguments the simplest conclusion, from which they derived the comfort they were seeking. He longed for the hecklers to return, but they stayed away. Those who remained did so in order to petition a remote divinity for the health of their livestock and children, and to do their best to drown the efforts of a tone-deaf organist.

The Rector's evenings always ended the same. It didn't matter whether he'd been attending a meeting of the PCC or drinking two or three stiff gin and tonics before a TV dinner: he always returned to his study to work. Through the power of his formidable concentration he would draw together the resources of his mind, scattered by alcohol, and read and write and think into the early hours. He read voraciously and wrote so much they had to have a regular order of biros for him down at the shop, but mostly he leaned back in his chair and took upon himself the burden of thought, as he lit another cigarette. He always used matches: every summer the white elephant stall at the village fête included one or two lighters that someone had had the inspiration of giving the Rector for Christmas, having noticed the poor man get through a box of matches a day. He always gave them away because he figured that if he had a lighter it would make it more difficult to give up smoking, which was something he intended to do at the earliest opportunity. Every time it occurred to him, however, he put it off for a couple of days, in a constant see-saw struggle, and cursed his weakness.

The trouble was he needed to smoke to help him concentrate in his search for truth, even though he was coming increasingly to suspect the very notion. Truth was, for him, synonymous with the Absolute, with God, but he knew this assumption depended upon the accident of his birth at a particular time, in a particular culture. He lacked the humility of the mystics, and as for the Indian yogis and the Buddhist saints whose sweet lives he read in paperback, he could not believe that they were born with egos. His had tormented him all his life. He had tried to annihilate it with prayer and hunt it down through rational argument, but it had always eluded him, slinking into the shadows to lick its wounds and recuperate, its eyes, malicious, glinting in the darkness.

He could never fully relax and submit himself to the will of God, that was the problem. Perhaps, he conceded, he was secretly scared of laying the silent offering of his self at God's door, in case it wasn't answered. Even now, at his age, he found the idea of there being no God made him feel nauseous: it was as if some necessary precondition of life, like gravity or air, had vanished, and he felt dizzy.

Sometimes he became so engrossed, so lost, in his nights of speculation, that dawn surprised him at his desk, and he would walk outside to be greeted by a cacophony of birds unaware of his contemplation, with bruised rings around his eyes.

And once, in the middle of the night he left his coffee to boil dry in the pan, confused by too much gin and too much thought, just to stretch his legs, and fell asleep. He was woken in the morning, in the field beyond his overgrown vegetable garden, by a cow's warm breath on his face.

CHAPTER EIGHT

Ice-Cream

'Do you want to come to church Sunday?' I asked Johnathan, as we lay by the pool, tired and bored. It was Tuesday, 11 September. We should have been back at school a week now. 'You can walk round by grandfather's back fields, no one'll see you. And the congregation's all senile anyway.'

Johnathan raised his left eyebrow and smirked. 'Really, Alison,' he said in his superior manner, 'we *are* nearly at the end of the twentieth century, you know. We gave up p-p-primitive religion *eons* ago.' Then his eyebrow dropped and his eyes widened. 'How about coming to visit? Father's making jam. We picked tons of blackberries yesterday.'

When Johnathan's father, the 15th Viscount Teignmouth, sold the estate to a property developer who then went bust, he moved his family into the old Lodge. When you looked at the estate from up at the beech tree the Lodge seemed like a little toy compared to the big boarded-up house, and I imagined Johnathan and his parents walking around inside it like giants in a doll's house, having to bend over as they moved around, folding limbs into miniature furniture.

Now as Johnathan led me through the front door I saw what an illusion that had been: the Lodge was as large as our farmhouse and the rooms, although their ceilings weren't that much higher than Johnathan's crumpled mop of hair, were all wide and spacious. But what was even more surprising was the furniture: none of it looked real, because every wooden sideboard, bookcase, table, chair and chest of drawers was covered in intricate carved patterns or decorated with wandering strips of delicate beading. No single surface was left straight and simple but had been finished off in ridiculous, fanciful curls by a wandering jig-saw. It looked like make-believe furniture, from the set of one of the television series mother liked to watch about scandal and dignity among the aristocracy. I realized that the big house must have been full of such furniture on all five floors, in all the huge rooms and all along the wide corridors, a mind-boggling prospect. And Johnathan's father just kept back a minimum amount, the most or, maybe, the least valuable.

The walls were covered in stacks of books, leather-bound like the few on grandmother's mantelpiece, but here were hundreds, thousands, leaving space only for the sash-cord windows and here and there a narrow upright strip of wall jam-packed with dim portraits of Johnathan's ancestors.

'And don't make any t-t-tedious jokes about family resemblance. Come on through to the kitchen,' said Johnathan.

There were crammed bookshelves dotted all around the kitchen, too, interspersed with a bewildering variety of enormous cups and saucers and silver salvers, weighing scales and flowery jugs, mixing bowls and plates as wide as you could carry. From the ceiling hung bunches of dried herbs. The room smelled sweet and musty, of old books and rosemary and coriander.

Johnathan's father was standing at the range, an Aga just like ours, which made him look even odder, a man in corduroy trousers and a brown jumper with frayed elbows, with an apron tied around his back.

'Father, this is Alison Freemantle. Alison, this is my father.' He turned round. He was the same height as his son, with the same unkempt mop of brown hair and a blue spotted bow-tie above an apron emblazoned with a picture of the Eiffel Tower and the words J'AIME PARIS in bright red and blue.

'Pleased to meet you, my dear,' he said. 'My goodness, and you're the youngest, aren't you? How's your father?'

What a strange question. What could he know about Daddy? 'He's all right,' I said.

'That's good. Do remember me to him. Now, would you two care to help me? Or are you as big a layabout as my son, Alison?'

*

Johnathan's mother had trained to be a social worker and his father did all the housework. He had a collection of notebooks filled with his own grandmother's recipes and was using them, according to Johnathan, as the basis for research into the lost art of English cooking. Johnathan said they didn't see much of his mother, who came home from work late and exhausted, and he'd given up talking to her about anything because she only interrupted and told him of people whose problems were unimaginably greater than any of his trivial anxieties and he should realize how fortunate he was.

Johnathan's father fetched a cardboard box of dusty jam-jars and filled the sink with hot, suddy water. We rolled up our sleeves and sponged the jars clean: their Mayonnaise and Peanut Butter labels slid off the hot glass and floated scummily in the sink. Johnathan's father quartered a couple of lemons, twisted a muslin sachet around them and lowered it on a piece of string into the vast pan of bubbling apples and blackberries. His face, already ruddy from the heat, was reddened further by the glow from the volcanic fruit.

'Come on, you two. We need them dried as well. Here's a cloth, Alison.'

Soon the draining-board was covered with gleaming jam-jars. Johnathan's father took a saucer and spooned a little jam onto it.

'Just a smidgin,' he said absently, and then to me: 'Now just prod it with your finger.'

The skin on the jam crinkled. 'It's ready!' he cried. 'Let's not waste time. You hold the jars, Johnathan, I'll pour it.'

The sizzling jam made the jars hot, but Johnathan didn't flinch. He was enjoying himself. I sealed the jars, easing rubber bands over their necks, although they tried to slide up my fingers, while the Viscount wrote labels and stuck them on.

'We'd better test it, don't you think?' he suggested, when he'd licked the last label, and we sipped tea with a thick wedge of home-made white bread and warm jam.

Dozily vindictive wasps darted at me, tiny blackandyellow

69

bullies, as I walked home along the lane. When I got in mother sent me straight out again to look for eggs. The hens were scrawny and dishevelled, and pecked at each other when I scattered a handful of corn each morning. They kept themselves alive only by extracting some illusory nutrition from the grit they pecked from the farmyard and passed through their digestive tracts, producing smooth and perfectly shaped eggshells that had no yolk inside. They'd scrutinize me, beady eyes full of resentment, and take their revenge by dreaming up new places to lay their useless eggs, watching with inscrutable satisfaction as I searched in all the corners of the barn and underneath rusting machinery, amongst the remnants of straw and on the stone lintels, between discarded feed bags and in the back of the trailer. But there were always some I wouldn't find for weeks, without realizing how old they were, like the one Ian picked up at breakfast one day to prove you couldn't crack an egg by squeezing its ends, such was the extraordinary strength of its shape, it just happened to be a physical impossibility, Ian said, a fact he'd proved in the early hours by mathematical calculation, only for Tom to take it from him, stand up and close his fist: rotten egg-white exploded between his fingers and polluted the kitchen with an acrid stench that put everyone off their breakfast and took mother all morning to scrub off the walls.

I threw pebbles at the hens and that made them jump and squawk. They couldn't fly because mother clipped their wings with an old pair of scissors. What I really wanted was to learn how to slaughter them properly. One day in June mother said she was going to kill a scrawny, featherless chicken that was being picked on by the others, and I thought I'd surprise her. I cornered it in the yard and tried to wring its thin neck like I'd seen her do so often. It wasn't difficult. But then instead of dying it jumped up and beetled around the yard making a hell of a racket, with its head lolling to one side. Mother came out and finished it off with a cleaver, and forbade me to touch the chickens again.

'Just collect the bloody eggs, girl!' she shouted. 'Can't you do nothin' right?'

I found one solitary egg and gave it to mother and then I heard the ice-cream van coming from a long way off, its tune losing coherence in the thin air and sounding like the accordion player at the previous year's barn dance.

'Oh stop moaning,' said mother; she gave me some money and I ran across the yard. Whenever we heard that lopsided tune it made our mouths water, but after the first couple of weeks of that parch-mouthed summer it augured only disappointment, for the laconic ice-cream man had fast run out of everything except the bland cornet-wafers that grown-ups preferred. He made no apologies, blaming his shortage on us for overbuying, and he never smiled even though he could keep cool by putting his hands in his ice-box.

Three times a week we heard his wonky bell, and every time had to go through the same charade:

'Choc split, please.'

'Ain't got no choc splits,' he replied lugubriously.

'Lemon sparkle then.'

'Ain't got they neither.'

'You got nut cream?'

'No.'

We soon tired of his litany of unavailable delights, and demanded to know what he did have, but he wouldn't be forestalled.

'Just ask, that's all, and I'll tell you.'

'You got chocwhoppers?'

'No.'

'What about orange maid?'

'No.'

We knew he was playing us along. He wasn't an ice-cream man at all, his real job was to teach us by example the Devon sense of humour. But our greed and the fact that he didn't give the game away with so much as a smile or a smirk combined to tantalize us right to the last fanciful delicacy. Then, hands in pockets, we'd slope away from his van. He waited a few crucial seconds, and then called after us: 'I got wafers. Get yer mum one.'

Mother always acted surprised. She'd give me some more money for lemonade as consolation and retreat to the cool little scullery with her wafer, where she could savour each lick before it melted. Daddy was pleased with his too but he swallowed it in a couple of gollops like a dog, while I scurried off to the shop.

It was always dim in Elsie's tiny front room. Even during that brightest of summers, when the sun sought out forgotten shadows in the nooks and crannies of ill-thought-out cottages, revealing long-lost pencils and socks and out-of-date coins, still she kept the blinds down and a low-wattage light bulb always on. Elsie and Stuart, her fiancé, were sitting in their easy chairs on either side of the room, surrounded by shelves of chocolate bars developing a white bloom, and teeth-cracking gobstoppers and liquorice chews that still cost a halfpenny, so that you had to buy two at a time. The shop never closed, even when they went to bed. We used to wait till the lights went out and then go in: they were the last people to lock their doors. The bell above the door brought one or the other of them stumbling down through the dark in their night dress, to sell you a small Kit-Kat or a bubble-gum and then go back to bed.

They'd been holding hands across the small space in the middle of the room, but I crept up to the door and as I opened it their hands snapped apart like an overstretched rubber band.

When I asked for a bottle of lemonade Stuart struggled grimly to his feet. Both he and Elsie grew smaller every year, and that summer we were all three the same height for the first and last time. Stuart hobbled out to the back shed; he'd only recently stopped making deliveries, incipient arthritis exacerbated by the steep paths of the village.

Elsie stared at me through pebble-glass spectacles, her eyes huge like an owl's. Stuart shuffled back with a dusty bottle. I opened it back home and found a yellowy film sitting on top of the liquid. Once I put a bottle of lemonade in the freezer overnight, but the piskies got in there like they got everywhere else and blew it up. So now I filled a big cider mug with ice, which inspired a whisper of bubbles in the flat lemonade, and I drank without stopping.

*

That was the summer when even abstemious men, soon to be joined by my brother Tom, at the end of another useless, dried-up day, would walk over the back of Rydon Farm at dusk to slake their thirst in the pub at Ashton. Some evenings the car park would be empty but the pub full. They imposed their taciturn nature on the clientele, who became incensed at having the good-humoured atmosphere that hung in their pub shot through with tables of sullen silence. An age-old animosity, towards men whose ancestors had left their poachers' bullets in the church door during the Civil War, bubbled up in the present, at first in sarcastic comments in the Public Bar and beer spilt by accident. It grew into threats by the dartboard, developed into scuffles in the Gentlemen's toilet, and culminated one Friday night in a magnificent brawl in the car park, which it took a vanload of policemen to break up, made the front-page headline of the Exeter *Express and Echo*, brought condemnation, from the local Member of Parliament, of the escalation of rural violence, and was the one real respite that Tom would have from his despair.

While I drank my lemonade in the kitchen the boys relaxed before tea in front of the six o'clock news. I could hear them cursing at the screen, their voices less lifelike than the sound of distant warfare between the police and the miners coming from the picket-lines.

'Go on, give 'im one, the fat bastard!' said Ian.

I could hear the rattling of shields, and men chanting like animals. It sounded as if they were just along the lane, coming down out of the forest.

'Look at the size of they bloody horses!' said grandfather.

'He'll break the bastard's skull like that,' said Ian.

'Christ Almighty,' Tom murmured, and they went silent.

Really, though, I didn't bother with television, I don't know why; I hardly ever watched TV. I knew it wasn't as good as it had been before I was born, when it was brought to the village as one of grandmother's miracles of electricity. She said they'd discovered how to show people's auras, only colour pictures were so confusing they'd lost the art. She said

73

they'd been able to confirm that history is a spiral, and that the future is present in the past, by showing snow falling on a summer's day. That was back when her cataracts were only partial, and now she was glad she couldn't watch any more, so she took her place at table in plenty of time for tea, joined by the rest of us when mother announced that it was ready. Only grandfather wasn't there, because even in that summer of sombre evenings when there was no work to be done, he had little inclination to come in before dusk, and would busy himself taking down some wire fencing and putting it up again a fraction tighter, or inspecting the disenchanted three-month-old lambs he'd inspected the evening before, or some such other superfluous task, in order to avoid having to join his family indoors before dusk.

Mother dolloped helpings of cauliflower cheese with mashed potato and scraggy carrots onto our plates, and poured pint mugs of tea for Ian and Tom.

'I was lookin' at the orchard s'afternoon,' she told them. 'We'll not get much off of they apples and pears.'

'True, 'tis too late for they, whatever 'appens,' replied Ian. 'The wheat'll be all right though, 'tis the late crop I's worried about.'

'What about the animals? The sheep's is got no flesh under their wool, mother,' said Tom. 'I still don't know why us got so many; they'll starve if this goes on much longer.'

'That don't matter. I told 'ee enough times, bay,' said Ian, grinning, 'us gets the subsidy for puttin' 'em out on the hill, not bringin' 'em back in.'

'Well, they's just skin and bones. If it dudn't rain soon grandfather says 'twill be worse than last time, when the earth swallowed lambs, and they only went out at dusk to pick up the dead cows –'

'– you's always so pessimistic, bay,' mother interrupted. 'Long's us can keep our stock alive while others' is dyin', come the end of all this we'll be well all right.'

'Course we will, Tom,' I said.

'Don't cheek your older brother, Alison,' said mother.

'Stupid maid,' said Tom, his mouth full of a chomped-up mess of cauliflower.

74

I ignored him and nudged Daddy. 'What's that you got in your pocket? There's always somethin'.' He managed to hide things there when I wasn't looking.

Now his face turned quizzical as he felt around and produced three small toads in his palm, which he laid on the table. They hopped off in different directions. Mother sat rigidly upright as if it was a personal insult, then smiled smugly, to show that she had a sense of humour, and grandmother screwed up her face in concentration, trying to make out by the sounds what was going on; Ian and I fell about giggling while Tom, ever practical, leaned over and picked each of them up.

'What'll you do with 'em?' I cried. 'Don't you kill 'em!'

'I'll just put 'em outside.'

'I wanna take 'em to the stream,' I pleaded.

'They wants a pond, not a stream,' he pointed out.

'Tom, let Alison take 'em, why not?' Ian suggested.

I made a bowl with my hands and the toads huddled in a slimy cluster. Daddy followed me outside and came with me to the goldfish pond in the garden of the empty house next door, not yet occupied by summer visitors.

I set the toads down beside the olid water. They hovered there like tiny garden ornaments, petrified by indecision. 'Go on and swim then,' I told them, but they wouldn't move, so we left them to it. I gave Daddy my clammy hand on the way back: he was trembling. But as we crossed the farmyard I realized it was me.

Mother was washing up. I heard Daddy say: ''Er's got the crinkum crankums.'

'I'm all right,' I said.

'You better get on up to bed, maid, you looks tired,' said mother.

My room was growing dark but it was still light outside as I sat on the window-sill; nightfall would bring only fleeting relief in that oven of a summer, when even my insides seemed to be cooking. At least it started me reading, as I tried to take my mind away from physical discomfort with the only books we had in the house, grandmother's single shelf of leather-bound English literature she'd brought with her from her father's house up on the moor. They were the one thing that saved my face with Johnathan, who as we lay on the rock by the quarry pool discussed the habits and opinions of characters from books as if they were personal friends, since he didn't have any real-life ones of his own.

'I don't care what anyone says, Mishkin isn't stupid. He's just surrounded by savages,' he said, adding, 'as indeed we are, Alison.'

'I suppose so,' I agreed in as noncommittal a voice as I could.

'But Raskolnikov is a more profound man altogether. God,' he shuddered, in his crackly, half-broken voice, 'he looked into the blackness of the human soul and entered it. I don't know if I could have k-k-killed her, do you, Alison?'

'Oh, I don't know,' I mumbled, 'it's hard to say.'

'But you must have asked yourself,' he insisted.

'Really, Johnathan, I prefer the Brontë sisters, like I've told you before.'

'You've probably read inferior editions,' he said in his superior manner. 'Remind me to lend you my Magarshack translations. I think you'll find the introductions helpful.'

I climbed into bed, bent my knees up and leaned a book against them, and tried to lose myself in *Middlemarch*, while beneath me the others slumped in front of the TV and Daddy would be sitting on the step by the back door, stroking the dogs in the dusk. Gradually they'd amble away to the barn, except for Tinker, the eldest, who nestled into Daddy's thigh. A motorbike roared into the village and swung into the farmyard, its white beam brushing across the front of the house. Pamela got off and gave her helmet to the rider, and strolled up to the house as he rode away. As she passed Daddy she bent down and picked a fluff of thistledown off his lapel, then she opened the door and a yellow light leapt across the farmyard to the hedge on the other side of the lane.

The evening was thick and sticky. Outside, Tinker had entered a dog's pretend sleep pressed against Daddy's legs.

Daddy gazed ahead into the gathering darkness, feeling nothing but a glaze of unquestioning calm over the world. My head was filling up with dust, and my eyelids were too heavy to keep up. I let the weight of the book push my legs out flat, and I rolled away from it as I drifted into sleep.

CHAPTER NINE

Burning the Stubble

In the premature dawn that fooled the cockerel an uneven morning mist draped itself like sheets over the church and houses up on the ridge opposite. It made the village look abandoned, like the house next door in winter, whereas in reality it was the most active part of the day, when people took heart from that moisture, as if God had breathed on the window pane of his world, and undertook strenuous tasks. Mother sent me into the fields up on the hill behind the house to pick mushrooms: unaffected by the drought, they appeared overnight like warts on the earth's skin; grandmother wondered whether they, too, might be susceptible to hypnosis, but they didn't seem to need it.

From up there on the tops I could see, off to my left, Mike Howard spreading silage on his pasture, and down in the village mother plucking a chicken in the yard, covered in its feathers, as if she herself were a moulting angel; I could see all too clearly fields littered with farmers' trash; discarded plastic fertilizer bags, orange nylon string, unused ends of mesh fencing and coils of barbed wire. Grandfather pottered about the meadow next to the barn, gathering up the rubbish like an impatient beachcomber, grabbing things with anger but also a little guilt, since his grandsons were no more careless than he'd been, it was just that in his day things were made out of canvas and twine, which rotted into the earth.

I could see Douglas Westcott in the distance lifting rams out of hedges that they'd caught their horns in trying to escape, convinced the next pasture must be better than this one, and Tom hanging a gate over in grandfather's land by the rectory, surrounded by bales of black hay, like giant sheep pellets, scattered by the new combine that Ian had bought in time for the harvest. I could see Maria, too, hanging up a newcomer family's washing in another breezeless morning, and they were all unable to stop themselves from reforming the daily, useless optimism that today might be different. It never was. The sun assumed its fierce midday throne by eight o'clock, to further torment the village, and fast burned off the mist and the dew, the mere memory of which, later in the day, was enough to make a person's mouth water.

The granite works gave out face-masks and initiated a four-day week because of the lingering cloud of dust that clogged even the office workers' lungs. Milk curdled in the churn and was refused by the collecting lorries. Men were sucked into the discomfort of their own flesh and stayed at home, where they sat swatting mosquitoes on their sweaty skin and suffered with their wives the awful sounds of dry wood, robbed of all its sap, splitting as heat opened the grain, and of starlings thudding against window-panes.

The starlings appeared in the village one evening as darkness fell, choosing the yew tree in the churchyard to tumble into out of the sky at dusk, like a pack of black cards sprinkled from the heavens. They made us think that grandmother might have been right after all when she said that time was changing direction, it had run out of momentum up the spiral and was falling back down again, because the starlings were like a reminder of the newcomers' disastrous barbecue back in June, to which they'd invited each other; a pile of news-papers awaiting the dustman caught fire and a scattered flock of charred pieces of paper rose into the sky and dirtied sheets drying on clothes-lines, spread a fine film of black dust in all the rooms in all the houses of the village, and ruined Granny Sims' six-monthly perm.

For some days the newcomers had stayed indoors, and when they had to go out they tiptoed around the village like unwelcome guests, and drove their silent cars off to work. Things turned right around, though, after the early harvest, because that was the time for Ian to do the job he enjoyed more than any other, the one he was best at, the one job he knew he could do better than Tom: burning the stubble of the cornfields. Ian subscribed to all the farming magazines, listened to the radio programmes over his early morning cup of tea, and sought advice from fertilizer salesmen and agricultural engineers for ways of improving our yield of cows and crops. But whenever anyone suggested that burning stubble was old-fashioned and wasteful, it was better to turn it over or dig it up or leave it be, then he folded the magazine or switched off the radio, saying: 'Come on Tom, us better be gettin' down to work afore 'tis time to stop,' and Tom would have to gulp down his tea and stumble out after his brother into the semi-darkness of dawn.

Ian looked forward all year to that season, and when it came he took his time, to his grandfather's dismay and his brother's annoyance, since there was still a back-breaking load of other things to do before they could relax, and celebrate the harvest festival. But Ian wouldn't be hurried, and in the end they left him to it, as they did every year, grandfather telling him: 'Don't you worry, bay, us'll take care of the sheep-dipping ourselves, you take yer time, you must be an artist or somethin' I suppose, us'll collect up the hay on ours own. 'Ow the 'eck did us get all this land anyway, 'twas better when the farm was small.'

Ian took no notice of them, because he knew you couldn't rush it if you wanted to do it properly, and that was the only way he wanted to do it; other farmers just lit up some chaff in a corner of a field according to which way the wind was blowing, and left the flames to drift across of their own accord. But Ian spent all day preparing lines of hay around the edges of the field, in order to burn from the outside in: if he judged it correctly the fire would speed towards the centre at an accelerating pace and combust with a bang in the middle of the field, and it was all over in an instant. He would prepare all the fields during the day and rush around setting light to them at dusk, because that was when it was most dramatic, and what he aimed for was to have them explode as close together as possible.

That summer the stubble was so dry Ian was glad to see grandfather leave, because he was worried a spark from his pipe might set it alight before he was ready. He worked all day making his lines of hay, and studying the dimensions of the fields, their contours, and the barely perceptible breezes. He didn't really trust anyone else to help him but he knew he couldn't do everything himself, so when the time came he got me to lend a hand.

We ran along the hedges with torches, and the stubble crackled and flamed. He never paused then, because there was no time for error: he decided where to start and we circled the field with fire, leapt into his van, and tore off to the next one. There were six in all, and we managed to cover each of them before the first one combusted and boomed around the Valley, while we lay spreadeagled by the van, drenched in sweat and panting like dogs. Then another one exploded, and another, like the big guns of an almighty battle, making Corporal Alcock's heart stop with nostalgic terror, Jane's dad wake up thinking he was late for work on the night shift at the quarry, grandfather curse and bite his lip, and Douglas Westcott remember the earthquake that surprised him in Mexico City.

They made the Rector climb through the skylight with his cigarettes and gin and tonic, to stand on the roof of the rectory and watch the sun go down crimson behind a patch-work of golden fields, scorched and smouldering with orange flame and drifting clouds of smoke, crackling and blowing. He thought it was the most beautiful thing he'd ever seen, and for some reason he couldn't quite work out it made him contemplate his own death. He went back down to his study and took out his Bible, and found the passage that was nagging at him, in The Wisdom of Solomon:

> As gold in the furnace hath he tried them, and received them as a burnt offering.
> And in the time of their visitation they shall shine, and run to and fro like sparks among the stubble.

He scribbled it on a scrap of paper, which he absent-mindedly handed to me a couple of days later, when I asked him for a bookmark.

The next morning it was the newcomers' turn to wake up with the black soot of burnt stubble on the carpets and furniture in their houses, and across the metallic paintwork of their saloon cars. With the communal energy of outsiders they visited us on a rota basis to complain to grandfather at such an unsociable habit, they wrote letters to the *Mid-Devon Advertiser* and the Exeter *Express and Echo* pointing out the safety hazards of this antiquated rural practice, and they organized a petition protesting at the damage done to the ozone layer, which they gave to the Rector, as their local councillor, to hand in to Teignbridge District Council. He listened to their resentment, took the petition from them, returned to his study, tore it up and threw it in his waste-paper basket.

On Thursday a parcel of books was delivered with my name on it by a conscientious headmaster who'd taken an oath that forbade him to strike. The family all volunteered to help with my postponed education, but in the end they all made excuses except Ian, who laid them out on the kitchen table but then just stared at the pages of the mathematics book in disbelief. After what seemed like hours he closed it and gave it me back, saying: 'They don't know what they's lettin' theirselves in for.'

The only person who was any help was Johnathan, who'd spent two weeks of every summer in France, and down at the quarry pool he tested me in my first attempts to learn the vocabulary of another language.

'Concentrate!' he urged me. 'Surely you want to read *L'Etranger* in the original.'

'Lay who?' I asked.

Johnathan raised both his eyebrows at once, and sighed. 'Albert Camus. He played in goal for the Algerian *national* team. One of the g-g-greats, Alison. Really!'

I began to wonder whether the Comprehensive in Newton

Abbot that I'd passed by for years, whenever we went in for a Saturday shop, was anything more than a façade whose pretence was kept up by everybody older than me, and was as much of a mirage as when schools had been the impossible dream of rural philanthropists: grandmother, whose memory had been sharpening as if to compensate for the muddiness of her sight, told me that at this rate our own children would have to end up teaching us, just like her mother-in-law who had taught her illiterate parents after the village school was built. Her father became such a scholard that he spoilt his ballot paper in the next election by signing his initials, instead of the X that he assumed was merely intended to represent the mark of an uneducated man. Grandmother suggested that one of the newcomer women start up a dame school at home, and she reminded the Rector, when he came to give her sick communion now that she could no longer hobble to the services, of one of his predecessors who'd taught children in the church in a previous epoch. But the Rector declined her proposal: 'I may be a priest, Mrs Freemantle,' he told her, 'and we'll doubtless be the last workers in the country to form our own union, but I'm no strike breaker.'

He tried to explain how reasonable the teachers' demands were, and how, what's more, every child should receive an equal education paid for out of income taxes, 'because education's not something the rich should be able to buy, surely, Mrs Freemantle, like a swimming pool or an expensive toy for their children, free and equal education's the measure of a civilized society and the way things are going if that woman carries on, the poor will have to pay for their own pencils and rubbers, and we'll be back to before the Second World War'.

Grandmother was unimpressed. She considered cruelty to children unforgivable, and refusing to teach them in order to demand higher wages she thought the lowest form of blackmail. She said that if she believed in capital punishment she'd recommend that they were shot, but since she didn't then she thought they should be banished from the kingdom, a humane punishment that she regretted had fallen into disuse.

The Rector realized the futility of arguing with her. As an

afterthought he told her how, soon after his arrival in the village, he'd been invited to become a governor of the Primary School in Chudleigh: back then there was still a grammar school in Newton Abbot and a secondary modern in Kingsteignton, and Chudleigh Primary held the record, in the county of Devon, of eight years without a single pass in the eleven-plus exam. The Rector did two things: he accepted a place on the Board of Governors, and he also bowed to his wife's demands that they send their children to schools in Exeter, because he didn't feel able to insist that their children's education be hostage to his principles.

Grandmother cackled with delight: 'You's a good man, Rector, a good man. But your head spends most of its time in the clouds.'

Unaware, as the world ground creaking to a halt, that the past was catching us up, and with it people's long since discarded memories, we lived a carefree existence. The younger kids in dark skirts spun cartwheels on the Brown, like dwarf nuns pleading for respite from the sun's divine punishment, or chased after a shrinking football, repeatedly punctured by Nan Dyer's mad terrier, which the boys had to repair by soldering it with matches. Some of the older ones, though, those with obstinate parents reluctant to submit to the sun's tyranny, were still assigned futile tasks: they planted a patchwork of tiny vegetable plots along the bank of the trickling stream until the day its last drops evaporated before their very eyes; they were then given improbable dowsing rods cut from hawthorn by old Martin the hedge-layer, and despatched in the vague direction of supposed sites of ancient wells. When I told grandmother she said she was sure she could remember coming across maps showing their locations, and she directed me to chests of drawers unopened in a generation. But there were no maps at their bottoms, only brittle sheets of old newspaper that crumbled to the touch.

Bigger boys accompanied their fathers to dying woods around the edge of the parish, because people were agreeing with grandmother that history is a spiral, and just like in 1976 the summer was so long it was burning up autumn altogether and would again be immediately followed by a harsh winter, and so the insistent hum that droned throughout those months was augmented for a while by the whine of chainsaws, cutting down the copses and spinneys that anyway, when you thought about it, only took up valuable space on arable land. They ripped up everything with their chainsaws: beech and ash, birch and elder, everything, that is, except oak, whose wood's no good for burning. The oaks were left and the ground ploughed up around them, sad, solitary trees in an emptying landscape of dusty soil.

CHAPTER TEN

Mirror

All along the Teign river beyond the quarry pool, willows stood along the far bank. You couldn't imagine how they got there, they looked so out of place, but one of the Viscounts' gardeners must have planted them, hundreds of years ago. By now they were old and stunted creatures, with varicose barks, twisted and splitting, rubbed against by generations of cows; their branches drooped sadly over the water.

The river was so dried up that on Friday morning Johnathan and I played jumping games across it, and when other children came down he hid in the cradles of the willow trees, watching.

Back at the pool we dislodged the widowman heron from his rock jutting out over the water; he retreated to a pile of granite rubble and regarded us mournfully, while sometimes one of the grown-ups, Maria in her red scarf or Yvonne, Jane's tall, skinny mum, with her fruit-picking basket, kept an eye on us through the telescope up on the cliff, as we dived into the black water.

If we screwed up our eyes, though, we could see that they'd soon lifted the telescope away from us, to gaze upon the long and slender waterfall that had been the 9th Viscount Teignmouth's lifelong dream and celebrated achievement. It was fed by a leat built to the Viscount's precise specifications by a dozen infantry veterans of Wellington's victorious army at Quatre-Bras who, sensing the furious revenge imminent at Waterloo, deserted camp and made their way home to London, which they reached at the same time as the news of Napoleon's final defeat.

They fled together to the spongy margin of Dartmoor,

where the engineering Viscount found them lurking in his pine woods and offered them work in his great enterprise. His and Johnathan's ancestor, the very first Viscount, had been a cabin boy with Sir Francis Drake, and the 9th Viscount was a follower of the great engineer.

The deserters worked like Trojans building that leat which began at a spring below the volcanic extrusion of heaped boulders of Houndtor and was directed across open heather, over the sloping granite past Manaton, through the combes behind Hennock and finally into the familial acres of pine forest. Using skills of dam building, irrigation and hydrography learned in the universities of Europe but improved upon by the obsessive neuropathy of a gifted aristocrat, the Viscount worked out a precisely detailed route whose falls harnessed energy sufficient to drive water up succeeding rises, and it wasn't until two generations later that an itinerant cartographer ingratiated himself with the then 11th Viscount by proving that the leat rose across its entirety by a height of twenty feet, for the engineering Viscount's route had been so complicated, with its ups and downs and unders and overs and around the corners, that it had fooled even gravity.

But apart from this unintentional miracle the waterfall was a failure, with not even the wit of an authentic folly; for the 9th Viscount had actually intended that the water should supply the house, if needs be, as a precaution against drought, such as that suffered in 1750 when footmen expired on their carriages and the water-closets all clogged up, so that breezes carried across the Valley odours of aristocratic excrement, stirring in the peasants of our village at their decimated harvest forgotten rumours of equality spread by those Levellers who had passed nearby in their flight to exile in Cornwall. But by an ironic hydrological error the power generated by the long gush of the cascade was insufficient to push the water back up under the terraced lawns to the house.

Furthermore, the 9th Viscount had imagined the spectacle created by narrowing the final flow of water from the leat through a carefully moulded clay funnel would emerge as a fluid representation of knowledge and art and manners, as the inevitable impulse of refinement inherent in civilization, broadening imperceptibly but unerringly during the progress of its own momentum. Instead it only made immature youths pee in their pants, and farmers' wives sometimes went to the beech tree on the pretext of checking on the swimmers or gathering blackberries thereabouts but really to watch through the telescope as the sun, filtering intermittently through illusive cirrus clouds, made the slender cataract seem to weave and ripple in its ineluctable glissade, and although the sight itself, in the silent isolation of the lens, was no more than an abstract display of light and movement, the women felt themselves gliding above the sawdust of an urban dance-floor, rustic unease blurred by Norman Calvados, waltzing in the arms of a tall, slender mute whose joints were made not of bone but of honey.

We could have drowned all at once and not been noticed, but we couldn't see any danger. After shouting and screaming as we splashed around we'd file quietly up the dried bed of the stream and back into the village. We each settled into our own thoughts, disturbed only by the strange boom that came from the church bell even though no one was ringing it. Behind us the heron resumed his vigil as the quarry pool digested our raucous and bubbly laughter and recomposed the placid, inscrutable black mirror of its surface.

There were no mirrors in our house; not since Daddy, losing his temper for the first time in his life, had stormed through all the rooms and smashed every last one, after lifting a soapy shaving brush and seeing not the sultana eyes and smooth, nineteen-year-old complexion of his own face, but someone else entirely. For a few seconds he stood, trembling, and stared back at brown berry pupils stranded in bloodshot whites, crows' feet picked out at the side of each eye and beneath them a single crease holding up a crescent of puffy, aubergine-coloured skin. From his precise jaw, pouches of flesh were pushing out at the jowls. Lazily parted lips revealed blackened teeth, and the apple-red ruddiness of his cheeks was blotted with mulberry splotches.

88

Daddy wrenched the mirror off the wall and smashed it on the basin, and then stormed through the house, mindless of the children he startled awake: no one said a word, not even Ian, who thought he'd discarded fear the year before when he fought with Joanna Simmons, leader of the newcomers' children. But like his brother and sisters he was struck dumb by our father's unheard of fury. I was only a toddler then, but mother said that even I held my breath until Daddy had completed his destruction, before summoning it for a high-pitched scream that echoed in the shards of glass scattered on every floor.

At the time mother said nothing, her immediate response being to blame herself, seeing Daddy's actions as the bizarre anger of an uncomplaining man in this strange village, anger directed at her and her unknowing transgressions, which grandmother would only later explain to her: allowing me to see my reflection before reaching my first birthday, or failing to veil the mirrors after the death of grandfather's sister. So she said nothing. Then one morning she awoke to find him sitting up in bed and scrutinizing her with a puzzled expression, and she felt all the substance of her being sucked out.

At first Daddy's amnesia had been intermittent. He'd start a job but move on to another before it was finished, leaving a trail of uncompleted tasks at the end of the day that grandfather had to clear up. When there was a pause in conversation he changed the subject, as if trying to prove how quick-thinking he was, and he would further bewilder mealtimes by asking, no sooner had he finished, what time was tea going to be ready, and what's more how come no one's done the washing-up, we can't eat off dirty plates. It got worse: he would plummet through the years, to find himself stranded at some point in the past, unaware of his predicament and eager for a future that had already occurred.

Dr Buckle at Chudleigh was harsh in his diagnosis. 'It's the cider, Mrs Freemantle. Stop him drinking and these lapses won't trouble him any more.' Mother felt everything she'd tried to ignore rise up from her liver. In the very first month of their marriage he'd disappeared one evening and she eventually found him in the barn, an empty flagon beside his unconscious body.

'Is it me?' she'd sobbed the next morning.

''Tis me, my lover,' he'd replied, pulling her to him with the tenderness he'd never entirely lose. But while she dissolved gratefully into his reassuring arms, he continued to seek the oblivion of rough cider, melting into the night and drinking himself unconscious.

'Why?' she pleaded.

And he would look away and say: 'I couldn't tell 'ee.'

After the initial shock, mother managed to convince herself it didn't threaten her: it was Daddy's secret, solitary weakness that dragged him off into the darkness but returned him more loving than ever. She was too grateful to him not to ignore it, too grateful to the school classmate who ignored her but whom she'd never forgotten, and who suddenly reappeared seven years later at her front door. He'd walked across the Valley and up through Teign Village, where net curtains were lifted for prying eyes, so that even before he reached Hennock she'd heard on the grapevine that he was heading that way, and wondered with envy who he was visiting.

He knocked on her door and her heart jumped.

'Do 'ee want to walk up the reservoirs with me?' he'd smiled. And so they walked, swapping news but talking less and less, though his smile said enough as they circled the reservoirs that damp autumn afternoon, their fingers imperceptibly becoming entwined.

'I'll be back next Sunday,' Daddy told her at her gate.

It was in unconscious imitation of his own father that Daddy courted a woman from outside the village. Although she wasn't a stranger, as grandmother had been, since she'd been to the same school as everyone else in the Valley, and neither did she possess grandmother's provocative beauty, still the women of the village resented her intrusion. They suspected her of having crept up on Daddy and seduced him while he was working alone in one of the hidden fields near the river, unwilling to accept that she was Daddy's own, enigmatic choice.

That habit the men of our line had of bringing wives into the village from outside was one of the things that set our family apart. Another was the practice of reasoning with their children instead of beating them, a practice that had been widely derided but which continued for three generations, right up until mother destroyed a tradition she herself had strained harder than anyone to continue, when on the first of October she would lose control and strap me, as her own father had done to her.

Grandfather made new windows for the entire house as a wedding present, and grandmother moved their things out of the main bedroom to give way to the bride. Daddy joined grandfather in his workshop to carve the parts of the bed they would share, and took his advice: 'Make it good and big, bay; sometimes you'll want all the space you can get for love, an' other times you'll need all that space to put between you.'

On the morning after their wedding night Daddy woke early. He didn't want to wake his bride, gently snoring beside him, and he wondered what to do with himself. Then he noticed her shoes lying where she'd kicked them off, in the middle of the room. He took them, along with all the other pairs she'd put in the wardrobe, downstairs to the kitchen. When she came down to make breakfast she found the table covered with rows of shining shoes.

From then on Daddy polished shoes every day, before he did anything else. He found it a pleasing way to wake up, and he continued as his children grew, placing Ian's toddler's sandals beside grandfather's heavy workman's boots. Mother told me that she sometimes found him transfixed by the sight of his children's tiny shoes on the kitchen table, and when he realized she was there he would blush and hide his watery eyes from her as he gathered them up.

He'd been locked in the past for months at a time when Dr Buckle at last referred him, too late, to a neurologist in Exeter.

'He's suffering from alcoholic degeneration of the mamil-lary bodies,' the specialist told mother. 'He won't recover his memory.'

While white strands were appearing in his unruly crown of hair Daddy himself was growing younger, percolating through his own past until amnesia gripped him for good at an isolated, unchanging moment in his childhood, present joining the lost past as daily experience soaked like receding water into the sands of forgetting. That was my Daddy, a man constantly disorientated by a world where people grew old overnight and moved house without warning, where everyday objects became mysterious totems withholding their true meaning, so that I'd come across him switching a light on and off in amazement or trying to speed up the brewing tea with mother's liquidizer, because he'd gone back to live in a world before the day that electricity came to the village, on which cows danced in the meadow that ran down to the stream.

Somehow we remained at least faintly familiar to him, as if our daily contact contained some coagulant that could partially plug the haemorrhage of memory, but even so, you sensed that it was like the disconcerting familiarity felt on meeting a stranger in a dream.

Coming back from the quarry pool through the vibrant heat haze that Friday morning I felt myself as if invisible, the cells of my body insinuating themselves into the thickening air, as I came into the yard. Mother was hanging up white sheets on the washing-line. Over at the barn Daddy was passing the last bales of hay down from the loft, a task so repetitive that there weren't sufficient intervals in which to forget the rest of the chore. Reappearing from the shadows gripping another bale by its twine and using his knee to swing it out from the loft, before letting it drop to Ian, Daddy was imbued with an illusory decisiveness and strength. Mother grasped a sheet and leaned into it, and regret stole her breath away. She stayed that way, breathing hard.

'Mother!' Ian's voice snapped her out of herself. He came

across to her. 'Us is at the end of the early crop, near's
dammit. We've got a week's feed left. I didn't want to say
nothin' las' night, but you ought to know. 'Cos then we either
buys or slaughters.'

He climbed onto his tractor and manoeuvred away. Daddy
was sitting at the loft door, legs dangling, waiting for something to occur to him. Mother hurriedly pegged the rest of
the washing onto the line, returned to the kitchen, and rolled
herself a cigarette from the tobacco Ian kept in an old cigar
box on the mantelpiece. When Ian was a boy and smoked in
secret, she used to confiscate his cigarettes whenever she
caught him puffing in the worksheds. After he'd gone to bed
she smoked them herself. She never came to look like a
smoker, though; she looked like a young girl still learning
how to.

She inhaled the smoke deep into her lonely lungs. She had
no friends in the village, and she never once returned to
Hennock after Daddy brought her to the farm past the
jealous scrutiny of the other women; their suspicion, though,
only encouraged her pride and she carried herself aloof from
them all: the intimacy with her one man was enough for her.
In the early years of their marriage they'd meet by chance in
the bedroom, drawn by a mutual whim, and mother would
re-emerge into a friendly world with her body lighter. Recently, she'd noticed how her limbs had grown clumsy, and
would knock into things for no good reason.

Mother rolled herself another cigarette, and as she put the
lid back on the box her attention was caught by the framed
set of school photographs that made us all look the same age.
Mother picked it up and placed it on the table beside her as
she lit her cigarette and inhaled the coarse smoke. Disappointment rose inside of her; she felt it hiss through her throat
with the smoke as she studied those pictures of her children,
from whom Daddy had hidden his drinking, teaching Ian
chess with the set given him years before by auntie Sarah's
grandchildren from Bristol, and taking Pamela with him on
his long Sunday walks around the parish, which encouraged
her gregariousness, as the walks became for her simply the

route from one remote farm to another, where she could renew acquaintance with friends; the flowers and birds and boundaries that Daddy pointed out held no interest for Pamela and were instantly forgotten.

It was true that he never saw much of Tom, who even as a small boy would beg to go off and help grandfather mending fences, dipping sheep, or dismantling tractor engines, invariably coming in long after his bedtime and resenting the daylight hours he had to spend at school, aching for the weekends, and beyond them the holidays, and further ahead to when he'd be able to spend all of his time tending the animals and the land.

So that when their father was swept through the house in his wind of confusion, breaking all the mirrors, my brothers and sister awoke convinced they were still dreaming.

And mother had no idea who to turn to. There was no question of her approaching grandmother: Daddy was her favourite child, and mother was sure she'd hear nothing said against him, would only blame mother for anything wrong, even more than she did herself. Finally she swallowed her pride and, even though ever since the previous Granny Sims had died the sewing circle had been steadily losing its power, she had to talk to someone. In Granny Sims' front room half a dozen elderly women sat around dropping stitches and reliving the times when what was decided in that circle, from the buying and selling of land and livestock to prospective marriages, was invariably carried out. Mother took along some socks and darning wool, and the older women, as self-important as their predecessors even as their influence waned, leaned back in the armchairs, lace chair coverings like aureolae behind their heads, so that they resembled the fading saints on the church screen. Mother told her story and when she'd finished, after a period of silence punctuated by the clicking of knitting needles, Granny Sims leaned forward and told her: 'You're a woman. This is yours to bear.'

Mother stubbed her cigarette out in the bottom of a teacup, squashing it with her thumb as if by putting out every tiny ember she might extinguish her thoughts. But it was no use. Watching from the dim passageway, I saw her pick up the photos that made us seem like quadruplets: Ian, their chess prodigy for whom anything was possible, but who relented to the pressure from his grandfather and uncles to take over the farm that they'd been propping up until he left school. Mother sent off for prospectuses from every university and polytechnic in the country, but Ian did no more than leaf silently through them in the evenings. Still addicted to the mathematical perfection of chess, but with no opponent of sufficiently high calibre in the area, he'd entered the chimerical labyrinths of chess problems, staying up half the night in his bedroom poring over the inanimate pieces on their chequered board, though always reappearing before dawn to dispel the heavy cloud of fatigue from his shoulders with mugs of bitter tea, before setting off into the fields.

Pamela at least would escape, but then she'd been born without ties. Mother remembered the words of the old Granny Sims, who looked at her baby after the christening and told her: 'She'll cut the cord, Deborah; you can always tell.'

She possessed a freedom the rest of us lacked, as if she had just come to visit one day and had stayed a bit longer than expected. It occurred to me that maybe my own sister was in fact the guest I had been expecting. Her freedom showed in all sorts of small ways: she'd never acquired the modesty that others had, who would be embarrassed by opening the bathroom door and finding her there naked, washing her hair in the basin or painting her toenails. In fact she took over the communal rooms as if they were set aside for her personal use. Whereas the rest of us trooped in and out of the bathroom, she set up camp there, with her tray of bath oils, scented soaps, essential perfumes, facial cleansers and toners, moisturizing creams, shampoos and conditioners and massage lotions. She squirted into the bath drops of oil and scented water from various containers and ran the taps, spreading through the house aromas of lavender, coconut and roses. When the bath was full and steaming she immersed herself and stayed there, deaf to the pleas of her family, whose bladders were bursting and who'd been waiting half an hour already, because she couldn't see why they wouldn't come in and use the facilities anyway; she didn't mind.

She liked me to read to her from her magazines while she lay in the bath, allowing her skin to luxuriate in the essential oils of mint and oranges, massaging herself in the water. The articles she most enjoyed were quizzes designed to ascertain whether or not she was a woman who loved too much, or a human doormat, or chased her best friends' boyfriends, or had the problem of being a successful businesswoman but a failure in love. She answered them all, carefully selecting the answer to each question, and I ticked them off as the pages of the magazine became damp and soggy in the sauna of a bathroom, until the biro refused to work any more.

She stood up to wash her hair under the shower attachment Ian had installed, although he'd never got round to fixing a plastic curtain rail around the bath, so that the water sprayed all over the floor. Pam stood under the jet of water with her eyes closed, her body foamy with shower gel, with a smile on her face. She always peed when she took a shower: she couldn't help herself; relaxing under the water that coursed over her body, she let go of the water inside her.

When she finally evacuated the bathroom, to the relief of her family, they found a scene of mayhem in which some natural disaster had occurred: water was dripping off the ceiling, the floor was flooded, towels had disappeared, soap was stuck to the bottom of the bath, the tops of the toothpaste tubes had vanished, and suddenly we were all out of toilet paper.

It was the same in the kitchen: there was an unwritten rule that we ate our meals together at the same time every day, breakfast at seven-fifteen and dinner at six-thirty. But Pam took less and less notice: she swept downstairs only when she heard the newcomers who gave her a lift to Exeter beeping their horn in the lane, and she grabbed whatever was on the table as she passed. In the evenings she rarely came home till late, and mother gave up putting a plate in the oven for her, because it always ended up in the pigswill. Yet mother never reproached her. She knew she'd missed the opportunity, and exactly when it had arisen: one Saturday evening five years before, when she was fifteen years old, Pamela had asked to be excused from the supper table early, because she was going out. Mother assumed she'd be off to watch television in one of the other girls' houses, or to play in one of their rooms, as she and her friends usually did. We were finishing dessert when she reappeared in the kitchen with mascaraed eyes and vermilion lips, a pair of black net gloves that went up to her elbows and matched her tights, a black lycra dress which hugged all the curves that showed she'd become a woman, and a certain perfume whose scent caused her older brother to stop breathing. The fact was she'd grown up overnight: her father didn't recognize her, and mother was too astonished to say anything before Pam had walked across the kitchen and through the door, said 'See you later' over her shoulder, and got onto the back of a stranger's motorbike revving up in the lane. And having missed her opportunity then, instead of pouring out her cold anger, burning her daughter's precocious wardrobe and tying her down to a regime of punishment, as everyone expected, mother simply accepted the fact that Pamela lived according to different rules from the rest of us, and from then on treated her as an equal.

I wanted to be like her, but I knew that I wasn't. I wasn't like any of them.

Pamela had more friends outside the village than within; she'd done a secretarial course in Exeter and now had a job there, commuting with a carload of the outsiders who'd moved into the new houses on the steep slope below the church. She was brought home by young men who, if they stayed at all, would take a glass of sherry in the front room with a look of amused condescension they made no effort to conceal.

Mother knew that one of these days Pamela would leave with one of them, carelessly, without a backward glance. No one minded.

Tom was Pamela's opposite, bound to the land from birth. Long before puberty on his skin the scent of animals lingered and sometimes, doing up his tie or wiping a midge from his eye, mother caught the smell of new-mown hay on his breath.

He inherited his grandfather's shyness: as a child, mother feared he was retarded because he showed no sign of speaking, until she surprised him in the barn repeating to the pigs the same stories that she'd told him, and she realized that it was just talking to other human beings that made him feel uneasy. The things that more forward children were shy about as they got older, though, Tom was unaware of. He'd belch without warning and fart without shame, filling the kitchen with a first-thing-in-the-morning pestilential smell, oblivious to mother's eyes raised to heaven in exasperation. Even if there was company he'd break wind with the sound of a trombone, without batting an eyelid. He blew his nose by pressing a finger against one nostril and blowing, then repeating it with the other, and he'd do it anywhere so long as it was out of doors. And if he wanted to pee, even if he was with other people, he'd turn around without saying a word, step forward a pace or two, unzip his fly, and water the grass. He didn't see anything wrong with such behaviour, because he'd learned it from the animals. But if someone asked him a question that required an answer he'd blush just like grandfather from his hairline to his collar and fumble with the words, as if they were slippery things sliding around on his tongue.

Ian was tall and stringy, with the wiry strength of his father and grandfather; Tom, on the other hand, had been given his body and his sluggish metabolism by the maternal line of our family. He was like an overgrown cherub, heavy-lidded and heavy-limbed, neither soft nor hard, neither fat nor muscular, but rather built of undefined muscle, or substantial fat, as solid and strong as a bull. Ian and Tom had never fought as youngsters: Tom wouldn't have dreamed of doing so. He never contradicted his older brother, who did the accounts, decided crop rotation, ordered foodstuffs and conferred with the vet. But Tom knew things that could never be learned. During the lambing season he stayed out day and night, and when a tardy cow was brought into the barn it was he who extended his arm into its slippery womb and eased the birth of a calf.

*

One Saturday back in May Ian had asked me to check the cows in the far pasture. Half the herd were heavy with calf, ponderous in their movement, passing through time itself at a different pace, appropriate to their weight and condition. I stood on the lower rung of the gate. The sun was slanting across the field and the cows had scattered themselves across it, grazing. I was about to leave when I realized that, without fuss or warning, no more than thirty feet from me a cow was giving birth: she stopped grazing and started to drop her calf, just like that, still chewing the cud. But it didn't come out all at once: the top of its head appeared, and then a little more, and then all of its head up to the shoulders. There it stayed, its eyes closed, half in the world and half still in its mother's womb, as if reluctant to wake up from the long sleep of gestation into the bright light of life. Its mother, too, looked unsure, not quite able to make up her mind whether or not to let go of the companion who'd shared her body.

It was in case of just such an eventuality that Ian had sent me there, and I knew I should jump off the gate and run home to tell him it'd started, so they could bring them into the barn, and Tom could help them with his inborn skills of a midwife. I knew I should; but I was transfixed.

It seemed like ages I stood there, gripping tighter the bars of the gate, silently urging the cow to push, mother, push it out of you, but nothing was happening, the calf was stuck and I was getting worried when quite suddenly it came sliding out all at once, afterbirth breaking up around it, tumbling into existence trailing its umbilical cord like a kite-string.

What happened next I'd never seen or even heard of before: while the calf was being born none of the other cows took the slightest notice. Now, though, although neither mother nor calf had made a sound, one or two of the other cows lifted their heads and ambled over, and when they reached the calf they began to lick it. It wasn't just the nearest ones that came first: they sensed what was happening quite separately from each other, and odd ones would stop grazing and make their way over from different parts of the field.

Soon a circle had formed around the calf, not just licking it but even, it seemed, pushing it with their tongues. After ten or fifteen minutes it made its first attempt to stand up, as if only because it was being pestered to by the cows. It got just half-way up before its spindly legs gave way and it collapsed in a heap, confounded. But they wouldn't leave it alone, instead urging it with their tongues to have another go: this time it nearly stood up straight before capitulating once more to the power of gravity.

But it wasn't to be defeated. The other cows began to leave it alone now, and it carried on between short rests. I wondered at the instinct embedded in its mind, new-born after nine months sleeping in its mother's belly, that compelled it so soon to struggle through that ordeal and stand on its own four legs. At last like a weightlifter it locked its knees, but then staggered giddily and keeled over; it took another few attempts before it could stand up straight and strong, by which time the other cows had all drifted away to graze, leaving its mother to finish licking it clean.

I told Ian the first calf was born, and that I'd seen how the other cows came round to welcome it into life and help it get used to reality.

'That!' said Tom, dismissing it with one syllable. 'Cows always does that with the first one. They smells the placenta. Can't resist its taste.'

When she got to my photograph I don't know what mother thought; she just stared at the picture. But after a few moments she turned the photos face down on the table. Three stubs had accumulated at the bottom of the teacup. Mother was motionless, unbreathing: the pulsating silence gathered around her.

'Why, dear God, do it only get harder?'

She walked to the door and shielded her eyes. Daddy was no longer at the loft. The stifling heat throbbed against her temples, and the memory of one damp autumn afternoon made her shudder.

*

The sun squeezed the air out of the house. Invisible birds hovered in the shadows, their wings fluttering as they kept their balance. I ran past mother and out into the world.

CHAPTER ELEVEN

The Lonely Hunter

During the week Ian dressed as scruffily, as practically, as any farmer, in tee-shirt, jeans and wellington boots. His week's work ended around midday on Saturday, in good time for football in the afternoon. It was his abiding worry that he'd be late for kick-off, because at the last minute some crisis always seemed to occur – a sheep was lost, the trailer needed emptying – and he'd come crashing into the kitchen crying: 'Mother, where's me shin-pads? Where've you put the first team strip? What did I do with my liniment?' It was the one time of the week we saw Ian flustered, the lid blown off the top of his nervous stomach by the fear of missing his football. Mother and Pamela and grandmother and I, eating the last of our lunch, awaited his panic-stricken entrance every Saturday.

'Should be here any minute,' Pam would say, glancing at the clock, and we'd all giggle.

''Asn't 'e got 'is kit ready again this week, silly bay?' asked grandmother.

When the door burst open we erupted into laughter, which only increased his alarm. 'Don't be stupid, mother,' he wailed, 'I'm late. Someone's stolen my shorts. Help me, mother.'

She would get up from the table slowly, with the smug assurance of a mother when she knows she's indispensable.

'Hurry up, will you,' Ian cried, checking his watch and playing with his hair, 'I's late,' as she proceeded with calm authority to collect his socks from off the drying-rack, his shirt from the linen cupboard, his jock-strap from the top drawer of his chest, his scuffed and wrinkled football boots from the corner of the hallway where he'd dropped them the week before, and his tie-ups from off the mantelpiece, because not only did she know where the piskies hid things but she also had a mother's memory, constantly taking stock and readjusting, for the location of objects around the house.

Ian scooped his kit from her arms and stuffed everything into a carrier bag, whose handles usually ripped open as he dashed out of the house, so that he wasted precious seconds retrieving a boot from the dust before throwing the bag into his yellow van and jumping in after it. He lifted the door on to its hinges even as he released the clutch, and bump-started the van as it rolled towards the lane.

In the event, Ian was invariably the first to arrive at the pitch, with time to stick the corner flags in and put the nets up before anyone else appeared. He accepted those chores as a captain's responsibility. He played for the Christow team, who ignored the sun and continued without a break throughout the year, organizing friendlies from May to September. Cricket wasn't a game taken seriously in the Valley, and was played by a team of soft-bellied newcomers and one or two older farmers, in a field next to the pub at Ashton. Tom had no interest in either sport, but he lent a hand when it was Ian's turn to mark out the pitch, and a couple of times a year they took the tractor over to drag the grasscutter or the roller across the ground. That summer more than ever before they should have left the pitch alone to recuperate from the battering it took in the winter and spring, but Ian promised the Christow Village Hall Committee he'd returf it in time for the Agricultural Show, and so they continued to play every week. By June the goalmouths were two dried-up craters, and the only green grass left on the pitch lay in thin strips along each flank. By July these too had disappeared, and the entire playing field had become a dusty desert, scattered with knee-scraping pebbles and grit. And although each match began with pristine white lines, they were scuffed off within minutes of the kick-off.

Quite apart from the disastrous state of the pitch, it was madness to play football, of all things, in the fiery heat of those months. While everyone around them was adopting the continental habit of taking a nap in the early hours of the afternoon, and the whole Valley assumed a slumbering silence, Ian and his friends were dashing up and down the Christow playing field. They lost so much liquid they had to place bottles along the touchline and behind the goal, taking quick swigs whenever there was a lull in the action.

Ian and the rest of his side gradually adjusted to the conditions. The teams who came into the Valley, though, from the Newton Abbot end or from Exeter direction, were unable to alter their tactics of English footballers: they still slid and rammed into bone-crunching tackles, the ball simply a cushion with which to legitimize their violence; and they still hurtled without pause up and down and across the pitch, the ball like the thread of an argument they could not quite follow. At half-time the Christow players calmly drank tea and sucked oranges, while their opponents, on the other side of the pitch, lay gasping like fish for air, their lungs on fire, bleeding from gashed knees and scraped shins and elbows.

Ian's team occasionally found themselves a goal or two behind at half-time, but they never once lost: the second half of every one of the friendlies they played during that summer became a clinical annihilation of the opposition, because they developed a new style of play, languid and skilful, based on accurate passing and control. They worked the ball in intricate patterns indirectly forward, and their opponents ran themselves into the ground chasing after the ball's shadow, so that it was as if they were playing the game as it had been played during the days when it was first shown on television, as grandfather described, when there were never less than two balls on the pitch.

It was Ian who masterminded their new approach from his position as sweeper, and every week he obtained more satisfaction from the game he loved, as a dream unfolded in reality before him. At the beginning of the summer they were watched by the usual handful of spectators: Gerry, their manager, with his bucket and sponge; two or three of the most loyal wives or girlfriends, sweltering in the heat; some younger lads who longed to grow big enough to get into the team, including Johnathan, the would-have-been 16th

Viscount, who kicked his football across the fields to watch in silence, talking to no one because he was scared they'd make fun of his undisguisable accent. He was the one who persuaded me to go along, and I did, not because I wanted to watch grown men thump a piece of leather round a field but because it was an opportunity to be with Johnathan without it being in secret, since no one else from our village went to the matches. The only other spectator was a rusty-coloured dog from the bungalows opposite Christow village hall, who escaped out of its house to come belting over to the touchline, where it bided its time before dashing onto the pitch and attempting to bite the ball.

Gradually, though, people waking from their Devonian siestas began to trickle down through the village in time for the second half, and as the summer wore on the touchline became lined with spectators, and by then I was glad to be among them since I'd come to see that it really was the beautiful game Ian had always claimed it to be. I in turn told the Rector, so that in the end he drove me over in his Triumph Vitesse, picking up Johnathan by the old Lodge gates.

The following season, watched by a crowd of rarely less than a hundred supporters at every home game, Christow were to win Division Two of the Exeter and District League without losing a single match (though they were knocked out of the Cup by their arch-rivals in a game of unprecedented violence, that came to be known as the Mudbath of Teign Village); and when, some years later, the World Cup was illuminated by the beautiful football of the Africans, football followers in our part of the country were confused, because they recognized 'the Christow style'.

After the games, Ian never stayed to shower with his mates or swill lager with them in the Artichoke. He came straight home and ran a scalding bath so deep that when he lowered his body into it the water spilled over the rim of the tub. He lay there half an hour or more, the water restoring peace to his limbs, reliving the game in his mind's eye and imagining further improvements to his team's tactics, which he would suggest at the following Wednesday evening training session. From the moment he'd finished work Ian's Saturdays adhered to an unchanging pattern. He finally climbed out of the bath, the fingers and toes of his wiry, tanned body all wrinkled, and wrapped a towel around his waist. He didn't bother to dry himself, because in the heat of that summer drops of water evaporated on his skin and his hair shaped itself into loose brown curls, while he shaved.

Back in his room Ian took out the same double-breasted black suit he wore every Saturday evening from under his mattress, where it had lain all week, pressed by the heavy old mattress and the intermittent, additional weight of his body. It was the same suit grandfather had got married in, fifty years before, and he'd passed it on to Ian for his eighteenth birthday, when his own body had shrunk so much grandfather felt foolish wearing his bridegroom's clothes. Ian laid it out on the bed and placed beside it his white cotton shirt, ironed by mother, with its subtle, barely discernible patterning. From his chest of drawers he selected one of his two pairs of maroon woollen socks, his matching maroon braces, and his gold cufflinks, and from the cupboard he picked his pride and joy, a pair of hand-sewn black brogues.

Ian cherished those shoes as if he was of an earlier generation, whose children had to spend their summers barefoot, developing thickly callused soles, and for whom wearing shoes was the highest luxury. He unthreaded the laces and polished the brogues, bringing up a shine with a buffing pad. Then he turned them over and hammered in some new metal studs, from a little bowl he kept on top of the chest of drawers. That habit seemed to be out of character for Ian: the metal studs rang out on the road, signalling his approach in an ostentatious manner, and at night his footsteps struck sparks in the darkness. When the erratic engine of his van coming home woke me in the early hours of Sunday morning, its headlights spilling across the ceiling, I could tell from his echoing footsteps in the yard what sort of mood he was in: it was usually a good one, his stride long and loose, and I'd fall asleep again while downstairs in the kitchen he drank the cups of tea of a man with no particular wish for the night to end. But on rare occasions his tread was terse, and he'd clump up the stairs and straight to bed.

When Ian had relaced his shoes and placed them on the bed he'd roll a cigarette, and smoke it pacing abstractedly around the room, still with a towel wrapped round his waist, relishing those preparations for his night out. Only when he'd stubbed out the butt of his cigarette did he get dressed. Unlike virtually all his contemporaries Ian never wore men's perfume. The younger blokes went out reeking of cheap aftershave, the married men splashed themselves with a more expensive cologne, and the greasers rubbed their bodies as well as their leathers with patchouli oil. But Ian must have known that he was one of those men whose sweat smells sweet, just as Daddy's did. The other thing he never wore was a tie: he thought they were undignified, too much like a halter or a lead, appropriate for an animal but not for human beings. He simply did up the top button of his shirt, and went out like that.

He never took Tom with him, and Tom was too shy to ask. He'd be sat in front of the television, but his ear was cocked like a dog's for the sound of Ian's preparations in the room above, the hammering of his metal studs and the faint pad of his bare-foot anticipation, and Tom watched out of the corner of his eye when Ian came downstairs in his antiquated suit that somehow looked brand new. While Ian had been playing football, Tom would have been pottering around the farm, hoping that this Saturday of all Saturdays his older brother would casually ask if he wanted to come along too, would advise him on what to wear, would teach him how to hold his drink, how to talk to girls, how to avoid fights and how to conduct them, and all the other mysteries of adult entertainment. Once Ian had returned from his game and was getting himself ready, Tom had the mounting conviction that this would indeed be his initiatory evening, and his body began to churn up inside with dread at the prospect, so much so that sometimes he disappeared into the fields again, on the pretext of completing some unfinished job, until he knew Ian would have gone out. But Ian never did ask Tom if he'd like to go with him, because he was a lone hunter and the thought never crossed his mind, and as soon as he'd left, alone, Tom's anxiety evaporated from his body, only to be replaced by a deadening weight of disappointment, which would grow heavier and heavier as the evening progressed in front of dreadful television programmes in the company of his parents, his grandparents, and me, his younger sister.

After tea Ian sat outside with grandfather and Daddy: they dragged their seats from the table and drank small glasses of Calvados in the warm evening, as the sun went down on the far side of Dartmoor. It was the only time of the week they talked together; well, Ian talked, and grandfather said a bit, and Daddy just drank his fruit juice and didn't even look like he was listening.

'See unemployment's nigh on three an' a half million now,' said Ian.

'Aye; bastards, not lettin' a man work,' said grandfather.

The Rector had told me there were a hundred and twenty-seven people in the village, on the Parish Roll. I asked Ian what three and a half million was divided by a hundred and twenty-seven, so I could get a good idea of how many people that was, but he ignored me.

'Word is the Honeywills is in trouble,' he told grandfather.

'See about buyin' their fields up by the forest,' grandfather said. 'That's good grazin' up there.'

'I already 'ad a word,' said Ian.

Ian rolled a cigarette and grandfather filled his pipe; then he laughed to himself and looked at me and said: 'Watch you don't talk to strangers, maid.'

'What strangers?' I asked.

'There's bound to be some about,' he declared. 'When I were a lad, in the thirties, they used to get lost on their way to Plymouth and walk through the valley. They 'ad to walk, see, they didn't 'ave no money. Used to ask for work without breaking stride, whoever they passed.

'"Any odd jobs?" they said, just out of habit. You'd say hello to 'em or nod, like, and all they'd say was "Any odd jobs?" They wouldn't look at you or even break stride, they wouldn't.'

He paused, then laughed again.

'Us found one of them in the orchard,' he said.

'What did you do, grandad?' I asked, already knowing the answer, because grandmother had told it me before.

'Father give 'im a good bloody hiding, thievin' bastard.'

It must have been the alcohol made grandfather so talkative. He emptied his small glass in straight swigs and refilled it, while Ian sipped his slowly and left it only half-drunk. He got up, bid us good evening, and walked over to his van, checking in his pockets as he approached it and invariably finding that he'd forgotten something vital, his silver lighter or his battered tobacco tin or his slim sheaf of cash folded over a rubber band, and swiftly returned inside to fetch it.

I was too young to understand then why girls were drawn to Ian, whereas they never gave Tom a second glance. It was only later I realized he had a lover's smile, which is one of complicity.

Whenever there was one being held, Ian drove back along the Valley to the Christow disco, in the village hall. They were organized by the manager of the football team, Gerry, and his wife Jean, who owned the best grocery store in that village. Gerry stood on the door and took the money, tattooing people's hands with a purple-inked date stamp in case they wanted to go in and out during the evening. Jean kept an eye on the flow of alcohol from the bar extension, and also broke up the fights: devoid of physical fear, she dived between the flailing limbs of drunken greasers, who were so shocked at being manhandled by a woman that they forgot why they'd started fighting in the first place and apologized for their behaviour.

Kids too young to buy alcohol from the bar, where they knew everyone's age, bribed older brothers or sisters to get them a bottle of Clan Dew from the Artichoke. A mixture of rough Scotch whisky and sweet English wine, they drank it in the lanes and threw it up in the hedgerows, before returning to the hall to dance unsteadily to the same records that had been played for years. Despite occasional experiments, Jean and Gerry always came back round to booking a balding DJ from Newton Abbot, who played the latest hit records but had the insight to throw in the odd heavy metal song from the seventies, or better still one by Gary Glitter, and then all the men who'd been leaning against the wall, cupping their beer and gazing vacantly at the girls who were dancing together, would come forward and jerk their bodies in rhythmic, stilted movements.

Ian was one of the few to resist even the beat of nostalgia. He felt uncomfortable dancing, because he was unable to relax his instincts of a predator. In fact he didn't enjoy discos at all: he disliked the music, and the fact that it was broadcast loud enough to bruise your eardrums made it even worse; he disliked the flashing lights and the frenetic atmosphere, as if courtship required suspension of the senses. He preferred to talk his way into a girl's heart, gently, but instead he had to shout at her above the din, and rely on his wicked smile. He also suffered from an inferiority complex about his dancing, and was bemused by how girls seemed to be able to do twice as much with their bodies as he could do with his, with no apparent effort; whereas he was exhausted by his useless attempts.

For Ian, the fast records were simply there to fill the soundtrack of the time before the slow ones, which the DJ had the good sense to start playing in plenty of time before midnight. Ian leaned back against the wall, sipping his beer to make it last, and choosing with his eyes a girl for the evening. He gave her half an hour to acknowledge his gaze in the way he recognized, and if she didn't then he'd choose another without a second thought. Now and then one of the blokes from the football team would join him, to yell in his ear with beery breath, or a past girlfriend would buy him a drink, hoping to persuade him into a resumption of their relationship. He never succumbed. When he did see the same girl for more than a couple of weeks he did his best to keep their affair a casual one, seeing her only on Saturday nights, never in the week, but still mother had got used to tearful phone calls from girls who couldn't understand how someone so sweet, who'd smiled that complicitous smile, with whom they'd danced close together to songs whose every lyric proclaimed eternal, undying love, did not wish to spend every moment ever after with them, as they did with him. She did her best to console them, being careful not to offer a morsel of encouragement. Her son was a heartbreaker. He preferred a different girl every week, and if towards midnight he was without a partner, or if it was clear to his seducer's instinct that the girl he'd been buying drinks for and dancing the slow dances with would not want to share their love later on, then he'd ease away from her, and end the evening with one of the plain and generous farm girls still dancing with each other.

In winter Ian would take his partner by the hand and they'd slip past the side of the stage, vibrating from the decibels of the speakers, and into the committee room at the end of the hall. Or if the DJ was already packing up his equipment they'd clamber into the back of Ian's van, with the engine ticking over to keep the heater going, and make uncomfortable love in amongst empty grain sacks and strands of bailer twine, and the nutty smell of animal feed. That summer he made love where he most enjoyed it, out in the open, with grass underneath and open sky above, because that was where he could most easily lose himself.

It was Pamela who told me that, shaking her head in disapproval.

'How do you know?' I asked her.

'Word gets around,' she said. 'That's the trouble with our brothers, Ali, they're as ignorant as each other in their different ways. Mind you don't take no notice of them. I'll take you to Exeter with me when you're a bit bigger.'

Ian didn't know why he never became attached to his fleeting girlfriends. The only advice Daddy had ever given him in such matters had fallen off his tongue one day some years before, as sometimes happened, the words as if of their own accord appearing for a moment on the tabula rasa of his memory. Ian had taken Daddy to help him patch up some fencing in the copse by the top field, getting him to hold off-cuts while he nailed them against tree stumps. As Ian bent to pick up some nails from the box at his feet, Daddy touched his arm and said: 'When you gives a girl the push, bay, make sure her thinks she's done it to you.' Then he turned and picked up another plank of wood, as if nothing out of the ordinary had happened. When Daddy said such things, in rare and inappropriate moments of lucidity, they had a peculiar force, like the first sentences constructed by infants in their acquisition of language. And, just as they vanished again from his memory as soon as he'd said them, so they imprinted themselves upon ours, and became a part of our family mythology.

That solitary piece of advice from a father to his son was something Ian took to heart and followed so assiduously that none of his girlfriends harboured resentment towards him. Whenever he met one he'd say hello and give some innocuous compliment and smile in his way, and they'd feel only tender pity towards him and wonder what it was that had made them break it off.

Ian had lost count of his girlfriends by the time he was twenty, although he always appeared to recognize them, even those whose faces he'd only seen distorted by the flashing lights of a disco and in the shadows of the Christow Hall committee room. He'd taken his pick from the girls of the Valley, as well as from the clusters from outside who came to the football club discos. If there wasn't one being held, he'd drive right through the Valley and on to Moretonhampstead, a large village on the edge of the moor which had more pubs than houses, or else he'd turn left when he reached the Valley road and go all the way down to Torquay, which was full of northern girls on holiday, with hotel rooms of their own. The only thing he never did was to go east, to Exeter, because that was Pamela's stamping ground, and they had some sort of unspoken agreement to keep out of each other's territories. The exotic nightclubs she described to me on her lazy Sundays at home were like forbidden zones to Ian, but with no attraction, while Pam thought that when Ian went out to his farmers' dances it wasn't so much to go to a party as to take a step back in time.

CHAPTER TWELVE

Superstition

'These yur's the dog days,' said grandfather on Monday. Buildings were swimming in the heat. Ian stopped smoking during the day, his throat raw, and Tom took to using a handkerchief for the first time in his uncivilized life, to wipe away the sweat that streamed into his eyes. On Tuesday at noon Tinker staggered across the yard like she was drunk, while down in the meadow some loose bullocks ate tiny, wrinkled apples, dropped and fermenting in the grass, and they chased each other kicking their heels in the air.

My earliest memory came back, from years before: mother woke me up in the middle of the night. The light was on in the hall. She wrapped me in a blanket and carried me downstairs; Ian and Pamela and Tom were already pulling their coats on and rubbing their eyes. Ian opened the front door. Rain was falling silently in the darkness. I had my arms round mother's neck, my legs wrapped round her body, as she led the way out of the yard. She was different then. I remember my head bobbing on her shoulder, that and the rain awakening me. Ian opened up a great black umbrella for himself and the other two, and they followed behind us, through the first field beside the lane and then away towards the orchard, the shapes of hedges and trees and the uneven ground revealing themselves as our eyes became accustomed to the darkness.

Suddenly mother stopped stock still. The others stumbling sleepily behind us bumped into her, and came around the sides of her to see if we'd reached our destination. We were still in the middle of the field, able to distinguish only the ground, for a few feet around us, in the darkness that had settled over the earth.

The rain was falling so softly each drop was as light as a snowflake and made no sound as it alighted upon the orbiting earth. Then out of the all-encompassing silence came the sound of breathing. We all held our breaths, instinctively. Footsteps became audible, coming closer towards us, walking at a heavy and ponderous pace. Breathing, deep and impatient, was almost upon us as a form began to materialize, dark as the night itself, as if the night itself were creating life from out of its formless immensity. But that was no human being appearing before us: instead, grandfather's big black bull, that I would come to know and fear as long as he was alive, passed in front of us, so close I could have reached out and touched his huge flanks.

We waited till he'd been swallowed up by the night that bore him, and then we waited some more, before we dared to breathe again. Then without a word mother set off again, and we crossed the ditch by the orchard over a bridge of mossy wooden planks, the rain audible for the first time pattering as it joined the water in the stream.

It was at that moment that the smell entered my nostrils. But mother didn't stop there. She carried right on into the middle of the orchard, through the ghostly trees, and there she made us stand and told us to close our eyes, the better to savour the painfully sweet scent of apple blossom that the softly falling rain had teased into the night air.

I found it difficult waking up in the mornings: I rolled out of bed but sleep still clung to me like a spider's web, so that I performed my chores before school like a sleepwalker. But I was shaken awake that unfortunate Wednesday when I stumbled over to the chicken coop with a bucket of water and a pan of corn and found them all dead, every last one, the laying hens, the pullets, the bantams and the cockerel too. Only when I looked closer did I see that there were two chickens left alive on their roosts, catatonic from terror, beady eyes staring straight ahead. Mother wrung their necks and ordered me to stay in my room for the rest of the day for leaving the door of the coop open the night before, her hands shaking with anger as she restrained herself from lifting the wooden spoon she was holding.

It was a sure sign that this was a summer unlike any other when birds' carcasses became a frequent sight, since birds go off to die in secret. Now, though, they appeared on the lawn, in the yard and on the Brown. Even Douglas Westcott, who knew all about animals, had never come across this peculiar catastrophe. He'd hand-reared wild mink by virtue of acquainting them with his voice before their eyes opened; when he went fishing he put maggots in his mouth to warm them and make them wriggle; and when the last Viscount had died it was Douglas who was hired to catch the pigeons who lived on the roof and dye them purple for the period of mourning. But he couldn't work out what was happening now; he wasn't even convinced it was a fox had destroyed our chicken brood: he'd noticed how scarce foxes had become, and those that were around were friendly, 'like they used to be, when there was rabies', he claimed.

People were beginning to agree that the things going wrong were the fault of the flea-ridden children and the lawless dogs of the hippies who'd arrived back in June, having been forcefully diverted from their original destination, Stonehenge. They arrived in time for the summer solstice, aware of the pagan fire festival we carried out despite the derision of a succession of Rectors, not because anyone actually believed in it but simply because it was exciting. That year, though, no one wanted to have anything to do with a pact with the sun of any sort, so the disappointed hippies had to enact the ritual on their own, drawing a flaming tar-barrel in an old wagon by long ropes. We watched from the Brown and applauded the display for its authenticity, especially the extent to which it imperilled the thatch on the Old Rectory.

The trouble was that the hippies didn't know the lanes in the village: they nearly ran themselves over going down Broad Lane, and their fun ended when they tried to pull the flaming wagon up Rattle Street. They got it a quarter of the way up and called for all the women to join in, half-way up they yelled for their children, they were heaving and grunting and ascending inch by inch, they got three-quarters of the way up and called with panic in their voices for more help, so we kids on the Brown ran over and put our hands on the ropes and we dragged that wagon which was getting heavier as it burned, not lighter, we dragged it inch by inch until we were within a hair's breadth of the top of the lane, when all of a sudden everyone knew simultaneously that they had no strength left. We all let go of the ropes at the same instant, they slithered through and burned our fingers, and we could only collapse on the steep tarmac as the wagon rolled away from us, gathering speed down Rattle Street, hurtling downhill to explode in a chaos of splintering wood and hissing steam in the shallow brook.

The hippies decided to stay, parking their small convoy of miraculous wrecks in the lane behind the rectory, and fetching water from the tap in the churchyard that never dried up, even though it wasn't on the mains and all the streams were disappearing into thin air.

Ian joined a small group of men with mattocks, their blades filed sharp as scythes, to look for brooks whose courses they could divert. Their heavy boots rang on the earth like it was hollow.

''Tis so 'ard the moles 'as all suffocated,' old Martin the hedge-layer told me.

'P'raps they've just gone down deeper,' I suggested.

'Well, let's 'ope the buggers get lost and don't find their way back,' he spat. A compulsive spitter, his palate dried out by that desiccated summer, old Martin hawked deeper and deeper, until he was finally cured of the habit when he began spitting globules of blood.

When drops of blood were found on bread taken from the oven grandmother said it was a sure sign the plague, after a three-hundred-year respite, was going to return before rain ever would, but when a spot appeared on the harvest loaf in the church Granny Sims confused it with the stigmata of the saints and revived her mother's biannual petition for the incense and holy water of High Church ritual. Her claim that this was God's reminder that He was omnipotent and could make it rain for believers whenever he wanted to inspired a revival of piety, and that Sunday the church was unusually crowded for early morning communion even though it was a service with no hymns. But the Rector belonged to the coincidental tradition of nonconformist priests stretching back beyond the limits of memory, and that week he made a visit to every house in the village and exhausted himself denouncing superstition, which he would have liked to rid the world of.

'Do you want the church to be empty, then?' one of the newcomers asked him, smiling.

'Yes,' he solemnly replied.

The Rector's arguments were successful, not through their logic, which was all the more convincing because his days as a theological student were coming back to him, with their evenings of intense, chimerical debate which intoxicated in the small hours over black coffee and cigarettes but had vanished in the morning, leaving behind only throbbing temples; he succeeded not through arguments that only one or two of the newcomers and perhaps Ian could follow, but because of his persistence, refusing to leave the easy chairs by the stoves and drinking tea and smoking until they agreed with him that God's omnipotence was not incompatible with free will, that whereas predestination was an archaic concept which meant you might as well lie in bed all day because you were guided inexorably by the ultimate destiny of your soul, predetermination allowed you to choose whether to get out of bed on the left or the right side, according to the dictates of your conscience, and continue through the day in similar free fashion, suitable for the freeborn farmers of Devon, and the way God meant it to be.

'Pelagius told us so, after all,' he argued, 'and it's been confirmed by the quantum physicists, as you've doubtless heard,' and people furrowed their brows and nodded agreement.

So that by the time of the harvest dance a week later, even though the blood on the loaf had sprouted a bright, flowery fungus, only one or two of Granny Sims' most loyal cronies still joined with her in agitating among the women for the institution of daily Mass and the recruitment of choirboys from among the idle schoolchildren.

Tom had watched Susanna for years, for as long as he could remember. Her family had moved into the very first of the newcomers' houses built on the slope down from the church, across from us. I was only a toddler then: huge yellow bulldozers, driven by dwarves, transformed the earth from one day to the next, gouging out lunar craters and creating whole new platforms of soil. Mother had to go round our house every evening before tea, cursing the bulldozers and pickup-trucks as she righted lopsided pictures that had trembled askew.

Susanna must have been hardly school age, and Tom still at Primary. Some time between then and when she left Primary herself to go to Newton Abbot, Tom first noticed her, and he began without realizing it to watch out for her. He watched her every morning, surreptitiously through the crowd as they gathered around the telephone box by the Brown, until Fred drove him and the older kids off to meet the school bus. It never occurred to him even then to talk to her. Tom didn't speak to people.

Later, after Tom had been released from school to spend his life in the fields and Susanna had been given her pony, she appeared to him less often but more distinctly. He would hear the horse's hooves first, and his body flexed.

His older brother Ian handled animals like the vet did, no more than was necessary, calmly assessing them as he did so. Tom, though, manhandled them. Whether he was setting a fleece-sodden ewe back on her feet or backing a bullock through pens with his shoulder, he did so with all his might, grunting, pitting his own weight against theirs. And he loved the feel of them: the thick matted wool of the sheep, which he grasped in handfuls in order to lift them, and the chunky flanks of the cows, their thick breath smelling of new-mown hay.

Tom would be alerted from his labours by the sound of horses' hooves, and he'd look up, eyes darting like an owl:

he'd watched her cantering through driving rain, he'd watched her flying across snow, he'd watched her splashing through spongy meadows after a storm, her jodhpurs flecked with mud. She was only fifteen but she was mistress of her mount; her authority was absolute, the pony's obedience unquestioning. Tom had seen her one winter morning leading him back to the stable after a hard ride: he was glistening with sweat that evaporated in the cold air all around him and Susanna was enveloped in the steam that poured, intermittently, from his nostrils.

She was able to ride her pony almost anywhere with impunity. I don't suppose she was ever aware of how strange that was. The farmers who would normally have bellowed without a second thought at anyone else were curiously spellbound by the sight of this carefree maiden, her long blonde hair billowing behind her as she cantered across their land, and they would watch her scattering sheep or making holes in hedges that she'd unsuccessfully tried to clear, and let her go by with no more than a friendly wave.

Ever since May, though, Tom had seen her differently from before, her form now indistinct through heat haze, an incomplete mirage. His imagination had to define her, to fill in what he could no longer see, and he found her more mesmerizing, and more distant from him, than ever.

Although nobody could really believe it was possible, the air was getting drier. The old bell in the church made its strange boom when no one had touched it, and Daddy said he was being bitten by the door handles. It must have been around then that grandmother told me her electric theory of memory. She said it was just one of the mysteries of life that electricity had clarified for her, when she realized that memory wasn't stored in some hidden corner of the skull; grandmother saw in all its simplicity the truth that events don't evaporate as soon as they're over but simply change form, existing in magnetic fields in the air. The brain acts as a receiver, tuning in to memories.

'That's what dreams are,' she told me, 'when we're asleep

we mixes up our own and other people's experiences by mistake.'

'What about Daddy?' I asked.

'The cider rusted up 'is receiver, poor love. His memories is scattered on the wind.'

CHAPTER THIRTEEN

Barn-Dancing

That summer Geraldine Honeywill was pregnant and she ate so many carrots she turned orange. Mother eventually let Daddy go out without his heavy jacket, and he was soon as brown as the rest of us, and almost as dark as the first black people ever to stay in the village, a Barbadian family who rented the diplomat's house next door, in order to enjoy an English autumn. Their son showed the village boys how to play cricket properly, and so for the first time the football was put away at the height of summer. But although he taught them the techniques of spin and off-cut, and how to appeal with conviction, what couldn't be taught was how to be slow and quick at the same time, with the languid bones of a cat.

The older women in the village, when they passed the Brown, were reminded of the dusky babies born in neighbouring villages during the Second World War, when American troops were temporarily stationed in Exeter, who were taken round and shown off by proud grandparents. Only the father of this Barbadian family was unhappy. A judge in Barbados, he never forgot the face of someone he'd sentenced, and on only his second day in the village he recognized Douglas Westcott, whom he'd once confined to a night in the cells in Bridgetown for drunk and disorderly conduct and threatening behaviour with intent to commit violence to a person's person in a public place. He spent the remainder of their stay inside, sheltering from the English climate that he'd dreamed of for forty-eight years but which now turned out to be so disappointingly like his own, and from the imagined revenge of Douglas Westcott. He didn't even come out later on during the virus of indifference when Douglas smiled, and he certainly wasn't going to risk a possible scene at the barn dance. He let his magnificent wife and young son and daughter go but he stayed at home, the only other person in the village apart from grandmother, who refused Ian's offer to drive her the short distance.

'I've seen enough dancing for one life,' she decided. 'Midsummer madness 'tis. Makes me dizzy at my age.'

At the harvest festival dance that forlorn summer men forgot their predicament for the evening, and like every other year people's mothers danced with other people's fathers in Joseph Howard's barn, though there was no hay to play in, and they had to make do with holding each other's hands as they staggered home. It was to be the evening that Tom plucked up the courage to approach Susanna Simmons. He watched all evening, as he'd watched for years, with a lump in his throat that felt like a mixture of sadness and danger.

Grandmother stated categorically that the dances were no good no more, not since the last of the church musicians, with their scraping fiddles and their wheezy harmonium, but no one really believed her. The band, which included the Chagford piano tuner on accordion, still attended by one or two persistent mosquitoes, was led by a short, toothless man who called out the same steps that had been entirely forgotten from the year before and the year before that. Daddy found himself on an equal footing with everyone else, though he took it for granted and so did they. The only people who knew the steps were Miss Branham and Miss Tuck, who took the men's parts with us girls for the first few dances, while the men stood sullenly around the walls of the barn and the band gradually whipped up a whirlpool of fiddles and skirts and sweat and cider.

We took our plastic cups of lemonade and coke up to the hay loft and looked down upon our parents and uncles and aunts and neighbours, amazed at their laughter, sullen faces cracking open when they got the steps right, and even wider when they got them wrong.

One by one the men were persuaded by other men's wives

to join in, and they fell off the sides of the barn like currants into mother's cake mix. Mike Hutchings danced with Yvonne Ashplant and Jim Ashplant danced with Sylvia Hutchings. Old Martin, who wanted to partner everyone, was frustrated that there wasn't time for that many dances even if they kept going all night, until he recalled that you couldn't stay with one partner for the duration of a dance even if you wanted to but got passed on from one to another, and then he enjoyed himself more than anyone, grinning through a glaze of sweat. Stuart and Elsie hobbled around energetically, in decrepit imitation of an ancient ardour whose promise they'd never ful-filled.

Douglas Westcott, meanwhile, was so astounded by the Barbadian judge's magnificent wife that she awoke in him for the duration of a square dance the excitement of his one and only, impetuous entanglement many years before, when he'd gone to the estate to slaughter the peacocks, and been brought a tray of tea by the Portuguese maid. Maria, who'd come to live in the old poet's shack when the estate was sold, had become a grey-haired and distinguished matron who still refused to learn a word of English. She and Douglas barely recognized each other at the dance, and felt no emotion. Instead, people manoeuvred her and the Rector together, because their innocent love affair was an open secret obvious to everyone but they themselves.

Pamela had brought along two or three young men from her rehearsals, and they patiently took turns partnering her. And even mother, only half-ignored by the other women on this evening of a half-truce, danced not just with Daddy but with his brothers-in-law too.

Tom, though, hung around the bar run by Corporal Alcock, because the proximity of so many people gave him goose-pimples, along with other men unable even on this once-a-year occasion to shake off their discomfort in the company of others: Douglas, whose family had been so upset by the deterioration in his manners since his return that one by one they'd left Shilhay Farm; and grandfather, who leaned against the bar downing glasses of cider not a single one of which he paid for. They were bought by other men old enough to remember him as a sinewy youth stepping forward and knocking out the Cornish bully of a foreman at the quarry, before the Christmas Eve when it filled up with water.

With the beginning of each new dance Tom postponed his approach until the next one, and observed a succession of partners hold Susanna tightly and join in the swirling mayhem. Tom watched morosely as the hours spun by, drinking steadily, leaving his place against one of the pillars only to step outside and pee against the wall of the barn. After a while he wasn't sure whether the chaos of dancers were spinning round or whether they were mannequins striking poses around which he and the other spectators hugging the walls of the barn were spinning. Only his stomach was still, but he could feel rising from its depths an inexplicable bubble of anger: he found himself scrutinizing the faces of the other men and he could perceive there, in the leering faces of his friends, in the dogs' eyes of lonely farmers, in the lecherous lips of the old men and even in the mournful gaze of the piano tuner on the accordion a lascivious desire for the prettiest girl in the village. He managed to get outside just before the bubble burst and emptied his stomach in a corner of the Howards' yard. He floated back into the barn as the caller announced the last waltz. Pausing only to cadge a polo mint off Corporal Alcock, Tom asked Susanna Simmons if he could have this dance. The piano tuner was already unstrapping his accordion.

'I'm afraid it's taken,' she replied, nodding towards him.

Without a second's hesitation Tom strode over: 'Put that thing back on or I'll break yer neck,' he told him. 'And play it well,' he added, 'or I'll break yer fingers.'

He returned to Susanna's side. ''E forgot. 'E's gotta play 'is concertina on this one too. 'E apologizes, like, and asks you to let me take 'is place.'

My practical brother had never danced a step in his life, uninterested in something that didn't have a function, but he melted without fear into the precisely flowing movements of

125

her body, and by a miracle of intuition concealed his clumsiness.

Mother took me and Daddy home while the rest of the world stayed awake. I didn't want to go to sleep. I was spongy with fruit punch, but the music was still giddy in my head. I sat on the window-sill. There was only a sliver of moon, but by then the sky was so clear and the air so thin that night became like another day, in the lucid light of a lunar morning. It was so hot people found it impossible to sleep with anything touching their skin: they discarded pyjamas and nighties, then blankets, until by June we all slept covered with a single cotton sheet. Mother flung hers off in the stew of 2 a.m., and was shocked when she awoke to discover herself naked to the world.

Some people caught Ian's disease, insomnia, as if reverting to the rhythms of poachers. They'd thresh around in bed, having thrown off sheets and clothes but still trapped in the discomfort of their own sweaty skins, changing position constantly, resentful of their partner's peaceful breathing and infuriated to find they'd forgotten the simplest of childish skills, that of falling asleep.

Now, though, the village was alive with people making their way home from the dance, figures stumbling along the lane and disembodied voices shrieking and cursing.

One person going in the other direction, trudging home out of the village, was the solid silhouette of Douglas Westcott, who that summer resumed his youthful habit of scrutinizing the night sky for falling stars. Grandmother told me that his leaving home in a huff many years before, after being chided by his father for his bestial table manners, was only a pretext to go in search of a fallen angel he'd seen plummet through the sky. He was convinced she was the woman he'd loved in his previous life, who'd thrown herself into the quarry pool because they weren't allowed to love each other. He scanned the faces of those in the vicinity in which he thought she'd landed, and gradually widened his search in ever expanding circles, figuring that traces of her landing would be evident in ripples. He'd reach a new port on some godforsaken continent and become excited by an aching familiarity in the sailors' bars and the bakeries and the oddly surfaced streets, and he'd begin looking for her in the market place and in the temples and by the stream where they did their washing, until it slowly dawned on him that he'd been here before, and the only spoor he was following was his own; Douglas returned home with no hope, only to have it resuscitated that inscrutable summer when the sky was so clear that stars flickered like candles.

The last distant shouts of drunken revellers died down. A brief deceptive breeze fluttered up from the Valley and over in the copse between the old and new rectories the pine trees swooned.

The very last people walking out were Tom and Susanna Simmons, round and round the village, looking into each other's eyes, gleaming with wine, their footsteps a dry whisper in the lunar silence, until they were finally swallowed up by moonshadow at the Simmons' front door. After a long time the door opened and blew the shadow away. Susanna stepped inside, and the shadow returned, then Tom emerged into the moonlight and made his way home, but I'd fallen asleep before he reached the house.

CHAPTER FOURTEEN

Geographies of the Unconscious

Mother told me that when she was heavily pregnant with me she was walking back one day along the lane from the shop, when Douglas Westcott stepped out of nowhere. They both slowed down, like you do, and mother said hello; but Douglas didn't say anything, he only fixed his grim gaze at her enormous stomach she had to hold in front of her as she walked. She wasn't sure whether to feel flattered or uneasy, and she didn't move. He stared at her stomach, then he looked up at her face. He seemed to be asking for something with his eyes, for permission; mother smiled, she didn't know why. Douglas stepped forward, blushing but unflustered, and without a word put his hand on mother's belly. She let it rest there a while, then she put her palm over the back of his hand and guided it over her stretched skin to where he could feel me kicking.

He closed his eyes and felt the faint, irregular heartbeat of a baby treading water in the womb, pushing through into his hard palm. Then he withdrew his hand, opened his eyes, looked at mother again, to say thank you perhaps, she wasn't sure; and he stepped past her and walked away.

Who knows why he'd once left home the way he did? Grandmother knew his mother, but even she wasn't certain. No one knew for sure.

They said he was heartbroken by the Portuguese maid at the big house; they said he'd gone and fallen in love with the crazy woman who'd killed herself the year before he was born: it didn't matter to him she was long gone down to her watery grave, he thought he'd seen her in the sky, on a night of falling stars. Others, more matter of fact, said it was an old story, between him and his father: they feared and hated each other, the way sons and fathers sometimes do on the remote farms, where such emotions fester. His father was well known for his pride, which, added to the whole family's reclusiveness, meant he never asked anyone for anything: in the winter of '53, rather than ask for help, he bled his cattle, as he'd heard the Highlanders of Scotland did, and his wife made them strange blood cakes, which it was said gave Douglas the taste for it.

The pylons carrying electricity to the village marched across Douglas's fields. Jane and I stood underneath them to remind ourselves of what rain sounded like, but we kept a wary eye out for Douglas, in his dirty blue overalls, with his black curly hair. We were scared of his dogs, too: they snapped for no reason, because unless dogs grow up with children they think that they're adversaries.

They said that after his return Douglas kept a bag always packed, ready for immediate departure, even after the rest of his family had left him alone on the farm, and he must have known he'd never leave.

When he left his mother was devastated, and refused to talk to her husband, whom she blamed; but when she went into her departed son's room she realized that whether he'd known it or not, his whole life he'd been preparing for this moment.

He'd never made friends, not as a child nor as a youth nor yet as a man, because he didn't like talking to other people. His mother had seen how even in his third year he showed no excitement at the discovery of language, as her other infants had, rambling on interminably to their parents, their siblings, animals, dolls, fantasy companions, or just to themselves, delighting in the torrent of words that grew larger every day. Douglas never went through that stage. From his first utterances, which were 'mum', 'moo' and 'cut', he continued to speak only in terse, monosyllabic sentences, his speech in actual fact not so much the limited expression of an idiot, as people assumed, as a miracle of brevity and concision possible only for someone of rare intelligence, but hemmed in on all sides by the curse of shyness.

His mother patiently watched him grow up, hoping against hope that, unable or unwilling to express himself in words, the most common language and the most versatile, the one in which people threatened and bullied one another as well as being the one of the spirit, he'd come to adopt as his own one of the other languages that man had invented: music, the language of the soul; or mathematics, the language of the mind.

Instead he chose another. She remembered the very day he discovered it: he came home at the age of eight with a neatly folded piece of paper. 'Look what us done in school today, mother,' he said in a rare burst of loquaciousness that alerted her immediately, and on the kitchen table he unfolded a map of Great Britain on which his teacher had made them trace the major rivers, from their sources to the sea. She saw the gleam in his eye, the rigidity of his muscles in the first instance of a child's obsessive interest that he'd yet displayed. He didn't say anything, he just laid out the map for her, assuming she'd find it as fascinating as he plainly did, staring at it intently. Then he pointed at the south-west peninsula and told her: 'That's where us is, mother. 'Tis Devon there. And the stupid-shaped bit on the end, 'tis Cornwall.'

That was the beginning of Douglas's interest in maps, the very day he was smitten with the shape of the world. From then on he saved up the coppers his father gave him for the jobs he did on the farm, a farthing for every ten lambs' tails he docked, a halfpenny a week for helping to milk the cows, a penny for looking after all the chickens, and a bonus of sixpence at harvest, and he spent them on only one thing: while other children bought sweets, dolls and footballs, Douglas purchased nothing but maps, and not just modern atlases but historical ones too, without discrimination.

His father went to market in Newton Abbot every Wednesday, and Douglas made himself indispensable by doing more than a child should, even in those days: he took such an interest in their herd of cows and flock of sheep that his father came to rely on his small son's second opinion in the business of buying and selling, to the point where Douglas no longer had to argue the case for having the day off school, where you learned so much information that was no use to country people, and they drove together to market. In fact it was there, even more than at home, that the boy became what he had hitherto only pretended to be, a farmer, as he slipped through the cattle pens, assessing the meat on the flanks of bullocks, measuring himself against the animal arrogance of the bulls, eavesdropping on the whispered conversations of Dartmoor sheep-farmers striking clandestine deals, and learning to decipher the abnormal utterances of the auctioneer. He felt at home with the various animals, and also understood the curious comradeship of men whose common bonds were their profession and the discomfort they felt in each other's company.

Even so, while his father drank beer in the Anchor at lunchtime, Douglas made his way to browse in an antiquarian bookseller's on East Street, who soon discerned the unusual passion of the intense, taciturn farmer's boy who could barely read but who appeared in his bookshop every Wednesday without fail. Douglas was by far the youngest of his customers, and for that reason, if no other, the old bookseller looked out something he might be interested in and offered it to him at a fair price, rather than his customary starting price of a few shillings on top, because the boy clearly had no talent for bartering. And it was in that shop that Douglas bought the maps that would fill his room and fill his mind in parallel, in equal measure: a road map of the British Isles; an outline of the countries of Europe, with their shifting frontiers, the previous ones marked with a dashed line and the ones before that with dots, like the trails of glow-worms, growing fainter on the page; a survey map of the Russian wastes, drawn to estimate the mineral resources of Siberia; charts of the Chinese deserts; a relief map of the Himalayas;

Italian woodcuts of the *Geographica* of the Egyptian Claudius Ptolemy; reproduction clay tablets of field plans from the late Babylonian period.

As time went by Douglas learned to fly across the world and land wherever he wished. He studied ichnographies of the Pyramids; old Admiralty charts of the Cape of Good Hope; ancient Roman maps of the south coast of Britain, which they imagined to be the tip of a vast new continent with a fabulous wealth of gold and tin. On the happiest day of his young life Douglas was given, gratis, a facsimile of the first edition of a book of maps using Mercator's projection, published in 1568. He hung globes of various sizes from the ceiling, on which he also glued planispheres of the heavens. He would lie on his bed, charting his way across medieval oceans with his Venetian portolan atlas, or staring at the stars on his ceiling, lost in a distant corner of the world, awoken from his reveries only by his father hammering on the door and telling him to 'get on and muck out the pigs, you can't lie around all day, this is a farm not a hospital, it's time to milk the cows or the milk'll go sour in their udders, you lazy little sod, you.'

For his fourteenth birthday his mother gave him a plaster of Paris model of Atlas kneeling with the world on his shoulders. She'd come across it in Woolworths, which in those days sold everything, as they claimed it did, on one of the rare occasions she accompanied her husband and their middle son to Newton Abbot. It was no bigger than the heart of a cauliflower, Douglas would already be able to engulf it in the palm of his hand, but his mother was overjoyed when she saw it: his passion had long proved itself to be of more substance than simply one of the capricious obsessions that marked other childhoods, and she'd been looking out for a gift that would acknowledge the seriousness of his hobby and, in the giving, accord him an adult's respect. Sure enough, when Douglas untied the string and unwrapped the brown paper, he stood entranced before that cheap plaster reproduction of a second-rate sculpture of the Titan whose strength kept the world in its place. It became his most treasured possession, and would be the first thing he put into his tiny suitcase on the day he packed to leave.

All through his youth Douglas continued to purchase maps, bring them home and study them in his room. He had it all to himself, which was surprising since his older brother, George, had to share with the youngest, while their three sisters all huddled together in one big bed. But Douglas's solitary nature had declared itself as soon as he was born: he'd never cried for milk, he never smiled back at his mother when she played baby games with him, making faces or blowing raspberries into the soft flesh of his tummy: she felt foolish, and left him alone, which was what he seemed to prefer. What he was given he took without a word, but he never asked for anything. When he scraped his knees in the farmyard he didn't run into the house, looking for her instinctively to swallow up the pain and trauma in her open arms, but would turn and run in the opposite direction, away from people, like a cat, to lick his wounds alone.

When his next-born sister arrived Douglas was moved on from the cot at the end of his parents' bed and into his older brother's room. But as soon as he could walk he'd leave that space he found stifling, where he couldn't breathe properly the air that was dense with the thick night breath of another human being and with the confusion of their dreams. His mother would find him in the morning sleeping in front of the fire, or laid out under the kitchen table, or curled up in his father's tattered armchair, but when she asked him how he got there and what did he think he was playing at, he didn't know what she was talking about, he looked at her like she was mad but he looked a little frightened and confused too, and she realized that her second son was a sleepwalker. At first she put up with it, because she was gratified by the belief then prevalent that somnambulism was a sign of sensitivity, and like all farmers' wives she wanted at least one of her sons to find a station in life above the husbandry of animals. But when his nocturnal wanderings took him out of the house, and she had to enlist the other children's help before breakfast in looking for him, at first in the hay loft, then sleeping with a smile on his infantile face in the clean straw of the pigsty, and finally perched precariously and snoring on the roost in the chicken coop, she realized it was getting out of hand, and gave him his own room.

And that was where Douglas retreated every evening as a child and as a youth, slipping away unnoticed from the tea-table in the furtive manner of the solitary, with a glass of milk, to pore over the maps that he acquired so indiscriminately, they all fascinated him, because he understood intuitively what only the most perceptive cartographers in history had understood, that maps delineate not only the layout of the physical world but also the geography of the unconscious, that in their attempts at an ever more accurate portrayal of what exists in material reality the map-makers were also charting the evolution of the imagination, the pursuit of truth.

It was not in itself so strange for a Devon boy to be fascinated by the boundaries of the known world, and what lay beyond, for most of the finest sailors in the ships that had made England the greatest power in the world, from anonymous cabin boys and midshipmen to Sir Francis Drake, the finest of them all, had been Devonians. But none, so far as anyone knew, had ever come from our village. Indeed when the Rector once showed me the first entry in the Baptism Registry it was that of George Westcott, of Shilhay Farm, in 1552, even the same Christian name as Douglas's father and his elder brother. Their inheritance was a vision limited to the walls of the Valley, and if what propelled Douglas's passion was an atavistic impulse then it came from way back, from the migrating nomads of pre-history, and had survived, intact and untouched, like a pebble through the digestive tract of countless generations of peasants.

So that when Douglas decided to leave home, apparently because of his father's insulting remark, a pretext he would never admit to his family was not the real reason, he realized that he'd find her without any problem, because although he didn't know the rest of the Valley very well the world was his oyster, he knew it back to front and upside down, he knew it from an orthographic as well as a conic projection, he'd studied charts of the shifting sands of the desert commissioned by Lawrence of Arabia, he knew all twenty-three authenticated sources of the Nile, he knew by heart the contours of the Antarctic memorized before him by Scott, and he'd inscribed upon a set of plates filed to one side of his brain, indelibly, the routes of the sleepwalking tributaries of the numberless rivers of the Russian Taiga, mapped out by a team of military cartographers who were aided in their endeavours by the legendary trapper Dersu Uzala.

In actual fact his knowledge, which he imagined to be virtually complete and a guarantee of trouble-free travels, was a hopelessly confused and tattered mess, riddled with the errors of history and superseded by time. In his travels he would lose his way more often than Marco Polo. And his only successful journey would be the one back home.

CHAPTER FIFTEEN

Someone to Watch Over Me

Ploughshares dispersed the top layer of dusty soil then snapped like ice on the rock-hard earth beneath. The corn had risen thinner than in the days when its seeds were scattered by hand. The meagre crop of hay came ready-dried for the winter. But it made no difference to the festival. All the grown-ups celebrated harvest that withered summer with more indulgence than ever, even though there wasn't any, and the morning following the barn dance they all awoke gasping, their throats as dry as the fields, their bodies dehydrated. Even the old people who still went to early communion on the three Sundays in the month when there was no family service stayed at home that morning, unable to face the sun that hung like a gauntlet between them and the church, bringing great relief to the Rector, who could hear bells pealing in his head. Corporal Alcock readily agreed with his suggestion that with just the three of us we might as well go home, and he came up with an even better one of his own, that we dispense with the rest of the service all right, but at least they should celebrate communion itself, because there was enough wine in the chalice divided by two for a hair of the dog.

People's parents, if they got up at all, wandered from room to room holding their heads and moaning: 'Don't touch me.' In our house Ian lay on his bed trying to keep as still as possible, after the one Saturday night of the year he relaxed his hunter's instincts and allowed them to be flooded with alcohol, because it was spent in his own village. I pressed the mattress and he whimpered like a wounded dog. 'Scat, you little cow,' he murmured, eyes closed, unable to move. He was filled to the very brim with a volatile liquid that would spill over unless he retained perfect balance. If he shifted position a fraction the giddying whirlpool in his stomach began to turn again and his brain started thumping against his skull.

I escaped to go swim in the quarry pool. I stopped on the way for sherbet fizzes at the village shop, where old Elsie Sims too was nursing the worst hangover of her long life. She let out a groan as I entered, and refused to open her eyes behind her pebble specs, instead groping blindly amongst the boxes on a shelf behind her and trying to give me melting chocolate bars and the ancient cigars that only grandfather ever bought, two at a time every Christmas, all of which I refused until she eventually unearthed three packets of incorruptible sherbet fizzes, with their stalks of brittle liquorice.

I swam around for a while and then sat by the edge of the pool with my feet in the water, sucking liquorice dipped in sherbet, waiting. The sun was making its slow climb through the sky, barely perceptible but still the only sign of life. I didn't even know what I was waiting for. I hoped Johnathan would show up – of course he hadn't come to the barn dance – but there was no sign of him.

Life had come to a standstill and everyone else seemed happy to let it. Maybe I was just different but I couldn't stand it, this feeling of being in limbo, waiting for time to get going again, waiting for my life to start.

Then everything went dark and a voice said: 'Guess who.'

I grabbed his hands from my eyes and bent his little fingers back.

'Ow!' he yelled. 'Really, Alison, there's no need to hurt. I was only playing.'

We swam for a while and then lay on the rock and shared the rest of my sherbet. Drops of water made it sizzle on our palms.

'You're right, you know,' Johnathan agreed with me. 'Life has stopped and no one's noticed. They're all turning into Oblomovs. But we shouldn't really complain, actually.'

'Why the hell not?' I asked.

'Well, my mother says that Ethiopia's a *real* drought, and we should count our blessings.'

I was going to argue but he suddenly jumped up and said: 'Gosh, it's late, I've got to get back for, um, elevenses.' He grabbed his towel and said: 'What are you doing later?' But before I could answer he was scurrying away.

I couldn't hear a thing, but sure enough a minute later figures appeared by the beech tree, their voices bounced around the rocks, and they came scrambling down to the pool. I wished I'd brought a book with me so I could ignore them and read it. Chris Howard challenged me to a race across the pool: he wouldn't accept I was a faster swimmer, he pestered me for a rematch every chance he got. This time I slowed up at the end just enough to ensure a dead heat, 'cos I couldn't be bothered with him going on at me afterwards; but the little squirt, coughing water and spluttering for breath, claimed he'd touched the rock a fraction before me and he was waving his arms in victory like he'd just scored a goal. Luckily just then Jane, who'd been sunbathing with Susan aloof from the water, spotted some men clambering down the dry bed of the village stream, and yelled: 'Look! Who's that?'

As they got closer their bodies stopped shimmering and became recognizable: it was Corporal Alcock and Mike Howard, Chris's older brother. They ignored us: they opened the boxes they were carrying and set up a tripod by the pool like the school photographer's. The boys started showing off their backward somersault dives and Jane's fat little brother did his bomb jumps, but although Corporal Alcock looked through the sights it didn't have a camera, only a yo-yo underneath which he didn't bother with. He looked through the sights and scribbled in a tiny black notebook while Mike Howard walked around the pool with a striped pole. Then they went back up the slope, constantly stopping and marking new patterns together, as if they were calculating the choreography of some new strip-the-willow dance.

I went over to Jane and Susan, who were lying in their bikinis on stripy towels. 'Do you want to do something?' I asked.

Jane squinted at me and closed her eyes again. 'What?' she enquired flatly.

'I don't know,' I replied, 'anything.'

'Steve and Rod are comin' down soon, we're waiting for them.' She sat up. 'God, is it hot? Look at that,' she said, peeling her bikini pants away an inch or two and revealing the dazzling contrast between white skin and the deep chocolate brown of her suntan. 'Not bad, eh?'

She poured coconut oil into her palm and spread it over her legs. 'Do my shoulders, Ali,' she asked, 'and you takes some if you want. God, when's you going to get rid of that one-piece?'

I rubbed the oil into Jane's back and shoulders, while she and Susan made some joke about Gordon Honeywill, who was ostentatiously diving backwards off the heron's rock.

'I'm so bored,' I said. 'Don't you two want to do nothing?'

'Why don't you go practise holding your breath underwater with they mature young men over there?' said Susan, and Jane giggled along with her. I ignored them and walked away and picked up my stuff.

It would have been all right but Jane had to go one better. 'Or you could take your Dad to the swings,' she called after me, and the two of them collapsed into giggles again.

I snatched up a tiny pebble, turned and threw it at Jane, just to make her shut up. Even as it left my hand I realized the pebble was much bigger than I'd thought. It didn't go anywhere near Jane but flew away from me almost at right angles and struck Gordon's brother Robert smack on the forehead. The world stopped. People became silent, astonished statues. Then bright red blood came oozing out of Robert's head and he started screaming. Gordon looked at me and then his brother and then at me again, not knowing whether he should look after Robert or beat me up. While everyone else stood still Robert had already turned round and, a bloody hand clutching his forehead, was running back to the path home. I turned and ran in the opposite direction.

I reached the Lodge without realizing I was going there. I sat leaning against the front door, sweating, getting my breath back. I could hear voices inside; well, not voices exactly but dim, disconnected drones of people talking. My breathing returned to normal and I stood up. I raised my hand to knock on the door when suddenly my heart thumped and my brain blew a fuse: I recognized one of the voices inside: it was mother.

It was crazy, all upside down. What on earth was mother doing at my secret friend's house, the Viscount Teignmouth's house? None of our family had anything to do with them. My brain was scrambled but it was fizzing with streaks of energy, trying to make sense of things.

And in the midst of weird ideas and strange, dark images skating across my mind I forced some kind of sense. The truth was I knew mother was as unhappy as me in her own, quite different way. I knew that she needed someone to talk to, and there wasn't anyone in the village. And Johnathan's mother helped people with their problems. I wasn't stupid. I could see what was going through her mind.

We all need someone to talk to, and now I was eager with curiosity to hear what I knew I should hear, that 'he's my strength, that boy, I tried to get him to go away to college, to escape, but if he had I'd have died, he holds it all together and yet he worries me, I never know what he's thinking. What help does he get from grandfather, who goes around muttering to himself because he gave Ian control of the farm and Ian took it? Or Tom, for that matter? He's a bit soft but he's a good boy but what's he gone and done but fallen for one of the newcomer girls hardly older than his own little sister? Pamela I never know where she is, she goes her own way, no help to me nor no one else, like grandmother, who's getting to be a hindrance now, I can't trust her to cook a meal without mixing up the salt and the sugar or forgetting a joint in the hot oven to bake dry. And you can imagine what it's like having a child for a husband. You can imagine all what that's like.'

That was what I would hear. Mother could unburden herself at last. I crept along the wall to an open window, where I could hear her clearly:

'Why do we set so much store by our children? They's bound to disappoint us, we wants too much for them: happiness, success, wealth, everything.' So I was right; except her voice was calm and friendly.

'Us wants them to stay, and us wants them to leave,' she continued. 'The cord's cut, and the trouble begins.'

Then another voice spoke. But it wasn't a woman's at all; it was Johnathan's father's. 'Have another glass of ginger wine,' he said. 'One wants a hot drink in this heat, Deborah,' he remarked. I heard him pouring them, and then sitting down with a heavy sigh.

'And how's young Alison?' he asked. 'I couldn't believe how big Georgie's little baby had grown, even though I knew she was almost the same age as my boy.'

I couldn't take in much more. My eyes grew bigger, and I held my breath.

'Alison? Oh, 'er's all right. You know what they're like at that age. Sleeps every chance you let 'er or hides 'erself away in some book, or else she gets in the way all day with energy that drives you mad, a proper little ragrowster. I'll be glad when the damn school gets started, that's for sure.'

CHAPTER SIXTEEN

Fire in the Wilderness

Neither Johnathan nor I could work out how our parents knew each other, so we gave up talking about it, dismissing it as one of those infuriating adult mysteries that'll drive you scatty if you let them.

Now I decided it was time to show Johnathan where I lived, partly to share it with him, and partly because it made for another game. At breakfast on Monday, the first day of October, mother declared that she was going shopping at the hypermarket in Newton that morning, if anyone had any special requests.

'Some of they chocolate desserts, mother,' said Tom.

We'd worked out a system of signs, and I signalled to Johnathan to meet me at the pool. Once Fred had brought us back from the road, I changed out of my school clothes and ran all the way to the quarry pool to wait for Johnathan. I was streaming with sweat, my tee-shirt and shorts were drenched, and my hair was sticky. Brown-haired people had been bleached blond by the sun, but my raven's hair had just become still more black and shiny. The heat seemed to make it grow quicker, too; it reached half-way down my back.

In my impatience to get down to the pool I'd forgotten to pick up my swimmers, but now I needed to get myself into the water. If I'd jumped in with my clothes on they would have dried out by the time Johnathan was likely to turn up, but I felt so uncomfortable in them that on the spur of the moment I peeled them off and jumped in naked, for the first time since I was a little kid.

*

The Sunday before, after I'd helped the Rector home from church with his stuff, instead of taking off his dog-collar and relaxing he'd gulped down a mug of coffee and dashed straight out, obsessed by his efforts to cure the world of superstition.

Alone in the rectory, I found myself in the drawing-room, empty save for the great gilded mirror above the mantelpiece. It was almost the middle of the day, and the stillness of the hour was accentuated in that bare house. It seemed that furniture must absorb not only light but even air as well, for without any the walls became less solid, membraneous almost, the rooms like chambers of a heart filled not with blood but with air, gently palpitating in the heat of noon. I could feel my own heart beating, as I stood before the mirror.

There were none in our house because Daddy had broken them all, except for the one grandmother had brought in her dowry. It hung in the hallway by the front door, and Daddy had overlooked it in his tirade of destruction. Mother had lacked the courage to replace them, so we'd got into the habit of using hand-mirrors and hiding them from Daddy, Pamela a compact for making-up and the boys a double-sided magnifying mirror for shaving.

I stood in front of the Rector's antique mirror: its gold-leafed frame was so grand and ornate that it overshadowed the mirror itself: it was more like the overwrought frame of some magical doorway, which it pulled you towards. The effect was to bring you, in fact, to the glass, but with curiosity, far more than if you had simply glanced in a bare-framed mirror to check your hair.

The glass itself was backed not with silver but gold, which softened what it reflected, and it was flecked with bubbles. I imagined the uncontrolled breath of some apprentice glassblower much the same age as me, not yet a master of his craft, creeping into the red-hot liquid glass and preserved there in tiny bubbles on the surface of the mirror, like a drowning boy's, centuries after he had exhaled his last breath.

Alone in the rectory I stared at my reflection. A stranger stared back. I pulled my tee-shirt over my head, and stepped out of my shorts and pants. In the silence of noon, through

143

fragile air in which could be felt the slow beat of invisible wings, my reflection fluctuated in the glass.

'How can you tell the difference between self-knowledge and vanity?' I once asked the Rector.

'That depends upon whether or not you like what you see,' he replied, taking a puff on his cigarette.

I thought about this dispiriting reply. 'We're supposed to hate ourselves, aren't we?'

He blew the smoke quickly out of the side of his mouth, impatient to answer: 'Not at all, Alison. Don't you believe all that nonsense; truth is more complicated. We're made in God's image. We might tarnish it, but the potential remains, unspoilt, unspoilable. To know oneself is to discern that potential, or God, within us; but it's also to see our own weaknesses, which have to be overcome; it's to hate not ourselves, but our insufficiency.'

My form hovered in the glass. I couldn't see who I was any more. Or what I was going to be. I was trapped in the glass, trapped in time, in this very moment. I was caught within it. It was like the moment making strawberry jam when it stops bubbling and starts to roll, streaming in from the sides of the pan towards the middle, as if into a whirlpool of its own making: after a while you start testing teaspoonfuls to see whether or not it's set, and finally you get a dab that crinkles when you prod it. Somehow, while it was rolling around, the jam was changing its substance, but you couldn't tell it was going to come out right, it was just a molten lava of strawberries churning over. I put my hands over my breasts, palms cupping the two slight mounds. Between my fingers I felt my nipples, no longer dots on my chest but small brown teats, ringed by brown. I tried to imagine a baby sucking milk from them; I imagined a tongue, licking.

I'd already asked mother for a bra. 'Don't be stupid, maid,' she said. 'Don't be in such a hurry. You'll have the rest of your life for them things.'

I ran my hands slowly down my torso, over my navel,

across my belly. I was still stringy, and strong as wire, like Ian. I was impatient to become a woman, as Pam was, but I'd decided I didn't want her wide hips, her broad bottom, and her soft, protruding belly. I loved being able to run, climb, and dive in the water with the boys, twisting and somersaulting in the air.

I ran my fingers down, into the sparsely tufted mound below. When Pamela persuaded me to share a shower with her, to save water, and saw the first wispy curls, she hugged me under the jet, splashing water even more than usual across the bathroom floor.

'Remember that a woman's body's the most beautiful thing in the world,' she told me. She gave me her make-up mirror and a book about women's bodies, so that I could see for myself the wonderful things she said were going on inside me. She explained about periods, and made me promise to tell her when I found blood on my knickers. ''Tis the second big moment in a woman's life,' she said, 'after the first of being born, and before the third, which I'll tell you about later on.' She washed my hair, massaging the shampoo into my scalp, and she dried me with a towel afterwards, not like a brusque mother with her child but as someone admitting a friend to a secret society. I'd never felt closer to her, and felt a warmth of relief and comfort, knowing she'd be there to guide me into womanhood; I wouldn't have to ask mother anything. I hid one or two tears of gratitude into the towel as Pamela rubbed my hair, little suspecting that when the time came she'd be gone, forgetting me, and I'd have to face it alone.

There I stood, naked in front of the largest mirror in the whole village, fingers searching the shape of what I was becoming. I closed my eyes. Images flowed through my mind, without order or reason: Pamela in the shower, soap slipping down her body; Johnathan's back, trembling as he prepared to dive into the quarry pool; his limbs brushing against mine under the dark water. The warm point of pleasure became the centre, from which it spread outwards. Susanna's pony galloping, as if on fire, through muddy pasture; Douglas Westcott's big barrel body, standing in amongst his cows, shimmering through the heat haze; and then suddenly, panicky, the throaty sound of the Rector's Triumph Vitesse.

I opened my eyes. The car was roaring down the drive and round to the front of the house. I pulled on my clothes, before I heard him opening the front door of the rectory.

Now I was swimming naked in the quarry pool, and felt a part of the water, as if this was where I was meant to live, not walking around on the earth. It seemed an elementary error of evolution that we'd ever come out of the water, as grandfather maintained we once did. I wanted to return, and fell prey to the illusion that here I was at home, safe and free. Rolling over and slipping under now and then, I swam out into the middle of the pool. The sun had risen above the rockface beneath the beech tree, turning the pool into a sheet of glass which reverted to liquid where I swam, but solidified again behind me.

I lay on my back with my arms outstretched, keeping myself afloat with my feet, propelling myself slowly along. I could lie like this all day, I thought; soon I won't even have to make an effort to stay afloat, I'll be able to stretch my legs out too, and float like a human star, held by the water as if on its solicitous palm.

The cramp gripped my right thigh in a sudden vice of pain, and then panic. I'd never got cramp before, and didn't know what to do: I bent my knee and brought it up to my chest, feeling that the natural thing to do, while I tried to keep afloat splashing with one arm and the other leg. But the pain only grew more intense. It robbed me of my self-control: I couldn't think clearly of a way of using my functioning limbs to make for the bank; instead the pain dominated me. I was shrieking and crying, and splashing around, in agony and helpless. Everything had turned against me in an instant: my body, so still and free, had twisted, part of it in blinding agony and the rest a useless weight gravity would surely drag under; my mind, so content, was whirling in confusion and terror; and the water, that had held me so gently in its hand, had opened up, the pool a treacherous being with an evil mind of its own, threatening to engulf me. I took a mouthful of water, but no sooner had I spat it out than I gulped another, and swallowed. I felt nauseous and was forced into a fit of coughing. Then, suddenly, for the briefest possible moment, a strange calm overtook me, and I thought: 'So this is it; this is how a person dies.' But the moment passed, as the pain of the cramp, locked into my thigh, shot like fireworks through my brain, and I felt my head duck under again, water forcing itself into my mouth and nostrils, and the world slipped away from me, into darkness.

I was woken violently, my head jerked forward, spewing water. I was lying on my front, and felt a weight roll off my back. Then my eyes were closed as I retched again, coughing more water out of my stomach, as well as the food I'd eaten for breakfast. I was sick until I knew my stomach to be empty, and then my body tried to be sick some more. I kept my eyes closed, knowing that if I opened them I'd faint, waiting for the nausea to subside. Gradually I was able to take deeper breaths, until I felt normality return to my chest and limbs. Then, like a blind woman groping through her darkness, I felt around for the person I'd sensed kneeling silently beside me. I found his wet clothes and pulled myself towards him, and I cried a long time in his arms, trembling, and whimpering.

I got dressed without saying anything, and neither did he. What had happened was too big for us. We didn't know how to deal with such an event: it had thrust itself into our lives, like an earthquake, and now we were dumbstruck, going through the motions of breathing and moving and seeing, while its shockwaves reverberated through and around us.

I could only think of doing what I'd planned to do anyway, which was to show Johnathan our house. I'd not recovered the inclination to talk, so I took his hand, and he followed me without question.

We didn't go straight back up the stream but followed the old railway line a way and then cut up to circle around behind the village. We didn't see another human being: the whine of distant tractors came in and out of earshot, and we could see one, crawling like a fly across a quilt, turning the soil in a field over towards Ashton. From the crest of the hill up behind our farm we turned and looked back along the Valley, at the other villages set, like ours, in its sides. I spoke for the first time: 'Think yourself invisible.'

We dropped down the steep fields, jumping and springing, and reached the back of our house, panting for breath. We had no back door, so I went in round the front and opened a window in the kitchen for Johnathan to climb through.

I peeked into the sitting-room: grandmother was dozing in her chair.

'She's asleep, but we better whisper just in case,' I told Johnathan. I took him upstairs and into the bedrooms: my parents', with the great wooden bed Daddy had made for their wedding night, putting it together in the room itself because it was far too big to get through the door; Ian's, dominated by his insomniac's desk, every inch of it covered with receipts, bank statements and balance sheets of the farm's accounts, by his chess board, the pieces arranged in the middle of some problem he pondered in the small hours, and by half a dozen empty tea mugs and an overflowing ashtray; Pam's, less a bedroom than a boudoir, as she called it, a piece of purple material draped over the lampshade, scented with jasmine oil, and a brightly dyed African tablecloth pinned to the wall beside her bed, which was itself covered with a sheet of similar material and cushions, too, to make the bed look like a divan; Tom's, neat and bare as a hotel room, showing no signs of being inhabited except for the spare pair of heavy workman's boots in the middle of the floor and a strong smell of dirty socks; our grandparents', darker than any of the other rooms in the house, with its heavy furniture and muddy wallpaper.

'This is my room,' I said lastly. 'You can look around if you want.' I lay on the bed, while Johnathan inspected the contents of my room: a miniature desk on which sat pencil case and rubbers and the unread textbooks that the headmaster had brought; various toys and knick-knacks on the shelf and window-sill: a plastic monkey from a Christmas cracker, a fluffy duck from a slot machine on Teignmouth pier, a long grey feather the widowman heron had let drop on his rock, half of a clay pipe I'd found in a field. There were a few books beside my bed, which was covered with a floral duvet. On top of the wardrobe sat a row of smiling teddy bears and empty-headed dolls, while blu-tacked to the walls were posters of a black galloping horse and a sunset in the Mediterranean that I'd bought for myself in Newton Abbot market.

Those objects adorning my room, the only place in the world that was mine, where I could do exactly as I wished, suddenly appeared alien to me, and I realized why: they were the possessions of a child. As relics of childhood I might have felt affection for them, but as they were now they remained evidence of my own childishness. I wanted to tear the posters off the walls and sweep the things off the window-sill: they embarrassed me.

The only people outside the family who came into my room had been my friends in the village. Jane had stayed countless nights, and Susan May too: every time one of them had come into our house I felt a sense of superiority, because apart from the rectory, which didn't count, ours was the biggest house in the village, and none of my friends' families each had their own rooms like we did.

Now, though, I was seeing everything with new eyes, those of Johnathan, who was inspecting my room with his hands behind his back, like some member of royalty on television being shown round a flower show, unconsciously condescending. All the walls of our house moved in, compressing the rooms, and the furniture became the miserable wooden stock of peasants or the cheap plastic of people brought up without taste, because although Johnathan no longer lived in the old estate it was where he came from, the carefree whims of its occupants over the centuries still ran in his blood and the dimensions of its architecture were implanted in his mind. I realized, as I watched him from my bed, that all he felt now was pity, however well he might disguise it, and for the first time in my life I felt its correlative: shame. I felt it swelling through my body and burning my cheeks.

149

'Come on,' I said, swinging my legs off the bed, 'let's get something to drink.'

As we reached the bottom of the stairs grandmother's voice called out: 'Who's that? Is that you, maid?' I gestured to Johnathan to go on into the kitchen, and went to see her.

'It sounds like you's slopping around in your shoes again, Alison. 'Tis a lazy habit, I've told you that before. Tie 'em up proper.' Her milky eyes gazed vaguely in my direction.

'Yes, grandma.'

'And another thing: they says talking to yourself is the first sign of madness.'

'But you does it all the time, grandma,' I replied, unable to stop myself.

Her face cracked open in a wide grin. 'Ooh,' she said, 'you's a wicked girl. If I'd talked back to my elders like that I'd have been sent straight to my room. Anyway, 'tis different for me: I'm discussing things with my memories. When you're my age, they come back to life to help you see things straight.'

'I won't do it no more,' I promised. 'Do you want a cup of tea or something?'

'No thank you, girl. You git on.'

Johnathan was sitting at the kitchen table. I poured us each a glass of milk, and joined him. We sipped it silently. Then Johnathan frowned, and looked at me.

'Where do you keep all your books?' he whispered. 'I didn't see them, apart from a couple in your room.'

All our conversations came colliding into my mind, all the times I tried to bluff my way through ignorance. The feeling of shame that I'd tried to leave behind upstairs rushed back in an instant over me, but with it too came anger.

'We 'aven't got a library, *actually*, Johnathan. My family's not spent its lazy hours reading the great writers of the world, it's been too busy working, and making things, and sewing clothes and cooking and digging the garden and that.' The more words came out the more furious I got. 'They might have done a lot of reading, and playing of music, and a little painting of pictures of an afternoon, if they hadn't been too busy workin' the land what you lot used to own.'

Johnathan had gone a little pale, and shrank back in his chair.

'I'll tell you what us've got instead, and that's memories. My grandmother's the one what keeps them. And she's passing them on to me. See this 'ere table? Grandfather had his tonsils taken out on it; that little stain in the middle there's his blood. He was eight year old. See that bit of rock on the floor, holding the door open? 'Tis granite. Grandfather brought it home from the old quarry, your great-grandfather's quarry, before he got the sack for knockin' out the bastard foreman's teeth. It only flooded a couple or three months later. That's what we got, see, memories; 'tis better than stupid books.'

I got up from the table. 'Give me your glass. You don't know nothin', that's your trouble.' I rinsed the glasses in the sink, and glanced back at Johnathan. He had his look of a frightened rabbit, as if he was about to burst into tears. It made me feel mean and horrible but also made me want to slap him, to shock some colour and strength back into his pale cheeks.

'You an't got no fight in you, have you?' I said. Johnathan didn't even breathe. 'I never seen that in no one before.'

Just then I heard a cough, and became aware of grandmother, whom I'd entirely forgotten. With her dog-like hearing she must have heard every word I said. But before I had time to consider this, another familiar sound came from the yard: mother's car turning in from the lane. I rushed over to the window: she was turning the car round, to reverse it up to the front door; Daddy was sat beside her.

'Come on, quick,' I said to Johnathan, ushering him to the back window.

We ran across the fields. Grandmother once told me that the way I walked it looked like I'd rather be running. That's how I felt; it's how your body's meant to move. When the barefoot African schoolgirl, Zola Budd, almost shocked the world in the Olympics earlier in the summer Ian had said: 'Blimey, Alison, if you cut all your 'air off I could say that were you, near's dammit, runnin' over with our sandwiches.'

'And was 'alf as ugly as you is,' Tom added stupidly for good measure, without a smile.

Now Johnathan and I ran along away from the village, laughing as we ran. There was nothing funny, it was just the relief of outside and the air in our lungs made us laugh. Then we scrambled back up the ridge and over the other side, and across a sloping, charred field whose stubble I'd helped Ian to burn.

The back lane to Ashton passed only a couple of fields away, but you wouldn't have guessed. It was hardly used. We found some elderberries and a few blackberries in a hedge. Johnathan reached his arm right in, and then withdrew it.

'Look at this,' he said. In his purple-stained fingers he held a tiny, black-speckled bird's egg. 'What do you think it is?' he asked me.

'Put it back,' I told him.

'What sort is it?'

'I don't know. Put it back quick, or the mother'll smell you, and push it out of the nest.'

In the corner of the field there was an old barn, recently filled with hay from the harvest; it was just a wooden shell, and that was all it was ever used for.

'Let's go in and get some shade,' I suggested.

The door creaked open, and the musty-sweet smell of hay filled our nostrils. I'd never seen so little there, just after harvest: it was stacked high in the middle of the barn, but the sides were bare.

'What about rats?' Johnathan asked, frowning.

'Don't be such a scaredy-cat,' I told him.

'I'm not really very fond of them,' he admitted.

'They don't bite humans,' I assured him. He stepped inside. 'Well, not girls anyhow,' I added. He looked startled. 'Only joking. Get on.'

We clambered up onto the top of the hay, into a dim space below uneven rafters, and lay down. Sunlight poked in through holes and cracks in the walls but the roof was the old earth-covered type, from which grass grew on the outside, and it was dark up there.

We didn't talk, we just lay there, tired, thinking our own thoughts. Johnathan's breathing was barely audible beside me. After a while my neck and arms started getting itchy, and I sat up.

'Empty your pockets,' I said.

'Why?' he asked.

'Just to see.' It was a game I played with Daddy; something I couldn't understand was how boys' pockets were always full of things whereas girls' were mostly empty, but then we grew up and suddenly needed whole handbags to carry all our stuff.

He laid a dirty handkerchief out on the hay, and put onto it a referee's whistle, a box of matches, a penknife, some string, the stub of a candle and a small plastic box.

'What's in there?' I asked.

He looked a bit sheepish. 'My c-c-contact lenses, actually.'

'I didn't know you wore them.'

'Only for reading. I don't have to, but I'm supposed to.'

'That makes a lot of sense. What's the candle for?'

'I don't know. Anything. I just took it out of the candlestick on the dinner table to put a new one in.'

'Let's light it,' I suggested.

'In here? You must be joking, Alison.'

'We won't do anything.'

'It's dangerous; it'd be m-m-mad in here.'

I rolled my eyes to the ceiling. 'You's scared of everything, aren't you? We're not going to drop it, you know. Just hold it, and blow it out when we've finished.'

He looked at me a moment, his eyes both mistrustful and defiant. Then he picked up the candle, and handed me the matches. 'Go on, then.'

As I opened the box and picked out a match, I realized how foolish an act it was. The whole barn changed from a place where hay was being stored into a dark cavern of inflammable material.

I struck the match, and lit the candle. The wick was almost buried: we had to melt a little wax until there was enough string showing through to take flame. Drops of melted wax dripped into the hay. Our faces lit up yellow.

Perhaps I wanted to show Johnathan I wasn't going to be grateful to him for saving my life. Perhaps I'd lost all sense of caution after coming so close to drowning. I don't know.

There must have been a wispy strand of hay sticking out from a bale, hanging out into space. The flame caught the end and ran along it. Within a second or two the side of the bale was crackling orange fire. We leapt up and started beating it with our shoes, but that just sprayed sparks everywhere. Until you've been in a fire, you can't believe how quickly it spreads.

'We've got to get water,' cried Johnathan. He hopped down the bales to the ground and I tumbled after him. He ran outside, and dashed one way and then another, running to and fro, looking for what he knew wasn't there. It was like he had the energy and the clear head to deal with a crisis, except that this one had no solution, and that confused him. Then he stopped and looked back at the barn, and did the strangest thing: smoke was drifting out of the doorway; there were no flames visible outside, only a fierce crackling noise; Johnathan ran over and firmly closed both the doors of the barn. The crackling was reduced to a distant roar. My skin prickled but inside I felt nothing. I was empty. Johnathan ran over to me.

'You're the fastest runner,' he gasped. 'Go and tell them.' But I was empty, sinking. My knees went and I dropped on to them. My hands were spread out, palms to the ground.

'I'll go,' I heard Johnathan say, and his footsteps receding.

I didn't faint. I wanted to run and hide, but I had the guts at least to stay. Or maybe I was just hypnotized. The roar became louder and louder, and smoke curled out of every crack in the walls. Then the flames burst through and the whole thing went up. Like a beacon. I watched it burn. I imagined I saw grandfather coming out of the inferno, leading his father's pair of horses by their halters. The barn was a crackling, roaring mass of flame, showering sparks across the Valley, and a column of black smoke rose into the sky. The fire engine when it arrived couldn't reach the field because the lane was blocked by cars full of strangers, who'd been drawn from miles around to stand and stare. It stood a hundred yards away along the lane, its siren wailing, while the firemen, in their Roman helmets, joined the silent crowd and watched the barn being reduced to ashes.

Mother telephoned Johnathan's father. A beaten-up Morris Traveller pulled into the yard, and the 15th Viscount Teignmouth stepped out. He had a cook's apron on. He ignored Johnathan, who didn't say anything either, to his father or to mother or to me, but walked over to the car, got inside, and waited. The Viscount spoke with mother for a while and then left.

It was the first time she'd ever beaten me, despite regular threats, because she'd respected that tradition of the family she'd married into. But she didn't hesitate about using the strap now.

She made me lie naked on my bed, and hit me with Daddy's heavy leather belt all up the backs of my legs and on my bottom. I screamed with each whack, and mother shouted: 'SHUT UP! SHUT UP!' and hit harder.

I squeezed the pillow and bit into it, and her fury slackened. She didn't say anything else. She didn't need to: I knew I deserved it. After she stopped it throbbed so much I didn't dare move. She turned round in the doorway and said: 'I won't 'ave you seeing him again. I'll not have you leading that boy astray.' After she left, I sobbed until the throbbing became less intense, and I sank into the mercy of sleep.

The next few days I didn't say anything to anyone, and Johnathan kept his distance from me. I just kept my head low, and made sure not to look anyone in the eye. When they spoke to me it was in a dismissive tone of voice. People get into habits, and maybe we would have carried on like that for ever, if Ian hadn't come in to tea one day after talking on the telephone.

'Well, that's all wrapped up,' he announced. 'Us'll get a new barn for one that was falling down any year, and we'll get compensation for twenty ton of top quality hay.' He couldn't conceal his delight, and I could tell from his voice that he was looking towards me: 'Folks'll think you done it on purpose, maid; they'll say I put you up to it. Bah. They can think what they likes. Give us another cup of tea, mother.'

CHAPTER SEVENTEEN

Waves Lapping, Children Laughing

Whenever a bug went round, of chicken-pox or measles or some such children's virus, the first mother to discover the symptoms in her child would put word around the village, and the other women would bring their kids along to a party so that they could all catch it together and no one would miss out.

The Rector used to bring his noisy film projector and his collection of reels of the old silent comedies. We'd drink coke and eat sandwiches and then play games like sardines or pyramids, any that entailed us sticking close together, preferably in an enclosed space, where the virus could pass amongst us all. The Rector, meanwhile, would be threading his projector and pinning blackout material over the windows, and we'd squash into whosever front room it was, sitting three to a chair and cross-legged on the floor in front of the Rector, his projector clattering on a table, so we could fall ill and begin to get well again all at once, 'because laughter's the best healer,' he declared, 'look at me, I never get ill,' although to fellow adults he confided that it was his deadly diet of cigarettes and alcohol that staved off flu, tummy bugs and the common cold.

It was true that he was never really ill. He must have been more at risk from unfriendly germs than anyone, on account of his visits to hospitals, with their unhealthy atmosphere, and his home calls to the bedsides of the infirm, but no one could remember his ever spending a day in bed. If on odd occasions his complexion was pale with the unhappiness indicative of influenza then he only blew his nose abruptly, gritted his teeth and carried on, because he was already behind in his duties, always, a hundred obligations large and small pressed into his collar-bone and preyed on his mind: there were meetings to attend, plans to draw up, papers to sign, disputes to settle, people to placate, sermons to compose, prayers to choose and fears to alleviate, and if he lost a single day from his schedule then that would be it, he'd never catch up.

The Rector's only hope of fulfilling his infinite obligations was to adhere to a strict routine, yet such was the ad hoc and unpredictable nature of his ministry that only the Sunday services conformed to a pattern. Everything else arose unexpectedly and demanded to be seen to at once, so that he was having constantly to abandon his illusory schedule to deal with what always appeared to be urgent emergencies, however trivial they really were.

Those sick-party screenings, however, were one of the few disruptions he welcomed. He'd brought the projector with him when he came to the Valley, on the advice of his old tutor at theological college, who when the Rector told him he was leaving his industrial chaplaincy in Crewe to come to a hidden village in Devon recommended that he show film versions of biblical stories in Sunday School, because he should be careful not to leave the twentieth century behind him when he crossed over the Exe river, and cinema's moving frescoes were the language of the age.

That earnest idea proved but one of the Rector's many initial failures, but he was able to exchange the reels of ludicrous extracts from the Bible epics of Cecil B. de Mille for the silent comedies of his own childhood, that his mother had taken him and his two sisters to watch every Saturday morning, and thus he was able, with apostolic enthusiasm, to introduce slapstick humour to every child that grew up in the village during the years of his ministry.

Because we were all jumbled up together, aged from four to fourteen, the Rector made no attempt to introduce us to the various comedians in any particular order of accessibility. Instead he selected a different star, from his well-stocked library, for each screening, and would put on all of their reels that he owned as they came to hand. Only gradually, as each of us gained admittance to those sick parties and grew up with them, were we able to differentiate and classify the assorted comedians, and discover our own favourites. And they each became identified in our memories with particular illnesses (either because the symptoms presented themselves almost as soon as the bugs entered our susceptible young bodies, or more likely because in reality the virus had already spread amongst us from our everyday contact, and those screenings were in fact more ritual than function), so that even today, seeing Buster Keaton's beautiful face bemused by but stoical towards the conundrum of existence I can feel my head begin to swim. I remember Ben Turpin, cross-eyed and indignant at being beaten at draughts by a dog just like Tinker, and I can feel again the hot flush of scarlet fever. I associate Harold Lloyd with being surrounded by other kids scratching the irresistible itch of chicken-pox, that would leave my cousin Dorothy's face blotched for the rest of her life. And I remember watching my favourites, Laurel and Hardy, struggling with the cruel objects and heartless people of their world, while under my clothes the little red spots of measles were surreptitiously manifesting themselves.

Our mothers usually had to carry us home, less sick than simply exhausted from laughter. When we were better again we argued amongst ourselves over why the characters moved in such a jerky manner: we thought it was because the stories were all about city people, always rushing around, but then the Rector showed some Buster Keaton shorts set in the country, and everyone flew around in just the same state of panic. So we figured maybe that's how Americans were. When I asked Ian why all the people in the Rector's films were in such a hurry he remembered the same arguments from when he was a kid, and he told me what he and his friends had decided was the explanation, that people in those days didn't live as long as we do today, so of course they were busier, because they had to fit everything into a shorter timespan. Pamela, though, said that was rubbish, it was simple, they only chose actors who walked with a stutter, because they were funnier.

By my time, of course, television had come to every house, but those screenings for sick children were still as special as they must have been for Daddy when he was a boy, because when compilations of silent comedy were shown on TV they weren't nearly as funny. Mother could hardly bear to watch them: slapstick infuriated her. She scowled at the television, muttering under her breath: 'Ridiculous', 'How stupid', or, shutting her eyes and slapping her forehead: 'I don't believe it!' as another custard pie landed in someone's face. So I stopped watching them at home, reserving the pleasure for those communal sessions when we cried so many tears of laughter the salt burned our faces, and the Rector laughed loudest of all with his smoker's laugh, broken up by bursts of coughing; unlike people's parents he hadn't lost his sense of humour when he'd grown up. While our mothers drank tea in the kitchen we laughed ourselves sick and well at the same time, we laughed ourselves silly, all except my friend Jane Ashplant, who, as a roomful of children fell about all around her, watched the black and white clowns on the flickering screen in silent, rapt concentration.

Sick parties were the only interruptions to the Rector's end-lessly disrupted routine that he welcomed. Everything else he was asked to do was yet more unbearable weight on his shoulders. It was only madness that had prompted him, when his children were small, to bundle them into the car at a moment's notice, along with any friends they might be playing with at the time and any dogs excited by the commotion, for spontaneous excursions. His wife preferred to stay at home, glad of the solitude, and she would strip to her bra and knickers, pull on a pair of wellingtons, and spend a rewarding afternoon in the garden, watched by one farmer or another from across a field.

Even after the Rector's children had long grown up and left home he would still realize, suddenly, that he'd been working too long and too hard, and he'd throw compass, swimming trunks, a thermos of coffee, a bar of Kendal Mint Cake, a football and a pair of binoculars into his old army

rucksack and get not into his Triumph Vitesse but into the
van that he'd persuaded one of the well-off newcomers to
sponsor: the fact was he had no wish to escape alone, and
those abrupt flights from routine were so strongly associated
with his habit of an indulgent father that he felt it only
natural to share them with children. So he'd stop at the
Brown to see if there were any kids playing there, he'd squash
as many as would fit into the Commer van, buzz around the
village to tell our parents he was taking us off their hands for
the day, and drive out of the Valley. By the beginning of that
summer I'd been his server for six months, and went on every
one of his excursions: if I wasn't already in the rectory or at
the Brown at the moment of his sudden impulse, he drove
into the yard to look for me, and we all set off for the coast.

The Rector loved everything to do with the sea. He'd drive
us down to Teignmouth, where the river from our Valley
joined the ocean, park the van, and jump out of it crying:
'Last one in's a nincompoop!' We'd race down to the beach,
then wait for him to catch us up and choose a place to dump
our stuff. He trotted across the sand, his limp less severe than
usual, and plunged into the waves, to forget for a moment his
exile from the world in a hidden village in a forgotten Valley,
his bright white body floating in the salty sea, unprotected
stomach exposed to the merciless sun.

Coming from the Valley, brown and dusty, everything
burned up and dried out, all that water took a few moments
to believe. Daddy came with us one time. He changed into
his swimming trunks but when we all dashed into the sea he
hesitated in the shallows, wading sideways, to and fro, the
waves rippling around his knees, scared to come in any
further, looking warily out to sea as if it threatened to absorb
him. His own past was a still sea, vast and calm, from out of
which isolated memories would now and then bob up to the
surface. I wondered whether his memory came back to him in
dreams, that he would forget upon waking. I saw him sometimes on the sofa during sleepy afternoons, dreaming like
dogs do, twitching with apprehension or pleasure. He woke

up with a disconcerted expression, retaining some sense of his dreams even as they slipped through his fingers.

We played football on the beach, the boys eager for a game any time, anywhere, even though that's all most of them ever did back home. Then we went into the amusement arcade on the pier, full of machines for stealing a person's money without them noticing: there were one-armed bandits, mechanical shooting galleries, crane-grabs, computer games, slot machines, ring-a-goldfish and penny slides. The Rector got a double handful of five pences and coppers from the change kiosk and distributed them casually amongst us, ignoring complaints from those who had less than others.

'Don't be so ungrateful,' he said.

'But 'tidn't fair, Rector, 'er's got more than me.'

He shrugged without sympathy. 'Enjoy what you've got,' he'd tell us. 'Be content with that.'

He always made money from the machines, because he always stopped as soon as he was ahead, even if he'd put in a penny and got two pence back on his very first go: that would be it, he'd go straight back to the kiosk and cash in his own change. He was disappointed that none of us could ever follow his example, unaware that few people, especially children, possessed the willpower he took for granted.

He'd indulge us for our inevitable losses with toffee-apples and candy-floss and lead us along the promenade. We gaggled around him as he strolled along with his trousers rolled up, his dog-collar forgotten, a smile on his face as he inhaled the salty air and observed the unhealthy families down from the north for their holidays, the beach-huts with their paint blistered by the sun and salt, the wild dogs sniffing scents along the seafront, the tropical plants in the municipal gardens, and the crazy golf he always encouraged us to ask him to let us play, even though he enjoyed it more than any of us did.

One Saturday back in July we'd filled a boat to go mackerel fishing. The skipper was an old man with a face made of cowhide, and we chugged to and fro across the calm bay without a bite, the old man shaking his head and assuring us over and over that they were there somewhere, he was sure of it. We sat around the back and sides of the boat, yawning with boredom, our lines trailing uselessly behind, when suddenly Jane gave a yelp and stood up, her line trembling from her fingers. Within seconds everybody's was doing the same. We pulled them in and copied the way the Rector unhooked the petrified fish, tossed them into buckets in the middle of the boat, and then fed our lines back into the water. A moment later they were tugging again, mackerel throwing themselves onto the hooks, and we found ourselves immersed in a frenzied, floating slaughterhouse. The skipper had shut his outboard right down and was crawling through the water: it was obvious that we were passing across a vast shoal of mackerel beneath the boat. We couldn't see them, but the water had a silvery glint in it, below the surface.

Slithering fish accumulated in the middle of the boat, tossed there as if they'd jumped in of their own accord out of the sea. They'd soon filled the buckets to overflowing and were flapping and jerking around on the floorboards, eyes staring in terror at the air they couldn't breathe but tried to anyway, gulping it down in disbelief, while their bodies twisted in half, lay still, then twisted again. I dropped my line in the boat and tried to look away, as far out to sea as possible. We weren't squeamish people, but that frenzy had the same effect on the others, who, one after another, also dropped their lines or let them go into the water, to be hooked forever into the cheek of some unfortunate fish. By the time we'd passed out of the shoal only the Rector and Gordon Honeywill were still pulling them in, while the skipper sized up the writhing mass of fish in his boat with a rapacious, amazed expression on his leathery face.

We never went mackerel fishing again, though half the families in the village were delighted to have such a welcome treat on their plates at tea the next day. What the Rector really preferred was to catch shrimps and prawns in rock pools along the shore with a half-moon shrimping net. While we made sandcastles and buried each other on the beach he wandered off with his trousers rolled up, his stomach stopped churning and settled down as he hunted amongst the miniature watery worlds of sea anemones, pincer crabs, seaweed, limpets and shells in perfect pools left by the tides, and he'd not return until his bucket was full of shrimps in salt water that would spill over the rim in the van on the way back home, and which he would boil alive before shelling, and then consume in mouth-watering sandwiches as he watched the late-night film on the television in his kitchen.

Once or twice our expeditions took us up to the high tors on Dartmoor, with compass and maps, and once we went to the cinema in Exeter because there was a brief revival of the western. But wherever we went, we somehow always ended up by the sea at dusk, the Rector answering the call of a secret vocation, the salt in his nautical blood of a long line of sailors, he told me, left traces in his nostrils and its taste on his tongue, and we sat on the beach sipping the last tepid coffee from the thermos, beginning to shiver and huddle together, conspirators, trembling and giggling in our tiredness, all except the Rector, who sat off smoking and gazing out to sea, watching the waves break first past the end of the pier, the sound of their dull crash coming after, watching them break again below us and the water slide up the sand teasingly towards his feet, almost tickling them before withdrawing, invitingly, back into the godforsaken vastness of the ocean.

In contrast to the raucous journey down we returned in silence, curled up in the van, children and dogs, sand between our toes, unable to keep our eyes open as the Rector drove us home through the darkness.

CHAPTER EIGHTEEN

Tea

'Sit down a minute,' grandmother said, and she slurped the mug of milky tea I'd brought through to her. I wanted to get outside.

'It were the coldest winter in history,' she declared suddenly.

'What was?' I asked.

She took my hand in hers. 'The story I'll tell 'ee, stupid.'

'Oh,' I said. So I gave up and tried to snuggle up beside her, except that now I was bigger than she was.

'It were twenty-five year ago,' she began.

'Wait a minute,' I interrupted, 'I thought you said last year was the worst winter we ever had.'

'Nonsense, maid. This one were much colder.'

It was in the coldest and most prolonged winter in history, twenty-five years earlier, when the peacocks that patrolled the terraced lawns began to peck away at the bulbs and roots of hibernating flowers, that it occurred to the young 15th Viscount Teignmouth that those peacocks had probably never been husbanded since their ancestors' arrival, brought by the very first Viscount. There was certainly no one in his retinue of servants, so far as he knew, with responsibility for their management: they were simply left to themselves.

The Viscount tried to count them and found it an impossible task, confused by their fans, which they spread and then withdrew with baffling irregularity, but he figured there were around thirty. 'If I don't do something soon,' he thought, 'they'll have wiped out the lawns and the flower beds too, before spring ever arrives.'

He instructed his head gardener to hire the local slaughterer, and so early one morning Douglas Westcott walked across the Valley with his bag of tools. The world was white, covered not with snow but a layer of brittle frost; the entire earth was still, having retreated into the depths of its deep sleep. Douglas felt like an intruder, worried he might wake up the earth as he walked across it, his boots crunching in the silence. His escaping breath froze on the air, hinting at thoughts whose articulation remained trapped on his tongue.

He caught half a dozen peacocks in the same way that he did chickens, creeping up on them from behind, undaunted by the eyes of their fans watching him, and swooping down upon them with his coat wide open.

Maria was polishing a second-floor window when she saw him in the backyard behind the scullery, slicing the necks of those beautiful creatures with a cleaver, their final ghastly breaths shrieking from their windpipes and shattering every silence but his own. She was stung with pity, whether for him or for the peacocks she wasn't sure. In some confusion she descended to the kitchen and made a pot of tea. As soon as she stepped out of the scullery Douglas recognized her: she was the black-haired stranger in a black dress he'd watched from the corner of his furthest field, walking into the village with a wicker basket; she was the angel who'd been interfering with his dreams. As she set the tray down on the ground his mind went haywire and came to an irrevocable decision, and with the next swing of his cleaver he opened a deep gash across his hand.

As the winter wore on Douglas returned at regular intervals to kill another unfortunate bird, one only at a time, and afterwards he would make his way to Maria's tiny room, where she changed the dressing. After love Maria came back to the world as slowly as she could, and she made her sullen lover laugh as she smoked his pipe and chattered to him in her native language.

After spring came and plants and grass began to grow again, Douglas failed to return. Maria was neither surprised nor sad, only mystified by the way his absence made itself known inside her, tugging at one or other of her organs like a torn tendon, as if his absence had always been and would always be there, requiring his intrusion into her life to bruise it and make itself known. But she wasn't sad; she was almost relieved. Life was complicated enough without him. She assumed he'd come to the same conclusion: she didn't know he'd walked out of his front door and left home.

One Sunday in every month my aunts and uncles and cousins came in from their cottages and small farms at various points around the parish and squeezed into the kitchen for afternoon tea. We sat around what had begun as a small and sturdy deal table, the same one on which grandfather had had his tonsils removed, but as children and grandchildren were born so grandfather had added folding flaps and extendable leaves, and on those Sunday afternoons the little table sprouted out almost to the walls, along which we slid in and sat on benches.

It was the only time we got together specially, and you realized that all those people made up one family; the rest of the time you forgot it. We'd meet each other in normal day to day, in the lane or coming out of the shop, and we didn't feel anything special towards each other; no more than towards other people like Granny Sims, or Martin the hedge-layer. It was like everyone was related, or else that none of us were. And it was even harder to believe that all the mothers were Daddy's older sisters, the same little girls who'd once made grandfather so proud.

'Mother,' aunt Susan asked that Sunday, 'why on earth don't you and father buy a larger house, or else build an extension to the kitchen? Us is squashed up like frogspawn.'

She made the same suggestion every month, and grand-mother always gave the same reply: 'At our age? It saw you all in and 'twill see us out. In't that right, lover?' she asked grandfather, and he responded with an affirmative grunt, neither age nor the familiarity of his kin alleviating his shyness.

The men sweated uncomfortably and consumed in silence the mountains of paste sandwiches mother had prepared, while the women talked to each other across them.

167

'Where's Pamela this month?' enquired aunt Dorothy, the eldest.

'You knows perfectly well where 'er is, girl,' said aunt Shirley, and my other aunties giggled.

''Er's one for the boys all right,' said grandmother approvingly.

'Nothing wrong with that,' replied aunt Dorothy, 'but 'er shouldn't neglect the family.' Dorothy was the only one without a husband. She used to have one, but he left her before I was born. She always knew he would. They said she was so jealous she used to make him stay in all the time, and kept the windows shut so even his smell wouldn't get out. She knew other women were after him. When he left her, without any children, she got rid of all the old furniture, threw out the carpets and the curtains, burned the sheets, replaced the cutlery and lamps and everything else too, as well as redecorating from top to bottom, to rid the house of every last trace of him.

'Pamela's rehearsin',' said mother quickly. 'You know, for this amateur dramatics.'

'Rehearsin' with the leading man, more like,' said aunt Shirley. None of the men smiled except uncle Sidney, who enjoyed his wife's provocative humour.

Uncle Terence never laughed at anything. No one could remember when he'd become bad-tempered. His round face was cast in a permanent mould of misery, with a thin-lipped downturned crescent of a mouth, and his only son, Terry, who wasn't much older than me, was a copy of him.

Terence's wife, aunt Marjorie, was the ugliest of my aunts: she had a face that looked as if it had had an argument with itself; her features were all mismatched, put together higgledy-piggledy, like she had one person's nose but another's ears, and her eyes belonged to someone else again. She also had a penetrating glance and looked at you intently, making you think she knew things about you you'd never told anyone; it was years before I realized that was an illusion caused by myopia, which she admitted to no one, too vain to wear glasses.

While the women were chatting, the men got talking by asking uncle Terence questions, because his lack of humour was what they found funny.

'There's a curlew around top field,' uncle Sidney told him.

'He's a noisy old bird,' said uncle Terence, 'nearly as bad as that nightjar's churr: drives a man mazed. What with all the ivy leaves rustling in the breeze, what a miserable old row 'tis, a man can 'ardly sleep nowadays.'

'Susan made 'erself up a bag of pine needles helps her sleep,' said uncle Bill.

'Tche! Stink! Don't 'e bother with that.'

Grandmother said little at Sunday tea nowadays, fully occupied with picking her way through her food, refusing to take anyone's word that paste sandwiches and drop scones presented no possible danger since she'd heard of someone choking on a chicken bone. But somehow the tea pivoted around her. Her husband was so modest that, even while he was becoming richer and widely respected in the neighbouring villages, with each flap and leaf he added to the kitchen table he made his own place more and more remote from what could be identified as the head of the table, with the expanding surfaces shaped to the uneven walls of the room itself. If anyone's position was most distinctive it was that of grandmother, who like all the women of her line had shed in her senescence the weight assumed for the years of fertility and who, wedged into the tight corner near the door, with the table pointing like an arrow towards her, gave out an aura of ageless but receding wisdom from her silence embellished only by patient mastication.

'Alison,' said aunt Shirley, 'fill the pot up will you, me lover?'

We took butter straight from the fridge, but even so it soon melted on the drop scones.

'I 'eard a silage tank exploded over Ashton las' week,' said uncle Terence.

'Serves 'em right!' said aunt Shirley.

'Is you predictin', Terence?' asked aunt Susan. 'Is you bodin' omens?'

'No,' he denied it. 'I idn't worried 'bout what's to come, 'tis bad enough now. We lost two ewes last week.'

Gradually, as we munched drop scones and swallowed lukewarm tea, grandmother's silence settled over the table. The men looked down at their empty plates; the large women leaned back against the wall; grandmother chewed quietly.

I thought of our ewes, and tried to remember them in the spring with their lambs. The world was so different then it was like remembering a completely different place: the earth was still moist and soft from the winter thaw, and the young lambs, as they frolicked in the field along the lane, bounced vertically off the ground. They looked like the most carefree beings in existence, but if a human approached they became panic-stricken, like children in a party game, and ran into and across each other looking for their mothers. They usually made for the wrong ones, and became lost and bemused, until their ears suddenly picked up the distinctive bleating of their own mother, and then they would home in on her and attack her teats, berating her for deserting them, it seemed, as much as seeking the security of her milk.

Then I remembered how, when I was much younger, one of the ewes had died in the midst of giving birth. It was a thing that hardly ever happened, and grandfather was furious: he pulled the half-emerging lamb from the dead ewe's womb, cleaned it up himself, and brought it to the house. He came in the kitchen, handed it to his daughter-in-law without a word, and left, to carry on with the rest of the lambing.

I don't think mother was too sure what to do. She got me to put some rags in a cardboard box while she warmed a baby's bottle of powdered milk. The lamb was a runty little bundle of bone and wiry wool. He looked more sleepy than anything else, but he took the rubber teat and sucked without pause. Mother told me to hold the bottle.

'He can be your responsibility, Alison,' she said. 'I'll show you what to do. And you can think of a name for him for starters.'

I decided then and there to call him Smudge, because he wasn't white like he was supposed to be. After he was fed we put him in the bottom oven of the Aga, with the door open.

Runts get ignored if they're lucky, or more likely picked on. There was nearly always one chicken scrawnier than the rest, who'd peck its feathers for no good reason, for their own humourless amusement, proving you don't need any brains to be cruel. They'd send it flapping into a corner of the yard. Smudge was never going to be like that. He didn't learn the timidity of his species, which in reality is only a habit passed on from one generation to the next: without their example he followed me everywhere, curious and playful as a puppy, but bolder. Tinker was no longer allowed in the house, and when Smudge followed me into the yard – the dogs' territory – instead of submitting to their indignant inspection of this unwelcome guest he'd look them in the eye and stare them out until they turned tail, and left him alone. The only thing he wouldn't do was allow himself to be house-trained, and I had to go around scooping up his neat pellets off the carpets.

As soon as he was old enough to graze Smudge was reintroduced to his flock in the fields: they accepted him immediately, and he them, but he remained aloof. I took my friends to play with him: we approached quietly along the lane, and Jane or Susan May would slip through the rungs of the gate. The game was to see how far we could creep up on the flock before they noticed us. As soon as one of them did then they all knew simultaneously, through electricity as grandmother would say, their heads snapping back, mouths full of grass clamping shut. Then they scurried away all together towards a far corner of the field; all, that is, except one, Smudge, who was growing into a proud, twist-horned ram and who galloped instead in the opposite direction, straight towards us, to renew his acquaintance with our species. Jane always got the closest, so that she then had to run the furthest back to the gate, squealing with terror and delight, hotly pursued by that comical sheep that I'd fed from a bottle.

One day grandfather took him off for slaughter along with the other young rams, without thinking to tell me.

*

171

Uncle Bill blew his nose loudly, lowered his handkerchief, and inspected its contents; uncle Sidney and aunt Shirley stole glances at each other; thin aunt Susan, with her wide eyes like a bird, cupped her almost empty teacup. I rubbed my finger round the rim of my glass; when the hum started, moths closed their wings and dropped off the lampshade. Mother slapped my wrist.

After a while Ian leaned across and muttered something to grandfather, who nodded with evident relief, before standing up.

'Us is goin' to the barn,' he declared awkwardly, 'to talk farmin' matters.' He stepped outside with Ian, followed by his sons-in-law and grandsons. The sharp scent of their sweat lingered over the table as the women watched them through the window, thin wisps of smoke coming round the sides of their heads as they ambled towards the barn in their crumpled Sunday suits.

The women remained silent a moment more, feeling some part of themselves departing, some silent measure of their conversation. But departed also was the particular inhibition men caused, and they pushed their chairs back and relaxed. Some drank another cup of tea, while we cleared away around grandmother and washed up.

When aunt Dorothy went to the lavatory, aunt Shirley said: 'Have you been over her place recently? She's got another bloody dog.'

'Must have more than 'alf a dozen,' said aunt Marjorie. 'Why on earth's 'er want so many?'

'All I know is she started acquirin' them, like, when she knew she wan't goin' to get another man,' aunt Shirley replied, adding: 'And who's to say 'er made the wrong choice?' And they all laughed, hiding their faces when she came back in the room.

Of the men only Daddy stayed inside, obedient to the bias instilled in childhood when, as the only son, he'd grown up in a household so filled with women that their cycles came to coincide.

Terry was the only cousin almost as young as me and he

was as bad-tempered as his father. I'd given up on him ever since he'd declared in the spring that there were too many primroses about, so when we were sent outside to play I manoeuvred down to the back of the barn so that we could see what was going on.

Down in the shadows of the cavernous barn, its floor bare except for a dusty sprinkling of chaff, they sat around on barrels and beams. Ian was telling grandfather of the decision that was forcing itself upon them: to buy in hay at great cost, or to slaughter the animals.

'I wanted to tell you before us decided one way or t'other. Make sure you approved, like, grandfather. To be honest, I think there's only one choice.'

Grandfather narrowed his eyes, cleared his throat, and spat a gob of phlegm into the dust. ''Tidn't right,' he declared. 'Us built this whole farm on stock. Even in the bad summer not long after the war, when your father was born, when I 'ad to pick carcasses up myself and bring 'em home on the trailer, I waited for the autumn. It'll come.'

'But we can get these 'ere subsidies now, you never 'ad 'em –'

'– I knows that.'

'We 'ardly grows enough grain for ourselves. If we turn over fields from grazin' to grain, 'tis money for old rope.'

'You needs sheep for the 'illsides,' suggested uncle Sidney.

''Tidn't a proper farm without pigs, that's for sure,' uncle Bill added emphatically.

'I don't like it,' said uncle Terence.

'See, we're wastin' space leavin' animals out in the fields,' Ian explained. 'They should be inside, then the meat in't lost with runnin' about. Us could easy convert the sheds for starters.'

They sat around in the dimness, the barn, squeezed by the heat, gently pulsating with their various thoughts.

'I'll approve of this,' grandfather declared at length, having admitted to himself that it was too late to take back the authority he'd passed to his grandson. 'If you has to slaughter, do it now; keep back the best. Then you can feed they the hay you've got left. You can start the 'erd up again next year.'

With the confidence of one with no doubts about his own leadership, Ian turned to his brother. Tom nodded.

"'Tis agreed, grandfather,' Ian said. 'I'll get Douglas soon's he can.'

'Good, 'tis settled,' grandfather said as he stood up. 'Now, I needs all of you bays. Deborah wants the chicken hut moving. They's peckin' up nothin' but dust, and us can all lift it together.'

They stepped outside. Eyes narrowed against the glare of the sun, my uncles' heads were filled with the calculations of acres and tonnes and Common Market money. Terry joined them and I went back to the house, just as Daddy was helping grandmother into the sitting-room. He eased her gently into her chair by the fire, which she insisted she needed kept alight to stop from getting cold, even in that furnace of a summer. She gripped his hand, and her milky eyes gazed vaguely through him.

'You's a good bay,' she muttered hoarsely. 'Too good for this world.'

He smiled. 'So's you, grandma.'

'That's all right then, 'cos I'll not be much longer of it.'

'Course you will,' said her daughters, who were on the settee, and they made tutting noises.

'Put another log on the fire, Georgie,' grandmother asked. 'I shiver.'

Grandmother was looking straight at me, but she couldn't see.

'Grandma,' I asked her, 'mother says you won't 'ave an operation for your cataracts. Why not? It must be awful not to see proper.'

'No, maid, no, I don't want it,' she replied. 'I've already seen enough for one life.'

CHAPTER NINETEEN

Electric Summer

Things aren't simple. Things change. You see how people are, and you think they were always like that. You don't realize what people do to accommodate themselves in the world.

For one thing, it was hard to believe, looking at them now, but fifty years earlier grandmother had realized what a mistake she'd made within months of the wedding. She'd met the wiry, reserved farmer at a harvest dance in Moretonhampstead, and he courted her every Sunday, riding his cob up past the reservoirs to her father's house on the edge of Dartmoor. He arrived every week without fail, at first in the late autumn, when she showed him her favourite walks across the heather and round the Tors, and then into the winter when he appeared through sweeping rain like a phantom. He'd change into the spare clothes he brought wrapped in oilskin and spend the day silently watching grandmother and her sisters sew, smoking his clay pipe and refusing their invitations to play cards or sing around the piano.

Even when the snow cut them off from the world in January, still he came, forcing his horse through the waist-high drifts and bringing honey and fresh cream from the Valley. The house was in a small hamlet, and on Sunday mornings the inhabitants all sat at their windows, each week agreeing that this time he wouldn't make it, and then applauding him from behind the glass when horse and rider once more came stumbling through the snow.

Grandmother's father, manager of the mines behind Manaton, resented the young peasant whose farm was little more than a smallholding, but by the end of that winter he'd relented to the perseverance of his daughter's suitor. For her part, grandmother found his taciturnity a welcome relief from the garrulous hubbub of her large family, whose prattle, jovial and witty, could not conceal their lack of sensibility, and from which she had escaped as often as possible into the civilized worlds of her dead grandfather's library and the windswept, elemental moor. She sensed the wisdom behind silence, and furthermore her fiancé's determined wooing of her revealed a will as strong as her own: she knew that together they would improve and increase his small farm into the largest in the district.

As their wedding day approached they drew closer and closer together, as they planned their life and felt their separate destinies drawing into one. Grandfather prepared for her arrival in the farmhouse, his parents making way and moving out of the main bedroom, where he constructed a bed for grandmother and himself, while his two unmarried sisters shared the room at the end of the corridor. The dark building with its roof of threadbare thatch, the dusty farmyard, and the quaint, ramshackle outbuildings, seemed as beautiful to her as the pictures of Palladian villas she'd studied in a book in her grandfather's library.

Grandmother soon sensed the extent of her error. It was as if her husband had used up all the resolution he owned in capturing her, some manly imperative like yeast lifting shape and purpose from his latent will, which in the months following the wedding collapsed into lethargy. He barely had enough energy to sustain the farm, taking days over jobs even grandmother realized could be done in hours, haphazardly feeding the livestock, and apathetically leaving the meagre harvest until impending rain forced him to it. In the evenings he would come in long before dusk and drink tea from a pot left brewing by the fire, and after supper he would sit there again, beside his sisters silently knitting, smoking his pipe, occasionally leaning forward and riddling the poker among the embers, and she realized then the awful and obvious truth of his reticence, that he said nothing because his brain was merely a froth of indecision and in his mind there were no coherent thoughts worthy of expression.

During the first winter of their marriage grandmother forced herself to swallow the phlegm of her regret, rather than spit it resentfully at her irresolute partner, and she gradually digested the reality of her predicament. She felt stifled and oppressed. She thought she would scream in the silent evenings around the fire, and she dreamed of saddling the horse one night as soon as the snow melted, and riding back home. Close to defeat, only her pride sustained her: once she said she'd do something she did it, and no one had ever stopped her before, least of all herself.

One Tuesday morning at the beginning of March grandfather was drinking his first mug of tea of the day when his wife swept into the kitchen, still shivering in her nightdress, and opened the window wide, before moving on into the sitting-room. He followed her, bemused, as she strode around the house, through every room, ignoring his sisters who were still in bed, opening all the windows and exclaiming loudly:

'Out! All of you! Out of this house, because it's mine now, I'm the mistress here and from now on you can all find somewhere else to live!'

Grandfather was horrified. He thought his beautiful wife had gone mazed, and he was dismayed at the thought of people smugly nodding to him because he was foolish enough to ignore their warnings and court someone from so far away. But he let her finish, and followed her back into the kitchen, where she poured herself some tea.

Tentatively, he asked her: 'Will 'e tell me what you're doin'?'

'What do you think?' she replied. ''Tis one thing to live with all your relatives. I'm not about to share my house with your family's ghosts as well.' He was nonplussed by her logic. 'It's all right,' she told him as she left to go and get dressed, 'you can close the windows now.'

And as grandfather walked around shutting out the March wind that had blustered briefly through the house, he realized that his wife was stronger than he was, and that things were going to be different from now on.

They were. Grandmother decided that there were two of them, after all, and so that spring she joined her husband in every aspect of the running of the farm, castrating sheep as well as milking the cows, building fences just as she repaired the chicken coops; she took charge of the accounts, and went with him to market in Newton Abbot.

Gradually she rekindled in him his former spirit, and all that summer they worked outside from dawn to dusk, and then into the night together planning improved systems for irrigating their land, different crop rotations, and researching information on cattle breeding. They bought pigs and geese, and planted apple and pear trees in the tiny meadow across the brook. In July, a destitute labourer knocked on the farmhouse door and tried to sell them a ferret, producing pedigree charts which claimed to trace its lineage back to the very first pair introduced to Devon from Russia by Peter the Great, when as a young man he was sent to study the navigational skills of the British Navy in Plymouth. They bought the ferret and hired the labourer, and they needed him that harvest as they reaped from their meagre land a prodigious bounty.

It was after they had stored the grain and squeezed all the bales of hay and straw into the barn that grandmother confirmed she was pregnant, and they rejoiced at the evidence of their fecundity. Their optimism even provoked in her husband an expansion of his interests; he listened, entranced, as she read to him from books she'd brought with her, and they would discuss the names of characters as possible names for their child. He in turn told her some of the secrets of the farm, such as that theirs were the only hives for miles around because only their family knew of bee herbs, which had kept their bees free of foul-brood, a disease that periodically wiped out whole other colonies. He explained the necessity of greeting the rooks when they returned to the rookery in autumn, and informing them of any changes in the family or the ownership of the land, or otherwise bad luck would surely befall them.

Grandmother's first pregnancy, however, was a difficult one: she felt seasick, even in the middle months. Unable to help on the farm and encourage her husband she could only observe helplessly as his willpower once more waned. Even milking the cows nauseated her, and the fowl seemed to glance at her with contempt in their eyes when she carried herself across the farmyard scattering their corn. There were days when her husband came in for his midday meal, and then supped his tea by the fire long into the afternoon, deaf to her reproaches and mindless of the fading light.

Grandmother retreated into her confinement and the child in her womb, regretting that she couldn't carry it without it handicapping her and drop it easily in the field. She resented its existence, if only for its own sake; the circumstances of its birth were sabotaging its own future.

She knew that her husband would scrape a living for his family from the farm with the residue of responsibility that no peasant would abdicate. You could put little or much energy into the land and reap the same reward either way; to really profit took an almost savage commitment of will, and grandmother knew she would no longer be able to spare that amount of attention from the child almost ready to be born.

As the end of her term approached, grandmother became calm. She had to carry her overripe belly with both hands just to be able to walk about, but she felt at ease, somehow certain that her body, having accustomed itself to childbearing during the last few months, was ready to give birth without difficulty. When the child was due the then Granny Sims, village midwife, had one of her many grandchildren always ready to come and fetch her, anxious as she always was over a woman's first birth, and grandfather's sisters hovered around grandmother like irritating flies.

Grandmother's instinct, though, was correct: her waters broke as she was preparing supper, she told the family her

179

time was come, and she made her dignified way upstairs to the bed grandfather had made them.

The pain was intense but she controlled it with the breathing methods Granny Sims had taught her and with her own calm surety that all would be well, and in the early hours of the morning Granny Sims handed her a wailing baby girl, with a crop of hair black as her own, so small she couldn't believe such a tiny thing could have caused all that fuss inside her; she asked Granny Sims whether there wasn't another still hiding, as she automatically quieted the baby by putting it to her breast.

'Don't be silly,' Granny Sims replied, "er weighs a good seven pounds, I should say.'

A few days later grandmother weighed herself, too, on the scales in the barn with which grandfather assessed the worth of his sheep, and she found she'd gained over a stone since the last time she'd weighed herself, a year previously.

Grandmother continued to grow larger, without trying, with or without another baby in her belly, and she let her body put on the weight it seemed to require for those years of fertility. Every time she recovered from one birth sufficiently to want to lie with grandfather, she seemed to conceive another, and her children were all born within little more than a year of each other. The only trouble was, they were all girls. When they had three grandmother suggested that was enough for one family, and that they could take their time together in working out ways of enjoying the pleasures of marriage uninterrupted by their procreative consequences. For the first time since their wedding she sensed the muscles of her husband's willpower tense, something inside him steel itself, something like anger except that it never showed itself: it was an implacable resolve, the foundation of his character, that lived deep down inside him, too far from his tongue and his ear to argue with.

'Who's to inherit the farm?' he demanded.

'Why not one of the girls? Idn't nothing wrong with that.'

He shook his head. 'Some young bugger'll come along and marry 'er; take 'er name and the farm too. No, us 'as got to 'ave a bay.'

She knew, somehow, that there was no point in arguing. He'd made up his mind and there was no changing it, unless she was prepared to enter into a battle of attrition whose end might never come. She gave way, and her duly apparent pregnancy filled him with hope. Nature, however, was not so compliant: it was another girl, and so was the next.

Somewhere in the middle of my five aunts funnelling as if on tap, at similarly brief intervals, into the world, grandfather's father passed away, and he found himself the only male in a household of women and noisy baby girls who between them demanded the full attention of any man foolish enough to linger indoors. It was then that grandfather resumed his long working days out in the fields, except that this time it wasn't with the short-lived empire-building energy of a newly-wed but rather as an escape from his own family. More than anything else, he was driven into the fields by the sound of his daughters crying. He noticed that there was a moment, before the pain of a scraped knee or knocked elbow assailed them, just before they burst into tears, when their faces assumed a look of utter confusion and bemusement, as if asking: 'Why is life doing this to me?' It tore his heart in two, and not only could he do nothing to assuage their suffering, he seemed only to make it worse: when he lifted them up to offer them all the comfort he could give, they only cried all the more and called for their mother, who would calm them down, translate for him their strange toddlers' utterances into the English language, and set them right with a medicinal kiss.

And so he crept out of the house at dawn with a flask of tea, leaving with relief the pandemonium of women and children awakening, hearing the first of his babies behind him as he crossed the yard, crying even as she awoke, as if betrayed once more by reality. He didn't return until dusk, slipping in by the kitchen door to consume alone the enormous plateful of food left for him in the oven and tip-toeing upstairs to bed, where he waited, smoking his pipe, for grandmother to join him, and he would lose himself, murmuring with gratitude, in the welcoming expanse of her generous body.

Convinced for no good reason that their next child would be a son, grandfather wasn't worried when a year went by, and then a second, without grandmother becoming pregnant with her usual punctuality. In fact he took it as a good sign, proof that the cycle of regular female babies was about to be broken. He was discovering, meanwhile, a vocation for farming he'd never imagined he possessed. His reluctance to traipse home at the end of the day, even when darkness fell, became in part because there was always another job he wanted to do; ideas for improving the farm came to him as he immersed himself in its rhythms and laws and possibilities. 'Us only needs to buy they two bumpy fields over back, what Father Howard never uses, and us could keep back another twenty ewes next year,' he told grandmother as he pressed his head against her body. 'And there's a new cow I sin down Newton market, from up Scotland. Tough-lookin' thing 'tis, wide horns and long 'air. Reckon us could try a couple or three of they.'

He also surprised himself, even more, by the pleasure he began to take from the company of his daughters, limited as it was to Sundays, the day of rest. He watched his mother, his two sisters, his wife and their five daughters process across the yard in their best dresses, turn left along the lane, disappear behind the farm buildings, reappear beyond and turn right into the footpath up to the church. He read his Sunday newspaper while they were singing and praying to a God he himself found less believable every week, as the dictators spread their malign influence across Europe – a God, moreover, who'd inflicted upon each of his daughters in turn the needless agony of teething – smoking his pipe as he read the football reports and the political columns, and stirring himself to baste the joint slowly crackling in the oven.

When they returned, the women set to preparing dinner, and grandfather put on his bowler hat and led his daughters on a weekly constitutional around the village. Other men, equally uncomfortable in starched shirts and ill-fitting suits, most of whom, though, had accompanied their wives to church, were also strolling along the lanes. They would meet and cluster in small groups, and converse with each other about the pesky caterpillars chewing holes in their cabbages or the cut-throat traders who were banding together to keep down the price of mutton. And they would congratulate grandfather on his brood of little girls, making banal jokes about the troubles in store for the father of so many daughters.

That stroll around the village of a Sunday morning became grandfather's favourite moment of the week. It was the only time in his life that he overcame his shyness, raised above it by the pride he felt being out in public with his daughters; he greeted familiar faces over their garden gates and chatted with those he hardly knew without blushing, while tiny fingers insinuated themselves into his own callused hands and tugged at his trousers.

In the afternoon they followed him to his workbench in one of the sheds across the yard, where he made wooden toys for each of them in strict rotation: a car in the shape of a Bugatti for aunt Dorothy, the eldest; a doll's house for aunt Marjorie; a pram for her doll for aunt Susan. As their characters emerged distinctly from each other he was amazed at how different members of the same family could be from each other, more like animals than human beings, because he'd never been so close to other people. And he wondered why on earth he'd ever wanted a son.

The years passed. War raged across the Channel, while in this country whole cities were reduced to rubble by the Blitz, but it only impinged once upon the Valley, when a Heinkel appeared out of nowhere and unloaded its bombs on the granite works, doing a month's worth of blasting in an instant and killing three people. Grandmother was one of the few witnesses to that incident: her two eldest daughters had gone to play with some friends in the quarry pool, and she went to the beech tree to check up on them. She'd just taken the telescope from its place in the sawn-off branch when she heard the whine of an aeroplane's engine, but she didn't think anything of it because there was an airfield in Exeter and planes going to and coming from the west often passed overhead. It came into view, flying low through the Valley, at the same height as where she stood, and she made to wave to the pilot. She already had her arm raised when she saw, with disbelief, the markings of the enemy, and as the plane passed before her she stood, frozen, with her hand outstretched, and she thought she saw the pilot smile.

Some of the kids heard her scream, but only faintly; it's hard to make out what someone's saying, said aunt Marjorie, when you're seeing how long you can hold your breath underwater. Those that did looked up to see their large and ungainly mother scrambling down the slippery bed of the stream. Half-way down she stopped and waved her arms about, as if she'd gone loopy and was playing charades at a distance, pretending to be pushing someone away from her. Then she started shouting again and this time they could make out what she was saying: 'Run! Hide!' but that was all they heard, because her voice was drowned by the harsh whine of the aeroplane as it returned along the Valley, even lower than before. They stood still in the water at the edge of the pool as the plane bore down upon them, while grandmother up the bank was gesticulating wildly and yelling, but without making a sound, until she stopped, knowing it was too late now, forced to watch, helplessly, as the children stood naked in the water up to their thighs, and the pilot grinned.

And flew above them.

They all turned and watched him continue the few hundred yards till he was above the granite works, they saw the cluster of tiny bombs like sheep's pellets drop, they saw the earth ripped apart, and they felt dust raining down upon them, and across the surface of the quarry pool.

Few men from the village went off to fight; of those who did two died from their wounds the year after they came home, which is why our memorial commemorates those who gave their lives in the war of 1939–1946, according to the pattern set at the end of the Great War of 1914–1919.

There was never any question of grandfather going, the only man in the family, with nine dependants on top of his farmer's exemption. He just worked harder than ever, though never on a Sunday.

While grandfather indulged his daughters, it was grandmother who brought them up. Her mother-in-law passed away soon after the granite works was bombed, and grandmother plundered her wardrobe to make clothes for the girls, while instead of throwing potato peelings into the pigs' trough she made soup out of them, although in truth that was less out of necessity than a gesture of solidarity with women in the cities, who were the ones that really suffered.

It was one summer soon after the war that electricity came to the village. A row of pylons advanced along an avenue cut through Haldon Forest: two were planted, one at either end, in the Westcotts' water-meadow, and one day when it rained, shortly after the supply was connected, grandmother came across their cows dancing in the meadow that ran down to the stream.

Grandmother had a photograph of herself at that time, taken by the new Rector, standing behind the cake stall at the church fête. When I was little I confused the photograph with her description of the distorting mirrors on the pier on her one and only trip to Teignmouth, because I only knew grandmother as a bony old woman, her body angular and uninviting, except for her enormous hands, as big as grandfather's and almost as tough, the hands of a hard-working country woman.

Back then during the electric summer, though, when grandfather dismantled the generator and left it behind the house to rust, grandmother was large enough for all her daughters, none of them so small any more, to squeeze against her on the sofa when she read them a story. She was glad her childbearing days were over. She took no notice of the heaviness in her legs or her fluctuating appetite, and when it occurred to her that her period had not come on time, in fact was really, now she thought about it, long overdue, she accepted without regret the arrival of middle age.

But when, some weeks later, she suffered a particularly persistent attack of hiccups that arose not from her lungs but from somewhere beneath them she realized, suddenly, that it was not she who had them but someone else inside her.

She couldn't believe it. She was forty years old, her eldest daughter was sixteen and old enough to bear children herself, and besides, she'd not taken any precautions since the birth of their fifth girl, when they were still trying to have a son. Grandfather had gradually overcome his suspicion that a woman's cycle was less regular than those of the animals he husbanded, that she only made love during what only she knew to be her infertile days. They'd come to accept that her body had decided of its own accord that it had had enough of its most punishing duties, and would need no assistance to prevent them being imposed again.

Perhaps, she thought, it was an illusion created by electricity, the current was interfering with her insides, and she told herself that the little bumps and thuds that echoed from deep inside her ample body were no more than a mild case of indigestion. That night, though, when she went to join grandfather waiting patiently for her in their wide bed, and lay there with his head against her, stroking his hair, she confessed to herself that that itself was an illusion. She took grandfather's hand in hers and pressed it into the fleshy folds of her belly, to where she felt the baby kicking.

He was startled. 'What the 'eck's is goin' on in there?' he asked her, and she told him.

To her surprise he was immediately glad. 'Why not? Us 'ave got five daughters, and each one of them's my favourite. I don't mind a sixth.'

At that welcome response from her husband, grandmother let out a cry. He raised himself up on his elbow. 'Don't worry, lover,' he assured her, ''tidn't that many; one more won't make no difference.'

She gripped his arm. ''Tis comin'.'

'When?'

'Now!' she gasped, as she felt her abdomen squeeze itself and then let go, and her breath desert her.

'But no one knows,' he exclaimed, 'not Granny Sims nor no one. Us idn't ready.'

'*She*'s ready,' grandmother muttered, as sweat broke out on her forehead. 'Get me some 'ot water and towels.'

Grandfather ran downstairs, and as he gathered up things in the kitchen he reflected that at least the birth would be an easy one, like all the others.

When he returned upstairs she was breathing deeply, her eyes closed, the first spasms receding. He put the bowl and jug on the floor beside her, and said: 'I'll go drag out Granny Sims.'

'No,' she told him. 'Stay with me.' She opened her eyes, and he saw something he'd never seen in them before. 'I'm afraid, father.'

He had to swallow before he could speak. 'Don't be silly, lover, what's there to be afeared of? You knows each one's easier than the last. And the first was easy enough.'

She closed her eyes, as if the better to regulate her breathing, the old patterns Granny Sims had taught her long before slowly coming back to her, and then she opened them again.

'I know,' she said, ''tis silly. But don't leave me.' And she felt the contractions coming back again, as if rising through water in a cavern inside her; she squeezed her eyes shut, and when they broke on the surface she screamed through clenched teeth.

Time refused to pass: when you're happy it slips through your fingers, the bastard, but with pain it stops still. Cranks up on a ratchet and stops. If she only let go of my hand time would start up again, and this would all be soon over, grandfather thought, as her mounting pain transmitted itself to him through his numb fingers. She'd soon lost the last remnants of her self-control, and her every scream sent a cold shiver through his innards. At one point he heard, as she took a deep breath between screams, a quiet whimpering behind him, and he turned round to see his five daughters standing pressed against each other in the doorway, all of them petrified by the sight, and even more the sound, of their mother being tortured to death.

He pulled his hand from hers, and shooed them like geese along the corridor to the room his sisters still shared at the far end. He jerked the door open, flicked on the light, and without a word closed the door behind him and rushed back to the bedroom.

'What's happening?' she cried. 'What's the matter?'

'You're ready all right, lover, you's all ready. I reckon I can see 'er feet.'

'What do you mean, her feet?' she gasped.

'Keep pushin', lover. Don't stop.'

She no longer had any control over her breathing, inhaling and exhaling in sharp little breaths. 'I can't no more.' she whispered.

'One more time,' he urged her, 'one more time, woman.'

The waves of pain came back at her, but they didn't reach the surface any more. Instead of withstanding their force, of holding on for dear life as they grabbed and then tossed her without mercy, now she had to help them, to summon up willpower she no longer possessed and strength that had dissolved from the muscles of her body in order to urge her diaphragm downwards and push the child out of her uterus.

But that child, having gestated so unobtrusively in a dark corner of her womb, was reluctant to make its entry into the world. Every time she pushed, with all the dissipating energy she had left, so she felt it holding back inside her, matching its own minute strength against hers. And it was winning. She felt the latest wave of contractions once more recede and lay back on her pillow, exhausted, panting weakly.

If there was one thing above all on which grandfather had come to pride himself as a farmer, it was in the skill he would one day pass on to Tom, as a midwife of animals: he'd already helped more tardy cows than he could remember deliver their offspring, reaching into their slippery wombs to reposition an awkward calf and sometimes, in emergencies, roping their forelegs to a hook in the barn in order to enlist the aid of gravity. Sheep, too, whose lambs crossed their limbs inside their mothers, had no safer hands to help them in the whole of the parish. He accepted a stillborn calf or lamb not as a regular, inevitable occurrence but as a personal indictment of his methods, brooding over it for days, and he'd only ever lost one ewe.

He knew more about birth than anything else that came later in life. But as grandmother, her face drawn and ashen, lay back against the pillows, her breathing faint, he felt all his knowledge disintegrate and his authority fall apart, because he realized that the woman who'd made his life worthwhile was dying before his very eyes.

'Hold on, lover,' he told her, trying to suppress the panic that had erupted in his guts, 'I'm goin' to get 'elp.'

He took the stairs four at a time and ran outside. The light shocked him: the world had woken up as usual, with no regard for the terrible event being enacted during that night; the cockerel was strutting in his awkward, imperious manner amongst the brood of hens pecking in the yard, in the field sloping upwards from the lane dew glistened, and the songs of invisible birds greeted the dawn.

Grandfather ran across the yard and looked left and right along the lane. He couldn't think straight, his mind flustered beyond the power of reason. The lane was empty, and he could hear no sound of human presence in the deserted landscape. His blood pulsed through his veins and his brain was a froth of indecision. His knees were trembling: an irresistible urge to sink to the ground, weeping, came over him, and he was on the verge of succumbing to it when there was a bark beside him. It was his sheepdog, Tinker, who'd followed him out of the yard. Her ears were pricked up, and she was peering along the lane into the village. Grandfather followed her gaze, and saw an unmistakable silhouette come into view down Broad Lane.

*

Douglas Westcott was not yet fifteen years old, but he was already fully grown, with a hesitant beard black as his curly hair, built like a bull, and without any question the strongest man in the village.

His father, like most farmers, had a secondary trade, necessary in the interdependent world of the village: he was the slaughterer. Although Douglas's older brother, George, was the one who as a matter of course was expected to learn those skills from their father, it was Douglas who'd displayed a vocation. He used to follow his father silently around the farm and accompany him to other people's places, standing in his father's shadow with unnoticed curiosity so that he could acquire the skills of a slaughterer without having to have them explained. By the age of ten he could wring a chicken's neck with two fingers of one hand, and on his fourteenth birthday, the day he left school, when his mother gave him a statuette of Atlas holding the world on his shoulders, his father presented him with his own set of surgical instruments for the clinical despatch of animals' lives, and began to pass on his minor, domestic contracts.

Now he was returning from the stationmaster's house down in the Valley, having culled their mongrel's unwanted litter of puppies before dawn, so as not to upset the children, and he was making his way home through the village, glad that no one would be up at that hour to invade his privacy, when he saw farmer Freemantle running towards him in his pyjamas.

Grandfather grabbed Douglas's arm.

'Come with me, bay,' he cried, 'you's got to 'elp me,' and despite his size Douglas felt himself being dragged, so fast it was only their momentum that kept him from stumbling, by a madman three times his age and half his size.

As soon as they came bursting through the bedroom door Douglas realized what he'd been brought into: grandmother lay naked on the bed, her enormous belly gently rising and falling with her shallow breaths.

''Twill be all right, lover, we's got help,' grandfather spluttered, and she opened her eyes: all trace of fear had vanished from them, and although they were deeply bruised by pain and exhaustion it didn't, somehow, appear so. Rather, it was an expression of serenity she wore, of utter peace. She smiled, and then she closed her eyes again.

Grandfather turned to Douglas: ''Er child's killin' 'er,' he said, in a low, gritty voice. 'I don't care about the baby, but save my wife, bay. Please, save 'er.'

Douglas had never seen any woman naked before, much less one in this condition, beyond help. He was stricken with terror; his head shook itself.

'C-can't do nothin', Mister Freemantle,' he stammered.

'What do you mean, bay, you can't do nothin'?' Grandfather's eyes blazed. 'You save my woman's life, bay. Save 'er life, or I'm tellin' you I'll kill you myself.'

Douglas was still an overgrown child, but he knew enough to discern that the threat was sincere. He also knew that it was already too late.

'Get some spirit, then, and something to gag 'er,' he decided. 'And find a needle and thread.'

As grandfather rushed downstairs Douglas opened his bag and picked his finest blade, a thin scalpel, and he sharpened it with a spot of oil on his stone, with a few swift strokes, until knowing the sharpness of its razor's edge made him shudder. He approached the bed, and looked down on grandmother, who was gradually slipping into the deep sea of endless sleep, no longer conscious but with a sweet smile on her face because she was dreaming that she could swim like a seal underwater. She was lolling and rolling near the floor of a vast ocean, and when she looked up she perceived the sun shining through the water.

Douglas put his hand on her belly, and as he did so he realized that he knew, as if by magic, the complex architecture that lay beneath: he knew what he should find as his scalpel sliced through epidermis and corium, blood would spill from minute veins and arteries as the blade sliced through subcutaneous fat, into her endometrium, and beyond, into the womb itself, where, enveloped in a livid mass of placenta and amniotic fluid, he'd find the child, no doubt twisted around like calves sometimes are; perhaps strangling itself with its umbilical cord; perhaps already dead. He knew, as if the information were feeding itself through his fingers, how her bladder and kidneys would have been squashed into corners to accommodate the foetus, and how the miles of tubing that make up a person's innards would have shaped themselves discreetly around the swollen uterus. He knew these things that he never imagined he knew because his vocation, that of a slaughterer, required the most searching understanding of anatomy. At this moment, though, he felt more like an undertaker.

As soon as grandfather came back into the room with a steaming bowl in his hands, Douglas wiped the knife with spirit and said simply: 'All right.'

Grandfather stooped to his wife's side, ready with the gag and brandy, and watched with horror as Douglas's scalpel blade entered the surface of her skin, just below her rib cage, as if it were no more solid than water, disappearing right up to its handle, and then sliced down her belly as Douglas pulled it towards him.

Grandfather prayed to the God he despised that she would not wake up, scrutinizing her face now. For a moment he even regretted doing this: it was virtually a desecration of her body, and he should have let her die in peace. Then her face suddenly twisted as the pain of the knife communicated itself, and he saw for the first time how old she was. Her eyes remained closed, but tears dampened her face. His heart was pounding. He realized they were his tears, falling upon her. Her face unclenched itself as she again lost consciousness, and he felt engulfed in a wave of relief and of sorrow. Douglas's voice brought him back to the physical reality before him.

'What you say, bay?'

Douglas had been transformed in those brief moments in which he had prepared himself for this task, and when he opened her up it was with the detachment and authority of a surgeon. But what he found there reduced him once more to what he really was, a terrified fourteen-year-old boy. His bloody hands were shaking.

''Er's all t-t-tangled up inside,' he stuttered.

Grandfather pushed him out of the way, and plunged his hands into the hot stew of his wife's insides. The feel of her viscera seemed somehow familiar. He felt around and his fingers discovered the shape of another, tiny body, and he grasped it as gently as he could, and pulled it upwards, through the jumbled flesh and free, into the open air, where he held it by its feet.

'Cut the cord, bay!' he ordered.

Douglas obeyed him, nicking the umbilical cord with his scalpel, and with his thick and trembling fingers he tied a delicate knot in an instant, at the navel of the child who hung limply from grandfather's hand. Then grandfather drew back his free hand and slapped the child's back: it came to life with a pathetically weak but nevertheless imposing bawl. Cradling it in his arms he rushed once more along the corridor to his sisters' room, and pushed the door open: his two sisters and five daughters were huddled on one bed, cowering together, with the patience of fear. He handed the child to the first pair of hands that reached towards him, turned, and rushed back.

'Run to the phone box, Douglas. 999. Get the doctor. Get the 'ole fuckin' hospital.'

Grandfather felt for grandmother's pulse. As soon as he found it he didn't wait to gauge its strength but set to cleaning her up. He couldn't work out where all the blood had come from, and still came. He pulled the placenta out of her belly and threw it into a corner. Then he threaded a needle for the first time in his life, with black cotton, and started to sew together the loose folds of her skin with small, precise stitches, in rapt concentration, making as perfect a job as he possibly could, not because he imagined that in itself it was important but because he thought that as long as he was doing so she would stay alive, and he wanted to keep sewing until the ambulance came. He kept his mind concentrated by repeating under his breath, over and over like a prayer: 'Hang on, lover. Hang on.'

He bit the cotton, as he'd seen her do a hundred times, and was tying the ends of the last stitch when the ambulance arrived. Lost in his labour of love, he was the only person in the whole village who didn't hear the siren, the first time one had come into our part of the world. A small crowd had already gathered in the lane by the time they whisked her away, with grandfather still beside her, holding her hand as tightly as she'd earlier held his.

They kept her in the Royal Devon and Exeter Hospital for three weeks, and gave her two blood transfusions, as well as undoing and rethreading the stitches of her Caesarean wound, before allowing her home to take over the rearing of the child who'd been wet-nursed, meanwhile, by one of Granny Sims' granddaughters. They brought the baby to her when she limped, sorely, through the front door, and the first thing she did was to remove its clothes and nappy on the kitchen table, because she refused to believe what they'd told her until she saw it with her own eyes.

'All right,' she said in a hoarse voice, 'so you wasn't being funny. I'll say this though: if that's what 'tis like giving birth to a bay, I'm glad we had all girls before.'

And that's how Daddy came, unwillingly, into this world, and might be why, despite the fact that he almost killed her, he was the favourite of all her children, such is the logic of love.

CHAPTER TWENTY

Flight

The mosquitoes that followed the piano tuner in his travels weren't the only animals who lost their sense of direction in that incandescent heat and ended up in the Valley. When the reservoirs up behind Christow dried up, strange species of fish, the like of which had never been caught by the lugubrious fishermen who came out from Exeter on Sundays, were beached on the black silt: flat, rhomboidal fish so much like children's drawings even the warden doubted whether they had ever really been alive, as well as, so it was said, the still squirming freshwater eels of the Fens.

Back on our side of the Valley at the bottomless quarry pool the widowman heron was joined for one brief visit by a crane that glided over the pine woods to land like a cotton sheet. When I mentioned it to grandmother she told me about the young 14th Viscount, Johnathan's grandfather, who in the inter-war years designed and constructed in the estate stables a prototype aeroplane. The entire population of the village gathered around the beech tree to watch him fly from the ridge above the quarry pool. They listened in disbelief as he explained the direction of his flight and pointed down the Valley towards Christow, to a field where champagne was on ice. Excitement mounted as he put on his goggles and climbed into the cockpit, and when his valet spun the propeller they held their breath, keeping it in as the plane launched from the ridge and plummeted, spinning, into the quarry pool. They held their breath until it burst out of them, and they stayed watching the surface of the pool until it had fully recomposed its placid surface. They waited even longer, too, but even so half of them were half-way home, muttering in agreement about the stupidity of the young and wiping their eyes, when back at the pool the 14th Viscount's leather helmet bobbed up to the surface and his mouth gasped for air. For the rest of his short life people would ask him what it was like down there, and he told everybody the same thing, that below the surface it was dark, too dark to see, he fell and fell and the water grew colder as he struggled to climb out of the cockpit; the only sense of any use to him was touch, except that everything felt unreal. Still he fell, and just as he thought he was losing consciousness he saw a bright light far below. Just then he broke free from the cockpit, and swam up towards the surface. He couldn't rise fast enough through the black water, and was tormented by the possibility that he was going in the wrong direction. His lungs were two ravens clawing their way out of his rib cage while his head was nodding off to sleep, when suddenly he woke up at the surface of the quarry pool.

A few years later, in the middle of a war, the German plane appeared in the Valley. The pilot hadn't lost his way: the granite works down by Teign Village was secretly producing cement for concrete bunkers and buildings. There were anti-aircraft guns and a barrage balloon at the end of the Valley, by Chudleigh, but it was a quiet Saturday in June and the officers had gone to the races at Newton Abbot. The men on duty, who for months had been half-cursing, half-blessing their luck at being stationed far from the action in this tucked-away corner of the world, gaped at the plane with enemy markings that appeared out of the blue sky. They watched it approach and knew its target, and they had it in their sights: but no one dared to open fire without the order from one of their superiors. The plane came dipping and weaving, to evade the inevitable flak, but when it didn't materialize the plane soared up and overshot the quarry, as if the pilot was so surprised he forgot to attack it.

Grandmother was one of those who saw it reappear and, as if in malicious imitation of the 14th Viscount's intentions, the pilot dipped his wings as he skimmed through the Valley, before emptying the contents of his bomb carriage directly above the granite works.

Some years after that grandfather took a one-off trip with Joseph Howard to Hereford market, to see what sorts of bulls other farmers were buying. (It was on that trip that he saw, in their orchards, bottles tied to pear trees, an idea he stole for the apple liqueur we drank at Christmas.) On the way back they drove underneath a crop-spraying aeroplane as it crossed over the road, and when they got home the paint on grandfather's van was all blistered. He began to wonder what the chemicals must be doing to his own soil, but the promises and guarantees of the fertilizer salesmen helped him put it to the back of his mind until the village streams, just before they dried up in that hottest of summers, began to reflect weird, unnatural colours that no one – except grandfather – could quite take in because they didn't have words to describe them.

"Er Dad don't know 'er, 'er Dad don't know 'er.' The chant appeared in my head, an echo from the past coming up behind me, whenever I thought that the summer and the teachers' strike would end and I'd have to start Comprehensive. In the playground at Chudleigh they'd taunt me at break when they were bored, a ring of grinning faces surrounding me. "Er Dad don't know 'er, 'er Dad don't know 'er.'
    I tried to stand aloof and regard the wheeling bodies with a look of such scorn that they felt ashamed, and the hands would break. Sometimes anger blew through me like a note through a whistle and I'd thump one of them: then either the game would halt for a second, allowing me to push through the ring and stalk off, or else I'd be thrown the relief of combat, the taunting forgotten for a more exciting spectacle, and I'd use all the tricks my brothers had taught me. But there were other times when the baiting pierced all my resistance, and I'd feel it discharge into a rush of tears. Then there'd be contrition and sympathy that I resented as much as when I saw it implicit in the greeting of some adult in the village.

The one person I wanted to talk about it with was Johnathan, but it was only a week since we'd burned down the barn and we were both too scared to even look at each other, let alone speak, down at the Valley road. The others all knew what we'd done, of course, and if they saw us getting friendly again word was sure to get back to our parents. And I suppose because I couldn't talk to him, I wanted to all the more.

All through the summer, when the thought of school intruded, I prayed that the ridicule wouldn't follow me to Newton. By this time it was a month into the term and although the school had now apparently opened part-time, those of us out in the villages still weren't being admitted. It allowed me to hope that once the world began again my simple Daddy would have been forgotten along with other trivial details from the burned up past.

But what made me angry with myself was that it was the baiting I feared, the way it isolated me, and not its substance. It wasn't so bad having such a father. He had inherited his mother's generous and open nature, neither of which had been entirely lost. He'd never, so far as I could recall, scolded me, much less given me a beating. I knew well enough the sullen solitude of my friends' fathers, who came in from the fields at dusk, bringing their own sweat and that of animals into the living-room, where they sat back silently smoking, before wearily treading upstairs to take shelter in the refuge of their wives. I had a companion instead: was that so bad?

My own brother, Tom, would one day be one of those fathers, with nothing to say at mealtimes and no ideas for improvements to the farm, which he left to Ian, cruising on habit and instinct, only fired with an implacable will in pursuit of the woman he'd chosen. In the days following the dance, while other men worked on various schemes to bring water to the village, all as hare-brained as Corporal Alcock's plan to use capillary osmosis to draw the black water up from the quarry pool, Tom ignored them and spent his time sitting on my window-sill, scrutinizing the Simmons' house on the slope below the church. Since there was no school, Susanna's parents made her stay in and study, keeping school hours. Consulting his watch every few seconds, Tom would go to meet her at breaktimes and dinnertime, and they strolled around the village hand in hand. At the end of her imitation school day they'd disappear together, returning as the sun went down, faces triangular in the dusk. It got so I couldn't go to bed myself until I'd seen their goodnights taken care of, stepping into the shadow at her front door, then Susanna opening it and being swallowed up by the light inside.

Inside his soft cherub's body, Tom was imbued with the wiry farmers' strength of our family, that had enabled my brothers and cousins to make up half the village tug-of-war team that wiped the floor with the Devon and Cornwall Constabulary in their bulging blue track suits at the church fête the year before. He could do the physical work of three men, grandfather said, and at the busy times of the year went with four hours' sleep a night and was still the first one up to put the kettle on and set the day's first pot of tea brewing. But love wore him out: he nodded off on my window-sill, fell asleep in front of the television, yawned uncontrollably in the kitchen, and mother had to shake him awake with a mug of tea in bed in the mornings. He lost his appetite too, refusing meals, pushing his plate away with a look of disdain as if to make clear that so base an activity as eating was beneath him. He was under the illusion that love alone was sufficient, that their long-drawn-out kisses satisfied his hunger, although in the middle of the night he floated downstairs like a sleep-walker to raid the larder, consuming half loaves of bread, joints of meat and two pints of milk at a time, as he had as an adolescent. His eyes became bruised by fatigue, but inside brown rings the pupils shone like pebbles under water, and all they saw was Susanna Simmons, or portents of her. Love briefly overcame my brother's sullen reticence. He appreciated for the first time the loyal devotion of the sheepdogs, almost as steadfast as his own eternal offering of himself to her. He watched as no naturalist had ever done the sand martins as they peppered the sides of the sand quarry at the granite works with their transitory nests, because they also, for no obvious reason, reminded him of her, her unnatural perfection that made his heart flutter whenever he looked at her strong shoulders, her delicate wrists, or beheld the miraculous articulation of her joints. The hallucinatory breeze he thought he saw on Monday afternoon ripple through a field of late corn reminded him of Susanna down to the last detail; and he even listened with Daddy to the morning record and was amazed to discover that other men had known exactly how he felt.

Tom was not among the men who met round our kitchen table that Tuesday morning to scrutinize the minutely detailed plans that Ian had abandoned his chess to stay up all night working on. Even Daddy's brothers-in-law, whom we usually only saw on Sundays, came to help in the search for the water which, according to Granny Sims, the hippies had come with the express intention of stealing.

Uncle Sidney with his woman's voice was the most optimistic. 'There's water in the rocks if we could tap it. Us is mostly water ourselves, that's why we're such good conductors of electricity; 'tis everywhere, even now.'

Uncle Bill was adamant about the best source of water: ''Tis pourin' non-stop down that waterfall over the Valley. While our fields is crackin' up and the waterboard's puttin' standpipes in the village, there's water wastin' away.'

'How's us gonna get it over yere?' asked Mike Howard.

'Well, as everybody knows, over the length of its path from Houndtor it rises twenty feet, 'tis a proven fact. I can't see no reason why it shouldn't rise some more.'

'Not that much,' said Ian, 'it's not possible. Besides, 'tidn't our water.'

They crunched mother's biscuits. I looked down on them from the top of the fridge.

'I know!' uncle Sidney announced eagerly. 'Since it idn't ours us could steal it outright. At night. Form a chain with buckets. Men, women and children.'

They were all so struck with this idea that they scraped their chairs back and left then and there to go to the telescope and check the practicalities. On the way they met Tom, who'd gone off to gaze at the dawn mist clinging to the surface of the quarry pool like smoke on a mirror. His cousin Andrew, Sidney and Shirley's youngest son, sarcastically asked whether Tom would care to favour them with his opinion of their scheme.

'Who needs water?' he replied. 'Us can drink cider and wash in wine. They makes it in enormous lakes in Europe.'

CHAPTER TWENTY-ONE

Liquid

There were nights when something twisted inside me, some-times in my tummy but more often in my mind, and sprung me out of sleep like a fish from water. It twisted me into a confusion that was inseparable from pain. I curled up as tight as I could to contain it, and I could hear myself whimpering. I wanted to go and slide under the sheets and snuggle up beside Daddy, but I knew mother would sense me there. She slept with a frown on her face, as if expecting the worst even in her dreams. She'd say: 'No, you's too old for that sort of silliness, what's wrong with you, girl?', and she'd give me a glass of milk of magnesia and tuck me up back in my own bed.

Light seeped out from under Ian's door. I'd find him by his short-wave radio, like a castaway on the island of his insomnia, listening to the sounds of the sea in a pool of light spread by the desk-lamp. He twiddled the dials of the radio distractedly, as if only out of some obscure obligation keeping an ear open for people's voices from across the night, when really he preferred the company of the oceanic lament of inter-ference.

At such times, creeping noiselessly into his room, I would see Ian unguarded, unaware of himself, adrift, curling his hair with his finger as he scrutinized his chessboard, filled in balance sheets or browsed through one of Pamela's glossy magazines. He held his cigarette between his middle fingers so that it wouldn't drop if he fell asleep, would instead burn his fingers and wake him rather than set the room alight, a nightwatchman's habit he'd learned from the quarrymen. He looked like a stranger then: his features were much sharper than I imagined them to be, his eyes were closer together, his lips thinner, his nose narrow, his cheekbones and jawline sharp as a ferret's. Amongst people his smile, his speech, his gestures, just the fact of self-consciousness opened up and rounded his face. If I could have taken a photograph as I saw him then I wonder whether people would have recognized him.

As soon as he realized I was there he became himself again. 'Can't sleep, maid? You got those pains again, little lamb?' I didn't say anything, I just climbed onto his bed and succumbed to the urge, provoked by his sympathy, to start crying, and Ian pushed his chair back, saying: 'You wants me to make you feel better? I'll try.' He shook his head. 'What girls has to go through at your age. 'Tidn't right. Almost as bad as bays.' He picked up a jar of oil that he kept by the bed. 'Take yer 'jamas off, then, and lie on your front.'

His fingers travelled across my skin and kneaded it like dough; he pushed and squeezed according to the bone structure beneath: his fingers seemed to know of their own accord the underlying secrets of my anatomy, and they persuaded the pain and unhappiness out of my body. Gradually it let go its grip and let me melt back into sleep, while his radio continued to transmit the sound of the sea to my brother's lonely room.

Tom was the better looking of my brothers. But before Susanna kissed him he couldn't look at a girl without blushing. As a boy he'd developed the ability, learned from hen pheasants on shooting expeditions with grandfather, to blend into the background: at school he made himself invisible behind his desk. He could still recall vividly, viscerally, an occasion when he, alone in the class, knew the answer to a teacher's question. He wanted to rise from his anonymity and he urged himself, heart hammering against his chest, breaking out in sweat, his face reddening and a vein on his forehead pulsing, as if it would burst, he urged himself to put up his hand. But it was beyond him, the teacher broke the silence saying: 'I give up on you all,' the chance of glory passed and he had failed. It was even worse with girls. Remote and forbidding, they existed in a different dimension, and he had no idea how to make contact.

The night of the barn dance when Susanna kissed him, her warm mouth vinegary from too much stolen cider, Tom's life turned inside out: he appeared at breakfast with his neck covered in red bites, smiling like an idiot, and he giggled at inappropriate moments. He began talking to people, filled with an overpowering urge to tell them about the miracle of love, not to boast but rather with the philanthropy of an inventor, because he was sure he'd discovered it for the first time. Their absorption with each other was mutual. At first they spent as much time at her house as ours, unaware, as they were of everything else, of her father's disapproval: he had other ideas for his daughters than getting caught up with some farmer's boy, and knew that the one danger of moving his family into the village was of having those plans tampered with when they were still so young. He wanted to forbid her from seeing him, except that such parental dictatorship went against his principles.

They had a golden labrador who growled whenever Tom touched Susanna, and sometimes even when he only imagined doing so. Once, forgetting he was in someone else's house, Tom grabbed the dog by the scruff of its neck and led it outside, where dogs were supposed to live. That was too much for Susanna's father, who was horrified by such uncivilized behaviour: he brought the dog back inside and asked Tom to leave instead.

Tom didn't mind, and neither did Susanna. They assumed that everyone else was as happy as they were, since everyone looked happy to them. They could only stand being apart from each other because each parting was as delicious as coming together again, and they mapped out the routes of their days precisely, so that Tom could sound his tractor horn on his way to the sheep while Susanna was half-way through a French essay, and she in turn would wave to him from her horse at 2.48 p.m. as he tightened the electric fencing down in the meadows. They were intoxicated by each other. He told her the reason they got on so well was that she carried on her jeans her horse's sweat while he for his part could never entirely shake off the sharp scent of pigs, and as everyone knows horses and pigs are the two most compatible species of animal, able to be left to pasture together without fear of a quarrel. It was the first joke he'd ever been known to make.

Susanna was learning to play the trombone. After she'd said goodnight to Tom she didn't want to lose the warm and curious feeling that enveloped her, so she would practise on her trombone late at night. Her family complained that she was keeping them awake, but they couldn't force her to go to bed because they'd decided that when she reached the age of fourteen they'd treat her like an adult. So her mother went to a music shop in Exeter and bought a device for muffling the instrument. From then on Susanna played her trombone muted, and her family were able to sleep again, except that the music rose through the floorboards and infiltrated their dreams, saddening them as they slept.

In the course of his meticulous preparations for Saturday nights, Ian had never noticed Tom. It was as if he simply disappeared from view, melting into the furniture. It was just part of the process by which the whole world altered its appearance, as Ian unconsciously honed his instincts for the chase. His nostrils became sensitive to the trail of perfume, his ears attuned themselves to the rustle of a dress and to certain nuances of a woman's voice, his thick farmer's fingers took on the sensitivity of a masseur's, and his sight altered so blatantly that men fell as if out of focus to the periphery of his vision, as he prepared himself for his once a week night of a lonely hunter. Ian had never bothered himself with his younger brother's sentimental education, other than to pass on the solitary word of advice that he had received from Daddy, that when you leave a girl you should make her believe that she's left you. He assumed, if he ever thought about it at all, that a man has to find these things out for himself, as he had, or not learn them at all.

Now, though, Ian began to notice Tom, and he felt some brotherly pity as he saw him lose his grip, as he watched him falling into the abyss of love. He wondered how anyone could be so stupid, could so deceive themselves, and wanted to point out certain things so obvious it seemed impossible Tom had not learned them, if only from Ian's own example: that the weekend's the time for it, bay, the weekdays is for working; that women is what makes life worth living, but your life is your own and no one else's; that when you gets a woman started you better take her all the way, that's all, take her half-way there and drop her off and she'll hate yer guts, you can do a hundred different things, just make her happy, touch every part of her except her heart; that if you stays the night you might never leave, bay, always make sure there's an unlocked door; that you can make them cry 'cos they likes that sometimes, but if you ever hurts a woman then don't come to me for help, you deserves what you gets, you fatherless bastard.

Ian couldn't help himself from thinking these things as he saw his silent brother transformed before his eyes, an idiot grin creasing his fleshy jowls and his eyes ringed by the fatigue of an activity the fool had confused with love. He found he had to remind Tom how to perform simple tasks Tom knew better than he did: he'd put the wrong tools in the van, take straw instead of hay over to the sheep, and couple the plough to the tractor when what they needed was the binder to reap the spindly, useless corn of that summer's meagre harvest. When they went to check the pigs in the top field Tom electrocuted himself on the wire and, instead of kicking the nearest sow as he would normally have done, only giggled. And at odd moments of the day he would suddenly say: 'You carry on, Ian, I'll be back in a couple or three minutes.' At first Ian thought he'd got the collywobbles from drinking too much tap water and disappeared to relieve himself, but he soon discovered that Tom was running off to keep his fleeting rendezvous with Susanna in the midst of her studies.

In the evenings Ian had always been the one to nag Tom and grandfather to finish work and get back for tea, and he often ended up coming home alone and asking mother to put theirs in the oven, because Tom found it as painful as grandfather did to stop work before dusk had smudged the outlines of things and left them with no alternative but to return to people. Now, though, Tom would ask grandfather to check the time on his pocket watch from four o'clock onwards, and would admonish the others, saying: 'Us better get back, 'tidn't fair to keep mother waiting.'

Worst of all, though, Tom started talking. They'd always worked in silence, a silence learned from grandfather, speaking no more than was necessary for the accomplishment of each task: superfluous speech did not disturb the sounds of metal on wood, the rustle of dry grass manipulated by human hands, the tread of heavy boots echoing on the hard earth. In that silence the primeval language common to all farmers asserted itself over any more recently developed dialect, because it was one that animals understood, a vernacular of grunts, whoops, whistles and guttural commands, monosyllabic but possessed of infinite expressiveness through the variables of intonation, inflection and emphasis. When they spoke to each other during the day, outside the house, it was in a pidgin English, using ordinary words but tersely, isolated from each other in truncated sentences, using their farmers' primitive colloquial to give the meaning of what they were saying. It was a language of necessity, of only urgent communication above the roar of the tractor engine or across a field, so that when we joined them to help round up animals or stack the hay loft we were startled at the way they addressed each other, as if cursing, and we felt as if we'd just stepped into the aftermath of some almighty argument. In reality they each worked at a steady pace, with a steady heart, and had the respect for each other that came from everyday, mutual dependence.

Then suddenly Tom had broken ranks, the least likely to do so, lured by love from their unspoken agreement over the parsimony of language. He started chattering while they drank their first mug of tea by the stove, he carried on gibbering as they crossed the yard, he shouted over the noise of the tractor, and he drivelled on as they returned for breakfast. He spoke about anything and everything, garrulous as a two-year-old, as if Susanna had triggered off that phase of a child's development that he'd not gone through at the proper time. He commented on the weather, noting with apparent surprise that it was just the same as yesterday; he told them how he'd slept and what he'd dreamed; and he pointed out the various types of tree and flower they passed, as if none of them had seen such things before. 'Lookee there, grandfather, 'tis a hazel, innit?' he'd suggest. 'Well bugger me if that idn't a dandelion clock. Funny old things. Oi! See that? 'Twas a thrush. Right there in the 'edge. Got itself a nest in there I don't doubt. You can never tell with they old birds. Be a lot of ladybirds around, too. I don't know as I've ever seen so many's I 'ave today, like. You see 'em, Ian? Little things they is, in't they?'

Deprived of the sacrosanct silence in which to sip his first mug of sweet tea, grandfather never sloughed off the bad temper caused by having to wake up in the morning. After three days of Tom's loquacity grandfather caught Ian's arm as they left by the kitchen door, letting Tom carry on ahead, talking to himself.

'I idn't feeling too clever, bay. I think as I'll leave you to it today.'

'What's up, grandad?' Ian asked him. 'Illness in't never stopped you wanting to work.'

'Well, then, I'll tell 'ee, between you and me, like,' grand-father replied. 'I in't never 'eard a man so full of prattle. I can't stand it no more. I'll get on with some little jobs around the yard. E'll get over it, I don't doubt.'

Grandmother, in her throaty voice, whispered to me a secret, certain way to bring rain, sending me off to throw flour into the same spring that her mother-in-law had used to finally dispel the drought in 1911. Her directions were simple and precise and I followed them easily to a spring in a hidden corner of a field up behind Longbrook Farm. I threw the flour in and stirred up the water with a hazel-rod, and a mist arose. It was only a matter then of waiting for it to condense into a rain-bearing cloud.

I had faith in grandmother's pronouncements, even if no one else did. They'd first begun to take less notice of what she said the previous autumn, when she started to make surprise visits to her daughters, persuading grandfather to drive her on an itinerary dictated by the caprice of her dreams: she would dream that one of her offspring was ill or unhappy, pack her bags in the morning, and arrive unannounced on the doorstep in order to lend one or other of her daughters a hand for a few days, as she used to do when their children were small. They contrived at first to validate her intimations, out of the respect they had for her, saying: 'Yes, grandma, you're right, Andrew hasn't been feeling too clever; yes, grandma, it probably is the measles, even if he is twenty-seven now.' But instead of being a help she just got in the way and caused more trouble than she was worth, volunteering to prepare a meal but making a mess instead because she'd forgotten how long things took to cook and she couldn't read the recipe, so that half the ingredients were overdone and the rest were cold. In the end they lost their patience, and told grandfather not to bring her any more. When she asked him to he had to tell her a white lie, that the car had broken down again, and brought the telephone to her chair instead so that she could make sure her family were all right, and give them at least some verbal advice.

The truth was that she was losing substance, slipping into the background of the family, having occupied centre stage for fifty years. She spent most of the day in her armchair now, much of it asleep, hobbling ever more slowly through to the kitchen for meals. She paused in the doorways, holding on to the frames to check her balance and get her breath back. 'Come along, grandma,' said mother when she came up behind her, 'you're causing another bottleneck.'

I was all the more surprised, then, when I came home with Daddy on Tuesday afternoon and we found her inching her way across the yard. We ran over.

'What you doin', grandma?' I cried.

'I seen it, maid; 'tis yere,' she said.

'What is?'

'It's taking my spirit away, but I'm not ready.'

'Come on, grandma,' I said, 'us'll help you back inside.'

She gripped my arm with surprising force. 'No, maid. This is serious. I can see the thread pulling away. You can 'elp me or not, but I'm goin' after it.'

We carried her, Daddy and I: Daddy took her legs, I held her under her shoulders. She was so light we could have carried her for miles, even in that liquid-looking heat: she was no more than brittle bones and dried-up skin. We carried her across two fields, as she directed us, following something only she could see, into the apple orchard, where we caught up with her invisible spirit. We rested under a tree, Daddy and I nibbling sour fallers while grandmother closed her eyes and got her breath back. And then we picked her up again and carried her home, my grandmother, frail as a bird, holding on to life.

When grandfather stopped going out on the farm because Tom's voice bruised the inside of his head, he assumed that after a day or two Ian would give him the welcome news that Tom had recovered and was once again his usual taciturn, bearable company. What he hadn't considered was that it was only his unswerving schedule of strenuous work all the hours of daylight, every day of the week except Sundays, that had held back the onslaught of old age. His age had never meant anything to him: he was always surprised when he came in to breakfast to find presents and cards by his place at the table and to be told he was another year older. 'Don't seem a year since the last one,' was about all he could say, overcome with shyness by all our attention.

But once he stopped performing the punishing tasks of a farmer, lifting sheep on to the trailer, or carrying a hay-bale on each shoulder and another on his back, as he'd always done, and instead pottered around the farmyard doing nothing more strenuous than sharpening tools and sweeping out the sheds, he lost the wiry strength of his forebears. When, over a week later, the yard had less dust than the house, forcing the chickens out into the lane, and all the sash-cords had been replaced inside the house, grandfather was reduced to oiling the hinges of the barn doors, yawning with boredom, even though he'd done it the day before. And Tom was still rambling on.

So grandfather borrowed a wad of Pamela's cotton wool from the bathroom, stuffed bits in his ears, and rejoined his grandsons. He was horrified to find that he couldn't keep up with them. Walking over fields at their steady pace, the pace he himself had taken from his father and kept for seventy years, made his breathing come hard and reluctant. Trying to help them lift some hundredweight feed-bags he felt his pulse skipping like a frisky calf, and Ian saw him open his eyes wide and look to the sky as he slumped against the tractor wheel to steady himself. He felt his heartbeat calm down but too much, heavy and sluggish, as if there were silt in his veins.

That night, when grandmother came to bed, she found him lying there as usual, staring at the ceiling, as he waited for her. When she'd got undressed and joined him, taking his hand as always, his rough, flattened hands made too big, by a lifetime's physical labour, for his wiry body, as if they belonged to someone else, then he started to tell her of the events of the day. His eyes gazed at the ceiling as he spoke. At first he simply told her what he and the boys had done, noting the small changes since he'd last worked with them, two weeks previously, as if what was of interest was his getting back into the routine of things. He told her of the worrying state of the cows, their scrawny flanks embossed with ticks; he mentioned the latest EC subsidies on offer, reported on the farming page of that morning's paper; he commented on the drought-stricken pastures up on the ridge past the rectory, beyond the makeshift homes of the hippies, and he recalled the disastrous summer after the war that they'd seen through together, when the earth had swallowed lambs.

She knew that he was most talkative when he was most tired, and let him drone on. She was almost falling asleep, his voice growing distant, when he added, casually, as if an afterthought, that it had taken it out of him today, maybe he shouldn't have taken so much time off, though he'd soon get back into it, no doubt, he said. He described his symptoms, still gazing at the ceiling, and the only reason she realized that he'd wasted so many words just to get around to mentioning his erratic heartbeat and his unbalanced breath was when she felt that his big rough hand in hers was trembling. She squeezed it, and he turned his head towards her.

'I just wondered if you 'ad in mind one of your remedies, mother, get me back to normal, like,' he told her.

Grandmother turned back the covers. 'Come with me,' she said, taking him by the hand as she hobbled across the room. She opened the door of their bedroom, paused to make sure no one was still up, then led him downstairs. She turned the light on in the hallway, and stood him in the middle. Then she let go his hand, put her arms around his waist, and hugged him. 'You know I loves you,' she whispered into his shoulder. 'There weren't no other man for me.' And then she let him go, and began to unbutton his pyjama top. He offered no resistance, too confused for a moment to think of doing anything, because this was something she used to do long ago, in the very first years of their marriage, and he'd offered no resistance then. She slid his top off, then she bent over and undid the cord of his pyjama bottoms, which crumpled around his ankles. He looked down at them as she stepped to his side, and pulled off her own nightdress. When he looked up he found himself faced with his own reflection, and hers beside him, in the large mirror.

She looked at him in the glass: 'No one never told you, lover. Us've gone and got old now. There b'ain't no remedy for that.'

CHAPTER TWENTY-TWO

Sickness, Health

That same night of 9 October, which was also the night of the day that Ian led men off to work out how to steal water from the old estate waterfall, a summer sickness hit us so abruptly that no one had time to defend themselves. Everyone succumbed, apart from Gordon Honeywill's father, who worked at the sewage-farm towards Kingsteignton, and who'd not caught so much as a cold in fifteen years. For two days no one stepped out of their houses: no one fed their animals, Fred didn't deliver the milk, old Martin neglected the hedges and the church bells were silent. I lay on my bed, wishing I could die, leaving it only to crawl along the corridor to the bathroom, where there was someone else already doing what my own body had to do. But we were oblivious to each other in the misery of our sickness, and the tact and respect of each other's privacy that enables a family to live under the same roof were set aside.

As I lay on my bed the only sounds that came in from outside were the postman's van when he came to deliver the mail and to empty the post-box by the Brown, and an occasional car, by the uncertain sound of whose engine you could tell was probably lost. Otherwise there was only the steadily rising lament of geese and chickens and domestic pets, and from further away the resentful bleating of sheep, calling as if to God for sustenance.

On the third day the symptoms abated. I was the first in our family to recover: I woke up with a jolt, and lay on my back, still as the sarcophagus in the church, because to twitch a single muscle caused a throbbing, aching pain. So as I lay there I used the compass of my sixth sense, the mind's awareness of its own body, to gradually travel along my limbs and through my flesh, ascertaining with mounting surprise that my head didn't spin when I tried to formulate a thought, my throat was no longer as rough as sandpaper when I breathed, my sinuses were clear, my nose was no longer sore, and so on all the way down to my toes, which no longer ached, and with a yell of relief I sprang out of bed, ready again for normal life.

Having quickly dressed I sprang down the stairs three at a time, and found the living-room empty, exactly as it'd been left the evening before the evening before last, when we'd slunk upstairs without clearing up. It was a spooky sight, as if everyone had vanished in an instant, like Granny Sims' grandmother who'd died of spontaneous combustion, and whose descendants all prayed, during that hottest of summers, that it wasn't a hereditary condition.

There were scummy, half-drunk cups of coffee, an ashtray with the minute stubs of Ian's narrow rollies, the rind of an orange on the arm of a chair. The cushions on the sofa and armchairs, which were grouped around the television as if the furniture itself had been watching while we'd been upstairs, were all creased and squashed. It was a disturbing sight, because mother would always tidy up, either last thing at night or else, if her insomniac son was still glued to the late-night programmes, then first thing in the mornings before I was awake. She'd collect the utensils and wash up, plump up the cushions, hoover the carpet, and push the pieces of furniture back into their rightful pattern against the walls.

In the kitchen, the last evening meal hadn't been cleared away. All the plates on the table, though, were washed, even though their knives and forks still lay across them: they'd been licked clean by the cats. Filled with the newborn energy of recovery I did all the washing-up and wiped clean the kitchen surfaces. Then I put the kettle on, cut up a three-day-old loaf of bread and made breakfast. The aromas of toast and coffee spread through the house and woke the others from the spell of their sickness, and they appeared one by one around the table, mother and Tom both a little groggy still

214

and content with a cup of tea, but Ian and Pam bursting with my own hunger, and Daddy looking no different from usual, ready as ever to eat whatever he was given. Grandmother and grandfather didn't come down till the next day, because it takes old people a little longer to recover.

It transpired that the summer sickness hit everyone the same way, virulent but at least mercifully brief. Everyone, that is, except for the Rector. It picked him up and wrung him through and almost wiped him out completely. He blamed God rather than a virus because, as he openly admitted, he took pride in never having had a day's illness in the whole of his adult life, and this was the punishment for his hubris.

On the same morning as I was making breakfast, Maria da Graça too woke up in her one-roomed shack fully recovered. She opened the windows, and made a pot of continental coffee: not to drink, since it tasted foul and had the effect of making her shudder, but for its divine aroma, which soon dispelled the sickly odours of illness in the room. Out on the terrace that overlooked the rest of the village she refilled the bird feeders with monkey nuts and poured some questionable milk into saucers for those cats who came to visit her. Then she sat down in her white plastic garden chair, listening to the sounds of the village coming back to life as people began to resume their responsibilities. She drank a long glass of her home-made aqua libra, which was all she ever drank, concocted from ingredients that Granny Sims ordered specially for her: sparkling spring water, certain fruit juices, fruit and vegetable aromatic extracts, aqueous infusions of sunflower and sesame, tarragon and Siberian ginseng.

Maria drained her glass, and found that she was thinking of the Rector. So she put on her red shawl and walked to the rectory along the lane, past the Alcocks', the village hall, the church and into the drive. The rectory lawns were forlorn-looking shadows of their former selves, almost all the grass faded to a dry, lifeless brown, but still patterned in precise lines: Gordon Honeywill cut them every Saturday morning, with the Rector's old-fashioned tennis court mowing-machine, and the Rector paid him to carry on all through the summer, even after the grass had stopped growing in July, because he knew how much Gordon enjoyed doing it. I sometimes saw him at work when I visited the Rector: the same age and size as me, he steered the mower with intense concentration and effort, his tongue stuck out of his mouth and aping his mind, towards a cricket stump. When he reached it he'd leave the mower idling, carry the stump back across the lawn and place it ready for his next line. Then he'd return to the mower, swivel it round, and aim for the stump once more, his eyes fixed upon it. Although I tried to stop myself, in the end I couldn't help asking him why the hell he didn't use two stumps and get the job done in half the time.

He looked at me with furious eyes. 'You do your bloody things your way, maid,' he shouted; 'I does my things my way.'

Maria let herself into the rectory by the back door, as she did whenever she brought the Rector a jar of marmalade or a bag of her home-made fudge. She called out, but there was no reply. She carried on into the kitchen, which looked and smelled the same as usual, the kitchen of a bachelor, which is what it was: on the draining-board were the plates and utensils of a dozen TV dinners, and on top of the stove was a blue china coffee pot, a strainer sitting across its neck, and a saucepan with a thin layer of three-day-old coffee in the bottom. Maria smiled at the tools of his illogical coffee-making routine: he would make himself a fresh pot before breakfast and then reheat mugfuls in the saucepan, each one a little staler, a little more stewed and unenjoyable than the last, until the pot was empty, whereupon he'd make up a fresh one.

She walked along the corridor towards the only other downstairs room in use, the Rector's study. All the other, empty rooms' doors were open, filling the house with light. The deep green carpet in the hallway cushioned Maria's footsteps as she approached the open study door, hesitated, and listened for the sound of his writing, his cuff scudding fitfully across paper, or for the striking of a match. She liked to listen to the sounds of his concentration when she paid him a call. Sometimes there would be silence, and she'd put her head round the door to see him sitting at his desk but turned sideways, gazing out of the window. Now, Maria stepped into the room and found he wasn't there, but when she came back into the hallway she was seized by the conviction that he was somewhere in the house.

The staircase reached the first floor by climbing around the walls. Three-quarters of the way up it turned, ran along for a few feet on a small landing which overlooked the hallway, beside a high sash window with a built-in seat below, and then turned again for the last few steps to the first floor. As Maria passed the sash window she had the strange sensation of a soul fluttering around like an invisible swallow, searching for an open window. She hurried along the upstairs corridor towards the furthest room, quickening her pace, until she reached the door and opened it, whereupon she was thrown backwards, across the corridor and into the bathroom, by an unbearable stench which even as she staggered back she knew was not that of death but of someone so sick they couldn't even drag themselves a few yards to the toilet bowl. It took Maria a moment to compose herself, and as she did so she could hear the Rector praying to himself. She steeled herself against the smell and strode into the room, and what she saw melted her heart: the Rector was spread across the bed, arms outstretched; he looked as if his body, in damp pyjamas, was pinning itself down. The sheets were all scrunched up and spilling over the side of the bed, and were sullied with vomit and excrement. And the Rector, oblivious to everything outside the parameters of the pain and nausea that engulfed him, unaware of anything except the certainty that he was beyond all hope, was quietly moaning to himself.

Moving as briskly as possible Maria collected a bowl of hot water and soap, a sponge and towel, and she rootled through the cupboards for fresh sheets and pyjamas. Only then did she go over to the Rector and put her hand on his forehead, and murmur some soothing words to him in her native Portuguese. The Rector appeared barely to respond at all, except that he ceased his incantatory moaning and his eyes fluttered open, then closed again. Maria assumed he was still lost in his fever so high it burned her hand.

In fact her icy palm and soft undertones did reach him, soughing across the hallucinatory landscape of his delirium from far, far away, from the other side of his eyelids, which were themselves a long way away from him. With a tremendous effort of coordination he was able to flick them open, and that was when he knew, instantly, that he'd passed the worst of it and come out on the other side of death, because an angel in the far corner of the room was speaking in the celestial language, and watching over him.

'That's interesting,' he thought to himself, 'how different perspective is in the next dimension,' before he slipped once more under the waves and lost consciousness.

Maria gently peeled the Rector's pyjamas from his limbs, and pulled the sheet and the sweat-soaked pillowcases off the bed. Then she eased a towel under his body, which was much lighter than she expected, and she began to clean him. At first she proceeded cautiously, almost fearfully, not out of embarrassment, to which she was immune, but with the timidity people feel handling an infant: he seemed so fragile and helpless she thought she might break something. Soon, though, her fingers and hands took on an authority of their own, manipulating him with the efficiency of a trained nurse, as she realized he was more robust than she'd thought.

She dipped the sponge into warm water, lathered it, and soaped his skin. His body was white and hairless, and he had an old man's skin, soft and loose. His athlete's stomach, once a hard wall of muscle, had slowly loosened and subsided over the years spent at his desk. He had a long white scar running from his right hip part way down his thigh: the scar tissue was like blistered skin, as if a hot fishbone had been branded into his hip. It crinkled when she rolled him over. She soaped his bottom and his genitals: his circumcised penis was stubby and shapeless, and Maria smiled to herself, as she had at each one of the few men she'd seen naked. When she'd wiped him clean with the flannel she dried him with the softest towel she could find, put fresh sheets on the bed, and dressed him in a clean pair of pyjamas.

The soiled linen was in a heap on the floor. Maria opened wide the window, scooped up the bundle and tossed it outside, unknowingly prefiguring an incident that would occur two days later in our house, when mother would come into my room to find the floor strewn with toys I no longer wanted, despite her repeated orders to tidy them up. And just as instantly as Maria, her anger as immediate as Maria's curious commonsense, mother would open the window and throw them all outside to land broken and scattered in the yard. '*Now* you can clear them up,' she said; and I shovelled them into a dustbin.

When the Rector woke up again, an hour or so later, he was surprised to find that heaven, at least in his immediate environment, was in fact a replica of earth, before he corrected himself as he realized that it could only be the other way round. He looked around the room, but his guardian angel was nowhere to be seen, which irked him for a moment until he realized how arrogant that was, making demands in such a place, and so he attempted to give himself over to the will and mercy of God: he lay still, eyes closed, trying not to think of anything in particular. He was aware that he felt wonderful, his body at peace with itself in a way he'd forgotten was possible; in fact he felt weightless, and wondered quite what it meant to have a body in the afterlife. What he didn't know was that he was simply basking in the brief, illusory haven of wellbeing that a sick man finds himself in when he first awakes, especially in a fresh pair of pyjamas. Instead he confused himself by pondering the consequences of waking up dead: how was he to communicate with the angel if and when she returned? Would he have to learn a new language, and if so would it be as difficult and frustrating as the European languages he misused on holiday, or as expressive as Serbo-Croat? Or would he suddenly start speaking in the angelic tongue himself, like those Pentecostal evangelists who lured the foolish and the vulnerable to their services in the community centre in Chudleigh? He was aghast at the idea, but it was replaced by another: what on earth did he himself look like now? He was seized with curiosity and, determined to find a mirror, lifted his head from the pillow, and his feverish mind, befuddled by brief exposure to the incongruities of life after death, exploded into complete bewilderment, for how could there be pain in the hereafter? It was inconceivable, the pantheon of Greek gods paraded past his mind's eye, because something or someone had gripped his head in a pair of tongs and was squeezing it as hard as they could. He groaned and fell back on to the bed, hoping he could slip back into the state of grace he'd just occupied. But there was no relief. Instead his body came back to agonizing life: all his limbs ached, his heart raced, his stomach churned and his lungs burned. It hurt just to breathe, each breath sending a ripple of aching around his torso, and even the pull of gravity hurt, pressing the mattress against those parts of his body with which it made contact. He began to moan as he realized what a dreadful illusion had overcome him and wondered who could have done such a thing, though he already knew who his chief suspect was, himself, and he tried to work out why an angel had come to visit him when she'd only done so like a mortal woman, in order to desert him.

In fact, Maria was in the kitchen, having had the bright idea of giving the Rector a cup of coffee. Not only would its aroma dispel the odour of sickness that lingered in his bedroom, as it had in her shack, but she knew that his favourite drink would revive him. She made a fresh pot and carried it on a tray with milk and sugar, bearing it before her like a magic potion that would bring him back to life. The wonderful aroma preceded her, wafting along the hallway, up the stairwell, into all the empty rooms, and along the upstairs corridor. It reached the Rector's bedroom a few moments before she did, and so nauseated him that she found him leaning over the side of the bed, heaving as if overboard a thin stream of yellow sputum.

Maria took cushions from the Rector's armchair in the kitchen and made herself a bed in the next empty room along the corridor from his bedroom. While he was sleeping she collected spare clothes and a few bottles of aqua libra, and she pinned a note to the door of her shack to the effect that she would be unavailable for house cleaning, sewing and ironing until further notice, an act typical of her thoughtfulness except that it was in a language no one understood.

The Rector inhabited a feverish domain that shifted as treacherously as a Dartmoor bog. Maria took his temperature often, placing the thermometer under his arm, and it soared up and down from one minute to the next. The morning after her arrival he became aware of her presence, and thanked her gratefully for coming to save him from his distress, but then he seemed to spot a light out of the corner of his sickness and he followed it like an ignis fatuus on the moor, picking his way from one clump of moss to another until he stepped on nothing and disappeared from reality: Maria again assumed the guise of an angel and the Rector's brow furrowed in confusion at further theological anomalies of the state he found himself in. He wondered whether he was in an uncharted region of *Limbus patrum*, once upon a time inhabited by the saints of the Old Covenant as they waited for Christ's coming and his redemption of the world; unused for two thousand years, perhaps it was again being filled with a new, obscure category of unredeemed souls, of whom he was one.

He'd explained to me the authenticated territories of limbo when I asked him what had happened to the souls of all the newborn babies buried in the graveyard, and he told me about *Limbus infantium*, the everlasting state of those who die unregenerate, including unbaptized infants, who were still in their state of original sin but were innocent of personal guilt. They were believed to be excluded from supernatural beatitude, he said, not bothering to conceal his irreverent grin as he did so, 'but according to Aquinas, Alison, they enjoy full natural happiness, whatever that means, apart from the fact that intelligent men, whatever other idiotic things they say, have always regarded happiness as of secondary importance'.

The Rector enjoyed telling me of beliefs upon which he

poured scorn. He recounted with distaste Saint Augustine's teachings on the subject, written in disagreement with Pelagius, whom the Rector had studied in theological college and regarded as a close colleague: Augustine taught that all who die unbaptized suffer some degree of positive punishment. 'For eternity, mind!' the Rector spat at me. 'Forever, Alison! Now what sort of merciful God would think up such a thing?'

Now, though, the Rector, in the delirium of a flu so virulent it was as if all the minor illnesses he'd avoided through his lethal diet had caught up with him all at once; now he wondered whether he'd been wise to dismiss the wrathful God of the Old Testament. For some reason the story of Abraham and Isaac came to him: regarded as a paradigm of faith, it had always made him uncomfortable. The God he had come to believe in would never demand such a sacrifice, and could not therefore use the threat of it as a test. The Rector had already pondered the point exhaustively when his own son was a child, and had come to the conclusion then that if ordered to kill him simply to prove his faith he'd dismiss the emissary as a false messenger. His own faith was built on quite different foundations; life itself was God-given, and was more precious than any dogma. But what if he were wrong? Despite his lifelong battle with his own ego, his attempts to annihilate it in the crucible of prayer, so that he would be able to present himself to God possessed only of a faith of the purest simplicity, perhaps intrinsic to the nature of those struggles was in fact an overweening emphasis on his own powers of reason to hack a path towards the truth. In which case God would tear off the mask of mercy that the Rector had erroneously clothed him with and, laughing the harsh laughter of the God of the patriarchs, consign him to the punishing flames.

These and other thoughts occupied the Rector in his molten fever. They formed themselves with pleasing lucidity in his mind, and as soon as he began to get better he longed to return to them, however spiritually uncomfortable their content, because reality was physically uncomfortable, which was even worse.

His gratitude towards Maria, meanwhile, was replaced by intense embarrassment at his realization of what she'd done for him. Horrified at the idea of her cleaning up the mess his body had produced, he blushed deeply. Maria saw the colour rush back into his pale cheeks and, gratified by this sign of recovery, smiled at him, which only increased his shame. Summoning up a strength that only humiliation could lend him, he swept back the covers, swung his legs out of bed and pushed past Maria in a flustered manner, thanking her profusely for all she'd done, 'but I'm fine now, Maria,' he stammered, 'I can look after myself.' He stood up and stepped forward.

'I'll get up and get dressed and I'll see you home,' he spluttered, still blushing, and then he found himself rooted to the spot as the room quite suddenly started to move, it spun round him, twice, and turned on its side, and although he thought he himself was still standing, the floor had come up to where the wall should have been and he was leaning against it. He could feel the carpet against his cheek. He closed his eyes and fell asleep.

Those next two days were the worst for the Rector. Unable to keep down even water his dignity spilled out of every orifice and, while he slept, from the entire surface of his being sweat poured into the sheets that Maria replaced three or four times a day, washing them by hand in the bath and hanging them out on the line in the overgrown vegetable garden. As weak as one of the Howards' newborn lambs, the Rector submitted to Maria's ministrations, as she mopped up the liquid faeces that he was unable to hold back and wiped acidic spittle that retched from his mouth, with a warm flannel. In between these inescapable ordeals of humiliation, the Rector recalled equally painful incidents from his life, such as the time when, as a seven-year-old schoolboy at Tyttenhanger Lodge, the Classics master had made him stand at the front of the class and recite the various tenses of the verb 'to be' in Latin, and reduced him to tears with his ridicule of the boy's mistakes. The memory still, more than sixty years later, made him burn with rage, and he wondered for how much longer he would have to carry such trivial instances of personal hurt with him. Through how many lives, he wondered, must we drag our failings and fears behind us?

On the afternoon of the third day after Maria's arrival, the Rector awoke with his pyjamas drenched in sweat and aching all over. His mouth felt like a dry quarry, his throat parched. Maria, who'd just herself awoken from a doze in the armchair in the kitchen, appeared with a glass of water. The Rector downed half of it in one gulp, and felt it stream down his gullet and into his stomach, which suddenly churned into motion like a cement mixer and sent the water back up the way it'd come. The Rector groaned and leaned forward, towards the towel Maria quickly held across his lap, and he spewed an infernal, foul-smelling liquid into the towel, the clear water transformed during its brief journey to his gut into a frothy, green-tinged stew. When his stomach had yet again emptied itself, its last sediment having dribbled from his lips, he fell back, exhausted.

His head felt detached from his body, but both were equally useless. He could hear, distantly, as one does on the edge of sleep, Maria running the bath taps, and thrusting the towel in and out of hot suddy water. And at that very moment he knew his degradation was over, for he felt not the slightest trace of shame. The last remnants of his pride had been sucked out of him then, and with a curious sensation of freedom he accepted all at once his old age, his sickness, his helplessness, the bilious discharges of his body that he'd not wanted anyone to see; but most of all he accepted Maria's unquestioning presence. The extent of her charity and the depth of her devotion became apparent, and in the face of it embarrassment was not only inappropriate, it was wrong. What this devotion meant he wasn't sure. Despite her career as a kitchen maid at the Viscount's estate, this was not the deferential loyalty of a servant towards her master, for theirs was a relationship of equals. It could only be love, of a kind that worried him. And as he lay there, worrying, so he began to get better.

*

Maria, meanwhile, had discovered with pleasure her talent for nursing. Once she'd got over the stench of the molten lava that poured from his bowels and the sickly-sweet contents of his stomach, she came to enjoy cleaning up his smooth, weak body, putting fresh linen on his bed, taking his temperature, giving him warm water scented with marjoram to settle his stomach, washing his soiled and sweaty pyjamas, and she even found some satisfaction in mopping up his mess. It never occurred to her to call a doctor. She treated him in practice as she'd always thought of him, as a child whose mind was too busy, which in reality was the main reason he ceased to be discomforted by her presence. She was also surprised by obscure envelopes of her memory which contained the lullabies and ballads her mother had once sung to Maria and her brothers and sisters. They'd folded over and remained tucked away during the intervening years, fragments of the tunes escaping from time to time, but now it was as if they were steamed open by the balsam, derived from essence of eucalyptus, that she made the Rector inhale to clear his sinuses and his mind, his head underneath a towel, so that he looked as if he were studying a part of himself in private. Maria sang the Rector to sleep in her husky, tuneful voice, and as his eyelids grew heavy she stroked his arm, and picked bits of fluff off his pyjamas.

Gradually the Rector's volatile organs calmed down. Time passed quickly, since there wasn't enough in which to decipher his inscrutable nurse's intentions, and he was soon able to keep down a breakfast of boiled egg and slices of thin toast, and other meals of thin broth and junket. The first time he reached the bathroom unaided he saw, as he sat on the toilet, feeling a little faint, white sheets on the line, swaying in the illusory breeze.

Maria knew he was irreversibly on the road to recovery when she found him smoking in bed, his first cigarette for a week, which made him feel light-headed. That afternoon he staggered downstairs to his study, clutching the banisters, to make a phone call, because the next day was Sunday, and he didn't want to risk fainting in the pulpit. He rang the Reverend Brian Dennis, who was a protégé of the Rector's from the days of his industrial chaplaincy in Crewe: Brian had been an apprentice electrician in the railway yards who, like me, had acted as one of the Rector's servers, and gone on to help organize the parish youth club. He kept in touch after the Rector moved to Devon, and followed him some years later to set up his own business in Torquay. His piety was matched only by his pursuit of unattached women: wherever he went two or three would accompany him. The Rector helped him through theological exams, which he reckoned, as he told me more than once, to be one of his most notable achievements, since not only was Brian's grasp of doctrinal matters tenuous, but his spelling was worse. He would drive up from Torquay on midweek evenings with his essays, and his silent girlfriends drank gin and tonic while the Rector corrected the mistakes of a dyslexic, which he would recount to me when he was in a good mood. 'Did you realize, Alison, that Moses rose up and led his people out of Eggpyt?' he would say, chuckling. 'And are you aware that Jesus carried his cross towards the Cavalry?' he howled with laughter. 'Do you believe in immaculate contraception, girl?' he spluttered, coughing his smoker's laughter. 'Have you read the parable,' he asked, bent double with amusement, 'the parable of the lost ship?'

Brian had passed his exams – by virtue, the Rector maintained, of a clerical error – and was ordained, but remained a lay preacher. He would fill in when the Rector took one of his rare holidays, and the Rector also occasionally invited him to give the sermon at services the Rector himself was taking. The chief reason he did so was something only I was aware of. The Rector would never have admitted it to anyone, least of all himself, but it was obvious to me: I had only to watch him, from my place in the chancel, while Brian was speaking to the congregation. Whereas the Rector addressed fellow human beings equally burdened with the profound challenge of existence, Brian treated us as if we were his children, and Jesus was a kind uncle we'd not seen for a long time but who might just be coming to visit. Whatever the text he started from, each of Brian's sermons became a homily to Jesus.

'You see, friends,' he would say in his strange northerner's accent, 'they couldn't see what they were doing. They were blind to their own sinfulness, and we know why, don't we?' He would pause, and scan the scattered faces before him with an expression of sad reproach. 'It was greed that blinded them, wasn't it? And we all know about that. We know we're all greedy sometimes, when we shouldn't be. But instead of punishing them, what did Jesus do, ay? He understood them, because he understands people, and he forgave them. Now isn't that wonderful? Don't we know how hard it is to forgive people who've done us wrong? But Jesus could. And he was showing us how to, wasn't he?'

I'd look over at the Rector, sitting in the empty choir stalls, and I was the only one in the church who could discern in his bearing the assumption of superiority. His affection for Brian was untainted by his dismissal of Brian's childish theology, and the reason he liked to have him preach was so that his parishioners would realize how fortunate they were that every other Sunday they had someone prepared to face up to the unavoidable problems of faith. In reality virtually everyone was grateful to be given sermons they could understand, and which were always comforting, unlike the Rector's, which if you could follow them at all only meant that you left the church with more on your mind than when you went in.

So now the Rector telephoned Brian. He was the most reliable man the Rector had ever met, and he knew that Brian would alter any other plans he might have and somehow arrange things so that he could come to the village with his compatible girlfriends, different ones each time and more, the Rector insisted, ever since he'd started wearing dog-collar and vestments. They'd fill the front pew and betray their inexperience in church by standing up and sitting down at the wrong moments, but during the sermon they would gaze up at Brian in the pulpit above them as if his words were actually coded messages, unique for each one of them.

By Monday the Rector had gained sufficient strength to dress himself and get up. He thought he'd surprise Maria as he appeared in the kitchen, but she'd already laid his place for breakfast. Afterwards, he stumbled in the corridor on his way to the study, and only Maria's precipitous reactions saved him from falling over. Ever since his hip had started giving him trouble, bone rubbing against bone, he'd walked with a limp, and he'd become accustomed to the moderate but constant pain. I'd given him a walking stick which old Martin cut for me: the Rector used it occasionally, walking on the moor, to test the ground in boggy areas, but otherwise he scorned it. Now, though, after Maria had steadied him, he fetched the walking stick from the porch and employed it as an aid to help him keep his balance, and he was not to be seen without it again.

As he got better the Rector fretted all the more over Maria: he knew that the experience had changed things between them, and that the stage of convalescence had been reached when they would look at each other and he would have to thank her. But how? In what manner? She would doubtless stand, mute and unworried as usual, while he floundered around trying to find the right thing to say, and all she'd do would be to step forward and pick a hair off his lapel. He imagined it, and already felt awkward.

Not long before the moment came the Rector, back at his desk sorting through his mail and wondering where to start work, heard a clinking of bottles in the kitchen. He picked up his empty mug and walking stick and made his way towards the kitchen. As he passed the open door of the old dining-room he saw her walking away across the lawn, with a carrier bag full of her empty aqua libra bottles, and he realized with a tremulous wave of relief that Maria, inscrutable as ever, had gone back home without even saying goodbye. His life had returned to normal.

A couple of hours later he was licking stamps, having answered all the mail with his own concise letters, and was planning to take them to the post-box and then walk around the village to find out what had happened while he was ill, when the door of his study opened wide and Maria put her head round and spoke to him in words he didn't understand.

She disappeared. Disconcerted, the Rector got up and limped into the corridor, to find it filled with children, of whom I was one, each of us holding something of Maria's: a black bin-bag of clothes, a cardboard box with her herb jars, a plastic bag of toiletries, while Gordon Honeywill carried on his shoulder the foam rubber, rolled up and tied with string, that served as Maria's mattress.

From her shack Maria had seen us down at the Brown playing football. I was the only girl, summoned to play in goal, but there were seven or eight boys there, chasing their sweaty dreams. Maria came down and walked right into the middle of the game, avoiding the ball by a fraction as it fell out of the sky from one of Gordon's enormous punts. She spoke to us all, then started walking back again. We didn't have a clue what she wanted, and were about to resume the game when she turned round and beckoned us to follow her. And so, half an hour later, she led us in a line, our arms full, the short distance from her shack to the rectory.

The Rector watched Maria march up the stairs, followed by her bearers. As I passed him he looked at me quizzically, and I shrugged my shoulders. Maria had us put down her things in the room along the corridor, the one she'd slept in, and gave each of us a piece of her mouth-watering fudge. The others all trooped out of the back door, but I dropped back and slipped into the old drawing-room, with its huge mirror, just to sit on the floor in that empty space and peaceful atmosphere.

So I heard Maria's footsteps coming down the stairs, and through the wide crack between the door and its frame I could see the Rector standing at the bottom. He waited until Maria had reached the second step up and was facing him, their eyes level with each other. His wrinkled face had a mystified expression.

'What's going on, Maria?' he asked her, and she answered him matter of factly, explaining things to him in detail, with emphatic gestures, as straightforwardly as she could, like someone giving directions to a driver lost in a strange city. When she'd finished she looked the Rector in the eye, smiled a wide open smile of satisfaction, took the Rector's white handkerchief from the chest pocket of his jacket, licked it, and wiped a fleck of jam from the side of his mouth.

The Rector felt heat rise up his body and burn his cheeks, but this was anger, not shame. He had to close his eyes, tilt his head back and take a deep breath, or he feared he might lose his temper. He could hardly believe that at his age he could feel such exasperation, but he did do and that was that. In fact he was almost trembling with it, for he was exasperated beyond measure by everything about the woman who stood grinning in front of him, on the other side of his closed eyelids. He was exasperated by her presumption, by her matter of factness, by the excruciating language barrier she refused to take down, even though everyone knew she'd been here so long she must know as much English as they did. He was exasperated by the fact that he never knew what she was thinking, by her inappropriate smiles, and by the streaks of grey in her hair. He opened his eyes. She was no longer grinning at him. He stood there not knowing what to do or say. She raised her eyebrows. And just as his anger had risen, the Rector felt it slide off him and, exasperated above all by the love he felt for her, he opened his arms, and I slipped away through the door on to the verandah.

CHAPTER TWENTY-THREE

The Confusion of Dreams

The thunder came from a long way away. It came rolling through the Devon valleys and combes, feeling its way towards our village, a slow, mysterious booming not from the heavens but rolling low across the earth. A single fork of lightning struck a moment later, like the crack of a whip in the dry atmosphere: it struck a tree beneath which three horses stood sleeping, one of which was Susanna's palomino pony. Their carcasses were found there in the morning, by the smoking tree stump.

When I threw open the curtains and saw the pony calmly grazing, it took me a moment to realize I'd only been dreaming.

Mother came into my room in the middle of the morning. 'You're not in reading again, girl! I've told you enough times, surrounded by all this mess an' all. Why don't you get out and play? What's Jane or Susan doing?'

'They're boring,' I moaned, without looking up. The only person I wanted to see was Johnathan, but I couldn't tell mother that.

'Well, I'm sure you're full of fun, turning into a cabbage. It's not healthy for a girl your age, you should be outside.'

'There's no point. I think I'm a *lushni ludi*, mother.'

'And what might that mean, may I ask?'

'I'm one of the superfluous men,' I told her.

'Don't you cheek your mother, young lady!' she said, grabbing the book from my hands. 'Come on! Out! There's plenty of chores need doing.'

*

231

I suppose other people didn't know you could go into the church whenever you liked. It was the only cool place left. Grandmother pointed out that in previous times they brewed and stored the parish ale in the church and that the priests used to keep wool or corn from their tithes there too, which got farmers talking amongst themselves about leaving the milk for the collecting lorries in the nave overnight. But no one had yet suggested it to the Rector in case it all reminded him of his own long overdue tithes, which he seemed to have forgotten. In fact, they often came to mind at this time of year: he'd only neglected to collect them out of modesty, having been privately lobbying the Bishop for a revival of the Norman custom whereby tithes in the parish of an unpopular incumbent could be paid to any neighbouring priest.

The church was never locked. People still remembered the PCC meeting that took place in the days when atheists first began stealing from churches: Granny Sims had got on to the agenda a motion that the church be locked from Sunday to Sunday, with keys given out only to regular churchgoers prepared to recite the Athanasian Creed. In the ensuing discussion it was only by resorting to the underhand trick of losing his temper that the Rector persuaded them to postpone the vote until the next meeting. In the interim he deposited, in a bank, the chalice and paten left behind by Buckfast Abbey, the cup given by the 1st Viscount Teignmouth with his coat of arms on the side, the pewter collection-plate that was said to have been used by the Romans, the stoup which Corporal Alcock lined up for last so that he could drain it, and the nickel-plated candlesticks that a gullible Rector had once bought off the same didicois whom grandmother could remember, passing through the village on their wagons that were like rooms turned inside out with everything hanging off the outside of the walls. The Rector deposited all those church utensils in a bank vault in Exeter and bought cheap replacements, so that the notion of putting a lock on the door of an inviolable sanctuary need never again arise.

Sometimes when I went I'd find the Rector there too, because when he wasn't in his study surrounded by twenty-six empty rooms, wrestling with an opponent whose limbs were made of liquid, he'd limp over to the church to have it out with Him face to face. He'd be walking between the pews looking at the ground and gesticulating, an unlit cigarette in his fingers, mouthing words of reproach he felt towards his Maker whose Creation contained so many baffling flaws.

Usually, though, I was alone in that cool sanctuary of stone, so dry that all the hymn books were crumbling but which retained its damp, ecclesiastical smell, that hung heavy in people's sinuses and antagonized their incipient rheumatism.

The day of my recovery from the summer flu, a flaming Friday, I stole out of the heat into the church, and sat in a pew in the middle. I cooled down deliciously, eyes closed, and had just become comfortable with my body again when the air began to tremble. It felt thin, like they say it gets on the top of mountains, as if it no longer held enough oxygen to support life. What happens to space when the air goes? Invisible birds were beating their wings, and would at any moment become visible. But then I realized that far from being a sign of some imminent apparition, those wings were the sign of life's departure. The air became empty of itself, it became a vacuum: I realized with horror that I was in Limbo. There was no time in there, so I could have been trapped for a second or a century, but the vacuum was shattered with the implosion of all the stained glass windows, coloured shards of glass cascading into the church.

My eyes blinked wide open like a cat's.

It was around then that I spent time with grandmother as we waited for the flour cloud to turn into rain, renewing the intimacy that had been reduced by her blindness. I read to her from holiday brochures that Pamela picked up from travel agents in town. She liked to hear descriptions of places she'd never shown any desire to visit: maybe she was doing it for my benefit, to open up my horizons.

She used to call me her little sparrow, yet just as I was growing faster than ever before, so that all my pairs of jeans

233

had a creased white ring around the bottom of the legs where mother had already let them down, and were still too short for me, it was grandmother who was becoming bird-like, her clothes like a bird's feathers inside of which there's hardly anything.

When I was little she would sit me on her lap and whisper: 'Who's my favourite granddaughter, then?' and fondle my shining black hair, which hadn't been seen in our family for three generations. Grandmother had had the first photograph in the whole village, which people stared at for ages before suddenly recognizing her mother-in-law, standing beside her out-of-focus son on Teignmouth pier. Grandmother saw the picture on her bedside table every night before turning out the light, and for a long time had assumed the inky black hair to be lost in history. But it had reasserted itself in me after taking a rest, and it made me stand out in her eyes among all her grandchildren.

That was before the thickening of her cataracts, which we didn't notice at first and which she wouldn't admit to. She had difficulty picking bones from her food, but insisted that she ate so slowly on the advice of the Prime Minister at the time of her infancy, who advocated chewing each mouthful thirty-two times to aid digestion, and after she'd repeated it a few times we all forgot that she hadn't always done so. After a while the rest of the family realized they didn't have time to be polite at every single meal, and soon even on Sundays we'd clear the tea away around her and leave the table, where she remained, chewing through the afternoon.

Grandmother's eyes went milky, but no one suspected what it meant. We didn't realize that she'd learned to identify people across a room by their smell. Even when she stopped reading, we accepted her claim that she'd read enough about other people, who after all only repeated the same old ideas and made the same mistakes. Her worsening arthritis seemed like a sufficient reason to stay indoors, and she left the house only to hobble to church, along a route she'd memorized over the years without trying, until, despite copper bracelets to ward off arthritis and a magnet hidden under the bedclothes to draw out rheumatism, she said she found the path too steep, and the Rector began bringing communion to her at home.

Gradually, however, once she'd stopped reading she began to lose interest in life; she'd never listened to the radio, unnerved by being unable to put faces to all those disembodied voices. Daddy came to spend hours beside her, the two of them holding hands and gazing ahead into an unpopulated blur, and it was Daddy, in fact, who inadvertently discovered that she was blind and saved her from dying of boredom, when he asked her how many lonely people there were, and she replied without thinking: 'About as many as there be white hairs on your 'ead.' Daddy ran through to the kitchen and blurted out: 'Come quick, grandmother's blinded, 'er thinks my hair's gone grey.'

Even though she was only speaking the truth, all at once things fell into place: why she insisted on taking a mug of tea in her hands rather than have it put on a table beside her, no matter how hot it was, and why she'd given up knitting after a lifetime making pullovers and woollen socks for her numerous offspring, which she claimed was because the clicking of the needles was beginning to get on her nerves after seventy years of the sound.

At first grandmother denied her blindness, not out of pride but because she dreaded becoming a burden, so Ian devised a series of tests: the first was a card with letters decreasing in size, as he'd remembered from the school optician's visits, but although grandmother could only make out the two largest letters at the top she closed her eyes and concentrated her mind and guessed the rest correctly. Then Ian beckoned her to the window and asked her to say which vehicles were in what position around the farmyard, but again she was right despite the fact that the scene was no more than a blur before her, because she assumed that they would be parked now just as they had been the last time she'd seen them, since people are above all creatures of habit, her own family no exception. It was only with his third and final test that Ian caught grandmother out, when he brought his brother and sisters into the room and asked her the colour of our hair.

With enormous relief, saved from her one fear, that of being a burden on her family, grandmother distinguished us easily by our smell and correctly announced the hair-colour of each of us until she got to Pamela, who was at the end of the line. All Ian said was: 'Wrong! Us'll come closer.' We took a step towards her each time, but she carried on getting it wrong, growing more and more stupefied. It didn't occur to her that Pamela might have dyed her brown hair with peroxide.

Forced to accept reality, things got better for her after that, not worse, and she didn't become the burden she feared. Grandfather constructed at his carpenter's bench a complicated contraption for reading with, which consisted of three magnifying glasses, a pair of thick pebble spectacles and an angle-poise lamp with an extra powerful bulb. Mother got her larger and larger type books from the mobile library, and grandmother regained her appetite for life.

During those days when I sat with her, waiting vainly for rain to fall out of flour, I held her hand and asked her why she'd refused spectacles for so long. 'No one should see their own chillern growin' old,' she replied. I lent her my walkman, and Pamela got her some talking book cassettes from Exeter Library, and grandmother fell asleep in her chair with the headphones on and dreamed of the members of her family acting out scenes from the plays of William Shakespeare.

During those forlorn days, when it became clear that nothing would bring the rain before it was ready, Tom received a blow that no one had prepared him for: overnight, Susanna became indifferent to him. Her pupils no longer grew larger when they stepped into the shadows together. She didn't mind whether he came to see her at breaktimes or not, and when they parted and he said: 'See you later, then?' she replied: 'If you want to,' or 'Why not?' She didn't refuse him, but let her hand flop limply in his, and her languid lack of response when he kissed her was worse than any rejection. After the euphoria of his discovery of love her indifference was more than he could bear, but everything was so dried up by that stage of the summer that he couldn't find any of the tears that he wanted to cry. On one occasion he kissed her and found it was the saddest thing he'd ever done, and he bit her lip: but even then she made no response, just tasted the blood on her tongue, with no expression of anger or even curiosity. Disconsolate, and with no one to turn to, it was then that Tom followed the other men over the fields to the pub at Ashton.

Tom wasn't the only one to lose his groundless optimism of the morning twilight, that today might be different. During those next few days there was nothing but confusion, as people lost hope and with it reality. Fred Sims' addiction to sneezing was worse than ever as he bumped us down the hill to a phantom coach supposed to take us to a non-existent school, while his crates of milk curdled in the phone box. Wasps and hornets bumped into each other in the air. The old bell in the church boomed when you least expected it. The animals, even as their ribs stuck out, were getting restless, and Ian and Tom exerted themselves in the false dawn to put up an extra barrier of electrified wire around the fields; Daddy kept on becoming intrigued and touching the buzzing wire, which throbbed unpleasantly through his organs, but he'd forget by the time he saw another one. Fortunately Tinker learned to growl when he went near and so distract him.

It wasn't only nettles and coltsfoot, meanwhile, that flourished without water in the arid soil. Rhubarb with leaves the size of tablecloths spread themselves across lawns, and the tomato plants that mother dug into the bed at the kitchen door multiplied along the side of the house and climbed the walls like wisteria. She picked a bucketful of green ones in the morning and put them on the window-sills. The following day they'd all be as red as the letterbox, and I've never in my life tasted such sweet tomatoes.

'Love apples, us used to call them. Is they fruit or vegetables?' grandmother asked me. 'Nobody knows, see. And they never will, neither, until they're too clever for their own good.'

'Don't you know, grandma?'

'Course I do, maid,' she replied. 'They's sweet little vegetables, that's what they is.'

People even got confused over time itself, especially in our house where the piano tuner, distracted by the mosquitoes that accompanied him, had left behind one of his metronomes by mistake, and it mocked us with its sardonic version of time rocking back and forth, back and forth, without going anywhere.

'If you set that thing going one more time, girl, you'll be for it!' mother shouted through from the kitchen.

CHAPTER TWENTY-FOUR

Slaughter

Monday was a somnolent morning, when even Pamela seemed to have plenty of time for breakfast before leaving in a state of calm. After she'd gone the rest of us sipped tea and Ian said:

'Us'll need everyone's help herding. We'll bring 'em into the farmyard.'

'Surely the abattoir lorries can go right up to the fields?' mother asked.

'Course they will, mother,' he replied, 'but there's some they won't give us nothin' for. Douglas 'as got to slaughter they.'

Mother was puzzled. 'What are we going to do with the carcasses?'

'Fill the freezers, mother.'

'Don't be stupid, bay. Us can fit a few joints in, what about the rest?'

Ian was reluctant, and he was looking into his mug of tea. 'Bury them.'

'Bury them? Where? Ian, you can't – '

'– Don't you worry,' he interrupted: he looked her in the eye. 'Mother, we idn't payin' good money to no knacker who'll sell 'em for glue. Mike Howard's going to use 'is digger; Douglas is coming round s'mornin'.'

Mother looked like her head was caught up in a cobweb of perplexity. She sat down.

Ian stood up. 'Bring Dad and Alison up top field. See you there.' Tom left with him. The dogs joined them as they crossed the yard. The silence in the kitchen was tightened by their departing figures, as we sipped our lukewarm tea. Then mother pushed her chair back and rose purposefully to her feet. 'Okay, you two, let's get ready.'

I collected the tea mugs. As mother rinsed them at the sink I put a hand on her back. Mother relaxed her hands in the water, eyes gazing into it. She took a deep breath and exhaled it slowly. 'Whatever you might hope for in this life, girl,' she said, 'don't expect to understand men. At some point they stops growing up, like, but they still carries on in another direction. My father, my husband, now my own sons. They all baffles me.'

She might have added the dogs to her list. They followed their own precise but ludicrous logic, describing huge superfluous arcs in pursuit of a breakaway heifer. And the cattle followed another, even stupider, pattern, thus thrown into terrified confusion by Ian and Daddy flapping their arms as if trying to take flight and Tom yelling hypnotic chants, and by the dogs veering in upon their flanks and nipping their pasterns. With panic in their eyes the herd were driven along the lane, the flurry of hooves further ruining the melted tarmac.

Douglas was waiting in the farmyard, sitting impassively on a barrel by the barn with his old leather doctor's bag, as the herd were brought wheeling into the yard in a splatter of gravel, their hooves sticky with tar.

Ian sent Daddy and me over to guard the fence by mother's sorry-looking vegetable garden, while mother put lightweight gates across the front entrance. Tom ordered the dogs to their place by the kitchen door.

'We'll let 'em calm down a while,' Ian ordered. He went over to Douglas, while mother went in to make tea.

''Tidn't too many?' Ian asked, gesturing to the remnant of his herd, no more than twenty, only the most scrawny and sorrowful, that were worth nothing to the abattoir, whose ribs pushed out through their sad hides, and who'd been abandoned even by parasites, the last of whom had gladly jumped on to any of the dogs that'd got close enough during the drive.

Douglas, facing the sun, had lowered his head. 'No,' he replied, without raising it.

*

Grandfather wasn't helping us with the cows: I found out later that he'd refused to, and instead gone for a long walk around the village. He saw uncle Sidney and his children ripping out the hedges between the fields of their farm ready to sow wheat, like the Saxons who cut down the high hedges to make their large continental fields that were so unsuitable for Devon, and were soon divided up again; he heard uncle Terence and Terry with their chain-saws laying to waste the small copse in the dip between three fields and he thought of the riots that had taken place when threshing machines were introduced in the previous century; and going past the hippies, who already had to walk around in groups, grandfather remembered the first men from the Labour Party who arrived without warning in the square and tried to inspire people with the chimera of democracy. Word soon got round and they were sent packing with bloodied noses, not because the villagers were inculcated with the gentry's Tory views, or even because they disagreed with the idea that people were equal, but because they wanted to be left alone by outsiders.

'So, she's right,' he thought, 'time's stopped still, and we're going backwards.'

In his beet field behind the church he took a handful of earth and, closing his fist, felt not the rich reddy soil of his heartland but sandy, dusty topsoil slip through his fingers. 'What's happening to our land, mother?' he cried.

Tom broke open the last bale of hay and strewed handfuls round the yard. Gradually the panic in the eyes of the cattle contracted. While we drank tea, replacing the sweat that poured from us in that cauldron of a morning but dried instantly on our skins in the strangely metallic heat, Douglas set up his tools in the depths of the barn. He plugged in his gun, and called out to Ian from the shadows: 'Bring the first one in, bay.'

Ian didn't move, but simply nodded to Tom, suspecting that there was an appropriate order to the slaughter, and that Tom might guess it by instinct. Tom walked over to a sad old cow, her udders shrivelled, and looped a makeshift halter of bailer twine over her neck. He slapped her bony haunches and led her to the barn.

'What's they doing?' Daddy asked me.

I knew how everyone protected him with tact and white lies. ''Tis slaughtering, Daddy. Douglas is killin' the cows, 'cos there's nothin' for them to eat.'

Daddy looked confused, and began to march away. 'I'm going for a walk,' he declared. His eyes were brim-full with moisture. Succumbing to a sudden, irresistible urge, I gripped his arm and pushed him gently: tears spilled from his eyes and ran down his face.

'They's only cows, Daddy,' I said. 'You's got to stay yere, help me keep 'em from goin' on the vegetables.'

Reluctantly he stepped back, and gazed towards the barn, where shadows swallowed first Tom and then the gaunt cow he was leading. Ian didn't follow him: he hesitated outside. I ran across the yard, past Ian and into the barn, and swung the doors shut behind me.

Douglas put the gun to the cow's forehead and squeezed the trigger. Her knees buckled, and spindly legs gave out. She sank forward, and then rolled over like a floppy doll. Outside, only Daddy discerned the flutter that shimmered through the herd, like a faint breeze through a field of corn.

Tom pulled tight a slip-knot over the hind legs of the carcass and strung her up on the pulley, which we swung along the freshly oiled track that ran round to the back door of the barn, where we dropped the carcass into the trailer that Mike Howard had parked there.

I opened the front doors of the barn, and the cows in the yard stopped chewing and looked at me with dumb suspicion. Tom walked straight through the herd to a maverick at its centre, and put his halter over its neck. He had chosen the strongest of that sorry group: although as emaciated as all the others there was a measure of defiance still in the rigid uprightness of his neck. Tom turned to lead him to the barn but he stood his ground, pulling Tom up short. Tom turned round: there was resentment at the edges of the bullock's widened eyes as well as fear. Tom, narrowing his own eyes, growled: 'The reaper's yere. Your time's up.' The bullock stared back at him a moment longer, then opened his mouth and let out a long, mournful low, a rising note of anger that surrendered to a resigned moo. Tom felt himself enveloped in a sweet cloud of freshly mown hay, and he led the bullock to the barn.

Flies and delirious mosquitoes gathered at the back of the barn. The sun didn't move. Mother picked weeds from cracks in the concrete.

Half the herd in the farmyard had been destroyed: a patch of blood where each animal fell had spread out. The barn was gradually being filled with a curious odour that sat with a metallic taste on my tongue. I watched Douglas intently: at the back door of the barn, before we lowered each corpse into the trailer, he selected a bistoury from the set of surgical instruments given to him on his fourteenth birthday. With the razor-sharp blade Douglas spilled the last residue of life from the animal, blood splattering his apron. I was mesmerized: Douglas had never changed, his bovine bulk, carrying the functional fat of farmers, was ageless, his black curly hair peppered lightly grey. I'd never heard him utter a sentence of more than four words, and we children had always avoided him as much as he had us. But now, watching him handle those instruments in his ham-like hands with an unbelievable delicacy and precision, despatching a herd of unfortunate cows as if in reality he was making some subtle improvement to their lives, I felt the urge to take one of his scalpels myself and cut through the lengths of bailer twine that tightened his buttonless jacket, to lean into the sweat-suffused shirts and the delicacy of those enormous hands.

Meanwhile, we'd strung up another limp and rickety cow and pulled it along the track to the back door. Douglas pressed two fingers against its throat, then bent over his bag of instruments and picked out a catling. He pulled taut the end of a length of twine that tumbled from his pocket and checked the sharpness of the blade. I stepped round the

243

hanging carcass to stand beside him as he lifted the neat tool, almost lost in his fleshy fingers, to the animal's neck.

I inhaled deeply his sweat, run so deep into the fabric of his clothes that it had lost its ammoniacal tang and become a tantalizing sweet scent: I wanted to bury my face in his firm barrel of flesh. Douglas made a deep incision on one side of the animal's neck and drew the catling in a graceful curve across to the other side, cleanly slicing through the animal's flesh. Most of the purple blood gurgled onto Douglas's filthy apron, but I felt drops of it sprinkle over my face and eyelids. The metallic taste on my tongue grew heavy and filled my mouth, and I felt myself suffocating in the heavy odours that had replaced all the air in the barn. I turned and ran through the dense cloud of death, ignoring Tom's command to come back, and swung the barn doors open.

The ten remaining cattle had been standing motionless, in a state of resignation, but as the barn doors groaned on their hinges and, coming into the fierce sunlight, I tried to wipe the blood from my eyelids, the herd was hit by the malodorous promise of extinction. All at once they began turning and lowing, and pawing the ground.

'Close in on 'em!' shouted Ian, but within seconds their shapes were lost in a vortex of dust. We were all forced back, choking. Tom came running out of the barn and up to Ian, who held a handkerchief over his mouth and was stepping indecisively back and forth.

'Drop back, drop back,' Tom told him. The dogs were already alert, and at his whistle they flew forward, round the whirlwind in the middle of the yard, and to his feet. He stationed the dogs and members of his family in a wide circle around the cows, and watched anxiously, as we waited for them to calm down.

Douglas took advantage of the respite to sharpen his instruments. The flurry of resistance outside didn't bother him: he was a patient man. Usually he brought along his own animal, a spindly, ageless cow, to lead the others through, but he'd figured that the sun would have squeezed all courage from the cattle, or that even if they sensed the danger they might gladly relinquish their tormented existence. He'd reckoned without a lablolly girl.

He sharpened a bistoury with a tiny file, too small even for a woman's nails. He rarely did such work nowadays, most farmers becoming fearful of the law and taking their animals to the shambles at Longdown. Sometimes, though, he'd set out his instruments on the kitchen table and bring up their edge, just for the pleasure of working them down along an infinite line of degrees of sharpness. 'You wants to get the atoms on the edge dancin' single-file,' his father had told him. Blunt knives he found infuriating and more than once, as a child, he'd grabbed one from his mother's hand as she sliced vegetables or chopped meat, and taken it off to sharpen its blade.

Filing his scalpels by Mike Howard's trailer, the carcasses giving off in the hot sun a faint, gamey aroma whilst a dark stain spread slowly out across the floor of the barn, Douglas felt himself, as he did every time, the executioner not just of these few cattle on our farm but of all the animals he'd ever slaughtered: his life arranged itself about those occasions, and concertinaed in upon them, accumulating them all in the present moment. He remembered the Sunday ferreting expeditions with his father, rabbits bounding from their holes and slamming up against an invisible wall as he pulled the trigger of his Mauser; he remembered all the Saturday mornings his mother had asked him to bring a chicken in, and how by the time he'd reached double figures he could break their scrawny necks with an imperceptible twist of two fingers, so that as he held them by their feet and they flapped a desperate farewell to existence other children already began to keep their distance; he remembered every unwanted litter of mongrels that the squeamish newcomers asked him to dispose of, and which he would take home in a feedbag over his shoulder, stun with one swing of a club and drop into a bucket of water; and finally, always last even though by now it had happened over twenty-five years before, he remembered that unconscionable winter when he was hired to slaughter the peacocks, on the 14th Viscount's estate, that were eating up the hibernating vegetation. He remembered through his impenetrable silence the screeching uttered from their windpipes when he sliced off their necks, and he remembered, with a pain that squeezed his insides, Maria, the gypsy-like kitchen maid for whom he'd opened a gash on his hand, and who after love chattered to him in her native Portuguese and made him laugh.

At that moment Maria was standing on the rectory verandah, looking across the village at the spiral of dust rising from our farmyard: she'd stepped outside when she felt her eyes unaccountably moisten, and she was stung with pity for other people's sons and daughters. She became aware of a metallic taste on her tongue and tried to spit it out, but it stayed. Then she saw the cyclone of dust lifting.

'What the 'ell's this?' cried Ian, as a gap appeared between the bottom of the swirling cloud and the ground.

'Buggered if I know,' said Tom.

The cloud continued to rise, until it was so far off the ground that the dogs ran across the yard beneath it, and Daddy bent forward and followed them.

Mother caught him on the other side just as the animals' hooves appeared from the bottom of the cloud, and gradually more and more of their bodies came into view as they slowly floated back down to the ground. Above them the cloud continued to rise but, deprived of its bovine dynamo, it was losing its spiral shape and cohesion, the particles gradually scattering across the sky.

The cattle were drenched in a sticky sweat to which dust had adhered, and their eyes were once more dull and lifeless. Then Tom suddenly exclaimed: 'But there's only nine of the buggers!' We all looked up at the high, dispersing cloud, and each wondered whether we could really believe what we thought we saw in the chaotic atoms of dust: the faintest suggestion of the skeletal frame of one fleshless old cow. And although Ian swore us all to secrecy, for fear of incurring the ridicule of the other farming families, people would tell their children, years later, of the time when knots of toads spent all summer searching for their stolen ponds and a cow floated over the village.

*

Mother helped Tom with the rest of the herd. I sat on an overturned drum and leaned back against the wall of the barn, eyes closed. The blood on my face and clothes had coagulated, clotted by the dry sun into faint crimson splotches, and the confusion I'd felt prickle throughout my body was now breaking out through my skin.

Ian still looked uncomfortable. He went into the kitchen and reappeared a moment later rolling a cigarette between his thumbs and forefingers. Daddy was there by the door: he fixed his gaze on the cigarette as Ian walked up to him, amazed that not a whisker of tobacco was dropped. Ian licked the sticky edge of the paper and rolled it tight.

'What's the matter, Dad?' he asked.

Daddy thought for a moment. 'I don't know,' he replied. Their voices carried across the farmyard as if across a room.

'Well, Dad, I tell you. I've just made the best, or the bloody worst, decision of my life,' said Ian, glad to be able to unburden his conscience to someone who'd then forget it. 'I've 'ad the most part of our 'erd killed so's us can plough up for grain and get they subsidies. If I'd left it another day grandfather would never have allowed it: cos this summer's comin' to an end. And I knew it. The air's all heavy.'

He was right. What Ian had calculated through the long, dehydrated nights for weeks past, weighing up the endlessly variable permutations of livestock, bales of hay, acres of field, tonnes of grain and guaranteed money, of a grandfather's conservatism, a mother's sentiment, the envy of uncles and the likelihood of rain, calculated with the fearful analysis of a chess player who knows that despite his most thorough concentration and computation there always lies just beyond the extent of his reason, in the infinity of permutations, the move that will beat him; what Ian had calculated seemed to have come true with eerily perfect timing.

The desiccated air filled up with moisture like a sponge. Darkness fell. Daddy, sitting outside with the dogs, was making a fist with his hand, as if under the illusion that he'd be able to squeeze water out of the very air, when Mike Howard appeared out of the dusk. Ian and Tom came out to join him, and the three of them walked round the back of the barn. We heard the tractor splutter into life and the trailer bumping into the lane, but they didn't use any headlights.

A single dry crackle of thunder ricocheted across the sky.

Mother took the sheets in off the line; dried up flowers opened their petals like mouths to catch the impending rain; it was so humid our clothes slid around our skins, the air was heavy and oppressive, and the sun set leaving trails of indigo and yellow along the horizon; the Honeywills put their donkey in the garage because it didn't like lightning, and newcomers' dogs hid under the sofas; the Rector set an old watering-can in the middle of the floor of the largest empty bedroom; deer whose thirst had brought them out into the open retreated back into the forest; Corporal Alcock called for ringers to meet in the belfry ready to peal the bells when the thunderstorm started; birds stopped singing and flies stopped buzzing and there was an eerie silence as the world held its breath.

Ian and Tom came home grinning and opened a bottle of Calvados, and they poured everyone a glass. It burned my throat. Then grandfather walked slowly into the yard, smoking his pipe, and we stopped laughing. He ignored us and went straight inside, but we heard him tell grandmother: 'Howards' cows is lying down in their field: 'tis going to rain tonight,' before carrying on upstairs to bed.

That was enough for me. I ran off with Daddy so we could stand under the rain together when it came, any minute now, that was for sure, and we skipped up to the Brown, excited as everyone else in the village.

And we were all wrong.

CHAPTER TWENTY-FIVE

Dust

The certainty felt by people, plants and animals of the imminence of rain was no more than a dream, a nocturnal illusion caused by something we ate, perhaps the yoghurt that no one liked but mother made to use up the spoiled milk, or possibly the hens' eggs that left an aftertaste of onions. Perhaps it was caused by the same piskies who in grandmother's day brought heather honey down from the moor and spread it on the underside of bedsteads, just to make people's mouths water as they slept. But it must have been an illusion, because we were woken as usual by the cockerel's crowing and rushed to our windows, thrilled by the prospect of rain, only to be greeted by the same slow infusion of blue into the sky, the same tentative breath of dew on the newcomers' lawns that vanished beneath one's gaze, and the chickens in our farmyard pecking in the same dust.

The disappointment was palpable: everyone shared grandfather's foul early morning mood, except that no amount of tea would dispel it. Ian was muttering about some dog that was chasing sheep, and that night a number of the hippies' truck windows were shattered by stones that came out of the darkness. But it didn't last long. People just began to lose hope, because they thought things would never change. The combe in which the village was set had become a cauldron, and like a dish stewed too long people's feelings evaporated. Only Tom found any consolation, as he realized that Susanna had simply been the first to suffer and that her apathy towards him wasn't personal after all. He no longer found it painful to watch her riding her pony endlessly across sad pastures as if lost, and he held her languid hand in his with patient pity. In a way he was happier and more in love than ever, as they spent the whole afternoon lost on the sofa, moving as if under water.

Animals were no better off than people: the dogs slunk along the sides of the buildings, staying in the shadows; the chickens started laying perfectly good eggs in semi-transparent, soft shells that were more like skin. I took one up to grandmother, who'd decided to stay in bed for the day, for her to feel too, but she said it made her uncomfortable, and I told her about the illness that was sapping people's feelings. She wanted to know the symptoms.

'Do it begin with a sense of foreboding?' she asked.

'Yes,' I said.

'Do people feel a dead weight in the stomach?'

'Like a melon – '

I wasn't able to get any further before grandmother interrupted me, alarmed, her milky eyes open wide.

'I knew it!' she exclaimed. ''Tis the return of the sweating sickness. I knew it when I felt the dust in my nostrils.'

I suppose mother must have overheard. When I came out of grandmother's room she'd already started sweeping up the cobwebby dust that settled on surfaces when no one was looking. She worked methodically through the house, sweeping the dust into a pan with a soft brush, moving quietly and slowly so as not to unsettle the dust before she could catch it, and filling three bin-liners. But the next morning there was a new layer covering the furniture in all the rooms, so she started again. This ridiculous activity was no defence against the indifference that had infiltrated the village, but at least it gave mother herself a few days' respite, as the dust that settled invisibly as soon as she'd swept it away so infuriated her that her desire to outfight it became an implacable obsession, which soon spread to other aspects of cleanliness. She polished the windows so fervently that swallows stunned themselves against the shiny glass and one night a barn owl broke clean through a window pane. We noticed him at breakfast the next morning, sitting stock still on the clothes rail above the stove and scrutinizing us with melancholy eyes.

That seemed to puncture mother's delusion, and she ceased caring about the indefatigable piskies of the dust. Pamela, too, succumbed. I drove with her to the clinic at Chudleigh to make sure she didn't fall asleep at the wheel when she went to get a sick note. Dr Buckle said it was glandular fever and prepared an injection. As the needle sank into her arm and the useless medicine entered her blood Pamela simply smiled at him, and I knew that it was getting late.

It was then that the hippies left, not because they were intimidated, since people's hostility had evaporated, but because they were worried that the indifference would confuse the effect of their Moroccan hashish. They almost left behind one of their number, a bearded giant of a man who had trodden softly across the farmyard to see if we could sell him some eggs for the journey and somehow ended up at grandmother's bedside. He stayed for hours. I went to tell him his friends were leaving.

'That's not a real aura, Nicholas,' she was telling him, "tis only static.'

'No, man, that's where you're wrong,' he replied softly. 'It's the blue electric membrane.'

He stood up and bent over to kiss her goodbye before he left, dwarfing her. She looked like a precocious child because she still wore spectacles, more out of her old habit of trying to fool people that she could see than because they helped her focus. We'd had to tell her that they were steaming up, and Dr Buckle had diagnosed glaucoma: 'If she doesn't have this extremely minor operation,' he told grandfather, 'there'll be a build-up of pressure behind the eye until it pops.'

'What's the use?' she complained. "Tis like cuttin' the toenails of an amputated leg.' In the end she'd relented: the ophthalmologist made a slight incision, and fluid spurted out, and for days she'd had to hold cotton wool swabs to her eyes. We couldn't work out where all the fluid was coming from.

Just as at first the exertion of love had kept Tom in bed in the mornings, so too did the languor of indifference, and it wasn't long before Ian caught it off him, spending more and more of the day dozing in his room. He was able to keep a tenuous grip on reality only in the middle of the night, when the heat was just bearably stultifying, by exerting his ferocious concentration on endless games of chess against his computer. Pamela, on the other hand, wasn't bothered about missed rehearsals, and strangers appeared in the farmyard on motorbikes and in Mini cars to ask after her. Daddy chatted to them until they became confused and drove away.

Daddy seemed to be immune, or else I couldn't see the difference. We sat outside the back door at dusk with the dogs and sucked orange-squash ice-cubes from the freezer, which numbed our mouths briefly against the metallic taste on our tongues.

That night everyone was startled awake by the sound of a siren whooping through the darkness. At first I thought Tom must have left the television on, while others looked out of their windows for signs of another fire. But it was only a police car taking a short cut through the village.

'At least we used to see the buggers when they came for their tip at Christmas,' grandfather complained, in a rare loquacious outburst, before going back to bed.

Grandmother had a smile on her face at breakfast. 'I heard the first 'orseman in the night,' she said mysteriously, and was disappointed when we told her about the modern sirens.

'That's the trouble, like I always said,' she declared, 'they should never 'ave replaced horses with cars.' Perhaps she was right. Her friend Nicholas and the other hippies had hardly got out of the village before their trucks started breaking down along the Valley road.

'On the other hand,' grandmother added, 'if there was as many horses as there is cars, we'd be knee deep in it be now.'

Mother shook her head. 'Shame,' she whispered to me. 'Your grandmother's lost more of 'er marbles than she can count.'

I wanted to kick mother's shin under the table, but then she said: 'What on earth *is* that bay doing out there? Bin there ever since I got up.'

Even as I turned round, my heart bucked. I looked out of

the window and there was Johnathan: whether out of politeness or timidity he was standing in the lane, staring at the
tarmac, and occasionally glancing up at our house.

'Don't you even think about it, Alison,' said mother,
adding: 'If he's not gone in ten minutes I'll give 'is father a
call.'

I tried to eat my toast but I couldn't swallow it. I sneaked
another look out of the window: he was still there, looking
pathetic. I tried to pluck up courage, and waited. Time
dragged heavy. Eventually mother got up. I summoned my
energy: she took the teapot over to the kettle and I jumped
out of my chair and ran into the hallway.

'Alison!' she yelled. 'You come back 'ere this *minute*!'

But I was out the front door and running, and no one
could catch me.

'Come on!' I gasped to Johnathan, and we ran along the
lane, up past the Old Rectory, and on into the copse below
the rectory vegetable garden.

We collapsed together and leaned against the trunk of a
pine tree. When I'd got some of my breath back I turned to
Johnathan and said: 'I thought you was *never* going to come
and see me again.'

But Johnathan didn't say anything. He looked startled, like
a rabbit caught in a car's headlights.

'You're not such a scaredy-cat after all,' I reassured him.

He still didn't say anything, he just sat staring at nothing. I
thought he was being a bit over-emotional. I was so glad to
see him, but I didn't want to make a big thing of it.

Then Johnathan put his hands over his face, and started to
tremble. I felt awkward, and regretted dashing out: after all,
I'd be in for it when I got home. I tried to think of
something to say, and I was about to suggest going hunting
for the Rector's wild cucumbers, when Johnathan stammered
something through his fingers.

'What?' I asked.

He took his hands away; his face was bloodless white. 'It
was ho-horrible,' he repeated.

'What was?'

'You n-never saw anything like it, Alison,' he stuttered. 'I saw it all.'

And then he told me: how he'd watched the hippies the night before, as they sought refuge in the deserted grounds of the old estate, silently pushing their vehicles through the Lodge gates and parking them on the terraced lawns. His mother had got him to help carry buckets of water from the outside tap, and to see if their babies needed anything.

In the morning they woke up to find the Valley road full of police vans. Johnathan's father went out in his pyjamas to see what they wanted and they told him it was none of his business, it wasn't his land any more and he'd better get back inside or he'd be charged with obstructing a police officer in the course of duty.

The police, who'd received some minor injuries in Tom's brawl at the Manor Inn car park, had come to evict the hippies in full riot gear. They smashed the windows of the converted buses, frightened the children, made the women cry and the dogs bleed, and forced Nicholas and his scruffy friends to leave, running through a gauntlet of swirling batons.

I had to hold Johnathan's hand to help him stop trembling, and then we both sat there not saying a word, staring ahead through the trees, both wondering what this world, that we were in such a hurry to be a part of, had in store for us.

CHAPTER TWENTY-SIX

Sleep

Granny Sims was convinced that people were suffering from a devil's sickness, so she and her sisters trailed round the village in the merciless midday sun with a petition calling for the revival of church sleep, or healing by dreams, in which people spent the night in the church and the martyrs of history appeared in their dreams with a cure. But no one could be bothered to sign it, so she withdrew to reword a petition that she'd been waiting years for the opportunity to unearth from the bottom of a drawer, calling for the reintroduction of Elizabethan laws that decreed compulsory church attendance on pain of the stocks. Her real upset, however, was yet to come.

It was then that Douglas Westcott began to invite people round to tea, starting with the Rector, who discovered a man so unselfish that the mirrors in his hallway and bathroom only reached up to his shoulders, because he was a full head taller than most people, so that even though he'd had no visitors in ten years he himself had to bend down to shave or brush his hair.

'P'rhaps he don't like to look at his own reflection,' I suggested, but the Rector disagreed.

'You're far too young to be cynical, Alison,' he told me in a disappointed tone of voice.

Douglas stayed behind after the early communion services to help Corporal Alcock blow out the candles, which spoiled half my fun, because I stayed too stacking the prayer books so that I could be there to watch Corporal Alcock's breath turn to flame. People's parents said it was no wonder, the way Corporal Alcock always took communion last, swallowing the remainder of the wine saying: 'Thank you, Rector'; but when the ulcer he'd suppressed for years suddenly exploded in his stomach it shook people for a brief moment from the stupor of indifference and made them feel sorry for what they'd said.

It was the Rector himself who shocked Granny Sims at the next Parochial Church Council meeting. All the members attended, but half of them gazed vacantly out of the window and the other half found their heads growing heavy with the very real weight of fatigue and so they propped them up on their elbows and nodded off. Only Granny Sims, her rigid piety bearing her across the sea of indifference in which everyone else was pleasantly drowning, and the Rector, with his mind always occupied, were able to give their customary attention to the matters in hand, until they reached Any Other Business, whereupon the Rector proposed Douglas Westcott as a new churchwarden and everyone woke up with a bump.

Joseph Howard had to use all his chairman's authority to bring some dignity to the discussion that followed, which confirmed the members of the PCC in their opinion of the Rector's estrangement from reality. He tried to explain, in the old school that muggy evening, the parable of the lost sheep, but despite the lucidity of his argument he made no impression, just as none of his predecessors, going all the way back to the Celtic missionaries who first preached under the same Gospel Oak whose roots still baffled old Martin when he had to dig a grave, had ever been able to explain it to people who couldn't see the sense in searching for some runty old stray when the rest of the flock needed seeing to.

The Rector lost his vote and from that moment on Granny Sims dropped her guard. But the Rector himself, fully recovered from his sickness, devoted more energy than ever to the welfare of his parishioners, relieved to dispense with the pretence of dealing with immortal souls and instead concentrate on the here and now of their bodies. I handed him the jug when he took the unbaptized and ritually immersed them in the quarry pool, to allow adults the relief of the ever icy water, and I passed round cups of tea when he held a storytelling session in the afternoon in the cool church to try to resuscitate people's appetite for life with narrative, using not old Biblical stories as expected but rather serializing instead the Russian novels of his youth, a chapter of which he would read over lunch and then retell in simpler language.

Even Johnathan came to church for that, although it was in the guise of a critic rather than a listener: to my relief and surprise he declared himself impressed by the Rector's literary taste.

'You might find it surprising that an old Anglo-Catholic priest could understand a t-t-tortured Orthodox agnostic, Alison,' he said in his almost-broken voice. 'But you see the real spiritual challenges are universal. I say, he did the G-G-Grand Inquisitor scene really well, don't you think?'

As far as the indifference was concerned, neither these nor the other tactics the Rector employed did any good at all, but he wasn't dismayed.

Grandmother said his dedication reminded her of what she'd been told about the plague, in which so many parish priests died amongst their people that in an episcopal decree of 1349, ordering the emergency relaxation of canonical rules, women were permitted to take confession from the dying.

I could see that grandmother was frustrated at her increasing invalidity, because she knew how useful she would be in such a crisis if only she were still active. She racked her brains thinking of a suitable plant for the Doctrine of Signatures, by which like cured like, the ear-shaped leaf of a cyclamen a cure for deafness and the little eyebright for blindness, but no matter how hard she tried she couldn't think of a flower that resembled indifference.

She did, however, tell me to warn people not to fall asleep during the day and that the consumption of olive oil might be fatal, when I accompanied the Rector round the village distributing orange-flavoured ice-cubes that Daddy and I had prepared in the freezer. The Rector hoped that they might counteract the numbness of the heat, but as he and Maria went from house to house, and people put gloves on when they answered the door because it had got so dry that they gave each other electric shocks when they shook hands, it gradually dawned even on the Rector that the time for last-minute remedies had passed.

Grandfather didn't talk to anyone in the mornings until after he'd had his first mug of tea in the kitchen. It was the only thing grandmother ever complained of about him, because she for her part always awoke refreshed by sleep, enjoyable dreams having replenished her store of good humour. Grandfather always woke first, a few minutes before her, and lay in bed trying to come to terms with another day. During those moments, alone, even more so than in the company of other people, he felt especially discomforted by life. It was as if the consciousness into which he awoke were a new suit a little too narrow across the shoulders, the trousers too short, waist too tight and squeezing his midriff. He was pinched by existence, and each day was faced with having to wear it in anew.

When a smile spread across grandmother's face grandfather knew she was about to wake up, and then he urged himself out of bed and began to get dressed. Grandmother opened her eyes, upon a world reassuringly familiar and full of promise. Her husband was sitting on his side of the bed, doing up his bootlaces; she took in his hunched, unfailing shoulders, his sloping backbone, his cropped white hair. 'Sleep well, my lover?' she asked, or ''Tis a beautiful morning.' But he never replied. The only response she received was the sight of his back rising and then disappearing from the room.

Grandmother would lie there then, disappointment seeping into her well of affection. Just once she wished his face to be beside hers when she awoke, his hand to welcome her into another day together, his voice to greet her, and such was her optimism that she failed to come to terms with the fact that he never would. Every morning of her married life, for a minute or two, she doubted that marriage: she blamed herself for succumbing too easily to his courtship, seduced by the tenacity of the silent farmer who forced his horse through waist-high snow drifts every Sunday afternoon of a long gone winter, to her father's house on the edge of the high moor; she regretted coming down from the wide vistas of that moor to this valley within a valley, dark and enclosed. And then she swept back the covers, interrupting herself with action, refusing to allow herself to ponder too deeply, because this after all was her life.

Recently, though, grandfather had begun to notice that grandmother was finding it harder each morning to emerge from the world of dreams. She seemed like a diver he'd seen in a wildlife programme, emerging from the sea with phosphorescence clinging to her body.

Now grandmother's dreams clung to her, and instead of addressing grandfather with her usual affectionate questions which so irritated him he had to leave the room, she spoke instead to her long dead sister, with whom she'd just been picnicking by Raven's Tor, or to a character in one of the books she'd left behind in her father's house. Instead of antagonizing him, in his bad humour, by being nice to him, she seemed to be barely aware of his presence. After a week of this behaviour grandfather had had enough: he stopped as he was leaving the room, turned round, and said: 'In't you even going to ask me how I is this morning? What the 'ell's up with 'ee?' And he marched off to the bathroom, more crabby than ever.

Grandmother's crepuscular confusion extended to the other end of the day, too, as she resumed the habit she'd once adopted as a young mother of walking through the house with a lantern to check on everyone sleeping. It was a habit she'd only stopped when Daddy married mother, and a new generation was born. Now she lit the paraffin lamp kept in the pantry and wandered through distorted shadows to rediscover, despite her almost total blindness, the calm, intense pleasure of gazing on the sleeping faces of the people she loved most. On one of those nights, though, mother woke suddenly to find herself being stared through by her mother-in-law, a stupid smile on her face, and she leapt angrily out of bed.

'What do you think you're doing, mother?' she cried, grabbing the lantern. 'You'll kill us all, you old fool.' Daddy woke then, and watched without comprehension as mother grabbed her arm, saying: 'Do 'ee want to burn the 'ole house down?' and led her off to grandfather, who was lying in bed, waiting for his wife to join him so that he could get to sleep.

'If you can't keep an eye on her,' mother told him, her temper at its shortest by being disturbed from deep sleep, 'maybe us should find her somewhere's where people can,' and she swept downstairs to hide the lantern at the back of the cupboard under the stairs.

Grandmother was fulfilling her own prediction that history had reached the top of its spiral and had changed direction: she was stepping backwards through her own life. When Daddy married mother and brought her into the house, grandmother and grandfather moved out of the main bedroom, to make room for the newlyweds, according to the family custom. Now, while grandfather awaited her, having retired first, grandmother would make her way to the wrong room, where she undressed, put on someone else's voluminous nightdress, and got into the wrong bed, mildly surprised to find it empty. Mother, infuriated, would wake her up and escort her back to her own room.

She was slipping into the margin. She became unaware of her own bodily needs and began to have little accidents: Pamela picked up incontinence pads from Chudleigh clinic, and they parked an ancient commode beside her bed. In the middle of the night mother and grandfather picked her up and put her on it, and she emptied herself without having to fully awaken.

Although grandmother stopped the briefly resumed, wandering night-time vigil, in the mornings her dreams clung to her all the more, and each day she grew visibly more confused when she turned round in the kitchen and her great-aunt Isabel wasn't there, or when she couldn't find her mother anywhere in the house to tell her a new word she'd discovered, or when she spoke to God and found that He was no longer in the mood to talk with her. 'I think God's asleep,' she confided to no one in particular, 'that's the trouble these days.'

On Thursday morning I was coming back into the house after another abortive attempt to attend school. I opened the door and almost knocked grandmother over: she'd been standing in the hallway. 'Sorry, grandma,' I said, 'I didn't see you there.' The door open, she was standing in full sunlight, against the shadowy background. Her milky eyes were more opaque than ever. 'The days is comin',' she murmured, 'when all what's hidden will appear.'

It took grandmother a little longer each day to come to terms with the logic of reality, until she stumbled through an entire day in a web of angels, piskies, childhood friends and her father, smiling at her with the smile of an idiot that fathers are unable to contain when they look at their favourite offspring.

She'd left us. We were the family she'd made. She'd given us all of her energy, her heart, her devotion. But now she turned her back on what she'd made, and returned to the family she'd left when she was still a girl.

I was still asleep the next morning when grandmother decided to die.

Mother didn't wake me as usual at three minutes past seven, but at four minutes past I woke anyway, and rose cloudily out of bed. On my way to the bathroom I noticed that the house was still in the grip of night's silence, even though it was light. Usually by the time I got up everyone else was moving around, but now there were none of the sounds of the cock crowing, the grandfather clock ticking, a tractor whining, dogs barking, crockery clinking. Only silence. I checked my watch: nearly ten past seven. In the passageway all the bedroom doors were open; I felt suddenly abandoned. Then at last I heard something: the distant sound of someone's exertion, a long way away, and I padded silently towards the open door of my grandparents' bedroom.

Grandmother was lying in bed, her eyes closed, not breathing. Grandfather was sat in his old grey dressing-gown, on a chair side-on to the bed, on the far side from me, both hands on the eiderdown, bent over. Pam was standing beside him, one hand on the back of his chair. Ian and mother both stood at the end of the bed, while Tom and Daddy were standing off away on the other side. They were all looking at grandmother as if waiting for her to say something, all of them frozen, except for grandfather: it was the first and last time I saw his tears. He wept as silently as he could, because even in this, the saddest moment of his life, he couldn't overcome his customary reserve and grieve openly. With a superhuman effort he held back his sorrow, his mouth clamped shut. Instead his sobs, forced up from the guts of his grief, broke in his throat, so that he looked as if a fishbone were stuck in his gullet. Tears, though, were not so easily thwarted. They brimmed out of his blue eyes and slid over his cheekbones.

I'd not looked at grandmother since my first glance took in the whole room. I didn't want to look at her. That's why I stared at grandfather. But the truth came up from inside me. From the doorway I ran to the bed and was on it before anyone could move, trying to bury myself in beside her, trying to lose myself in her. Ian dragged me off and carried me away; they said I was screaming and shaking. I don't remember. He took me into his room and let me cry with him.

That night Tom slept on the sofa downstairs, to give grandfather his bed. Grandfather couldn't sleep. The doctor had given him some sleeping pills but he ignored them. He missed the damp heat of her body and her shallow, anxious breathing. He calculated that from the age of twenty-four he'd not slept a single moment without her beside him, since even when he went to bed before her exhausted, in the middle of harvest or in the stupor of Christmas, he was unable to fall asleep until she was curled up beside him and the rhythm of her breathing had changed; and in the morning he always woke a few minutes before her, with a farmer's bad conscience, bad-temperedly rising through the darkness towards his first mug of tea. And he resolved there and then that he'd never again sleep without her. He got out of Tom's bed, pulled on his moth-eaten dressing-gown, and returned to their bedroom. There he pulled a chair from the wall up to the bed, took his tobacco pouch from the pocket of his dressing-gown, and filled his pipe. He felt calm, not in a smug or unfeeling way, but because the worst had happened, and now he knew what was to come. He recalled the disastrous summer after the war which almost destroyed the precarious economy of the farm, and how at the moment they understood the full extent of the crisis – their herd wasting away, crops failed – he'd experienced this same sense of utter calm, floating above the disaster and seeing it grow smaller and insignificant.

And as he sat smoking beside her, so he forgave grandmother for doing the one and only thing that in the fifty-six years of their marriage he'd ever asked her not to do, which was to die before him.

The next day a man came dressed in a piano tuner's clothes, and he spent an hour in grandmother's room with the door closed. The following day the man returned with two of his brothers, carrying a child's coffin. As soon as he saw it grandfather lost his temper and ordered them out of the house. Ian conciliated them out in the yard, till grandfather appeared with grandmother's wedding dress, neatly folded and wrapped in tissue paper.

'Use that to measure it this time,' he told them, turning on his heels, and as he slammed the door behind him he spat out: 'Disrespectful bastards.'

Grandmother died with so little fuss that none of us could quite take it in. We were stunned. We'd not prepared ourselves, having missed each of the many clues she'd laid before us in her thoughtful way, dismissing as further signs of second childhood her abstract asides, telling no one in particular that 'I've packed my bags,' 'We'll miss the last train if it don't come soon,' and 'I don't want no flowers, maid.'

It was the sight of the tiny coffin which so angered grandfather that made me realize she was really dead. I kept on remembering her as she was alive, with her smell of face powder, her large bony hands and her throaty voice, fixing an image of her in my mind to last me through the years ahead, to fill the gaping hole inside me, but each memory only made it worse. I needed to cry, to share the loss, but no one else wanted to. They must have been sad too but they wouldn't show it, they put rigid masks on their faces and bit their lips and went off to their rooms alone.

I ran all the way to Johnathan's house across the Valley in the dark, too distraught to be scared, and threw pebbles at his unlit window. Eventually the curtain opened, and then closed again immediately. For one desolate moment I thought he'd hidden himself deep under the bed-covers, but then the light went on around the curtains. Next thing he was at the front door in his pyjamas, ushering me inside.

I didn't give him a chance to ask me what I was doing: as soon as our eyes met I lost all self-control and fell forward into his skinny arms, engulfed in tears.

I must have made a racket. I was dimly aware that at some point the Viscount appeared on the stairs, a misty, bemused vision in his dressing-gown, and I heard Johnathan say: 'It's all right, father, I've got a visitor.'

He didn't say another word until I'd exhausted myself and all I had left were snuffly, choking breaths. Then he extricated his damp pyjama-top from my clammy embrace, poured a glass from his parents' drinks cabinet and said: 'Swallow this.' It was sour and burning. Then he took me upstairs, pulled my trainers and jeans off, and laid his duvet over me, and I sank into sleep beside him.

Grandfather had never allowed dogs inside the house. He'd been given his first one, a new-born puppy, for his first birthday, so that they could grow up together. The puppy, a black and white mongrel bitch called Nipper, soon outgrew him, but only for a brief period before he caught her up again, and grew up and away from her. She remained his shadow throughout his childhood, and before she'd died, at the age of fourteen, he'd replaced her with one of her identical granddaughters, the runt of the latest litter because they make the best sheepdogs. Her name was Tinker. That was the pattern for the rest of his life: he not only replaced each one as she grew old with one of her granddaughters, always a bitch, but he christened each one with the name of her grandmother's grandmother. For that reason, and the fact that he taught them to respond to the same gruff commands, grandfather almost convinced himself that he was accompanied throughout his long life by one or other of the same two dogs, reacting with the same quicksilver obedience to his commands, even before he'd uttered them, as they had when he was nine years old: nipping the heels of a lazy bullock; retrieving rabbits stunned by the invisible bullets of his .22 rifle; or selecting a sheep in the middle of a flock and circling it at such mesmerizing speed that it thought itself surrounded, and gave in.

Now, though, without telling anyone, he invited Tinker inside, to share his vigil at grandmother's side. He'd explained to me that to calculate a dog's age relative to a person's you had to multiply by seven, and by that reckoning Tinker was almost a hundred years old. She let herself in and out by the kitchen door, waiting patiently for someone to appear and open it, and then padding through without looking at us, shy as her master but proceeding with assurance of her right to go, now, where she'd not been allowed to since she was a small puppy and my companion.

She sat beside him, as he sat beside grandmother, with her paws crossed, glassy-eyed and blinking slowly. Now and then she climbed onto a chair by the window, put her front paws on the sill, and looked outside, eyes wide open, as if waiting for grandmother's spirit to return.

I knew it never would. They'd brought back a larger coffin, and grandmother looked lost inside it. The undertaker's embalming fluid had given her the complexion of waxed fruit. I tried not to look at her when I came, with a mug of sickly sweet tea or a feather for his pipe, to keep grandfather company. Members of the family came to the house, and they stood beside grandfather with a hand on his shoulder, expressing platitudes of sympathy he ignored, and coughing in the fug of tobacco smoke that filled the room. Word got round the village of how grandfather puffed on his pipe beside the body of his wife, and people tutted to each other at such behaviour.

Dusk was absorbing the light in the room, and we'd been sitting silently, when he suddenly said, without turning to me: "Er idn't gone, maid, 'er's waitin'.'

'What for, grandpa?'

'For me, maid. And 'twon't be too long, I can assure 'ee of that.'

'Then what, grandpa?'

'Then us'll be 'gether 'gain.' He spoke with calm finality, and there was no more to be said. I wanted to ask him where it was they were going to meet, what they'd do together. But I knew it would only irritate him. He had lost part of himself, and looked forward only to losing the rest, having decided to believe that in doing so he would in reality become whole again.

The next time he spoke I was dozing, but was brought back instantly by his quiet voice in the darkness.

'They says other men falls in love in springtime. Me, I met your grandmother in autumn, and I courted her through the winter: we was married in May, near enough sixty year ago, that's the reason us endured, like.' His voice began to waver. 'It don't make no sense, but they you plants September gets their roots in best. You could dig up an old vegetable garden been abandoned fifty year, and still bring up a stack of tatties on your fork.'

Grandfather coughed, and a gob of phlegm slid up his throat. He spat it into his handkerchief. 'Leave me now, maid. I wants to be alone with 'er.'

When the Rector came he didn't stay long. I took him upstairs to grandfather. I'd never seen just the two of them together before. They had little to say to each other. The

Rector was confident of his ability to lend comfort to the bereaved, even to those who rarely came to church, because at such a time they were glad to accept that the person they'd lost had not been wiped out but had moved on to a more important place, and that they too would join them there when the time came. But grandfather only listened politely, impassive, and when the Rector paused grandfather gave him a list of hymns she would have wanted sung at her funeral, and got up to see him out.

A long time ago grandfather had consented to attend confirmation classes because his mother, who sang in the choir when we still had one, long before the days of Corporal Alcock, insisted that he did so. But after his first communion at the age of thirteen, when he took his wafer and sip of wine from the purple-robed Bishop of Exeter, he determined never to go to church again except, reluctantly, for baptisms, weddings and funerals, and then only to please the women. He didn't even go with most of the other men of the village to midnight mass on Christmas Eve, when the damp smell and the scent of candles was overpowered by alcohol on the breath of unsteady men, who'd hurried back from the pub at Ashton. In our family it was different: each Sunday morning, until her arthritis forced her to accept sick communion at home, grandmother led her offspring to church while grandfather stayed behind, reading the Sunday papers that Fred delivered, and occasionally basting the roast.

Grandfather wasn't anti-religion, like some among his generation, who'd watched, as their parents and grandparents had watched with unceasing bitterness, the complicity between priest and Viscount, and who'd greeted the Rector with such hostility when he first arrived. It was just that little of what grandfather had read in Sunday School or sung in the hymns or heard from the pulpit made any sense to him. If God had ever existed at all He'd been only a fleeting visitor, like one of the magicians who entertained the crowd at Chudleigh Carnival for a brief period in grandfather's youth: he imagined God passing through the world of inanimate matter like a magnet across iron filings, causing them to dance into being, and then leaving the world to its fate and continuing on His journey. Responsible as God supposedly was for an infinity of stars, grandfather couldn't see how He would have had time to linger on earth and supervise its growing pains, maintaining a personal interest in every one of the millions who'd professed faith in Him.

Apart from this life-breathing God of a fleeting wind, grandfather didn't believe in the all-seeing and omnipotent Father of religion, because in his experience everything could be explained by nature. Its laws could be learned and respected, and when they were transgressed or tampered with then someone had to suffer. Certainly there were many things no one understood, but knowledge was something gradually accumulated in time: things that in his childhood were inconceivable had become commonplace during his lifetime: television, broadcasting events from the other side of the world even as they happened; travel, in God's footsteps, to other planets; automatic washing machines in almost every home; babies conceived in glass tubes; dead men's hearts sewn into other people's bodies, to pump an extra lifetime.

There were many things no one understood, but any fool could see that there was no limit to knowledge. Only people who knew more than was good for them imagined their knowledge to give them power over nature. Nature would always prove unpredictable; but that didn't mean it couldn't be predicted.

Here in the Valley, on the farms, they knew enough about the earth and about animals to copy their parents' customs, adding one or two of their own, to exist in an uneasy, mistrustful, respectful partnership with nature. At least that's how it used to be.

Neither did grandfather believe in life after death, because he couldn't see how something could live apart from its body, and he knew the difference between a body and a carcass because he'd seen so many hundreds, thousands of them in his life. When an animal died, whether it was human, bovine, or one of his beloved dogs, then that was it, the end of the story, and life was for the living. Grandmother's

sentimental attachment to the piskies and angels of her childhood had just been a weakness she'd not wanted to grow out
of, and which he'd patiently put up with without ever making
fun of her.

So when he told me that all he wanted was to rejoin her I
knew he'd not undergone an easy conversion, grasping in his
distress after dishonest consolation. What he meant was that
he knew he couldn't live without her and that he'd rather join
her in oblivion, in the darkness that awaited them, than
remain here without her.

In the days after the funeral, of which I have no memory at
all, except for Auntie Sarah's Toll rung on the bell as we
walked away from the grave, grandfather's habits gradually
resumed their normal pattern: when the cock first crowed he
rose as usual, washed and dressed in his vinegary silence,
drank a mug of sweet tea with Ian and Tom, and followed
them into the yard for their early morning chores before
breakfast. And so he carried on through the days, padding
like a somnambulist through his familiar routines, performing
superfluous tasks that didn't need doing that summer when
time stood still, with Tinker at his heel, as if nothing out of
the ordinary had occurred, showing no more sign of his grief.
He came back into the house at dusk, hung his cap on the
hook in the hallway, consumed the meal mother left for him
in the oven, and then watched television if there was a
wildlife programme on, before slipping upstairs without
saying goodnight, as was his habit.

Grandfather brushed his teeth, put on his pyjamas and
wrapped himself up in his grey woollen dressing-gown to
contain the shivers of an old man despite the unrelenting
temperature. The only thing different from normal was that
now Tinker came in with him and curled herself up at his
feet, blinking her heavy eyelids in the way that dogs do,
pretending they're not sleepy. He filled his pipe as usual for
his last smoke of the day, staring into the darkness through
the window he'd once made, while around him the members
of the household made their ways to their own bedrooms.

He showed us no sign of grief. But at night, while the rest of the world was sleeping, grandfather lay on his back and stared at the ceiling, not bothering to take off his dressing-gown or get under the covers, and half-way through the night he turned over and faced the wall. He was surprised by how little willpower it took to stay awake, having prepared himself as if for a swim from one side of the quarry pool to the other, braving the pull of the deep as he had as a young man, remembering well how cramp attacked your body only when you were stranded in the middle. He imagined that sleep, too, would drag him down when he was at his most vulnerable, at two a.m. in the dead calm of the night. Instead, having decided to stay awake, he found sleep exerted no pull on him, no yawns, no feeling of fatigue. His only problem was boredom. He'd never had reason to appreciate how long a night lasts. Now, with nothing to do the nights seemed interminable, and grandfather wondered how he'd make his way across them to the dawn. Boredom like he'd never known threatened to shrivel his spirit, and he had no resources with which to combat it: he refused to seek refuge in memories, because he didn't believe in living in the past, and neither could he escape into the future, for he had no plans at all. He fell back on his willpower, and rediscovered his implacable resolve of a youthful suitor, who'd forced his horse through waist-high drifts every Sunday of a distant winter, to persuade the young woman of the moor to become his bride. He told himself he was courting her now, except that instead of inviting her to join him in a new life, he was coming to rejoin her in death.

That was how grandfather kept himself awake until the world outside began to take shape in the first light of dawn, which came as a great relief but which he greeted nevertheless in cantankerous mood, resenting it out of habit even as it prised him from the torturous boredom of his bed.

Grandfather told no one of his sleepless nights, as he carried on throughout the day as usual, and no one noticed anything was wrong, because they were too wrapped up in themselves.

Ian was busy planning the final changes that he said would take the farm into the twenty-first century. 'Agriculture's an industry now,' he reminded us. 'We've got to compete with big business, and not just in this country but all of Europe too. Us'll have no more chickens pecking grit in the yard,' he said, as he drove off to consult with architects over building plans to house battery hens. 'Animals is a waste of land resource,' he said, 'cereals is where the money is today,' as he made a telephone call to book in good time the services of a crop-spraying aeroplane for the following summer.

As for Pamela, I hardly noticed that she hadn't been around until she appeared one Sunday in a hire-van, which she filled with the contents of her room before kissing us goodbye and going back to a flat she'd rented in Exeter. Tom, meanwhile, spent more time than ever with Susanna, and they never let go of each other. They were like two people blinded by some accident who needed the constant reassurance of touch to verify their bodies were still intact.

Then one evening it was announced on the local news that the strike was over and all the schools would be back to normal the following Monday. Mother looked over at me and said: 'What a mollywallops you is, Alison. We can't have you goin' off to school like that.'

'What're you on about?' I asked.

'Come with me,' she said, and took me into the kitchen, where she put a towel round my neck and sheets of newspaper on the floor. I couldn't believe it: she knew how grandmother went on about my hair being special in the family, but I was speechless before this callous act of sabotage. Long clumps of shiny black hair fell on my lap and on the floor around me. And I sat there in silent fury.

As soon as she'd finished I stormed out of the kitchen and looked in the mirror in the hallway, to discover with a shock that I wasn't me any more. My drastic haircut revealed a stranger who gaped back, with my eyes and mouth and nose and everything but they'd changed somehow, been refash-ioned into a bizarrely altered model of myself. As if my long hair had been covering up changes in me. And as I stared at my strange reflection mother called through from the kitchen, as if reading my mind: 'That's right: you're not a child any more, girl.'

It was Daddy who asked: 'What's up with the old man?' and we watched grandfather for a day or two. He'd told no one of his sleepless nights, but something in his manner betrayed him, a hesitancy in his movement, his limbs preoccupied. We all noticed it now, but we couldn't put a finger on its cause, so mother called out Dr Buckle. Grandfather didn't object to being examined: he stripped to his string vest and subjected himself to Dr Buckle's clumsy fingers tapping his hollow back, to the cold metal of his stethoscope, which made him tremble, and to a spatula pressed upon his tongue. Dr Buckle pronounced him fit as a fiddle, but in the kitchen he whispered to mother that his heartbeat seemed sluggish, and that it might be a good idea if he stopped smoking. And so it was that grandfather let mother take his pipe away, without a word of complaint relinquishing his one consolation, in what he'd decided were to be the last days of his life.

CHAPTER TWENTY-SEVEN

Brothers

As soon as he was strong enough the Rector had loaded the rest of Maria's belongings into the Commer parish van and brought them to the rectory. If he thought people would be scandalized he was wrong: no one batted an eyelid. The few who even noticed only wondered why he hadn't done it years ago. They'd seen it coming long before the Rector ever had, because although he'd preached his gospel of love to the world he'd lived so long without it himself he'd learned how to manage.

Now Maria moved into his house and into his life with so little fuss that the Rector had to pinch himself to realize she hadn't always inhabited them, except that he was experiencing emotions he'd not felt in forty years. At first he couldn't fathom what they were, until it finally dawned on him that he was in love. The confusing difference was that when he was a younger man, he recalled with painful nostalgia, those emotions had made themselves manifest by wreaking havoc throughout his body, making his spine tingle, his stomach churn, his mind spin, his kidneys overact, his knees tremble and his sense of balance go haywire. Now his feelings were concentrated in one single organ, his heart, which pumped warm and contented blood around his body.

Maria didn't try to change the Rector's way of life at all. She was as much a confirmed spinster as he was a reconstituted bachelor; she put her food in the fridge and explained in Portuguese that the bottom shelf was for her and the rest for him, and they even cooked separate meals.

At eight-thirty in the morning she left the house and didn't reappear until a quarter past five with a bundle of sheets she proceeded to iron in front of the mirror in the old drawing-room. Their lives ran parallel to each other until after supper, when they'd washed up their own utensils, one after the other, and the Rector had retreated to his study. Then Maria walked in, sat down in the armchair without even looking at him, and proceeded to read a book. The first evening the Rector found it difficult to concentrate on the sermon he was writing and kept looking at her because he felt her gaze burning his skin. But whenever he glanced in her direction he only found her engrossed in her reading. The second evening, however, he calmed down, and discovered that her quietly breathing presence made him feel better inside in some mysterious way and, if anything, helped him in his work.

At half past ten his concentration was broken by the firm thud of a book being closed and he looked up to see Maria rising from her seat. She stepped forward, said something in her native language, smiled, kissed him goodnight, and retired to her room next to his at the end of the upstairs corridor.

On the fourth day after her arrival the Rector was finishing his breakfast of bacon and eggs as Maria made to leave for work.

'Wait a minute,' he said, forgetting in his absent-minded way that she didn't understand a word he said. 'Look, Maria, there's no need for you to go and clean people's houses any more. My income's large enough for both our needs.'

Maria smiled at him. 'Don't be soft,' she said in a strange Portuguese–Devonian accent, 'I've not been supported by a man since I were nine year old. There in't no need to start now, silly.'

Grandfather tried to keep up with the boys, but when he realized about midway through the morning that he was only holding them up, he dropped back and let them get on with their work. He'd spend the rest of the day pottering around doing things he'd never done in his life before but found were quite useful, determined to leave the farm in as good a condition as possible, sure that Ian would realize his foolishness and scale down his ambition, while cursing himself for making the farm so much bigger than the one his father had passed on to him. It was something he'd never particularly wanted to do anyway, it had just happened, somehow. Now he sanded down and painted the door- and window-frames of the sheds and creosoted their beams, in preparation for the piglets they'd surely buy in the spring; he spent three days pruning the apple and pear trees in the orchard, so unsteady on the ladder that Daddy and I had to take turns standing on the bottom rung; and he went around setting light to clumps of dead grass at the foot of trees and along fences. I had to watch him then, too, in my last week before school, because Ian was sure he'd start a fire, since everything on the surface of the earth was tinder dry. But grandfather's little fires never got out of control: he understood the element. It was actually from him that Ian had inherited his skill at burning stubble.

Once he'd started, grandfather took to burning dried grass with an enthusiasm that was compulsive. He didn't even notice that I was there: he just went from one clump to another, tested the wind by licking his finger and holding it up in the air, and struck a match. He set off little pyres all over a field and left charred patches behind him; it was like he was making obsequies for grandmother. He'd found his own way of saying goodbye to her, all across their farm.

Then grandfather looked around and saw me. 'These bloody wasps is gettin' on my nerves, Alison,' he said. 'They's everywhere. Come on, I'll show you how to burn their nest, flush the buggers out for good.'

We found them drifting in and out of a hedge in the bank up behind the house, and grandfather pulled up some armfuls of dried grass: oblivious of wasps buzzing around his head he stuffed the grass into the hedge. I stood well back.

'Aren't you getting stung, grandpa?' I called.

'In't no use worryin' about that, maid. Go get a can of petrol out the barn.'

He emptied the entire contents over the wodge of grass. The air shimmered, and stank of petrol. He stepped back, grinning all over his face.

275

'You can't use half measures with these buggers,' he declared. He struck a match and flicked it towards the hedge. Nothing happened, so he did it again, but again the match died.

'Damn!' he said, and stepped forward. He struck another match and reached out with it: the petrol-soaked grass whooshed up in a rush of flame. Grandfather staggered back, his hair and eyebrows singed, but still grinning, while above the roar of the fire came the buzzing of angry wasps, as hundreds of them came out into the air and swarmed around in irate, confused circles.

'That'll do the job,' grandfather said, as he turned and hobbled back to the house. I picked up the empty petrol can and followed him.

That night I had a dream: it was soon after dawn, but everyone else was sleeping. A damp, early morning mist clung to the earth, bleaching the colours so that everything was a dull lifeless shade of grey or green, and muffling whatever sounds might have carried from the fields around. Then a distant, intermittent clacking entered the edges of my hearing. As it grew louder I recognized it as a horse's hooves approaching at a gallop, coming into the village along the road behind the almshouse. It grew louder and louder in that grey, dull silence and then appeared past the houses on fire, bright orange flames raging from its mane and back and tail, frenziedly galloping through the village.

Ian was left to withstand alone the barrage of drivel that poured from Tom's mouth, which he put up with stoically, keeping his irritation under control, until Tom started to explain the meaning of love. He wouldn't have minded if Tom had asked his advice on the subject, realizing in time the trap he had set for himself and appealing to Ian to help extricate him. That was what Ian had been expecting, and he'd prepared his answers, not out of smugness but compassion. What he never expected was for Tom to start explaining to him, his older brother, about love. He told him what it felt like, like an illness except that it was the opposite, and he told

276

him how to cope with the symptoms, which was to encourage them. He noted how strange it was, but true none the less, that when you really love someone the thing you most want to do is to die for them, and it was only a shame that no opportunity seemed to present itself. On the basis of Susanna's behaviour he told Ian what women were like, in what ways they were different from men and in what ways the same. Ian couldn't believe his ears. For the first day or two he smiled in response, his smile of complicity, acknowledging the joke, all the better for being such a meandering but sustained one, and welcome evidence of Tom's newfound sense of humour. Eventually, though, he was forced to admit that Tom was serious, his monotonous monologue was indeed intended to impart the wisdom of his experience, and he had no time for humour because it was more important to tell Ian that he'd discovered something new in the world, more precious than life itself, more nutritious than meat, more substantial than the earth, and yet it was invisible, can you believe that? If people would only listen to him they'd become richer than people in olden times did from the discovery of tin up on Dartmoor, because this was something people made out of nothing, just by being together, and if he called it love that didn't mean he was talking about the same thing people had talked about before when they used that word, it was just that he couldn't think of a better one.

'No, Ian,' he said, pausing for emphasis as Ian held another sheep down and Tom stood above him with the syringe. 'No, the thing is, when you really loves someone 'tis forever, like.'

Ian's irritation turned into anger. He bit his lip, but he felt the anger growing inside him. It increased as he glimpsed Tom and Susanna walking around the village arm in arm; it gave him a headache to catch them in the toolshed, Tom sitting on the workbench while Susanna blew her warm breath into his nostrils; he felt blood gather behind his eyeballs and tingle along his limbs as he watched from the window of his room, next to mine, as they said their lingering goodnights at her front door, disappearing into the shadow of the porch for a period that lengthened every night, until

277

she opened the door and disappeared into the light. His anger mounted right up to that Saturday evening, when he came downstairs dressed like an Edwardian artisan for his night of a stalker on the dance floor, and saw them curled up together on the sofa in front of the television, their limbs so intertwined it was as if they'd been spliced together. Ian bolted his supper down and left without taking his customary glass of Calvados with grandfather and Daddy, slamming shut the door of his yellow van and leaving a brushstroke of burnt rubber in the yard.

He never drank more than two pints of beer, sipping them slowly, because he could see no point in blurring the edges of pleasure. Now, though, he joined his footballing cronies at the bar and copied their uncivilized consumption of double whiskies followed by lager chasers. He'd never enjoyed their company outside the brief, intense intimacy of playing football together, but discovered now how much fun they were to be with when they were drunk, and he lost his bad feeling in their ribald bravado. His head felt light and hot at the same time, and he undid the top button of his shirt as men he'd never got to know before nudged him, shouted lewd references to certain girls in the hall, winked at each other, and argued their right to buy the next round.

The alcohol flooded his senses, and he felt his instincts of a hunter bob only briefly and then disappear beneath the surface. Two girls he recognized but whose names he could not recall asked him and his goalkeeper to dance, and he stumbled past flashing lights into a minefield of music, with its thumping bass and ear-splitting treble, stepping on their toes and falling against them until they abandoned him in the middle of the dance floor.

His friends greeted him back at the bar with admiration and laughter for such a clumsy show, their aloof captain one of the boys at last, no longer the stuck-up silent man they couldn't help respecting but they didn't have to like, who sneaked off with a different woman every week; here he was, having a drink with the lads and prepared to make a fool of himself. He put his arm around someone's shoulder, emptied his glass and smiled with bleary-eyed pleasure.

*

He hadn't even thought of Tom and Susanna for hours. His anger had dissipated, squeezed from his head by alcohol that took up all the space. He came back along the Valley road under the illusion that he was sober. The moon was not quite full, but it was so light that he considered cutting the lights of his van so that he could see more than just what their beam illuminated. There were no other cars about: he felt solid and sure, carefree and at ease. And then, precisely because he was so clear-headed he began to sense his anger with Tom rising once more. 'Dammit,' he thought, 'why should I make myself think of him?' But there was nothing he could do about it: his blood was pulsing more urgently and his muscles were tense, and he was unaware that his clenched knee was pressing the accelerator pedal down against the floor, as the road, raised up to avoid the spring thaw floods, passed the water meadows next to the river.

Some years earlier the Rector, late for a meeting of the Valley parishes joint Flower Festival committee, being held in Bridford, had roared along the Valley road in his Triumph Vitesse. He'd flashed past the Little Hyner lane at sixty miles an hour, past the Hyner Farm entrance at seventy, past the estate drive at eighty, and then entered the chicane in the road there. Unable to hold his lane, he'd had no option but to surrender to his fate and take the bend on the wrong side of the road, at which point he was passed by a car doing the same speed in the opposite direction, also on the wrong side of the road. At that moment the Rector understood that, against all logic, it was possible for God not only to direct the course of the universe but also to follow the destiny of each and every individual, by means of intermediaries in the form of guardian angels.

Now Ian entered the same chicane, coming the opposite way the Rector had then, cursing his brother under his beery breath, driving on automatic pilot. Suddenly his mind shifted and he became conscious of being behind the wheel, only because some bastard had gone and extended the curve of the road. He thought for a moment that the road had been turned into a cul-de-sac with a roundabout at the end, that he was going to be brought right around in a complete circle and be sent back towards Christow, because the bend seemed to be going on for ever. His skin went dry and his blood turned to ice, he was ready for anything, but he knew he was powerless: if he tried to turn the wheel any harder down the van would flip right over, and if he took his foot off the accelerator it would surely skid. Time, too, bent into an endless curve: he seemed to have an age in which to ponder his misfortune. In fact he wanted to roll a cigarette and contemplate the beauty of the car's unchangeable momentum, cruising in a lock-solid groove created by the combination of curvature, speed and gravity.

'H'm,' he thought to himself, ''tis invisible, like love.'

When he saw the road straighten out at last, up ahead, he knew it was too far away, too late, that he and his old van wouldn't make it, because the verge was suddenly coming closer.

'Fuck me, bay,' he said aloud, as both nearside wheels touched the verge, ''tidn't anger, bay,' as the wheels on his side lifted off the road, 'of all people, Ian Freemantle, you prick, you,' as he felt himself light and rising, away from his horrible mood, feeling lucid and light and relieved for the first time in weeks.

'So this is what jealousy feels like,' Ian said to himself, as the van was sprung from the grip of gravity, launched itself over the hedge and spun through the air in a vaulting arc, before falling towards the low-lying meadow.

When Ian woke up he didn't know where he was. He knew somehow that it was night, that he was enclosed in darkness, but there were bright lights directly above him. He was lying down but his legs were bent up towards his torso. There was a faint antiseptic smell, a smell of cleanliness. He could hear movement, footsteps, commotion of some kind, but he didn't know whether it was bustling around him, coming closer or fading into the distance. Trying to piece together the jigsaw he listened for nurses' voices, but heard none. Sensation began slowly to return to his body: he felt bruised somewhere but couldn't at first locate its source. Then he realized that it was all over: every one of his limbs was possessed of a dull ache. His hands and arms returned to his body, tingling with pins and needles. Something instinctive made him lean to his right while his right hand searched in the darkness, which he knew was stupid even as he shouldered the air beside him, except that sure enough he made contact with something, which gave way, and the door of his van dropped off its precarious hinges and clattered to the ground. The chaos into which he'd awoken fell into explicable shape: the van had ended up on its back, headlights pointing solemnly at the sky, as if searching forty years too late for a German plane that had once dipped, unchallenged, along this same Valley. He switched them off.

Ian lowered himself out of the van carefully and wearily. He could feel no bones broken, nor the dampness of blood, only a spreading bruise on both the outside and the inside of his skin. He began to walk tentatively away from the van, and could hear across the meadow the sound of cattle running together, scampering away from the metal comet that had landed in their pasture: so he'd been unconscious only a moment. He made straight towards the river, aiming to cross it at a place he knew, where a branch reached across the water. Then he would walk up past Rydon, enter our land through the copse by the top field, and drop to the back of the house.

As he walked Ian tried to remember what had happened, but something was missing. He recalled shouting goodnight to his mates at the hall, and coming back along the Valley road. It was clear and light, he thought; yes, of course, as it is now. He'd considered cutting the lights but thought better of it, just in case a silent police car was cruising through the area. Then he'd started thinking about something else, he was sure. He couldn't recall actually driving: it seemed to him that it wasn't that he'd forgotten driving along, but rather he'd done so automatically, and so would not have stored the images in his memory anyway. He was preoccupied with something else at the time, dammit, why couldn't he remember?

He was sure it was something important. He stopped by the river and rolled himself a cigarette. His pain trickled away as he racked his brains trying to remember, annoyed with himself but at the same time enjoying his mind's struggle because it was exactly like battling with a chess problem whose solution lurked just outside the margin of your intellectual capacity. 'Maybe this is how father feels all the time,' he thought.

Ian threw the glowing stub of his cigarette into the river and started walking again. Movement jogged the brain cells, which was why he paced to and fro across his room at night, to and fro past the chessboard on his desk, during his nights of a chess player's insomnia.

It came to him, though, not from his mind but from his gut, bile rising towards his heart, as anger once more began to consume him. 'Of course,' he thought, 'that sodding brother of mine, that's what's gettin' to me. Thinks he's William Shakespeare, Tom Crabtree and fuckin' Frank Sinatra, rolled into one. Tellin' me how things is!' And he walked on up past Rydon, cursing as he threaded his way through the penumbral landscape, his brother's happiness filling him with rage, having wiped from his memory his own uninformed, accurate diagnosis of the reason for that rage.

CHAPTER TWENTY-EIGHT

Blood and Water

Grandfather was deteriorating before our eyes. He lost weight he could ill afford to lose, his hair thinned out and revealed the shape of his skull. He was coming to resemble one of the drawings I'd done when I was a small girl, which still clung to the greasy wall above the cooker where mother had pinned them years before: spidery and crooked, as if the muscles and tendons and ligaments of his wasting body were no longer capable of supporting his frame, which was twisting into unlikely angles wrought by a combination of arthritis and grief.

He took to wandering off on his own, without a word to anyone, with each step planting a walking stick, which Tom had cut from an ash tree, on the ground before him like a cane beside sweet-peas, for without it his precarious limbs would surely waver and fall. Despite such slow progress, grandfather sometimes set off so early in the morning that by the time anyone thought to worry about his absence he'd hobbled clear out of the parish, and Ian and I had to drive around the lanes in ever widening circles, stopping to ask people whether they'd seen him. And whenever we described a frail old man who looked as if he was about to collapse, accompanied by an anxious sheepdog, we could barely reconcile our description with the grandfather we knew.

Usually we would meet him coming back home, not of his own accord but shepherded by Tinker, who used her nose to guide him in the right direction. On one occasion, though, after hours of driving, Ian and I found him at dusk on the bridge over the motorway below Chudleigh, in the middle of which grandfather stood leaning against the rail, waving his stick at drivers in the fast lane. Ian helped him into the passenger seat of one of the three new cars he'd just purchased in order to claim tax relief on capital investment, and we set off back home. The muffled engine glided along as silent as a hearse, but grandfather still shouted, because it was a farmer's habit of a lifetime to shout above the noise of the tractor, as he berated his grandson for treating him like a child.

I dreamed that the world was awash with water: everything was sinking beneath a biblical deluge. Only the roofs of the houses showed above the surface. It was a silent and deserted landscape, except for a cluster of hens perched on the ridge-tiles of the Honeywills' cottage, and the widowman heron on the thatch of the Old Rectory, staring impassively into the water.

I found myself on a raft, floating between the roofs. The world was empty. I woke up drenched in sweat and loneliness, the bed sheets soaked.

Grandfather had decided to leave as unobtrusively as grandmother: this time, though, I was the first one into his room. I stood by his head, looking down at his closed eyelids, his stubbly face, his proud nose and his hesitant white lips of a taciturn grandfather. I understood that he'd done exactly what he wanted to do, forcing his body, by sheer willpower, to relinquish his lonely soul into the nothingness where grandmother had already gone. One by one the others appeared and gathered round, mystified and silent.

I knew he'd done what he wanted to do, and it was out of happiness for him that my eyes filled up and a tear dripped on to one of his eyelids. Then we all gasped and stepped backwards, transfixed, as grandfather's eyes opened slowly and stared sleepily towards us. They were icy blue and translucent, and I felt my legs and my stomach go soft, when his eyes suddenly blinked and snapped into focus. He looked at me and then along at the rest of his family, raised himself up, and growled: 'What the 'eck's is going on? Can't a man get no sleep round yere without being interrupted?'

*

The telephone rang and I ignored it as usual till mother shouted through from the kitchen: 'Will you get off your backside and answer that, girl?'

I said yes and Johnathan's voice asked: 'May I speak to Alison, please?'

'It's me,' I said, shocked, not because it was Johnathan but because I'd never thought of talking to him or anyone else on the phone. My friends had always been from a few doors away, and the only time I ever dialled anyone was to make reluctant thank you calls to my aunts at Christmas. Suddenly a previously unconsidered method of communication, of immediate and intimate contact, opened up before me. No need to depend on surreptitious signals or chance rendezvous, we could just call each other any time we wanted. It was an entry into the adult world.

'I didn't recognize you,' Johnathan was saying.

'I had a haircut,' I replied.

There was silence at the other end of the line, then: 'I meant your voice.'

'It was a joke, Johnathan,' I told him.

'Listen,' he said, thinking it best to ignore me, 'father just decided we're going on holiday tomorrow, to Brittany.'

I thought he was joking. 'Didn't you hear? We're starting school Monday. We should've bin there *months* ago.'

'I know. I told father. He said: "Spontaneity's the keynote." You know what he's like.'

My heart sank. I was counting on us making a fresh start together. It was going to be bad enough anyway. 'Your family's all upside down,' I told him bitterly.

'I can't help it, Alison. Anyway, promise you'll help me catch up when I get back.'

'Maybe. I might have new friends by then, I might be too busy.'

There was silence at the other end. I could picture Johnathan's face, with that look of his like he was about to cry.

'Bring me back some French chocolate, and I might think about it,' I teased him.

'Don't worry about that,' he replied eagerly. 'Tell you what, I'll find some real Breton crêpe dentelles.'

'Don what?' I said. 'Sounds boring. No, it's chocolate or nothing.'

'All right, all right, no need to fret. I'll see you in a couple of weeks, then, okay?'

'S'pose so.' The line was quiet. Neither of us could think of anything to say.

'You can call me again if you like,' I said in the end. 'In fact, why don't you call me from France?'

'I'll try. See you then.'

'Bye.'

Pamela came to visit that evening; now it really was like having a guest in the house, she was such a stranger. She brought a bottle of red wine left over from some farewell party at the office where she worked. She opened it at supper and poured it into tumblers in equal measures, except for mine, which she diluted with water.

'That's what they do in France,' she told me, winking. 'Kids start on wine at seven year old.' I felt even more envious of Johnathan.

Tom lifted his glass and emptied it in one gulp before Pam could stop him. 'You're not meant to do that, stupid,' she admonished him. 'You're meant to savour it. Let your nose enjoy it first, then your tongue, before you let it go down your throat.' She showed us how, and we copied her.

Ian had hardly ever drunk wine before, apart from sparkling white wine that had stood in for champagne on various occasions, and the aftertaste of cheap red wine in one or two kisses. When he lifted his glass to his nose, though, and inhaled its perfume, he was stunned by a shock of recognition: for what he smelled in the bouquet was Susanna. She had brushed past him a hundred times in the hallway, she'd sat next to him at this table, but he'd never considered her as he did other women, with her own secret, intoxicating scent. It had never occurred to him that she had one. But here it suddenly was, caught like a spirit in the bottle of wine, her aroma filling his nostrils and lightening his head. He lowered the glass, pondering this provocative magic, and drank the wine in sombre mood.

It was a blazing Friday morning, the last before the postponed term at my new school was finally to begin, that Ian lost his head. Everyone was half-way through breakfast by the time I came tripping downstairs. There was a scampering sound coming from the sitting-room, and I pushed the door open to find one of the ginger cats taunting a sparrow. She was relaxing her grip long enough for it to think itself free and flap its wings and then pouncing again, her claws turned in, causing it no physical harm, only terror. I yelled: 'Scat!' She didn't move except to spin her head towards me and stare, eyes wide, and in that moment's distraction the sparrow broke free and rose. Too late the cat swiped her claw at air. The bird made straight for the light of the window and bashed against the glass, and then scurried against the pane as if frantically signalling to other birds outside. The ginger eyed me with calm hatred as I crossed the room. I was going to open the window, but the sparrow looked so pathetic in its stupidity and fear that I wanted to reassure it. In its fright it had smeared a streak of yellow against the glass. It was tiny in my hand: its wings beating gave it the illusion of a size and power it didn't have. It was insubstantial, less than a handful of feathers, skin and splintery bone, and startled eyes. I opened the window and launched it outside, and it flittered off towards the sun.

'What the 'eck's you doin', maid?'

Mother was standing in the doorway, shaking her head. 'I called you twice for breakfast. Don't know why I bothers.'

My brothers were leaving. 'You go on ahead with the tractor,' Ian told Tom. 'I'll catch 'ee up in the car, I needs to get some tobacco.'

'I'll wait for 'ee,' Tom replied.

'You get on, bay,' said Ian. 'I'll catch up with 'ee there. Take the dogs and the Benitrex, make a start. I'll see if Howards 'as got any syringes to spare.'

*

I dragged Daddy out and we went looking for someone to play with. But the village was like some enormous chicken house at night when the hens aren't exactly sleeping but you know they must be doing something similar.

Up at the Brown the telephone was ringing but no one answered. The front door of the almshouse was wide open but Nan Dyer had retreated into its shadows. The only other person outside was Douglas Westcott, who was sitting all alone chewing daisies in the middle of the Brown, as if he was wondering when the children were coming out to play.

The ringing of the telephone died behind us as we walked out of the empty village towards the quarry pool, brushing the hedges that were swallowing the lane because lately the heat had achieved an intensity that proved too much even for old Martin the hedge-layer. He sat with his sickle and hook in the small cottage whose location I could never make out, somewhere off the back lane to Chudleigh, searching through his memories to ascertain whether or not the notion that had just occurred to him was true: namely that all his life, while he had greeted people, introduced himself, initiated conversations, hailed passers-by, waved to motorists, let children run their hands over his nut-brown skull, invited dancing partners, given tips to gardeners and advice to pregnant women, escorted the elderly up the lane and made suggestions to farmers, no one had ever approached him, not really. 'Even the dogs growl at me,' he said to himself.

The only things thriving in that tropical heat were alien plants impervious to the lack of water. Colonies of coltsfoot covered whole fields overnight and giant rhubarb that no one could be bothered to cut sprouted, like rampant fungi, in odd places. A hoopoe was seen in the village for the first time since one of the Howards shot one almost two hundred years before. Crimson rashes of poppy reappeared in the stubble of wheatfields, their seeds all confused by the climate, while in the hedgerows impossibly tall nettles, whose stems could not support them, bent over and stung our necks.

Down at the pool the widowman heron stood on his rock, and he stayed where he was while we splashed around nearby.

I didn't mind skinny-dipping with Daddy, I liked him looking at me. Daddy had forgotten how to swim, so I had to keep an eye on him as he fooled around at the edge of the pool, but after he got tired I made the heron move and gave Daddy a diving demonstration, saving my backward somersault for last: as I curved backwards through the quivering heat I could feel my body trembling, not one beating heart but the accumulation of a million cells palpitating, before I sliced into the black water. I rolled and stretched beneath the surface and swam lazily, half-consciously, on top. Then Daddy went sniffing around the old mineworkings, and the widowman came back as I sat on a smooth flat stone underwater, and closed my eyes.

Elsie was already holding out a packet of Ian's brand before the bell on the door had stopped ringing. He fingered it as he got out his money: it rustled.

'Ain't you got none no more recent than this? 'Tis all dried up.'

'You sayin' we been kept it too long, bay? Buy it somewheres else if you don't like it: you's the only one what smokes that sort, I only orders it for you. 'Tidn't our fault anyways; what can you expect in this weather?'

'If I rolls one with this, 'twill fall out before I can light it.'

'Give up smokin', then.'

Stuart came in from the back room, dragging a box of groceries. 'Put a piece of orange peel in the tin,' he suggested. 'That's what some people does.' He stood up, holding his back and grimacing as he did so.

'How are you doin'?' Ian asked him.

'Ah, this bastard heat,' Stuart replied. 'Excuse me, miss.' He sat down in his easy chair. 'They says 'tis cold and rain makes arthritis bad, but not mine. It's never got me so good as now. I can't wait for the bastard rain.' He slapped his mouth. 'Excuse me, Elsie.' Then he got up again and went over to open the door. Stuart had always walked with bow-legs, but that summer it got more and more pronounced, as if his legs were stretching outwards to escape a pain whose source lay between his knees.

'Yes, give me rheumatism anytime, I don't mind that.'

'What's all in the box there?' Ian asked.

'Oh, I got to take it up village,' Stuart replied.

'I thought you stopped doing deliveries?' Ian asked him, looking at Elsie. She rolled her eyes, behind her thick spectacles.

'I told him he shouldn't oughta do it. You can't tell 'im nothin'.'

Stuart looked modestly at the floor. 'Well,' he said, 'just the odd one.' He raised his head. 'I'll charge 'em, mind. Add a pound or more on, delivery charge, like.'

'Who's it for?' Ian asked.

'Simmons, up the new 'ouses.'

'I'll drop it off on my way,' Ian suggested. He stepped forward and picked up the box. 'Tain't no trouble to me.'

He noticed the garage was empty, and for some reason he didn't fully understand he drove past and parked his car up around the corner of the Brown, and carried the box back down Broad Lane. Susanna answered the door. She had a pen in her hand and an abstract expression he recognized as his own, when someone disturbed his concentration at the chessboard.

'Where's the kitchen?' Ian demanded from behind the box. She stared at him.

'I just been in the shop. It's your mother's groceries.'

'Oh,' she said. 'Through here.' She turned, and as she did so Ian felt as if someone had struck a match inside his abdomen: her long blonde hair swirled lazily behind her, shadowing her body's turn. As it settled against her back Ian's gaze followed it down, past untidy split ends, past her white shirt to where it was tucked into her jeans, and settled on her bottom, which eased slightly sideways as she walked. His abdomen was made of wax, and was melting.

The fitted kitchen was bright and sparse. Must give you indigestion, eating in a room like this, he thought.

'I suppose you can put it on there, by the cooker,' Susanna gestured.

Ian did so, and turned, with his arm resting on top of the

box. Susanna smiled, and looked at her trainers, and looked out of the window, looked back at Ian, waiting for him to say something, then looked at her feet again.

But Ian didn't say anything. He was too busy looking at Susanna, taking her in as if she'd been away for many years. She was the same girl he'd seen the day before, intertwined with Tom, as they dragged each other under like a pair of drowning children, but overnight she'd changed, had been renovated, the complex architecture of her womanhood refashioned, and Ian lost his tongue and his self-awareness, engrossed in her perfect teeth, her adolescent cheeks, the discernible outline of her child's bra beneath her white shirt, the way she was standing now, self-conscious and fidgety, with her legs of a colt and her long blonde hair. She raised her head and her eyebrows together.

'Do you want paying? Mum's wallet's somewhere.'

'Who? Oh. Isn't she here?'

'She took the others shopping in Exeter.'

'Didn't you want to go too?'

'I had to stay and work. Boring.'

Sure, he thought. Didn't want to miss seeing Tom at lunchtime, more likely. 'Each time you sees someone you love, you loves 'em a little more,' Tom had informed him, with grave self-importance, on at least a dozen occasions.

'She keeps her wallet in one of these drawers.'

'Won't she 'ave it with her, if she went shopping?'

'This one's just money for bills.'

'Well, there bain't no need to pay me. She can see Elsie. I just dropped it off for 'er.'

'All right, then.' Susanna stood again, almost swaying on her feet. She hadn't yet learned the protocol of adult conversation. It was up to Ian to say that he was leaving: then she would see him out. She could only take her lead from him.

'You might give us a cup of coffee, though,' he suggested, giving her his smile that he knew wouldn't be refused. Her adolescent eyes barely glanced at him, but they glimpsed his smile.

Ian was her boyfriend's forbidding older brother, a lean

and scowling presence in the background of their happiness. The rest of Tom's family had welcomed her into our home, where she spent more and more time, and she never felt like an intruder, except now and then she noticed Ian glaring at Tom across the table when his hand on her leg made her giggle, or scowling at them as she sat on Tom's lap on the sofa watching TV, his thin lips set hard in an expression of distaste. His censorious countenance had made her shiver, but she'd dismissed it because it made no sense.

His smile transformed him, as if instantly erasing what had only been a mask of disapproval. She'd misjudged him: after all, Tom was so sweet and playful, how could his own brother be the opposite? No, it wasn't possible, and she chided herself for being so stupid.

They drank their coffee in the sitting-room. Susanna was sat on the sofa, Ian in one of the armchairs. He asked her about her school work, and he told her stories from his own schooldays, which seemed to him to have taken place a lifetime ago. He couldn't believe how irrelevant his studies were to his life since leaving school, and he heard himself admitting how much he regretted not staying on and going to college. 'You know what grandmother told me? "Everyone should study. You don't learn nothin', but it makes you think."' He made her laugh with stories of backward boys, wicked girls and scatterbrained teachers. She explained to him what it was like at an all-girls school, and he said he wished he'd gone to one. He asked her whether he might smoke and she said yes, flattered, as if it were her house and she had invited him, a guest, to take coffee with her.

Ian blew smoke rings. 'This one's for you,' he said, before dragging on the cigarette and releasing another small circle of smoke: they floated upwards, entrancing.

'Let me have a go?' she asked. 'How do you do it?' First, he said, she had to learn to roll the cigarette, and she was amazed at how adroitly his thick, callused farmer's fingers plucked the right amount of tobacco between the thumb and forefinger of his left hand and spread it along the paper; then with a brief flurry he twirled the paper, raised it to his mouth, licked the seal, and twirled it once more, and lo and behold he held another perfectly cylindrical cigarette.

Her fingers, by contrast, though slight and graceful by comparison, became ugly in their clumsiness. They might have been someone else's, so removed were they from her mind's instruction. She concentrated so hard Ian saw her mouth mimic her fingers' struggle, but all she ended up with was a misshapen taper with a scrap of tobacco plugged in one end.

Then Ian showed her how to blow rings. 'Use your tongue to make the hole,' he told her, 'and pretend you're a fish with your lips.' Some of the smoke escaped into her brain, and made her feel lightheaded. After a few abortive attempts she suddenly released a ring of smoke that floated gracefully upward.

'I did it!' she cried.

'You certainly got the skill,' he told her. 'Took me two months of trying afore I could do that.'

'No,' she laughed, knowing he was teasing her.

'True,' he insisted. 'Tell 'ee what: see if you can blow me one.'

'What's that?'

'Blow one t'wards me and I'll show you.'

He sat beside her on the sofa. 'Go on, just let it go in my direction.'

Susanna took another drag, collected the smoke in her mouth, poked her tongue into its midst, and opened her mouth in an inverted gulp. As the ring appeared, as perfect as the first, Ian was above her: he swallowed the smoke, smiled his complicitous smile, and blew it out again, not in a ring this time but a tiny globe of smoke.

'I want to do that!' she demanded, handing him the rollie. 'Go on. It's my turn.' She knelt on the sofa.

'You ready?' he asked.

'Go on,' she said. He sucked in a mouthful of smoke and raised his head towards her. She was ready, flexed in concentration above him. He moved his mouth towards hers; her lips parted slowly. He inched upwards and stopped. He could smell, despite the acrid smoke in his mouth, a faint taste of apples on her breath. They hovered like two dragon-flies. Then Ian turned his head, blew the smoke shapeless into the air, and brought himself back to face Susanna. She didn't move. Ian brought his lips again closer, and stopped again. She felt his four-day stubble brush her chin. Again they trembled, barely a thought apart; and then Susanna edged towards Ian, and their lips met.

They were still kissing when Ian's ears suddenly twitched and his mind hauled itself, as if out of water, back to reality: he'd heard the tractor engine, firing on three cylinders. He lifted his hands and put his fingers in her ears, and while Tom blew the horn of his tractor three times as he passed by, using their secret code of lovers, grinning to himself, Susanna was sinking in the quicksand of a kiss, the like of which she'd never tasted before.

In the quarry pool I sat in the shallows on a smooth flat stone underwater, up to my nose, knees held up to my chest. I wanted to rock to sleep in that patch of warm water. From out of the sheer blue sky some scattered drops of water landed on the pool. I stayed as still as I could, I didn't know why, but I had to. Somewhere deep inside of me a thin, hot thread was being drawn through my body. I didn't know what was happening, until I began to bleed into the water; my blood spread out into the quarry pool and was absorbed by it. I thought I was dying, but it was more like being born. It didn't hurt; I wasn't scared. I thought: 'Things won't be the same any more.' There was a taste on my tongue more metallic than ever. I thought: 'The world is turning. I better stay.' The sun was fierce and the air as hot and humid as a greenhouse above the glassy water. I closed my eyes.

Tom wasn't bothered by Ian's not joining him at the field. He noted vaguely that he was alone, but assumed something had cropped up, and so he told the sheep about the meaning of love as he gripped them between his legs and inspected their eyes and teeth, and injected them with antibiotics to immunize them against the side-effects of the antibiotics they'd been given earlier on in the summer.

He broke off at eleven o'clock, unhitching the trailer and rumbling the tractor back into the village. As he passed Susanna's he pressed the horn, three times, in his daily declaration of love, grinning to himself at the wealth of meaning enclosed within that clarion call, a straightforward one for the rest of the world but with so many secret meanings for Susanna, and the horn echoed around the village.

Ian held his arm around her. She lay with her back against him, her face buried in a cushion. He stared at the ceiling, lying as still as possible, trying to breathe as silently and as unobtrusively as his body would allow, hoping to stop time that way and give himself some time to think and make some sense of the confusion in which he was immersed. He wanted to disappear, he wanted to die, but the truth was he'd never felt so awfully alive. The one thing he'd not considered, had not imagined for a single moment, was that the two of them were still virgins, that their fumbled puppy-love caresses and endless, swooning kisses went only so far and never further, by unspoken mutual consent.

He should have realized before it was too late, he told himself; then he might have been able to turn back. How could he have failed to interpret the clues? For they were clear and repeated, in the way she kissed him with ardour, the way she blew up his nostrils which he found both strange and unpleasant, the sound she let escape from her mouth as he nibbled her ear-lobe, the way she guided his hand inside her bra, all these things, in contrast to the way she froze when his fingers slid to the bottom of her belly. So he withdrew them and returned them to her young girl's breasts, and then he lowered his mouth, and she again moved in a way he admired in women, increasing her own pleasure. But when he unzipped her jeans and put his hand on her thigh he might have had electric fingers, for she was paralysed, she turned from a cat into a sparrow, her body fragile, her neck trembling.

He should have realized. But he was no longer sure of anything. Never before had he been so involved, so overcome, in the act of making love. From his very first time, with one of the ephemeral farm girls who worked for Miss Branham and Miss Tuck and who took pity on his shy smile, he'd discovered a composure, a command over himself and the situation, as if sex was a hand-held plough he steered by instinct. Now, though, he felt himself pulled along a furrow he hadn't chosen. His body was doing the same things it had always done but his mind was not free, no longer the calculating mind of a lonely hunter but enmeshed in the act, inspired as he was by the closest thing to love he'd ever experienced, which was jealousy of his younger brother.

As soon as it was over he became himself again. He held her out of duty, and was about to move, as soon as it was possible to do so without revealing his cruel nature too openly, when Susanna got up first. Without saying anything she disappeared. He pulled his clothes on, gathered his tobacco tin and lighter, and took the ashtray to the kitchen to empty it, obeying his furtive instincts. He found her there, sitting naked at the kitchen table, staring out of the window. He was ten years older than she was but he felt much younger. He was going to say goodbye, but his mouth was dry and his tongue stuck to his palate.

When I pulled myself out of the pool I knew I'd left part of myself behind, dissolving in the water. I'd changed, had gone into the water a stringy girl but the changes bubbling inside me had moved into a new phase, like strawberry jam rolling. I came out with more substance. I didn't know who I was any more, but I knew there was someone there, and that I would find her.

On the way back Daddy and I paused to look through the telescope, at the ragged peacocks on the terraced lawns of the boarded-up estate. The waterfall cascaded silently in shadow. Daddy looked sad.

'What's the matter?' I asked.

'I don't know,' he replied.

Tom had long ago taught me to throw. I extended the telescope to its full length and hurled it as far as I could. It spun out away from the cliff and fell, spinning all the way, towards the quarry pool, which it entered with a barely audible splash.

'Come on,' I said. 'Let's get back.'

'Mother,' I said, 'I got something to tell you.'

'Tell me lunchtime, Alison. I've got to finish this washing and ironing first. Get your father to help you put that lot on the line; bring in what's already on there.'

I sat down. 'What's up with you, girl? I want another load dry before lunch.'

I had to tell someone. 'When's Ian coming back?'

'He's in already. Come in in a foul mood and went straight up to his room. Didn't answer me when I asked him what sandwiches he wanted. If he chooses to be like that, he can go hungry.'

Tom completed his inspection of the flock and hurried back to Susanna's, where he parked the tractor and trailer carelessly in the lane outside, with the thoughtlessness of love, forcing other drivers to take a detour round by Rattle Street.

Sometimes Susanna was already outside, waiting for him, and they would set off together for their hour-long stroll in the midday sun, blinded by each other. Sometimes, though, she'd still be at her desk, struggling with an essay. He knew that today her mother and sisters were probably still in Exeter, so he let himself in through the front door, trying to make up his mind as he did so whether to call out or to creep up and surprise her. It was the smoke he smelled first. It was invisible but he hit it like a wall: its stale odour clung to the room, familiar and unsettling. He walked straight through the sitting-room but his glance took in the green packet of Rizlas on the coffee table, and the blood stains on the dishevelled cushions on the sofa. Susanna was in the kitchen, in her white shirt and jeans, standing at the sink with her back to him, staring out of the window. She didn't turn round.

I put the clothes pegs in their bag, which I'd hooked to

Daddy's trouser belt, and he followed behind me along the clothes line, strung across the lawn, so as I could drape the dry clothes over his impassive shoulders. The clothes were so dry they were light as paper, and Daddy looked like a farmer at harvest in one of grandfather's old photographs, garments piled high on his shoulders like a huge forkful of hay. I was unpegging the last of grandfather's white underpants when Tom drove the tractor and trailer clattering in from the lane. As he brought it to a halt Ian appeared in the front doorway. Tom jumped down from the cab and his face was disfigured by tears.

Tom's tears were not for her, nor even for himself: they came because he knew he had to fight his older brother, and Ian knew it too. He'd been smoking in his room, curling his hair with his forefinger, stupefied with remorse, and he wanted to say he was sorry, it was all a big mistake, Tom, you're my brother and I hurt you just because you was happy. And I beg your forgiveness, ask me anything I'll do it, I'll leave like Douglas did only I'll never return, the farm's yours, I'll take my suit and my chess set and I'll be gone forever. But he knew he couldn't, that a primitive code of honour as old as our world forbade it, and before Tom had turned off the tractor engine Ian was already stepping outside.

Tom was crying for what his brother was forcing him to do, but his tears did not dilute his resolution. As they met, mother too appeared out of the kitchen door, a few yards away. None of us knew what was happening, but she'd glanced up and seen Ian pass along the hallway, his body hunched, and she'd smelled the rank odour of fear that escaped from Ian's body, the only sign that betrayed what was about to take place, because he couldn't conceal it.

Ian gestured to the barn, and Tom led the way across the yard. Mother didn't say anything, she opened her mouth as if to speak but no words came out. She followed after them but stopped half-way, and she watched them stride inside and the doors swing shut behind them.

There were some muffled sounds. A dog barked. It was

over in less than a minute. Tom emerged from the barn and came towards the house, still crying, his knuckles cut and bloodied. Mother waited until he'd passed by her, and hurried over. I left Daddy, immobile beneath the load of washing, and ran after her, but I stayed outside the barn. When she came out and found me there she grabbed my arm like I'd done something wrong and pulled me with her towards the house.

'Take Daddy, go see Maria, give her half a dozen eggs for the Rector. Don't hurry. Should take you a couple of hours.'

When we came back, at dusk, the house was deserted. Even grandfather was gone. I found us some food and tried to ring Pamela, but there was no answer at her flat.

'I'm frightened, Daddy,' I said.

He looked at me with a worried expression. 'So am I then,' he said.

'We better go to bed,' I told him. I made sure he cleaned his teeth and found his pyjamas under the pillow.

'Why's everything feel like you can't breathe?' he asked me.

'I think it's going to rain,' I replied.

I awoke feeling as if I'd slept in syrup. I blinked, and peered into the darkness, and I could make out Daddy's shadowy form drifting across my room to the window. Tinker had come in behind him, and sat down by the door. I joined Daddy and we both sat on the window-sill, and looked out into the murky night. An engorged cloud rested on the rim of hills around the village and its belly sank into the combe, enveloping the church tower over the other side. Suddenly it spat a tongue of lightning into the darkness. Daddy didn't move.

'You know what that is, Daddy?' I asked.

'It bites trees,' he replied.

The lightning brought yellow and purple shapes to life: below us in the farmyard grandfather was hobbling in from the lane; he looked as if he was miles away, in a different dimension.

A crack of thunder erupted up on Haldon and rolled down the hillside, shaking the trees and houses.

'Did you hear that?' I exclaimed.

'No, 'twas too loud,' said Daddy.

We gazed into the darkness, waiting for the intermittent illumination of the lightning. The air was heavier than ever: inside my chest, a butterfly started fluttering its wings, and I had to breathe deeper.

Then it was as if a fine scalpel had been drawn through the belly of the sky. It spilled open, and although that was the last thing we saw as the world went black, we could hear the rain roaring.

I stumbled over to the bed, with a pain inside, and I asked Daddy to sleep beside me. He lay down flat, staring upwards as always until his eyes closed of their own accord and the rhythm of his breathing changed.

I leaned, curled up, against his side: he was the only one who couldn't do anything, who I couldn't ask what was happening, who there was no use telling things to. But he was the only one who was there. The rain roared, from another world. Crying silently, I rocked myself to sleep. The summer was over.

CHAPTER TWENTY-NINE

Autumn

We woke to diagonal rain splattering like buckshot on the corrugated roofs of the sheds; it bounced in the yard, creating froth and steam, and made thousands of tiny rivulets which joined the dried-up stream that ran through the village and transformed it into a muddy torrent. God had woken up at last, with pins and needles. He shook himself awake and the rain fell.

A thrush hopped across the lawn pecking worms and grubs from the parched soil that was opening its pores to the rain. One worm in the bird's beak was its largest meal in months, but it didn't have the patience to actually stop and eat it: it dropped the worm to hop a little further and pick up a slug, but then dropped that too as it saw another worm wriggling from the soil. It was intoxicated.

The water drowned the horseflies and wasps, midges and mosquitoes that had tormented us all summer, but it also lifted another generation from the undergrowth. They rose, in between showers, doomed and dazed. With the rain came falling leaves, carpeting the surface of the earth: autumn had arrived all at once. The world smelled new again. It had been hammered by the sun as surely as a horseshoe at the blacksmith's at Ashton till it was bent and buckled out of shape. Now the rain revived it and the world stretched back to life with a great breath of relief, and its breath smelled of pine and mint, mushrooms and dead leaves.

Water coursed across the sloping fields, carrying with it the thin, crumbly crust of top soil, while below the surface irrigation trenches and underground streams gushed and roared towards the river. The earth was cleansing itself, as if it had had enough and was clearing out its system: the streams rushed along with an unwanted cargo of chemicals and fertilizers and poured them into the Teign river, which rose to within an inch of its banks and was covered with a toxic foam as it surged down the Valley and towards the sea. The earth didn't know that the rain itself was impure, and that the trees in the forest the following year would have the first tinge of pink in their leaves.

Ian spent the weekend in hospital and then, against the advice of the doctor, dressed himself slowly, overcoming the pain in his chest from his four cracked ribs, his eyes still so puffed up he could hardly see, his broken nose, his missing teeth and his wired-up jaw. He couldn't eat solids, and was spoon-fed a diet of soup, yoghurt and liquidized fruit by the nurses, Tom having done to his own brother what grandfather had done to the quarry foreman over sixty years earlier. After an hour Ian had succeeded in dressing himself, so they told us, except that he wasn't able to tie his shoelaces. He refused to let a nurse do it for him, though, and he limped slowly out of the ward.

He didn't come home, not even to collect his things. He just went away somewhere. He didn't tell mother where he was going and he didn't write when he got there. She understood that he'd done something awful, even though Tom had refused to say a word to her or anyone else, because when she visited Ian in hospital he made no effort to communicate with her, not even to raise his hand, had only stared straight ahead, ignoring her presence while curling his hair with the forefinger of his left hand, so stricken was he with remorse. Now she became worried for his safety and she persuaded the police to send two divers into the quarry pool, with a special request to do it quietly, and they tried without success to reach its bottom, suffering from what they called 'bends, only different', as their torches failed to function in the impenetrable darkness of its depths. The only thing they disturbed was the widowman heron, who stubbornly put up with them from a distance until late in the afternoon, when he launched himself on to the air and with the regal, captivating flapping of his wings disappeared from our Valley forever.

It was that autumn that my mother grew older. She'd stayed the same age all through my childhood, but now she entered middle age overnight. She lost weight, went grey, and the wrinkles that had only showed when she frowned now showed all the time. She'd tried hard to cope with life, but it had only grown more difficult. She was surrounded by men immobilized by circumstances beyond their control: grandfather sat in his armchair, Tom stared at the rain, and Daddy followed her round the house, dogging her footsteps. The one who had helped her was gone. His room gathered dust: it settled on his chessboard, his short-wave radio and his Edwardian brogues. She gathered up the balance sheets, tax returns and paper-clipped wedges of receipts from off his desk and spent three evenings at the kitchen table attempting to make sense of the farm's accounts. She was unable to do so: a bewildering quantity of figures moved themselves around, in and out of illogical columns which totalled different amounts every time she added them up, in a variety of permutations whose significance completely baffled her, except for her mounting conviction that we were hopelessly in debt and on the verge of bankruptcy. Finally she stuffed the papers into carrier bags and took them to the accountant in Exeter who she knew did the annual audit for Ian. She handed them over with trembling fingers and was unable to sleep, her mind teeming with numbers that always added up to a lot less than nothing.

Two days later the accountant rang her up because he was rather worried, he said, and she went stiff with fear. It's true, he said, that the taxation rate on such large sums of capital as ours was thankfully a lot less than it was five years ago, he chuckled, but a little more judicious investment could still save us from missing out on a great deal needlessly, and there were a number of options he could suggest if she'd like to come in and discuss them. Some day next week? Perhaps Monday? Was she still there? Mother gathered herself and took a deep breath.

'You mean we idn't in trouble?' she asked.

'In trouble, Mrs Freemantle?'

'We idn't going bankrupt?'

He laughed down the telephone. 'We've been auditing your family's accounts for over thirty years,' he assured her. 'You're far better off than you've ever been.'

'You mean us is rich?'

He paused. 'It's a somewhat relative description. But yes, I'd say you were rich.'

A solicitor had meanwhile made an appointment with mother and grandfather, who were read out a will grandmother had made at the beginning of the summer. She'd told no one, not even grandfather, who was furious, and they couldn't work out how or when she'd made her way to Exeter in secret, unless Ian had taken her there one day when everyone else was busy. To their amazement the will consisted of one single stipulation, namely that her secret savings of a lifetime – farthings saved from her pocket money, coppers kept back from the sale of hens' eggs, pennies left over from the housekeeping, and pounds put by from her pension – all accumulated out of her thrifty common sense and invested in a Post Office savings account, whose blue book we'd find underneath her blouses in the third drawer down, should be used to send me, her youngest grandchild, to a private school, so that I'd be the first in the family to take our wasted intelligence into the outside world.

They both drove home in a bad temper and refused to speak to me, until it dawned on them that the sum of three hundred and twenty-seven pounds mentioned by the solicitor, and confirmed in the little blue book, was a hopeless and insignificant amount, and in that light the sentiment of her last wish became a most endearing one. I didn't know why they'd been nasty to me and now I didn't know why they turned nice; only that this time it wasn't my fault.

I went for a walk by myself. I lay down in damp grass on top of the high ridge up behind the house. Moisture seeped through my clothing; it was in the air, too: it came in my breath and refreshed my throat and the insides of my lungs. I lay in the grass looking up at the overcast sky, trying to think of nothing. Then I realized the earth was slowly turning: it carried on turning half a circle until I was hanging on, looking down at the sky. The sky was waiting for me to fall into it, and the earth could have just dropped me off if it had wanted to. But it held on to me, and then turned back a half circle again to how it had been before, and I closed my eyes, thinking of my Daddy, wondering why the sweetest person in my life had drunk himself stupid and left me to fend for myself. There was no answer.

'The cider drowned 'is memory, girl, that's what 'twas,' mother said when I got home and for the first time plucked up the courage to question her.

'But why did 'e take to it in the *first* place?' I asked her.

'Truth is, I don't know, Alison. Men 'as secrets eat 'em up inside. Sometimes it eats a girt big 'ole, and they tries to flood it.'

She sent me out to get eggs for tea, and I searched in the dark corners of the barn. I could hear a chicken brooding in the shadows. My eyes got used to the darkness and I squeezed my hand under the hen and felt around for an egg there, daring the hen to peck my arm. Suddenly a voice said:

'Looking for one of these, by any chance?'

I spun round. Johnathan stood there, holding out a brown egg smeared with shit and straw.

'What on earth's you doing here?' I asked him. 'I thought you was in France.'

'We spent four days in Dover,' he said, smiling. 'The dockers wouldn't let anyone on the ferry.'

'Blimey,' I said. 'I bet your mum was mad.'

'She was,' he agreed. 'She got so cross she joined the picket line on the second day. It took father another two days to persuade her to come home.'

They'd got back the night before and Johnathan had gone straight to school in the morning. He wanted to know why I wasn't there, and I broke the news that I was being sent away to boarding school. He had his look like he was about to cry, and I felt sorry too, but then he started laughing.

'With our family backgrounds,' he chuckled. 'And here am I starting at Comprehensive while you're off to Public School.'

'What's so funny about it?' I demanded, but he just carried on chuckling to himself. Then he stopped abruptly.

'But when am I going to see you?' he asked in a distraught voice.

'Don't be silly,' I replied, and then I thought about it myself. 'It'll be Christmas soon,' I said, not convincing either of us.

We sat against the wall of the barn. The chaff on the floor was itchy on our legs. The hen was clucking behind us. Rain dripped through the roof in various places, plonking into small puddles.

I fingered the dust beside me, between us, and doodled nondescript patterns. Johnathan was doing the same thing. We watched our fingers get closer. They didn't belong to us. Our hands touched each other.

We sat there, our fingers playing together silently, feeling strange. My mind was both blank and teeming, thoughts like thick clouds scudding. After a long time we plucked up the courage to look at each other, and then we closed our eyes and our lips moved together.

We held hands walking across the yard; it was only from the barn to the front door, but it felt like Johnathan was walking me home.

'We're being separated by fate,' he said quietly, to himself rather than to me.

We stood by the door. The rain was drizzling.

'I know!' I said. 'We can *write* to each other.'

Johnathan was overjoyed at the idea. 'Oh, yes!' he agreed. 'We'll write amazing letters, Alison. I'll tell you everything.' His eyes lost focus: he looked like he was already planning his first one.

'Well,' I said eventually, 'I suppose I better go in.' We kept looking at each other as I opened the door behind me and he walked backwards. Then he turned and ran across the yard. His splashy footsteps receded, and I heard him whoop, once, in the lane.

*

306

Things happened fast. Grandfather spent all his time in his chair, with a grimace on his face. He switched the television on in the morning and kept it on all day but he wasn't really watching, not even the wildlife programmes. When he spoke it was only to complain of the pain in his joints, all rusted up by the rain. He agreed with mother's decision to respect grandmother's wishes and send me away to school; she was keen on the idea of getting me off her hands for my own good, and she assured me I had no say in the matter.

'You can see your friends in the holidays,' she said, 'and anyway, you'll make better ones there. You ought to wake up and realize how grateful you should be, girl. There's not many parents would make this sacrifice, so's you can learn the things we never did.' She managed to convince herself, if not me, and got carried away planning my education: she unearthed from the cupboard under the stairs the pile of prospectuses for universities and polytechnics that she'd once sent off for for Ian. When she realized they were useless she rang around a list of schools that still had places left in the intake for the term that had already begun. Undeterred by my nervous, feigned indifference she dragged me on a whistle-stop tour and was most impressed by a meandering, airy palace in Somerset whose pupils were locked in small cells to practise the piano after lessons and slept together in dormitories, which was a good thing, the matron explained, because the girls' individual dreams became confused, their cycles came to coincide, and they learned how to live together as adults.

We raced around Exeter and bought the prescribed uniform and new pairs of everything you could think of wearing, as well as a calculator and stationery, pens and compasses and rulers, a pocket camera, a matching set of suitcase and travelling bag, a hockey stick and a tennis racket, a Latin and a French and an English dictionary in a giddy unprecedented spree that mother took, amazingly, in her matter-of-fact stride, peeling notes from her wallet like she was dealing cards.

Back home I packed slowly. The few possessions that had escaped mother's defenestration I threw away myself, sparing only grandmother's perished and rusting skates in the bottom of the wardrobe. I packed the book that Johnathan had given me, *Peter Abelard* by Helen Waddell, declaring with evangelistic excitement, all the more startling for erupting out of his customary reserve: 'You've got to start reading this before you even *eat*, Alison.'

I studied the covers. 'Oh, it's a love story,' I said.

Johnathan's cheeks burned with anger and embarrassment. 'It's n-n-not at all,' he'd replied. Then, correcting himself: 'Well in fact it *is* a love story, actually. But it happens to have been written by an-n-n angel.'

Tom took no notice of my imminent departure. He'd returned to the person he had been before his one, disillusioning love affair: he left the house early, kicking the chickens out of his way as he walked through the rain across the yard, and he worked dumbly and furiously all day unblocking irrigation trenches, patching up holes in the roofs of barns and sheds, and turning over fleece-sodden sheep who were lying with their legs in the air.

That last evening, when I'd finished packing after tea, I went to the rectory to say goodbye. I found Maria ironing sheets in the drawing-room and the Rector preparing a sermon in his study, surrounded by twenty-six rooms, each of them empty except for an extraordinary variety of buckets, cider barrels, pitchers and pos, plastic dustbins, crucibles and carafes, watering cans and a fish-tank, placed around the floors to catch the rain that dripped through the ceilings.

I told him I had to go away.

'That's a shame,' he said. 'People shouldn't have to leave home.' He paused. 'But maybe it's for the best.'

'Why?' I asked.

He looked at me a moment before answering, and lit himself a cigarette. 'Because your family can't give you what you need, Alison. Maybe you'll find people who can.'

Before I could work out what he meant exactly he asked if I was still the only one around here who could make a drinkable pot of coffee.

I brought him back a mug of his strong, bitter coffee and he said: 'I say, Alison. Did I tell you I recorded something on our tape-recorder? You won't believe it. I'll play it to you.'

I curled up in the armchair in his study while he rootled through a drawer and found the cassette he wanted. At first there was nothing on it except for the assorted sounds we'd always picked up: odd footsteps; the whoosh of a wing; a hollow tap; all in amongst the distant roaring of a storm.

'There it is,' he declared.

'What?'

'Listen.' I pricked up my ears: from far away came not footsteps but a jangling guitar, a gentle drum, a rhythmic drone.

'What on earth is it?' I asked.

'How would I know?' he smiled. 'But I do have an idea. I think they might be the lost songs of the disciples of Babaji. I must have mentioned them.'

'No you didn't.'

'Well, you should ask Maria. She knows more about them than I do.'

From far away came a man and a woman's voices, singing the saddest songs I'd ever heard, singing them so beautifully that even though the words were in a strange language you knew that what they were saying was that, despite everything, love is something real. Gradually they grew louder, and scratchy, like an old recording. I looked at the Rector: he grinned back at me. I didn't know whether he was grinning with delight at capturing something on his tape or more likely because he was teasing me, so I just leaned back and closed my eyes. I half opened them briefly, to see him turned back to his desk, continuing with his sermon, his concentration undisturbed by the sound of a distant, departed guru's disciples singing songs of praise from the other side of a storm. So I let my eyes close again, and as I drifted towards sleep I remember wishing I could stay there with him, in that room, that I didn't want to go either home or away from home, I didn't want to go anywhere; I wanted to stay, because I felt safe there, where he'd given me a place of safety between home and the world that was waiting. I wanted to say thank you, Rector, and I think I did, but I was so drowsy he may not have heard, before I sank into sleep.

I woke at dawn with a crick in my neck: mother would be furious. The tape-recorder was off and the Rector's chair was empty. I slipped out through the door on to the verandah, where I found Tinker waiting for me; she must have been there all night. I was stroking her behind the ears when I realized with a start that the Rector was standing at the far end of the verandah with his back to me, gazing, from there up on the ridge above the village, out across the Valley. I followed his gaze.

Dawn mist rising from the river was tangled in the treetops, obscuring the waterfall which became a barely perceptible glimmer of movement. Thick, low clouds inched across the sky, rearranging themselves into changing shapes of grey above muted leaves of russet and gold. Sporadic birdsong was beginning to fill the emptiness of the Valley. The Rector inhaled the smell of the soil, gently breathing; the whole Valley was gently breathing. And I suddenly became aware of the fact that, although she was hidden from me, Maria was standing in front of the Rector, leaning back against him, her hands resting on his arms around her shoulders. He stood so still, at peace at last in the valley of fallen leaves, the place of exile that had become his home; he stood so still, lost in the beauty and the strangeness of the earth.

I slapped Tinker's haunches and jumped off the verandah onto the wet skiddy grass, and ran across the lawn without looking back.